Suddenly a ringing neigh sounded above the wind's roar. There was a wild crash of hooves and a scream of terror. The Turic and the women whirled in time to see the winged mare Demira rocket forward through a door in the front of the wagon. Hands reached to grab her halter, but she screamed and reared, flailing her hooves over the heads of her enemies. The fabric covering her wings ripped and fell away; her wings spread like an eagle's, ready to launch.

"Catch her!" Zukhara shrieked. His words were lost in a crash of thunder.

The winged mare rolled her eyes at her rider. "Go!" shouted Kelene, and the mare obeyed. Like black thunder she charged the open gateway. Carried by her desperation, Demira spread her wings and threw herself into the teeth of the storm. At once the clouds opened, and the rain poured down in blinding sheets. In the blink of an eye, the Hunnuli had vanished.

OTHER TSR® BOOKS

BY MARY H. HERBERT

Dark Horse

Lightning's Daughter

Valorian

City of the Sorcerers

Mary H. Herbert

WINGED MAGIC
©1996 Mary H. Herbert
All Rights Reserved.

First Printing: March 1996
Printed in the United States of America.
Library of Congress Catalog Card Number: 95-62200

9 8 7 6 5 4 3 2 1

ISBN: 0-7869-0484-4
8253XXX1501

TSR, Inc.   TSR Ltd.
201 Sheridan Springs Rd.   120 Church End, Cherry Hinton
Lake Geneva, WI 53147   Cambridge CB1 3LB
United States of America   United Kingdom

To Mary Helene

Because every writer should have
a fan as wonderful as you.

Love, Mom

Prologue

The meara raised his head, his shapely ears pricked forward, and he turned his nose into the night wind. His nostrils flared wide at the chilled smells on the breeze. The winter camp of the clan lay close by in its sheltering basin between two tall, easy hills. Its heavy odors of leather, smoke, dogs, and humans were clear in every detail to the sensitive nose of the stallion. The humans peacefully slept, except for the outriders who rode guard duty around the scattered herds and the large cluster of tents, pens, small outbuildings, and the chieftain's timbered hall that marked the treld, or winter camp. The outrider near the meara's herd seemed to be dozing, too, for his head drooped over his chest and his horse stood relaxed.

The big stallion snorted irritably, his sides rippling like molten bronze from a tension he could not identify.

He had been chosen to be the meara, or king stallion, not only for his conformation, beauty, and speed, but also because of his fierce desire to protect his mares. Some unidentified sense in his mind whispered something was wrong. He could not understand what it was yet, and that disturbed him enough to set him trotting up a gentle slope and away from the treld to a spot from which he could survey the meadows.

Up on a rise, he lifted his head to the cold wind. Spring had come in name only, and the frost hung thick in the air. On the eastern horizon, a pale gold band of light heralded the coming day. The breeze stirred again, riffling the meara's heavy mane.

He breathed deeply of the biting cold and caught a taste of something new on the edge of the wind. There was a hint of softness, a faint wisp of warmth that hadn't been there before. The wind had swung around from the south, and its swirling tide bore the spicy scent of the Turic deserts far beyond the Altai River and the Ruad el Brashir grasslands. The stallion felt the coming change in the weather as surely as the cold that tingled in his nostrils.

But he realized the wind was not the object of his unease. Wind was a natural part of his existence; something else out there in the night was not. He inhaled again, and this time he caught another scent. It was faint and south of the treld, but it was unmistakable now: horses, many of them, and all strangers. A low sound rumbled deep in his chest.

His neck arched like a strung bow, he pranced along the edge of the meadow where his herd grazed to another hilltop south of the camp. He stopped there, for the scent was stronger and coming closer. He could smell other things, too: leather, metal, and the heavy scent of humans. Not clanspeople. These men smelled different, spicy like the desert.

The meara could hear them now. The strange horses'

pace abruptly broke into a gallop, and their hoofbeats pounded closer. In the dawning light, the stallion saw the horses rise over a distant slope in a long line and charge down the incline toward the sleeping treld. The soft light gleamed on the blades of many swords and on the polished tips of spears.

Wheeling, the meara bellowed a warning to his mares. He galloped back toward his herd while the strange horses thundered over the frozen grass. Somewhere in the camp, a guard shouted. Then another. A horn blew a frantic high note. More cries rang in the chilled dawn air, and men began to appear among the tents.

All the horses in the meadows were alert now, their heads raised to watch the unknown horsemen approach. The newcomers gave a great shout as their mounts reached the first tents on the southern end of the camp. Suddenly there were screams, and the wind became tainted with the smell of blood. The horses grew frightened. The meara alone paid no heed. His only thought was for his herd. Like a tornado he roared across the pasture, bellowing and snapping at the mares to get them moving.

They needed little urging. Neighing with fear, they cantered ahead of their king, away from the blood and the panic and toward the open grassland. No outrider tried to stop them, for the guards were galloping frantically back toward the treld.

Another horn blast cut across the gathering din of shouts, screams, and the clash of weapons. The meara hesitated, stirred by a faint memory from his younger years when he had been trained for battle. The song of the chieftain's horn had once been an important signal to his mind. His steps slowed, and he turned once to look back. In the brightening day he saw the treld consumed in chaos. The strangers were everywhere, their swords rising and falling among the struggling clanspeople.

Women and children scattered everywhere, and the people fought fiercely to defend their homes. Already smoke and flames rose from the chieftain's hall.

The stallion trumpeted a challenge. He waited for the chieftain's horn to call again, unaware that the horn lay broken in the bleeding hand of the dying chief. The wait became unbearable, the fear for his mares too great. The stallion turned away from the killing and galloped after the fleeing horses, driving them toward safety on the open sweeps of the Ramtharin Plains.

1

The wind blew from the south for three days, roaring with the first fanfare of spring across the frozen plains. It was a tossing, tumbling, tumultuous wind, a great warm ocean of air that tossed the trees, swirled the winter-cured grass, and swept in an irresistible current over the far-flung hills. Its warmth erased the last of the snow and filled the valleys with the rippling sheen of water.

In the winter trelds of the eleven clans of Valorian, the clanspeople shook out their rugs and bedding, aired their tents, and rejoiced in the change of the seasons. The clans' horses lifted their muzzles to the rushing wind and filled their nostrils with the warm, dry breath of the deserts far to the south. The mares waited patiently, knowing the Birthing was coming soon, but the youngsters kicked up their heels to race the wild wind.

In the brilliant blue sky above the high plateau of Moy Tura, one horse did more than lift her heels to the wind. A Hunnuli mare, as black as obsidian, raced to the abrupt edge of the highland and launched herself into the skirts of the wind. For a moment she tucked her front legs and dropped toward the rocky base several hundred feet below. Her rider, a young woman with hair as black as her Hunnuli's tail, gave a sharp cry of elation; then the horse spread her wings and rose high into the currents.

Wheeling, soaring, hearts high with release, horse and rider flew with the spring wind in the bright, clear light of the morning sun. They headed south on the tides of the air for several hours, until the mare was drenched in sweat and the rugged Himachal Mountains rose like a fortress wall to their right. Southward, where the wind continued to roar, the rolling grasslands faded away into the gray-blue horizon.

The young woman, Kelene, realized it was time to return home, but for a while longer she stared south into the wind. To the south lay Dangari Treld and the Isin River, and farther still lay the winter treld of the Khulinin Clan, the home of her parents, Lord Athlone and Lady Gabria.

Kelene shrugged her shoulders somewhat irritably. She had never imagined three or four years ago that she would move so far from home and miss her parents so deeply. As a girl she had avoided her parents' love and concern, much as a stubborn child would refuse a sour draught. It wasn't until she married and moved two hundred leagues away to Moy Tura that she realized how much of her mother and father's time and wisdom she missed.

"It would be nice," she said, unaware that she had spoken her wistful thought aloud.

The Hunnuli mare, a horse descended from an ancient and revered breed, cocked her ears back. *What would be nice?* she asked in the silent, telepathic communication that linked all Hunnuli to their riders.

Kelene started out of her reverie and laughed at her own musings. "To see my parents again. It has been so long; I was just thinking how nice it would be to keep flying south and surprise them with a visit."

The mare, Demira, snorted. *That would be a surprise. Especially to Rafnir. He's expecting you to help with the wells this afternoon.*

The reminder brought a grimace to Kelene's tanned face. Unexpectedly the delight in the morning dwindled, and she muttered between her teeth, "I am getting just a little tired of that ruin."

As if the words had opened a dam, her frustrations welled up uncontrollably, like gall in her throat. Kelene shook her head fiercely, trying to deny them. What did she have to be angry about? She had the most wonderful horse in the world, a winged mare who could fly her to any place she chose to go. She had a husband who adored her, parents who loved her, and a rare and gifted talent to heal that made her one of the most respected women in the clans. The weather was glorious, spring was on the way, and this flying ride was everything she had ever dreamed. So why, Kelene asked herself, why do I feel so dissatisfied?

She pondered that question while Demira winged her way home on the northern track of the wind. Truth to tell, Kelene decided, her frustration hadn't been a sudden thing brought on by the thought of her parents or the reminder of unpleasant work. It had been building, layer by thin, brittle layer, for quite some time, and that bothered her.

After all, she knew frustration and setbacks all too well. As a girl she had been crippled and willful, afraid of her own power and too stubborn to ask for help. Then three years ago during the clans' annual summer gathering, an old evil escaped and a virulent plague struck the clanspeople. In a desperate attempt to help, Kelene, her brother Savaron, his friend Rafnir, and several other magic-wielders journeyed with the sorcerer, Sayyed, to the forbidden ruins of Moy Tura to look for old healing records that could help save the clans.

Through the midst of the monumental tragedy, Kelene grew to become a competent, caring woman. She learned to accept her strengths and weaknesses and to use her gift of empathy and magic to her utmost. With Rafnir's help, she gave wings to Demira; she befriended the Korg, the sorcerer in the shape of a stone lion who guarded Moy Tura; and she learned to use the healing stones that helped cure her dying people.

When the dead were buried and clan life began to return to some semblance of normal, Kelene and Rafnir took her parents to Moy Tura and made a startling proposal: they wanted to rebuild the city. Kelene still remembered the exhilarating excitement and anticipation of their hopes and dreams. It would be a monumental task, but they had been empowered by their own optimism and newfound maturity.

That had been three years ago.

Demira's light thought teasingly interrupted her reverie. *Do you mean that ruin?*

Kelene glanced down and saw they had already reached the huge plateau that bore the ruins of Moy Tura on its flat crown. "Don't land yet," she said.

Obligingly the mare stretched out her wings to catch a rising draft and lazily circled the city.

Kelene sighed. From this bird's-eye view there certainly wasn't much to see. There wasn't much to see from the ground, either, even after three years of unending work. Moy Tura had proved to be a tougher problem to crack than either she or Rafnir had imagined.

At one time Moy Tura had been the jewel of the clans' realm and the center of wisdom and learning.

Magic-wielders, those people descended from the hero-warrior Valorian and born with the talent to wield the unseen, gods-given power of magic, built the city.

But over the years the clans grew fearful and suspicious of the sorcerers' powers. In one bloody, violent summer, the clanspeople turned against their magic-wielders and slaughtered every one they could find. A few fled into hiding, but Moy Tura was razed to the ground and magic was forbidden on pain of death. So it had remained for over two hundred years.

Until Mother came along, Kelene thought with a sudden grin. She still wasn't certain how Lady Gabria had done it. Gabria had faced incredible odds, including the massacre of her entire clan and the opposition of a clan chieftain turned sorcerer, and somehow returned magic to clan acceptance. It was her determination, strength, and courage that made it possible for Kelene to be where she was.

"But where am I now?" Kelene asked the sky above.

I believe you are with me above Moy Tura, Demira answered for the cloudless sky. When Kelene didn't respond to her teasing humor, the mare cast a quick look back. *You are certainly pensive today.*

Kelene's hands tightened on the leather flying harness Rafnir had made for her. It was the only tack the Hunnuli wore. "This morning was fun, Demira. I needed it."

But it has not helped.

Kelene snorted in disgust. "Moy Tura is still nothing more than a heap of rubble. For every building we clear out or rebuild, there are a hundred more to do. We can't get enough help. No one wants to leave their comfortable clan to come live in some cold, drafty, haunted pile of rock and, since the plague, there aren't even enough magic-wielders to go around the clans, let alone resettle Moy Tura. The clan chiefs won't support us. And where in Amara's name are the city wells? The Korg told us there were cisterns, but he couldn't remember where.

Why can't we find them?"

Kelene stumbled to a startled silence. She hadn't meant to explode with such an outburst; it just came pouring out, probably loosened by the first taste of spring after a long winter's drudgery.

Actually you have accomplished a great deal, Demira reminded her in a cool, matter-of-fact manner. *You learned the craft of healing, you are an accomplished sorceress, and you are the only clanswoman to do an inside loop.*

Kelene laughed at that. The "inside loop" was a trick she and Demira had accomplished—once. It had scared the wits out of them and sent Rafnir into fits of rage at their foolhardiness. He had promptly constructed the flying harness to hold Kelene on Demira's back and forbade them from flying without it. Kelene had to admit it proved very useful.

"Looking at it that way, you're right," Kelene conceded.

But Demira knew her rider's every nuance of speech and character. *It is not just the city that bothers you, is it? You have been there only three years. You knew it would not grow overnight.*

"No," said Kelene, her voice flat. "It is not just the city." She couldn't go on. There was one fear left she could not put voice to, one emptiness inside her that ached with a cold dread and made every other setback more difficult to face. After all, what good was building a home if there were no children to fill it? She had not said anything to Rafnir about her inability to bear babes, nor he to her, but she felt his disappointment and concern as poignantly as her own.

Perhaps that was why she was struck with such a desire to see Lady Gabria again. Her mother would provide a loving, sympathetic ear for her worries, and maybe she could suggest something Kelene had overlooked. Unfortunately, there was too much to do at

Moy Tura to even consider a journey to Khulinin Treld.

The young woman sighed again. The clans would be gathering at the Tir Samod in three months' time. Maybe Rafnir would agree to go this year. They needed various tools, herbs, and foodstuffs even magic couldn't supply, and they could use the time to talk to other magic-wielders. Surely there were a few who would be willing to give Moy Tura a helping hand. Kelene could then talk to her mother and share her anxieties. Until that time she would have to be patient. As Demira pointed out, neither cities nor babies grew overnight.

Kelene was about to ask Demira to land when the Hunnuli turned her head to the south. *Someone is coming,* she announced.

Kelene's spirits rose a little. It was always pleasant to see someone new. "Who?" she asked.

In reply the mare veered away from the ruins and followed the pale track of the old southern road where it cut across the top of the plateau. At the edge of the highland the trail dropped over to wend its way down to the lower grasslands. *He is there, on the lower trail. Coming fast.*

Kelene saw him then, a rider on a black horse cantering up to the foot of the plateau. Her heart caught a beat when she recognized the color of his clan cloak. Every clan had its own individual color to identify its members, a color that was always dyed into the comfortable, versatile cloaks the people wore. This rider, who was obviously heading for Moy Tura, wore the golden yellow of the Khulinin.

At Kelene's request, Demira landed at the top of the trail and waited for the rider to climb the plateau. Kelene tried not to fidget, yet she couldn't help straining to look over the edge. Her parents did not send messengers often, only when the news was important. She mused, too, over the coincidence of her wish to visit her parents and the arrival of their messenger on the same morning.

The rider came at last, his Hunnuli winded and sweating. He raised his head at Kelene's greeting and grinned a very tired and dusty reply. The stallion climbed the last few feet of the incline, topped the trail, and came to a grateful halt beside Demira.

"Kelene! I thought I saw a big black vulture hovering over that dead ruin." The rider's weathered face crinkled around his green eyes.

Demira snorted indignantly.

"Veneg," Kelene addressed the Hunnuli stallion. "How do you put up with him?"

He is rude only to people he likes. Everyone else he ignores, Veneg replied with tired good nature.

The young woman laughed. "Gaalney, he knows you too well." She paused, taking in for the first time the man's exhausted pallor, his dirty clothes, and the nearly empty travel packs on the Hunnuli's back. These two had traveled long and hard. "Are my—" she began to say.

Gaalney rushed to assure her. "Lord Athlone and Lady Gabria are fine and send their greetings. My message is ill news, but it is for Sayyed and Rafnir, as well as for you."

"Then save your words and tell them once before us all." She gestured north toward the city. "Come. There is food and drink in Moy Tura and a proper welcome."

Side by side the two Hunnuli cantered slowly along the old road to the city. The pace gave Kelene a little time to study the man beside her. Gaalney was a distant cousin to her father. He was a young man, rash at times, but with a dauntless courage that helped him excel in his studies of magic. He had stiff yellow hair cut much shorter than she remembered, full green eyes, and a thin mouth that always seemed to lift in a quirk of a smile. She also noticed he had a newly healed wound on his neck just below his ear.

They rode in silence until they reached the tumbled walls of the once-great city of the sorcerers. As they approached, Kelene glanced at Gaalney to see what his reaction would be. She was used to the massive entrance by now, but newcomers were always impressed. Gaalney was no exception.

The horses slowed to a walk, and Gaalney ran his eyes over the repaired stonework, whistling in appreciation. Kelene smiled. She, Rafnir, and the Korg had worked very hard to restore the old gateway. Although it was one of four entrances into Moy Tura, it was the only one they had repaired so far. Most visitors came on the southern road to this gate, and Rafnir wanted to give them a good first impression. The gate was a huge, arched opening between two powerful towers. Both towers had been rebuilt down to the decorative stonework around the defensive crenellations. The road was repaired and repaved with new stone slabs, the archway was cleaned of several hundred years' worth of grime and old debris, and a golden banner hung above the arch.

The best touch of all, to Kelene's mind, was the restoration of the two stone lions that had once guarded the gateway. Crouched in perpetual attention, the beasts stood to either side of the road and fixed their red-jeweled eyes on travelers who approached the city.

Gaalney looked at both lions and shook his head. "They're magnificent." The horses walked together through the gateway, and the young man waved a hand at the stone arch. "Is this any indication of your progress in the city?"

Kelene reached out to run her fingers along the cold, smooth stone. The old wards in the gates were still intact—they had saved her life once—and she felt their ancient potency tingle on the tips of her fingers. She drew strength from their presence, a power that had endured for generations, and she drove her own frustrations and worries back into the dark recesses of her mind from where the wind had shaken them loose. Smiling now, she rode Demira out from the shadow of the stone into the sunlight and pointed to the city walls that still lay in tumbled ruins.

"Well, no," she acknowledged. "That is more like the rest of the city. We've had some problems the past few years. Clanspeople have lost the art of working stone."

She did not elaborate further, allowing Gaalney to see for himself. The outlying areas of the city along the walls were as yet untouched. The buildings lay in crumbled heaps where the attackers and the elements had left them. In this part of Moy Tura only the main road was cleared and repaired. The rest of the wind-haunted ruins remained as they had since the Purge.

Gaalney was quiet as they rode. His eyes tracked back and forth over the devastation and slowly filled with wonder. "How can you live here?" he questioned. "All this would depress me too much."

His choice of words startled Kelene, and she freely admitted, "It depresses me, too, sometimes."

"Then why do you stay here? Why don't you come home?" Gaalney asked, voicing a question Kelene was certain a number of people had wondered.

Before she would form a sensible reply—if there was one—Gaalney's face transformed into a picture of delight. They had been riding along one of the major roads that led to the inner heart of the city where the primary public buildings had once stood. One such edifice sat to the left of the road in grand, shining eminence among the destroyed bones of its neighbors.

It was a temple, built three hundred years before to the glory of the holy quartet of gods worshiped by the clans. The Korg, before he died, had restored the temple as his gift to Kelene and Rafnir. With the last of his strength, before his worn and aged body had faded, he used his knowledge and magic to return the large temple to its previous magnificence. Now, shining in the sun, the white marble building sat as a fitting monument to the Korg and his wish to protect and restore his city. When he died, Kelene and Rafnir buried him at the foot of the large altar that graced the central sanctuary.

"And I thought all you had fixed was the gate," Gaalney laughed, obviously impressed.

Kelene, observing her cousin's delight, looked at the temple anew for the first time in a long while. She had been so used to working on other ruined buildings, she had momentarily forgotten how lovely this one was. She nodded and thought of her friend, the Korg. Two years after his death she still missed him deeply. "That is the Temple of the Gods," she explained. "The Korg hoped they would bless our efforts here in the city if we restored their sacred temple."

"And have they?"

"More or less," Kelene replied dryly. "Come on, Rafnir should be back at our house by now."

Gaalney made no reply but followed Kelene and Demira along the road, past a stone wall and several piles of rubble, to the wide central square of the city. The huge open space in the very heart of Moy Tura had once been a market and gathering place for the entire community. Its broad expanse was paved with slabs of granite, and at its center, where the four main roads of the city converged, a tall, black obelisk towered nearly twenty feet into the air. Atop the obelisk hung a golden rayed sun, the emblem of the goddess Amara.

Kelene watched the Khulinin sorcerer gaze around at the city of his ancestors, and she saw the subtle shift of expression on his face, from awe to anger. It was a change she had witnessed on many magic-wielders' faces. It would have been very difficult not to feel anything. The rage that had massacred an entire population still lay mutely evident in the shattered wreckage of the old square, where skeletons of walls and hollow foundations lined the open space.

The grand Sorcerers' Hall showed the worst of the attackers' fury, for its desecrated remains still had unmistakable signs of heat fractures and scorch marks from a large fire. It was known from the Korg's tale that the attackers had thrown hundreds of bodies into the burning Sorcerers' Hall—and Kelene believed it. Two hundred years had not been enough time in this semi-arid land to totally erase the bits of ash, remnants of bone, and the black stains of soot that still lay in the cracks and crevices of the ruined stones of the hall. She and Rafnir had made no attempt to restore any part of the old foundation.

But if the square had been the scene of tragedy, it was also the center of returning life—little to be sure, but life nonetheless. Turning away from the dead hall, Kelene pointed Gaalney toward a side street where he could see several restored buildings just off the square. At the corner of the street and facing the square was a house of some dignity, completely rebuilt, and gleaming in the sun like a pearl among dross. It was the house Kelene and Rafnir had chosen when they moved to Moy Tura. Broad, open, and airy, it was a comfortable abode for people used to living in cramped, movable tents. It had taken Kelene some time to adjust to the differences in housekeeping, but now she loved the house and called it home.

Gaalney's tired face lightened when he saw it.

"There is a guest hall down that street," Kelene told him. "You may leave your things there and clean up if you wish while I find Sayyed. Rafnir should be at our house for his midday meal. Join us there. If Veneg would like to rest, there is a stable by the guest hall or he can join the other horses out in the fields."

Gaalney's mouth lifted in his quirky smile. "Guest hall, huh? How many people do you have here?"

"Not enough," Kelene replied honestly. "We built the guest hall for the people who visit but don't want to stay. At the moment we have three historians from the Five Kingdoms, an architect from Pra Desh who is helping us learn to build, two bards, two healers, several exiles who are trying to earn their way back into the clans, and a priest from Clan Dangari. The rest of our residents, the permanent ones, equal all of eighteen."

Gaalney grimaced at the cold numbers. Even he as a newcomer could see eighteen permanent residents—no matter how many guests they might have—were not nearly enough to make a viable colony. He spoke his thanks for her information and turned his stallion down the road to the guest hall.

Demira trotted across the square toward the Sorcerers' Hall. Kelene did not need to tell her where to find Rafnir's father. Sayyed had been going to the same area almost every free moment since he'd arrived nearly two years ago. The mare bypassed the old foundations, walked up the main road, and turned left into the ruinous streets west of the hall.

Before the Purge the area had been one of the finer residential neighborhoods in the city. While a few of the houses had been destroyed in the fire that consumed the hall, many other homes had simply been plundered and left to rot.

One day, out of curiosity, Sayyed decided to see what he could find in the crumbled ruins. Beneath the decay and rubble, he was fascinated to discover a wealth of artifacts from the golden age of Moy Tura, and most important of all, a few precious relics and scrolls left by the magic-wielders themselves. He had been excavating ever since.

While some visitors thought Sayyed's work was rather frivolous compared to the rebuilding and everyday chores, Rafnir and Kelene found his self-appointed task invaluable. Useful items were kept by the colony, the magic relics were sent to Gabria, and the jewelry and rare items unearthed in good condition were readily traded by numerous clanspeople interested in their past or sold to merchants from Pra Desh who detoured from the main caravan routes to pay a visit to the city that had once been forbidden. The coin Sayyed raised went in turn to buy livestock and needed supplies for the tiny colony.

Magic-wielders though some of them were, the inhabitants of Moy Tura could not use magic to provide everything they needed. Living creatures like wool-bearing sheep or work horses could not be created, and unfamiliar things, such as carpentry tools or masonry equipment, could not be duplicated until they had some in hand to study. They also knew they could not function effectively if they used magic all the time. The gift of the gods was infinite, but mortals' ability to use it was not. Wielding magic was exhausting and sometimes dangerous, and the sorcerers had long ago learned that physical labor combined with a judicious use of magic was the safest and most effective way to get a job done.

That morning Sayyed was relying on simple muscle to accomplish his task. Kelene and Demira found him in the roofless room of a once-luxurious house. Sunlight poured into the ruin, washing the fallen rock and rotting floor timbers with a warm, golden light. The young woman slid off her horse and poked her head through a large gap in the wall. She saw Sayyed carefully lifting chunks of stone one by one from a pile by the far wall. Hot from his labor, Sayyed had removed his tunic and wore only his leggings and leather boots.

Kelene grinned at his bronzed back. Still slim, erect, and vigorous at forty-four, Sayyed was handsome enough to attract most women. Just below middle height, he had a short, neatly trimmed beard and sharp, piercing black eyes.

Once his face and eyes had been filled with gaiety

and mischievous good humor, until the plague struck the clans and claimed his beloved wife, Tam. Unable to bear the memories and sadness of her passing, he had left the Khulinin to live with his son and Kelene in Moy Tura. He had brought only Tam's animals, his Hunnuli, and a fierce desire to bury his grief in hard manual labor. He had found plenty to do in the ruins of the city.

Several dogs and one white cat lounged around Sayyed, patiently waiting for his attention. The dogs wagged their tails in greeting to Kelene; the white cat lifted her head with its jewel-green eyes and meowed softly.

The sorcerer turned his head to welcome Kelene. They had grown close since she saved his life three years before, but Kelene sensed a deep, aching loneliness in her father-in-law that nothing yet had filled.

"Kelene, you're back!" he exclaimed in a voice rich with excitement. "Come see what I found."

The woman held on to her message a moment more and hurried to see what he had discovered.

"There's an old chest under this pile," Sayyed explained. "A good one from what I can see. It's still intact." He smiled, a flash of white beneath the dust and the black beard. The value of the objects did not interest him. He enjoyed uncovering the mysteries, learning the secrets of the past, discovering new items that might be useful. He had no idea what was in the chest he'd found, and he could not wait to find out.

Kelene hated to disappoint him, but the exhaustion and urgency in Gaalney's demeanor forced her to say, "I'm sorry, but Gaalney is here with a message from Father to you and Rafnir."

Sayyed slowly straightened, the anticipation fading from his face. Without further question, he reached for his tunic. The dogs jumped to their feet. He scooped up the cat, then quickly followed Kelene and Demira back to the square, the dogs close at his heels.

When they reached the house, they found Gaalney, looking somewhat cleaner, and Rafnir standing in the garden behind the house. Nothing was blooming in the garden this early in the season, but on this warm, windy day, it was a pleasant place to sit, eat, and talk.

Rafnir, Kelene was pleased to see, had already provided bread, cheese, a bowl of fruit, and a pitcher of ale. Gaalney helped himself with a gusto.

Abruptly the young man broke off his meal and stared in astonishment at Kelene. "You're not limping!" he sputtered through a mouthful of bread.

"Of course, I'm not—" Kelene broke off and beamed. She hadn't seen Gaalney in three years. How could he have known what she had done to her crippled foot? "I used a spell similar to the one Lord Medb used and straightened the bones in my ankle and foot. It's not perfect, but I can walk now without pain."

Gaalney's surprise turned to delight, and he made her walk back and forth so he could admire her graceful stride. "Why didn't someone try that spell sooner?" he asked.

"No one had the skill to work on such complex bones until we found the healers' records here in the city, and Mother didn't want to risk experimenting on her own daughter." She stopped by Rafnir's side to give him a quick hug. His arm went around her waist and stayed there, strong and comforting against her back. "Rafnir gave me the strength to try," she went on, and her tone turned teasing. "He needed someone whole to climb those high towers since he's afraid of heights."

Rafnir chuckled and handed Kelene a mug of ale. The four made themselves comfortable on low seats, and while the others ate their meal, Gaalney gave them his message.

"How much news from the south have you heard up here?" he asked first.

"Little enough," Rafnir replied. "Most of our visitors

have either been here for a while or are from northern clans."

"Then you haven't heard the rumors of war with the Turics."

Sayyed straightened in his seat, his dark eyes sharp as dagger points. He was a half-breed, raised by his Turic father until the father rejected him because of his inborn talent to wield magic. Although he had lived with his mother's clans for over twenty-five years, he was still Turic in the far corners of his heart.

"The trouble started along the border last autumn," Gaalney went on. He leaned forward to rest his elbows on his knees, and all humor fled his face. "It was mild at first—a few horses stolen, travelers robbed—nothing out of the ordinary and no one was hurt. We thought it was just a few brigands, but the raids did not stop in the winter as they usually do. They got worse and more deadly. Wylfling Treld, Ferganan Treld, and Shadedron Treld have all suffered serious depredations from a large and well-organized band. Just last month a caravan returning north over the Altai River was ambushed. Everyone in the party was killed. The raiders have even reached as far north as the Khulinin grazing lands."

Kelene stirred. "Is that how you were wounded?"

Gaalney automatically touched the new scar on his neck. "I was in a group of outriders taking a yearling herd to the Blue Mountain meadows when we were attacked. An arrow pierced my neck. Veneg saved me, but we could not save the other men or the horses." His eyes burned darkly as he said, "Lord Athlone is furious. He has called for an emergency gathering of the council and has petitioned the Shar-Ja to meet with the clan leaders at Council Rock to settle these border clashes before emotions get out of control."

"Have the other chiefs been called?" Rafnir asked.

"I have already been to the Bahedin, Amnok, and Geldring. They are coming. You are my last stop."

Rafnir and Sayyed exchanged glances. The Shar-Ja was the ruling head of the Turic tribes. If Athlone felt it necessary to meet with him, the situation in the south was grim.

"Has the Shar-Ja agreed?" Sayyed inquired. The present Shar-Ja had held the throne of the Turics for nineteen years, and in all that time there had never been any serious trouble between tribe and clan. Sayyed found it rather odd that trouble was brewing now.

Gaalney answered, "We had not yet received a message when I left, but the Shar-Ja has always been steadfast in his friendship to the clans. The chiefs think he will come. That is why Lord Athlone requests that you three join him for the council. He wants your expertise and, as he said, 'the presence of three more powerful magic-wielders won't hurt.' "

Kelene remained silent and pondered the emotions that flew through her mind on the wind of Gaalney's news. Most of all she felt outrage at the Turics' greed and audacity. Peace with the Turics had always been tricky, but it was generations old and to risk it for the sake of livestock and plunder was folly. What was the point? The Turics were a numerous and thriving people. Their realm stretched for hundreds of leagues, from the Absarotan Mountains across the flat Ruad el Brashir grasslands to the Sea of Tannis, from the Altai River to the Kumkara Desert far, far to the south. The clans had very little the Turics did not have. So why would the tribesmen want to antagonize their neighbors? Were the raiders from a few disgruntled tribes along the boarder, or was the entire Turic nation preparing to sweep over the Ramtharin Plains?

Kelene's eyes turned to Rafnir. Even with a husband who was part Turic and a father-in-law who was half Turic, she knew very little about the southern tribes. The emotions on Rafnir's open face were clear enough though. There was still too much to do here: the cisterns had to be found, the few broodmares they had would foal soon, the herb and vegetable gardens Kelene had planned needed to be tilled and planted, and the new forge was about to be put into operation. How could all this be left for a journey that would take at least several months?

Kelene felt his frustration, too, but deep within her heart, in a small space reserved for herself, she found a pleased relief that she might be able to see Lady Gabria after all. Then her thoughts paused, and she asked Gaalney, "Why does Father want me to come? I do not speak Turic as Rafnir or Sayyed do, nor am I really needed at a council."

"Your reputation as a sorceress healer has spread beyond our borders," Gaalney replied. "It is rumored the Shar-Ja is ill from an unknown malady. His ambassador, who received our message, hinted the Shar-Ja might come to a meeting if you are there to examine him.

Kelene's dark eyes widened. "The tribes do not have skilled healers of their own?"

"Dozens of them," Sayyed said, suddenly rising to his feet. "But none like you." He offered his hand to her. "Will you come with me? You and Rafnir? Come see my father's people."

She gazed up at him and recognized a flicker of bright interest in his face that she had not seen in years. Rafnir must have noticed it too, for he stood and clasped his father's arm.

Kelene had no premonition of the coming events, no vision of disaster or pricking of the thumbs to warn her. She felt only the need to serve and the anticipation of a journey to the Khulinin. She took Sayyed's proffered hand and said to Gaalney, "We will come."

2

It took two days for Kelene, Rafnir and Sayyed to
pack and settle their immediate duties in Moy Tura. The
residents and some of the guests were dismayed by
their departure and the reasons for it, but the three
vowed to return as soon as possible and left leadership
of the tiny community in the capable hands of Bann, a
middle-aged widower, sorcerer, and the builder of the
new forge. Sayyed also very reluctantly left his dogs and
Tam's cat in the care of Bann's delighted son.

With Gaalney accompanying them, the three magic-
wielders mounted their Hunnuli in the dim light of a
chilly dawn and left Moy Tura for the journey to the
Goldrine River, where they would meet Lord Athlone
and the Khulinin delegation.

The warm, tumbling wind from the south had ended
the day before, leaving the way open for a change of

weather. The air had turned damp and cool; the great arch of open sky became a leaden ceiling of low-hanging clouds. There was no rain yet, but the horses smelled it, heavy and close in the morning air.

The riders pulled their golden cloaks close as the Hunnuli cantered across the plateau toward the road that led down to the plains. At the edge of the table-land, the other three horses slowed for the descent on the steep trail, while Demira sped forward alone. Like a huge black eagle, she launched herself over the sharp edge and soared into the air. She could not canter hour after hour with the endless ease of the other Hunnuli, for her lighter legs and body and her large wings made long runs too difficult. Yet, borne on the air's invisible hand, she sped far swifter than any land creature over the rolling plains.

Casually she wheeled overhead, waiting for the others to reach the lower trail. When the three stallions broke into a gallop on level ground, the winged mare turned south and led the way with the north wind at her tail.

* * * * *

They reached the Goldrine River three days later, after an uneventful though wet journey. Under a clearing sky, twilight deepened into night and a full moon sailed into the east.

Although the moon was full, Demira did not like to fly at night, so as soon as she spotted the fires of the Khulinin camp on the southern bank of the river and located a passable ford nearby, she joined the others on the ground.

Warm weather had begun melting snows in the Darkhorn Mountains, but the high waters and the swelling rains of late spring had not yet affected the Goldrine. Its waters ran shallow in the ford, making it easy for the four Hunnuli to cross. They trotted up the southern bank, swung left, and broke into a trot along the grassy, rolling valley toward the horseshoe-shaped bend in the river where the Khulinin camped.

They had not gone far when all four Hunnuli perked their ears forward. Soon, everyone could see the glow of the cooking fires and the solid shapes of the clan's small traveling tents.

Kelene tensed and leaned forward. Even from this distance out in the night, she could see the camp was in an uproar. Men ran back and forth, dark shapes darting through the dancing firelight. Horses neighed, and the harsh sound of raised voices mingled with the quieter noises of the river and the night insects.

Kelene heard a pounding of heavy hooves, and two more Hunnuli galloped out of the darkness to meet them. Nara, Gabria's beloved mare, and Eurus, Lord Athlone's proud stallion, neighed a strident call of both welcome and urgency then turned on their heels and escorted the newcomers rapidly into camp. Activity, light, and noise surrounded them as they rode in among the tents.

Kelene noticed the unexpected haste was not confused chaos, but alarmed organization as people moved rapidly to tear down the camp. Tents collapsed around her, packhorses were loaded, and supplies were repacked as quickly as possible.

In the midst of the frantic labor stood Lord Athlone, rigid with fury, a rolled scroll in one hand, a tattered scrap of fabric in the other. His dark hair was grizzled now, and deep lines etched his weathered face. Tall, strong of body and mind, he wore the authority of a clan chieftain with ease and passionate ability. Although forty-nine years of life and a close brush with the plague had slowed his endurance and stiffened his joints, his strength of command was unabated, and his eyes still studied the world like those of a vigilant hawk. He spotted Kelene and her companions, and his anger receded before his pleasure when he came to greet them.

Sayyed dismounted and, as senior clansman, saluted the chieftain. "Hail, Lord Athlone, we of Moy Tura answer your summons."

A smile broke over Athlone's face, warming his eyes from stone to brown earth. He returned the salutation and embraced his friend, his son-in-law, and last of all his only surviving daughter. Kelene returned his hug fiercely and let it linger for a moment longer before she let him go.

Like most magic-wielders, Kelene had certain abilities that were more developed than others. Her talent for healing came not only from a natural desire to ease pain, but also from a unique ability to sense other people's feelings. While she could not understand their thoughts, she could feel their emotions through the touch of her skin on theirs. During the past few years she had learned to control this gift until she could use it at will.

In the grip of her father's embrace, she opened her mind to his emotions for just one beat of her heart and felt his fury and sense of injustice. To her silent relief, there was no personal grief or the stunned shock of loss. "What happened, Father?" she asked worriedly.

Athlone stepped back, his hands clenched around the objects he carried. He lifted the scrap of fabric in one fist. In the firelight, they could all see the cloth was a piece of a light blue cloak splattered with darker smears and spots.

"This was brought to me just before you arrived," he said, darkly smoldering. "A large force of Turics attacked Ferganan Treld five days ago. Lord Tirek was killed, along with twenty-eight of his hearthguard and warriors, when he tried to protect the fleeing women and children. The raiders devastated the treld."

Kelene, Rafnir, Sayyed, and Gaalney stood shocked

by the ghastly news. The Hunnuli gathered around them, still and silent. Ferganan Treld, the winter camp of Clan Ferganan, sat in the fertile valley of the Altai River just north of the Turic realm. Of all the eleven clans, the Ferganan had the most amiable relationship with their Turic neighbors—in part because the Raid tribe that lived in the vicinity was ruled by Sayyed's father, the man who had married a Ferganan woman. That the raiders had turned so viciously on Lord Tirek's people was a betrayal of the worst sort to the generous, proud clanspeople. The rage on Lord Athlone's face was mirrored in the expressions of every chieftain in the clans when they heard the news.

At that moment Gabria and Savaron hurried through the fevered activity to the small group by the fire. The sorceress's face was troubled, yet she welcomed her friends with genuine delight and gathered her daughter close.

Kelene smiled, silently pleased to see how little her mother had changed the past few years. Gabria was still lithe and straight-backed, with clear green eyes and the hands of a young woman. True, the lines were etched deeper on her forehead and around her mouth, and her braided hair was more gray than gold, but what did that matter when the spirit was still resilient and the heart still sang with gratitude to Amara, the mother of all and the source of all bounty?

"What about me?" chided Kelene's brother.

Savaron, wearing the gold belt of a wer-tain, hugged her too. Tall, muscular, dark-haired and, to Kelene's eyes, handsome, her older brother had been leader of the clan warriors, the werod, since the plague when Wer-tain Rajanir had died. Savaron was married now, with two little boys and a wife he adored. Kelene marveled how much he had come to resemble their father as the years passed.

He held her out at arm's length. "Mother told me you

had healed your ankle, but she failed to mention how beautiful you've become." He let her go and playfully punched his friend, Rafnir, on the arm. "You two had better quit playing in your ruins and get to work on a family."

Kelene bit her lower lip to stifle a retort that she knew in her heart to be unnecessary. Savaron was always teasing her, but he would never deliberately hurt her if he knew the extent of her concern.

She was relieved when the levity in Savaron's eyes died, and he returned to the subject at hand. "The riders are ready to return to the treld," he informed the chieftain. "We leave at your command." He spoke reluctantly, plainly showing he was not happy with the decision.

Lord Athlone nodded once and turned to Sayyed. "You gave up your place in my hearthguard, but will you accept it again for as long as I need you? After this raid, I have decided to send Savaron back to reinforce the guard on the clan and the treld. I still need a strong arm by my side and a translator I can trust. We heard this morning the Shar-Ja has accepted our invitation to meet at Council Rock in ten days' time."

Sayyed's eyes glittered. His grim expression was yellow-lined in the firelight. Half Turic though he was, the Ferganan were his mother's kin, and many of them had become his friends over the years. His hand tightened on the hilt of his curved tulwar, a prize won during his rites of manhood in the Turic tribes. He bowed before the Khulinin. "I accept with honor," he said.

Rafnir, too, grasped his sword. "Lord Athlone, I have never taken the rites of the hearthguard, but I ask to be allowed to join your guard while you attend the council."

His request pleased the chieftain. "Granted," said Athlone with the hint of a smile. "And you may start tonight. We ride to meet the Dangari. Lord Bendinor passed us yesterday, but he is waiting for us so we may ride to Council Rock together. I intend to be there before the Turics, so they cannot have any nasty surprises ready for us."

The last of the tents had been packed already, and the warriors doused and buried the fires. In moments Savaron and half the troop of mounted warriors—eighty in all—cantered west toward Khulinin Treld, their pack animals and supplies close behind. In the darkness the magic-wielders mounted their Hunnuli and joined the remaining guard of clan warriors. At Athlone's quiet command, the Khulinin delegation set out, riding south and east to meet the contingent from Clan Dangari.

The Dangari chief, a middle-aged warrior of courage and sense, had sent the messenger bearing the news of the Ferganan attack to Lord Athlone. He had also suggested they travel together to Council Rock. Athlone readily agreed under the premise that no Turic, no matter how greedy, well armed, and vicious, would dare attack a large troop of clan warriors containing several trained magic-wielders. The addition of Lord Bendinor's men gave him the excuse he needed to send Savaron and half the werod guard back to the clan despite his son's arguments. The safety of the Khulinin was more important than a show of strength at the peace council.

The Khulinin met Lord Bendinor near dawn after a long, chilly, damp night. He led them to his temporary camp, fed them well, provided a tent for Lord Athlone, Gabria, and Kelene, and patiently waited while the Khulinin rested and cared for their horses.

Bendinor was a quiet man, capable, efficient, and well liked by his people. He had little of the charm and charisma of his predecessor, Lord Koshyn, but he and Lord Athlone respected each other, and even if friendship had not come yet, they had a useful working relationship. With unspoken consent, they had their clans ready to leave shortly after noon. Beneath their blue and gold banners, the two chiefs led their warriors south toward the Altai River and the meeting with the Turic tribes.

*　*　*　*　*

Council Rock had earned its name nearly two hundred years before when the chieftains of the Dark Horse Clans and the tribesmen of the Turics met to establish the Altai River as the formal boundary between the two nations. Since then it had been used occasionally as a meeting place between clan and tribe to solve minor disputes, trade negotiations, and border clashes.

Although its name was simple and obvious to the casual observer, the landmark was not so much a rock as an island in the middle of the river. Clanspeople who were curious about such things sometimes wondered where such an enormous chunk of rock had come from, but no one really knew. It had always been there, as far as anyone remembered, a tall, rounded boulder surrounded by water. Over the years a gravel bar had formed around the base of the rock. The gravel had caught more debris through seasons of flood and drought until a long, low island built up like a skirt around the massive rock. Local tales called it Altari's Throne, after the beautiful water maiden who was believed to be the soul and spirit of the stately Altai River.

The maiden's namesake, the Altai, was an old watercourse, running deep and staid through gently rolling hills. Over time it had formed a wide, fertile valley where groves of trees, lush meadows, and broad sweeps of marsh grew like a wide green ribbon across an otherwise semi-arid plain.

While early spring barely touched the northern grasslands, it spread its warm breath over the Altai valley. A pale green glowed along the riverbanks and meadows where the grass was sprouting in thick layers; the damp curves of abandoned river bends sparkled with the delicate whites, pinks, and blues of early wildflowers; and a haze of misty green buds spread through the scattered groves of trees.

Kelene drew a pleased breath when she saw the tranquil river from the air. She had not been this far south and had never learned to appreciate the beauty or the importance of the Altai valley. She turned her gaze farther south to the Turic lands that rolled away beyond her view. The landscape appeared much like the plains on the northern side of the river, but farther away the green faded to tan and eventually vanished in a brown-gold haze.

The sorceress and her Hunnuli completed their duty as scouts, and when Kelene reported to her father that the valley and the Council Rock were empty, Lord Athlone said with satisfaction, "We're first."

He and Lord Bendinor established their camp on a level rise across from the island, far enough removed to be out of arrow range from the ford, yet close enough that they could easily survey the island as well as the opposite bank. Guard posts were organized, and outriders were sent on patrols to watch for the approach of the other chieftains.

With Sayyed and Rafnir's help, and under the fascinated gaze of the Dangari men, Lord Athlone drew on the magic power steeped in the world around him and enlarged a traveling tent to resemble the large council tent that was used every year at the summer clan gathering. Willing hands raised the huge shelter on Council Rock and made it comfortable in preparation for the Shar-Ja's arrival.

Two days after their arrival at Council Rock, the Khulinin and Dangari welcomed three more clans. Lord Jamas brought a small contingent of brown-cloaked Wylfling. His treld to the west was the other clan whose lands bordered the Altai River. He had left most of his werod with the clan and brought only his hearthguard and an unabated anger at the depredations suffered by his clan during the winter. Lord Wendern of Clan Shadedron arrived next with a young, shattered-looking man barely out of boyhood, who looked as if he had aged years in the past few days. One Ferganan warrior stood with him.

Carrying his light blue cloak and weaponless, the young man bowed before the chieftains. "Hail, lords," he saluted them. Bruises discolored his face, and his arm hung in a crude sling. But the surface pain of his wounds was nothing to the grief that burned in his face. "I am Peoren, youngest son of Lord Tirek. I come to represent the Ferganan and to demand the weir-geld that is due us."

Lord Bendinor looked dubiously at Peoren and his lone guard. The boy looked barely sixteen or seventeen. "Are there no others to come with you, lad?"

Peoren drew himself up. "My father, an older brother, and the wer-tain were killed. Almost all of the hearthguard are either dead or wounded, my lord, except for Dos here, who vowed to attend me. I am the only male left in my family, and I felt it was my duty to attend this council even though I have not been accepted as chief. I decided the rest of the warriors were needed to guard the clan and help the women care for the wounded."

Kelene, who had been studying Peoren's bandaged arm, asked worriedly, "Where is your healer? He should have seen to your arm before you left camp."

The young man winced. "He was killed in the first surprise attack. We've been doing what we can."

"Are you certain you want to do this?" asked Athlone.

Lord Wendern, his long features masked with concern, stood beside Peoren. "I saw what was left of the treld. Peoren has done a man's job of organizing the clan and caring for his people. I feel he's earned the right to stand in his father's stead."

The sorcerer lord accepted his word, and the other chiefs made no further comment. Nor did the remaining chiefs when they joined the council. They came by twos and threes, traveling together with their mounted guards for convenience and safety. Another sorcerer, Kelene and Rafnir's friend Morad, came riding in with Lord Hendric of Clan Geldring.

Last to arrive were clans Amnok and Murjik, the two northernmost clans. The chiefs and their men came late in the night, weary from days of relentless travel to reach the council before the appointed day. They had only one day left before the Shar-Ja was due to arrive, and there was still much to do to prepare to meet the Turics.

The tribesmen, however, followed their own schedule. The following morning, only a few hours after the clan horns had blown to welcome Amara's sun, the horns blew again in warning. As the horn blasts died away, they were echoed by a blast of deeper horns that sounded from somewhere across the river beyond a long, low ridge.

The clansmen paused at their tasks for a brief moment, and in that space of silence they heard a distant murmur of sound: the dull thunder of hooves, the rumble of wagons, and the din of many voices. Over the gently rising hills they saw a wavering cloud of dust that rolled closer, spreading wider as it approached. The murmur of sound grew to a constant clamor.

"To your horses!" bellowed Lord Athlone in a voice that cracked like thunder.

Every man grabbed his weapons and ran to mount his horse. The standard bearers brought the chieftains' banners and took their places by the lords in a line along the northern riverbank. By the time the Turic vanguard rode into sight, the clans were ready, sitting in rank after rank behind their chiefs. The bright colors of their cloaks glowed in the morning light; their mail and weapons glinted like scattered pieces of silver. As the Turics came into view, the clansmen raised a forest of spears above their heads in salute.

At the forefront of the clan contingent sat Lord Athlone on his towering Hunnuli, Eurus. Beside him rode Gabria, Sayyed, Gaalney, Rafnir and Morad, representing the clan magic-wielders. Their black Hunnuli stood as an impregnable bulwark across the path to the river's ford.

From where he sat on Afer, Sayyed felt his heart twist at the sight of his father's people. He should have worn away the Turic in his mind by this time, but the blood of his fathers still clamored for recognition. The sight of the tribesmen, dressed in traditional burnooses and long, flowing robes and pants, and riding their sleek desert horses was enough to jolt more memories than he had believed still remained.

Although he deplored the viciousness of the attack that destroyed his mother's people at Ferganan Treld, he couldn't help but be pleased as the standards of the fifteen tribes came over the crest of the hill and lined up on the banks opposite the clans. There among the colored banners he saw the lion rampant on red, the emblem of the tribe of Raid. In twenty-six years of contentment and happiness among the clans, Sayyed had learned to forgive his father, the Raid-Ja, for rejecting him so many years ago, and he wondered now if any of his family still lived.

"By Amara's crown," he heard someone breathe in awe. "How many are there?"

Sayyed glanced at his son and saw interest and amazement play across his face. Although Rafnir could speak fluent Turic and understood Sayyed's devotion to the Turic god of ages, he was clan from boot to plaited hair. He did not really understand the strict and honor-bound codes of the Turic.

"The Turic believe it is necessary to show an opponent

their power and strength before negotiations of any peace treaty," Sayyed explained. "Because the Shar-Ja is with them, they have probably brought his entire retinue to prove to infidel clansmen that the Turic hold the upper hand."

Rafnir jerked his head around at the word "infidel," but the quick retort died on his lips when Sayyed winked at him. They both turned back to watch the vast procession. Even after his talk of retinues and shows of strength, Sayyed had to admit his words paled in comparison to the overwhelming numbers of horsemen, wagons, and chariots that gathered across the river.

The Turic had always outnumbered the people of Valorian, but Sayyed had not realized until now just how wide the discrepancy had become since the plague killed over three thousand clanspeople a few years before. This was not going to make negotiating a settlement for damages and peace any easier.

At that moment a ringing fanfare of trumpeters announced the arrival of the Shar-Ja. An enormous wooden wagon rumbled over the hill, drawn by a team of eight matched yellow horses, the sun-gold mounts of the desert monarch. A peaked roof covered the top, and the windows at the sides were hung with silk hangings of silver and blue. Elaborate carvings decorated the wagon from wheel to roof.

If the Shar-Ja rode inside the wagon, Sayyed couldn't tell, for the ruler did not reveal his presence. But flanking the vehicle rode the heavily armed troops of his royal guard, followed by a group of nobles and attendants.

The wagon creaked down the easy slope to the rows of Turic warriors and stopped nearly opposite Lord Athlone. A strange, wary silence fell over the valley as the two forces stared at each other across the water.

A clan horn suddenly sounded, pure and sweet, and Sayyed nudged Afer forward into the rushing water. The big Hunnuli splashed as far as the edge of the island, where he stopped and neighed a ringing welcome. Sayyed raised his hand palm outward in a gesture of peace. He felt a twinge of humor at his position. He had left his usual burnoose and tulwar in his tent and wore instead the clan cloak, tunic, leather-and-mail shirt, and the short sword favored by the clans. The Turics would take him for nothing more than a bilingual clan sorcerer.

"Hail, Rassidar al Festith, Shar-Ja of the Fifteen Tribes, Ruler of the Two Rivers, Overlord of the Kumkara Desert, and High Priest of the Sacred Rule," Sayyed bellowed in perfect Turic. Then he proceeded in impeccable tribal decorum to greet the representatives of the fifteen tribes. "The Eleven Clans of Valorian, Masters of the Ramtharin Plains, welcome you to Council Rock. May wisdom walk among our people and peace shine upon us," he concluded.

The words had no sooner left his lips than a winged shadow flitted over the gathered clansmen. A babble of excitement rose from the watching Turics when Demira, Kelene on her back, soared effortlessly overhead on a fresh spring breeze. Full of grace and beauty, she circled over the Turic ranks, then made a gentle landing on the island, beside Afer.

Sayyed grinned at them both. Kelene loved to make an entrance, and while the Turics had certainly heard of the winged Hunnuli, few had seen her until now. Her altered appearance was a peaceful reminder of the power of the clan magic-wielders.

The crowd near the Shar-Ja's wagon parted for a solitary rider who cantered his horse to the river's edge. Obviously a tall man, he sat his mount with practiced ease and total command. When he swept aside his burnoose he showed a face of middle years, swarthy, grim, and forged with resolution. His hair was knotted behind his head in the manner of the Turic people, and a trim beard etched his jaw with black. His deep-set eyes seemed sunk in shadow, and there was little sign of humor in his graven features.

"I am Zukhara, Emissary of the Shar-Ja and First High Counselor to the Throne of Shar. I bring greetings from His Highness." The man spoke, in polished Turic, from the far bank. It seemed he would not deign to yell, yet he made no effort to cross his half of the river to meet Sayyed and Kelene. The two of them could make out his words, but the clan chiefs could not hear him at all over the splashing flow of the river.

"Sadly, our monarch is weary from his hard journey. We ask to postpone any meeting until midday tomorrow. Then we will meet on the Council Rock."

"We?" Sayyed murmured. "Who is this man?"

The Shar-Ja's son? Afer suggested.

"No. The Shar-Yon is younger. And more personable, they say. This is a new counselor. I wonder where he came from?" Sayyed had tried to keep informed of Turic news and politics, until Tam died and he moved north to Moy Tura where he had lost interest in the world of his father. Now he regretted his ignorance. He bowed over Afer's neck to the Turic and replied, "We are willing to wait. Until tomorrow. May the Shar-Ja find rest and comfort." As soon as they received a reply, Sayyed and Kelene trotted their Hunnuli back to the clan lines.

"I'm not surprised," Lord Athlone responded when they told him the emissary's words. "In fact, I will be surprised if the Turics do not keep us kicking our heels for several more days."

"But we will wait," Peoren ground out. "I will wait for as long as it takes."

*   *   *   *   *

To everyone's annoyance, Lord Athlone's words proved correct. The Turics set up their camp in a wide meadow across the river and forced the clan chiefs to wait for four days before announcing the Shar-Ja was ready to hear their grievances. By that time even Lord Terod, the most complacent and timorous of the eleven chiefs, was swearing under his breath at the delay.

The time, though, gave the lords an opportunity to hear the full accounts of the raids on the southern clans, to plan their strategy, and to agree on their objectives. They kept a careful eye on the big camp across the river and made certain their own defenses were fully prepared.

Kelene, to her amusement, had discovered she and Gabria were the only two women in the entire camp of nearly two hundred men. The absence of other women was not a deliberate exclusion, for by rights established by Gabria many years before, the priestesses of Amara and the wives of clan chieftains were permitted to attend important clan meetings. But the ancient ritual of the Birthright, the women's festival of fertility and thanksgiving was about to be celebrated by every clan, and the other women had chosen to remain at the trelds for the very important sacred ceremony.

Kelene and Gabria, therefore, assumed the role of hostesses for the whole camp. They treated minor injuries, supervised the cooking, took water and ale to those too busy to stop their work, and settled a number of brief disputes among the proud and free-tongued clansmen. Kelene was so busy she had no time to talk privately with her mother. She contented herself with staying close to Gabria and sharing the older sorceress's companionship.

The day of the council came cool and windy with a cloudy sky and veiled sun. Soon after the morning meal, horns blew on both sides of the river, calling the start of the meeting.

The island was too small for every man to attend the council, so the ten chiefs and Peoren, with one guard apiece, represented the clans. Rafnir asked if he could represent Moy Tura at the council, and the chiefs, anxious to have as many sorcerers as possible with them, agreed. Kelene quickly offered to serve as wine bearer, for work at negotiating was always thirsty business. She stated boldly that she had been asked to come because of the Shar-Ja's poor health, and she wished to see for herself how the man fared. Lord Athlone had no objections, and Rafnir, who knew his wife well, merely shrugged his shoulders. Gabria stayed behind with Gaalney and Morad to keep watch from the river's bank.

In the Turic camp, a similar number of men—priests, counselors, and several tribal leaders—accompanied the Shar-Ja down to the river. The monarch rode in a little chair slung between two horses. He made no move and gave no smile as the entire group rode across their half of the ford.

The two forces met and dismounted on the island without exchanging a word. The clansmen watched as the Shar-Ja was helped from his litter by a solicitous young man and escorted into the big clan tent. Everyone else quickly followed, leaving their weapons at the entrance.

Although the Turics did not generally permit their women to attend councils, no one objected to Kelene's presence. They knew who she was, the healer, the sorceress, the rider of the winged mare, and Kelene realized their silence was a mark of their respect.

She stood mute beside Rafnir and curiously watched the Turics stride into the tent, their faces dark and taciturn. Everyone wore long robes in subdued colors and burnooses so white they seemed to gleam against the duller blues, browns, and grays of the robes. Only the Shar-Ja wore the pelt of a desert lion over his shoulder as a symbol of his authority, but many of the others wore silver-linked belts, brooches of gold, armbands, and chains of gold or silver. They were handsome men overall, dark-eyed, golden-skinned, with full, even features. They often wore their black hair in intricate knots and plaited their long beards.

Kelene recognized immediately the emissary who had spoken four days before. He stood a head over the tallest Turic in the tent, and his hooded eyes watched everything with a cold, avid gaze. He made no move to help the Shar-Ja but waited with ill-concealed impatience behind the others while the young man settled the Shar-Ja in a heavy wooden chair provided for that purpose and propped him comfortably with rugs and pillows.

Kelene craned around Lord Wendern's big head to see the Shar-Ja. She frowned when she finally got a close look at the man. Rumors of his ill-health were obviously true.

The Shar-Ja was barely fifty, yet he looked as old as seventy. A gray pallor clung to his face, and his skin hung loose over his shrunken frame. His hands shook as he pulled off his burnoose and revealed a ring of grayish hair that clung to the back of his balding head. Until recently he had been a powerful man, strong, athletic, and known for his just and firm government. In a society ruled by a strict code of conduct, the Shar-Ja was known as an honorable man.

So what, wondered Kelene, had brought on this rapid decline? She glanced at Sayyed, who stood beside her father, and saw that he, too, was frowning. He did not like the appearance of the Shar-Ja either. It seemed odd to Kelene that she had not been invited to attend to the monarch. She had understood that the Turic messenger had specifically asked for her to come to the council, yet sick as the Shar-Ja appeared to be, no one had bothered to request her assistance.

Kelene suddenly realized the tent was very quiet. Every man had taken his seat and was waiting for someone else to make the next move. Her father glanced at her and nodded once. Clan hospitality dictated that guests were sacrosanct and that any gathering, small or large, was always made more pleasant with food and drink. Because the clans had initiated the council, they considered the Turics their guests, even on an island that was essentially a no-man's-land. A fire had been laid in a central hearth to chase away the morning chill; rugs, stools, and pillows were provided for comfort; and trays of food, pottery cups, and wineskins had been left in the tent for refreshment.

Kelene stepped into the watchful silence and bowed politely to the Shar-Ja. She held herself tall and proud as she walked to the cache of food and wine. She had braided her long black hair in a matron's braid that hung to her waist and danced with its ties of jaunty green ribbons. Keeping her hands steady, she knelt, laid out the cups and trays, and poured a single measure of the heavy red wine. She paused only when a strong, sour smell reached her nose.

Her eyes narrowed as she tasted the wine and calmly swallowed it. Fools, she thought fiercely to herself. Someone had brought wine without bothering to check if it had spoiled on the journey.

Smoothly she took the cup to Lord Athlone to confirm her findings. His expression did not change at the bitter taste. He only glanced at his daughter and inclined his head as he handed the cup back to her. He had confidence that she would rectify the problem.

Kelene knew every eye was on her by that time. Clansmen and Turic alike were awaiting refreshments. There was really only one thing she could do. Serving the spoiled wine would insult the Turics and cast dishonor on the chiefs. Running back to the camp for more wine would take too long and could irritate the Shar-Ja and his counselors. She would have to use magic.

She knew the Turics did not approve of sorcery. They did not despise it with the fervent zeal of past generations of clanspeople, but like anything not understood, sorcery was condemned in Turic society. In order not to infuriate the already defensive tribesmen, she would have to work surreptitiously and pray no one noticed her spell.

She smoothed all expression off her face and looked about for a useful vessel. Fortunately someone had left a large pitcher with the wineskins, and Kelene carefully filled it to the brim with soured wine. With her hand over the pitcher's mouth, she thought of the finest beverage she could remember: a mead, a cool, light honey wine, delicately sweet as spring flowers, as golden as morning light, fermented from honey harvested from a bee colony she and Demira had found in the southern cliff face on Moy Tura's plateau. No one outside of Moy Tura had tasted that wine yet, but if she could duplicate it with magic, she was sure her father would approve.

Kelene concentrated on what she wanted. She felt the magic around her in the earth, the grass, the stone of Council Rock, and with her mind she pulled the magic into her will, shaped it to her design, and silently whispered her spell to clarify exactly what she wanted. When she pulled her hand away, the red wine was gone, replaced by a crystal yellow liquid that smelled of honey and spices.

Kelene tasted a little from her father's cup. The resulting mead was not as full-bodied and rich as the original, but it was delicious enough to be served to the clan chiefs and the Turic nobles.

She served her father first, to reassure the Turics that the wine and the food were not poisoned; then she swiftly and efficiently served the Shar-Ja, his men, the chieftains, and the clan warriors. That her mead was appreciated quickly became apparent by the low hum of conversation, the occasional quiet laughter, and a more relaxed atmosphere.

Besides Sayyed and Rafnir, a few clansmen from Clan Shadedron and Clan Wylfling could also speak Turic, and several Turics could converse in Clannish. Before long the two groups were passing plates of dried fruit and sweetcakes and exchanging wary compliments.

Kelene looked on with satisfaction. She quickly converted all the spoiled wine to mead, placed filled pitchers within reach of the men, and wordlessly sat beside Rafnir. Her husband took her hand and gave her a wink.

Finally the Shar-Ja raised his hand for quiet, and one by one the men fell silent. The clanspeople leaned forward, waiting for the Shar-Ja to speak and open the negotiations.

Instead he inclined his head to the young man beside him, relinquishing his authority. The man approached the stand, a square of space between the two groups where a person had the right to speak. In his midtwenties, he was a good-looking man with strong cheekbones and a thick cap of black hair tied in a single plait. He bowed to the clan chiefs. "I am Bashan al Rassidar, the Shar-Yon, eldest son of my father. In the name of Shar-Ja Rassidar, I welcome the Lords of the Eleven Clans," he began. His voice, firm and assured, spoke in credible Clannish and went on to greet each chief and apologize for the delay.

While she listened, Kelene stared intently at the Shar-Ja, who was watching his son with obvious pride—the father grooming his heir to assume the throne. Sooner than later, Kelene judged. There was too much gray shadow in the old man's face, too much lassitude in his body. If only she knew what was wrong.

A quiver of awareness ran up her backbone, a cold, trickling feeling that lifted the hairs on the back of her neck. She tensed, her eyes wide and her nostrils flared, her senses as alert as a wary deer's. She felt something odd, a surge of intensity in the air around her. Normally she could sense emotions only if she was in physical contact with a person, but she had honed her empathic talent until once in a while she could sense strong feelings from someone close by.

She concentrated all her ability on the strange tingling, and like a form taking shape in the mist, the emotions clarified in her mind: greed that shook her with its need and hatred as cold and implacable as a glacier. The focus of those feelings was not clear, only their intensity. Heat and ice raged unseen in a man's heart, and no one but she was the wiser.

Slowly she lifted her eyes and found herself drawn into the bitter, dark gaze of the man named Zukhara. He stared full into her face, devouring every detail of her features. Then he deliberately lifted his cup to salute her, and his thin mouth lifted in a smile that pulled his lips back from yellowish teeth, like the snarl of a waiting wolf.

Kelene's eyes flashed a bright and steely challenge.

Still smiling, Zukhara turned his gaze away from her, dismissing her as obviously as a master sends away a slave. Almost immediately the powerful sense of emotions faded from Kelene's mind.

She sat, feeling cold and oddly disturbed. The strength of the counselor's mind, the intensity of his emotions, and the unshakable presence of his arrogance were all enough to cast a gloomy shadow over her thoughts. None of the clansmen seemed to know who Zukhara was or where he came from, and Kelene began to seriously wonder why he had come to the council. Whom did he hate with such intensity?

She slowly sipped her drink and decided to forget her worries for now. She determined to keep an eye on Zukhara in the future, but at that moment the Shar-Yon was talking favorably of peace and the council was off to an auspicious beginning. Better to help the peacemakers build their bridges than fret over one individual.

3

There is a storm coming.

"What?" Kelene muttered from somewhere under Demira's belly. She gave the mare's front leg one last swipe with the brush and moved to the hind leg where reddish mud had caked into the ebony hair.

There is a storm coming, Demira repeated patiently. *From the north.*

Kelene did not doubt her. The Hunnuli's weather-sense was as infallible as their ability to judge human character. The sorceress continued brushing and asked, "Can you tell what it is?" A thunderstorm would be a pleasant change. The turbulent lightning storms provided a phenomenon for magic-wielders by enhancing the magic already present in the natural world. The increased power energized the magic-wielders by strengthening their spells and increasing their endurance to wield magic. She was disappointed, though, and a little alarmed when Demira answered, *Snow. It is already snowing beyond the Goldrine River. It will be here in a day or two.*

Kelene straightened and stared up at the huge arch of the sky. A solid, featureless sheet of cloud moved overhead, pushed by a steady wind from the north. The afternoon air was still mild, almost balmy, but Kelene knew that could change very quickly. This time of year, when winter and spring vied for rule of the plains, storms could be tricky and often treacherous.

"That's just what we need," she said irritably, stretching back under the mare to reach her inner hind leg.

"What's what we need?" asked a different voice.

Kelene glanced around Demira's leg and saw a familiar pair of boots and a red split-skirt, a red the same scarlet as that of the long-dead Corin clan. "A storm," she called out to Gabria, then popped up and flashed a grimace at her mother over the mare's folded wings. "Demira tells me a storm is moving this way."

Picking up another horse brush, Gabria began to polish Demira's other side. "Nara said the same thing. It will probably turn to sleet or freezing rain by the time it reaches us . . . which will make things only slightly more chilly and uncomfortable around here than it already is."

Kelene grunted in agreement. "I don't understand what's the matter with the Turics. There's a strong undercurrent of tension in their midst that has nothing to do with us. We've had two days of meetings and have accomplished nothing. It's almost as if the Turics are afraid of saying much for fear of spooking someone."

"Who?"

"I don't know," Kelene replied. "It isn't the Shar-Ja. He almost never reacts. He sits in his chair and dozes half the time. Bashan, the Shar-Yon, is doing his best to push a settlement through, but the others keep blocking him with petty gripes and details." She paused. She had not mentioned her misgivings about Zukhara to anyone, but perhaps her mother could give her a different perspective on the counselor. "There is one man . . . even the Shar-Yon treads carefully around him."

"The emissary Zukhara?" Gabria guessed.

"You know of him?"

"Sayyed and Rafnir told me about him," Gabria hesitated, then added, "Sayyed said this man stares at you during the meetings."

To that Kelene shrugged. She hadn't realized anyone else had noticed. "He stares, but he says nothing. Perhaps he is only curious—and ill mannered."

He is not just curious, Demira put in. *There is a taint about him I do not like. He will not come near the Hunnuli when we wait on the island for the council to end. The other Turics have spoken to us; the Shar-Ja has patted my neck. But this Zukhara stays away from us.*

Kelene's brows lowered. "I didn't notice that. I wonder why?"

Gabria leaned against Demira's warm wing and turned a concerned eye on her daughter. "Have you heard the Turics speak of the Fel Azureth?"

It seemed a simple question, but Kelene caught a distinct note of worry in her mother's voice. She shook her head, the horse brush forgotten in her hands.

"The Azureth have surfaced only recently. It is a fanatical religious group sworn to the overthrow of the Shar-Ja's throne and a return to the ancient practices of the Prophet Sargun."

"Why hasn't the Shar-Ja done anything about them?"

"I don't think he can," Gabria said sadly. "He's too sick. His son has been handling many of his responsibilities, but he is too inexperienced to deal with such organized fanatics. The Azureth are very secretive. Even their leader, whom they call Fel Karak, is unknown to all but a few of the most trusted members. They are well organized, well supplied, heavily armed, and very dangerous."

Kelene was both fascinated and alarmed. "But I thought the Shar-Ja was respected by his people. Have the tribes done anything to stop these rebels?"

"Our sources tell us the tribes are too busy trying to survive themselves."

"Our sources?" Kelene chuckled. "Sounds so mysterious."

Gabria's fair face lit with a gleam of humor. "It's amazing what you can learn from caravan drovers, traveling bards, merchants, and traders. They love to talk when you bring them in off the cold plains and give them a hot meal and a dry bed. We learned much this winter about the Fel Azureth and the tribes' troubles." She shook her head, and the humor faded from her green eyes. "They haven't had good rain in two years. The land is dry, and the rivers are low. The Shar-Ja has done little to help. The tribes grow so desperate, even this extremist group looks promising to some."

"And you and Father think this Fel Azureth may have something to do with the attacks on our people?" Kelene suggested shrewdly.

Gabria nodded. "That was one reason why he asked for this council, to spur the Shar-Ja into some sort of action against these fanatics before their raids lead us into war."

"Then perhaps we'll see some reaction today at council," Kelene said. "Peoren is going to have his say about the attack on his clan. He has been very patient so far, but I think he's about to explode."

"Just be careful of Zukhara," said Gabria with motherly fervor.

Kelene's eyes narrowed as a new thought occurred to her. "Do you think he has some connection with the Fel Azureth?"

"No one knows. But as Demira pointed out, there is

a taint about him."

Across the river a horn blew a sonorous note to call the clans and the tribes to council. Another meeting was about to begin. Demira's ears swept forward as Eurus, Tibor, and Afer cantered by to meet Lord Athlone, Rafnir, and Sayyed. The little Hunnuli nickered impatiently while Kelene gathered her combs and brushes, restored them to the carry bag, and handed them to Gabria.

Kelene took leave of her mother and trotted Demira down to the river to join the clan chiefs. This time she paid close attention to Counselor Zukhara when he arrived with the Turic delegation. Just as Demira described, while other Turics admired the magnificent Hunnuli, Zukhara held well back, keeping the Shar-Ja and Bashan between himself and the black horses.

Interesting, thought Kelene. Was he afraid of them? Or was he just not interested? Did he know of the Hunnuli's intuitive ability to read human character?

Keenly aware of Zukhara, Kelene followed the men into the council tent. She noted that he seemed to avoid the Shar-Ja and his son, as if he did not want to associate with them. He refused to sit but stood aloof, his hands clasped behind his back, his long legs apart and braced for a lengthy wait. The other tribal leaders were deferential to him, yet Kelene saw many of them eye him with subtle wariness or shift their gaze away from him completely.

The sorceress pursed her lips in thought while she poured and served refreshments as usual. The wine was good this time, a light crisp fermentation from the Khulinin's own reserves, and the Turics appreciated it.

Only Zukhara turned it down. When she came to him, he grasped her tray in both hands, forcing her to stop in front of him. He was so tall she had to lift her eyes to see his face, and when she did so, with a bold, angry glare, he curled his lips in that condescending smile that so rankled her.

"What, no mead today, my lady?" he said softly. "Not even for me?" His long fingers suddenly grasped her right wrist and twisted it upward to expose the diamond splinter that lay beneath the skin of her forearm. He studied it, tracing his finger along its glowing length.

The splinter was a slender sliver of diamond, embedded in the wrist of a magic-wielder when he or she completed training. It was a powerful emblem, and to Kelene, a personal one that should not be revealed and examined without her consent. Her face flamed red at the man's audacity, but she controlled her famous temper for the sanctity of the council and deftly twisted her arm out of his grasp. "Not today, Counselor Zukhara," she replied with frosty calm and turned away before her father or her husband came forward to protest the man's rudeness. It wasn't until she finished serving the refreshments and sat down that she realized Zukhara had spoken to her in perfect Clannish.

She was still inwardly seething when Peoren took the stand before the council to describe the surprise attack on his treld. Eight days of rest, Kelene's gentle ministrations, and his own youthful energy had worked wonders on the boy's battered countenance and his sense of maturity. Although only sixteen, he had left his boyhood behind on the bloodied fields of Ferganan Treld, and he stood before the gathered chiefs and tribesmen with the determination and authority of an adult. Knowing he had the support of the ten chieftains, he launched into a passionate and detailed description of the tragedy. Sayyed translated for him and did not change or leave out a single word.

At first there was little reaction from the Shar-Ja or his nobles—which little surprised the clansmen. The Turics had shown almost no emotions to any of the previous complaints. But as Peoren continued with the account of his father's last stand and the bravery and sacrifice of his hearthguard, the Turics began to grow restive and visibly upset. Their impassive faces darkened in anger; their heads turned toward one another to exchange agitated whispers.

Kelene, her attention still centered on the tall counselor, noticed Zukhara was the only one who remained unmoved. In fact, his expression had the look of a man who had heard the tale before and lost all interest.

"Your Highness," Peoren was saying to the Shar-Ja, "to my knowledge, our two peoples have not declared war upon one another, nor has there been a state of animosity between us. My father died not understanding why his neighbors and those he called friends were killing his people." The young man took a step forward and held out the bloodied scrap of blue cloak sent to Lord Athlone. His pale gray eyes flashed like steel. "There was no reason for your people to attack mine, Highness. Therefore I demand weir-geld, blood money to be paid for the deaths in our clan. Thirty-six people were dead when I left and several more were badly wounded. If we are not recompensed as stated by our clan laws, we the Ferganan will wage a blood feud until every Turic in that raiding party is dead."

The Turics were silent now, their faces grim and intent. They knew Peoren was deadly serious. Blood feuds were sacred to clan society; revenge was a survivor's right and honor.

Kelene held her breath while she waited for the Turics' response. How they dealt with Peoren's demands would tell a great deal about who was truly responsible for the raids across the border. If the tribal leaders were softening the clans for war, they would brush over the Ferganan's claims as unimportant. But if Lady Gabria was right and the rebel extremists were attacking the southern clans, then the Turics would respond with honor and, Kelene hoped, with action.

The Shar-Yon started to stand, but his father gestured

to him to remain seated. Slowly the Turic overlord pushed himself to his feet and drew up to his full height. Some measure of his old vigor and spirit still remained in his beleaguered body, and he drew on that now to address Peoren and the clan chiefs.

"Young man, it is my deepest grief that this tragedy has come to pass," the Shar-Ja spoke. Although his hands trembled with the effort of standing upright, his glance was clear and his voice was still steady and powerful.

While Sayyed translated, the clansmen and Kelene gave the overlord their full attention, for this was the first time the Shar-Ja had spoken at the council.

"I did not know of the disaster," said the Shar-Ja, "and judging from the expressions of my advisors, I believe it is the first time many of them have heard of it, too. We knew a band of malcontents and rebels was marauding along the border, and men were sent to end these raids. But, to my disgrace, I did not follow through to be certain the raiders had been stopped. Obviously, my troops failed me." He paused there and cast a cold look of disapproval at Counselor Zukhara before turning back to the chiefs. "You must understand, difficulties have arisen from the two-year drought that has stricken our realm. My people grow desperate as we face another year of crop failure and dry wells. But it was never my intention that our problems would spill over onto you. My lord chieftains, I shall pay your weirgeld out of my own coffers, and any damages resulting from earlier raids will be paid by the marauders themselves or by the northern tribes who have harbored these thieves."

Several Turic nobles looked shocked, but the others inclined their heads in agreement. Whatever had held them back before had apparently been put aside for the moment, because most seemed to agree that a settlement was necessary.

As Sayyed finished translating the Shar-Ja's speech, a

murmur of approval ran through the ranks of clansmen, and a feeling of relief, too. Now they finally knew they were dealing with outlaws, not the entire Turic nation. Perhaps the Turic tribesmen, in spite of their overwhelming numbers, knew they had enough problems in their own land without incurring the wrath of the Dark Horse Clans and their magic-wielding sorcerers.

Peoren threw the scrap of cloak into the fire and bowed slightly to the Turic in acceptance. Lord Athlone and Lord Fiergan, the fiery, red-haired chief of Clan Reidhar, joined the youth. Sayyed accompanied them, as well, and as Lord Athlone made his reply, he translated the fluid, rolling tongue of the clans into the more abrupt and literal speech of the Turics.

The lord of the Khulinin formally thanked the Shar-Ja for his generosity and presented the Turic scribe with a complete list of damages, stolen property, and lives lost among the four clans hit by the rebel marauders.

"Shar-Ja," Athlone continued civilly, "we did not come to this council just to make demands. We offer a renewal of peace, a treaty of cooperation between our peoples. Let us offer vows of alliance, if not friendship, to you and your nation. We are not rich in goods or many in numbers, but what we have we share with our neighbors."

Kelene lifted her chin, her senses suddenly attuned to those around her. She felt that strange tingling in her spine again, the furious hot and cold emotions of a man with a powerful mind. Immediately her eyes sought Zukhara, and although he had not moved or changed expression, she knew the rage came from him as surely as heat emanated from a fire.

"What in Sorh's name is he so angry about?" she murmured to herself.

Whatever infuriated the tall man, he did not make any indication or show any obvious sign of his fury to the rest of the council. Like a statue he stood aside from the proceedings and merely watched. Only Kelene had an inkling of the volcano behind his deep-set eyes.

Kelene studied him worriedly and wondered if she should warn Rafnir or her father. But what could she tell them? That the counselor was rude to her and angry about something? That was less than useful. Not every Turic was as diplomatic as the Shar-Ja or likely to be happy about a peace treaty. A few of the tribal leaders were sure to be disgruntled about the Shar-Ja's decision to make the northern tribes responsible for the damages to the clans. Perhaps Zukhara was one of those. Whatever his problem, he did not seem inclined to make trouble at this meeting, and because of that, Kelene decided to keep her peace—at least until she had a clearer cause to speak up. The Shar-Ja was speaking to her father again, so Kelene set her unproductive thoughts aside and turned her attention back to him.

"The present Treaty of Council Rock is thirty years old. It was signed, in fact, by your father, Lord Savaric, and by the lord of the dead Corin clan, Lord Dathlar." A ghost of a smile flitted over the old man's face. "Much has changed in thirty years, Lord Athlone. Your powers have become accepted above the Altai River and your magic-wielders work wonders. Perhaps it is time we craft a new treaty of peace. Magic such as yours would be a better ally than enemy."

The tremor in the Shar-Ja's hands became more pronounced, and his face faded to a bloodless pallor. He sank back into his chair, his strength gone.

Kelene jumped to her feet, deeply concerned by his appearance, but before she could get close to the Shar-Ja, Counselor Zukhara moved to block her path to the chair. He paid no attention to her, only gestured to the litter-bearers, who came instantly to the monarch's side.

"Forgive me if I do not stay to finish this," the Shar-Ja managed to say. "My son will speak for me, and you may write the treaty with him."

The chiefs bowed as the Shar-Ja was carried from the tent. Kelene did not know whether to feel annoyed that Zukhara went with him, preventing her from slipping out and trying to visit the overlord alone, or relieved that the counselor had gone. Without his imposing, negative presence, the whole tent seemed lighter, as if a dark cloud had moved from the face of the sun.

Maybe the other delegates felt it too, or maybe they were simply anxious to end the council. Whatever the reason, the afternoon flowed productively until dusk, when the clan chiefs and the Turic tribesmen called a halt to the meeting. Both sides had a copy of the rough draft of their treaty, hastily written by scribes and witnessed by all there. A final draft was to be completed and signed the next day.

As the chiefs left the tent, Lord Fiergan slapped Peoren on the back. "Good job, boy," he said gruffly. "Your father will rest at ease."

"Do you really think the Shar-Ja will pay?" Peoren asked anxiously, retrieving his short sword from the weapon rack by the front entrance.

"The overlord is a man of his word," Lord Athlone assured him.

"If he's allowed to keep his word," Kelene interjected.

The Amnok, Lord Terod, hoisted his eyebrows toward his thinning hair. "What do you mean by that? Who would prevent the Shar-Ja from fulfilling his promise?" he asked sharply.

Lord Bendinor, walking beside Athlone, jerked his head toward the Turic camp across the water. "If I had to make a guess, I'd say that rock-faced counselor, Zukhara. He hasn't done much talking during these meetings, but everyone walks on nails when he's around. He would bear watching."

Kelene hid a smile. She was beginning to like this shrewd and sensible Dangari.

The clansmen reached their horses and mounted for the return ride to camp.

Rafnir looked up at the sky that had darkened to a deep blue-gray. "Here it comes," he said and wiped off several wet splatters from his face.

More raindrops pattered on the rocks and speckled the water. The north wind freshened and roared among the trees, tossing their branches and making the trunks creak and groan. It pulled at the riders' cloaks and chilled man and horse with its sudden damp cold. Across the river, only a few small fires fought bravely against the wind and coming rain. The riders said no more but hurried back to the shelter of their tents and the hot meals awaiting them.

*　*　*　*　*

The rain fell through the night in steady sheets that swayed and danced in the wind. Lightning crackled a few times, and the magic-wielders felt their blood stir and the energy sing in their heads. But the storm cell moved in harness with the wind and was gone as quickly as it had arrived, leaving behind the steady rain and slowly dropping temperatures.

The thunder had faded and the lightning passed to the south when Gabria rose from her blankets beside Athlone and quietly stirred the embers in her small brazier back to life.

Kelene, wakeful beside Rafnir, saw the dim light beyond the sleeping curtain in the tent they shared with her parents, and she slipped out to join Gabria. The older sorceress silently brought out a second glazed mug, poured water for two into her pan, and spooned several heaps of her favorite tea into a teapot.

They huddled together around the small warmth of the brazier while the tent around them heaved in the blustery wind and the rain beat on the waterproofed fabric. They said nothing until the water boiled and Gabria poured it into the pot to steep.

Kelene saw with alarm that her mother's hands were trembling. "What's wrong?" she whispered, conscious of the men sleeping behind the curtains.

Gabria's eyes were huge in the dim light and rimmed with shadows. She shakily set her pot down and pulled her arms tight about her. She nodded gratefully when Kelene brought her gold cloak and wrapped it around her shoulders.

"Something has happened," she said in a soft tone that was terribly certain.

"What?"

"I don't know. I had a dream as dark and foreboding as this night, but nothing was clear."

A dream, Kelene thought, feeling the first stirrings of dread. Gabria's talent for magic sometimes manifested itself in prophetic dreams and visions. The problem was the dreams were not always clear enough to understand until it was too late. She thought about her mother's words and asked, "You said *has* happened. It cannot be stopped?"

"I fear not. I sense the Harbingers are near," Gabria replied in a hollow voice.

Kelene's heart turned cold. The Harbingers were the messengers of Lord Sorh, god and ruler of the Realm of the Dead. If the Harbingers had entered the mortal world, someone or several someones had died.

Already forewarned, neither she nor Gabria were surprised when a distant horn suddenly sang in the storm-wracked night. Somehow they had been expecting it.

It blared again, insistent and furious, until it was joined by others that blasted their warnings into the dark.

Gabria heaved a deep sigh and stood, ready to face what would come. The horns were Turic, and in her deepest sense of the unseen world she knew the Harbingers had arrived.

Behind her, Athlone and Rafnir sprang from their pallets, pulled on their boots, and reached for their swords. There was some advantage to sleeping in one's clothes, for the two men were racing for the tent flap before the horn blasts had ended.

"Wait," Gabria called. She and Kelene hurried into their boots and joined their husbands, cloaked and ready to go. Just outside under a canopy their four Hunnuli stood ready. The horses tossed their heads in agitation, and their star-bright eyes rolled in anger. Their breath steamed in the cold air.

Someone has used magic across the river, Eurus's deep masculine thoughts reached the four people.

"Oh, gods," groaned Athlone.

The Hunnuli carried their riders at a canter through the rain-soaked darkness to the river. Activity already stirred the clan camp, but Lord Athlone refused to wait. He urged Eurus on across the Altai. Water fountained beneath the Hunnuli's hooves as they charged through the ford to the opposite bank. Abruptly they came face-to-face with a solid phalanx of Turic guardsmen.

The guards lowered their spears to face the magicwielders, forming a deadly barrier across the road. Their actions were swift and angry, and their faces were cast in rage. Behind them, the Turic camp was an uproar of shouting voices and running men. Torches flickered everywhere in the rain, and armed guards rushed to defend the perimeters.

"Stop there, infidels!" a commander bellowed in credible Clannish.

Eurus slid to a halt, his hooves sliding in the muddy earth. Lord Athlone carefully unbuckled his sword and held it out to show he came in peace. "I am Athlone, Lord of the Khulinin. I came only to learn of your trouble and offer our help."

"I know you," the officer snapped. "You are one of those sorcerers, so you already know what disaster has overtaken us. Begone from here before I have your horses brought down."

Kelene felt her fury rise. Hunnuli were impervious to magic, but not to normal weapons. To her, the Turic's threat was underhanded and unwarranted. She opened her mouth to say so when another figure appeared on the path behind the guards. The tall form stopped when he saw the clanspeople and shook his fist at them.

"You!" he bellowed over the sounds of the storm. "Curse you for your deeds! What you have done this night will plunge our people into war!"

It took the magic-wielders a moment to recognize Zukhara in the wild night; then Athlone raised his voice. "Whatever has happened, Counselor, we have had no part in it. We came only to give our aid to the Shar-Ja."

"He will not see you," Zukhara answered wrathfully. "He lies crushed in grief. His eldest son, the Shar-Yon, is dead."

A small, heartsick moan escaped Gabria's lips, and she leaned over Nara's neck. Her dream had been right.

At that moment Sayyed galloped up on Afer, his head bare to the pouring rain. He had heard the counselor's last words, and his hand clenched tight on his stallion's mane. Like most clansmen, he was unafraid to speak his mind before his chief or any other figure of authority. Immediately he shouted back, "Prove it, Counselor! Show us the Shar-Yon's body that we may see you do not lie for your own devices!"

A roar of dissension burst from the guards, but Zukhara raised his hand to silence them. "I grant the Khulinin that right. Lord Athlone, you and your guard may enter if the others remain here. I want your word that you will keep your people under control. No weapons, no magic while you are in this camp."

Although the clanspeople could not see it, Zukhara's

mouth twisted into a smile of satisfaction while Lord Athlone gave his bond. "I must attend the Shar-Ja," Zukhara called. "Officer, take the infidels to the Shar-Yon, then escort them off our land." He turned on his heel and strode out of sight, his cloak snapping in the wind.

The commander of the guards looked as if he would burst with outrage, but the Turics were more reserved and strict in their ranks, and he managed to stifle his objections to trusting a clansman. Grudgingly the guards parted before the Hunnuli.

Athlone glanced apologetically at Gabria before jerking his head to Sayyed. The two men slid off their Hunnuli and followed the fuming commander. Five guards fell in behind them and followed them into the heart of the camp to the Shar-Yon's large tent.

On the riverbank, Gabria, Kelene, and Rafnir waited in growing impatience. The rain soaked them quickly in a cold, drenching downpour, and the Turic guards made no move to offer them shelter. The guardsmen simply stared balefully at them and kept their spears lowered. A long time passed before Athlone and Sayyed came trudging down the slope to rejoin them.

Both men were speechless with anger and frustration. Curtly they took leave of the Turics, remounted their Hunnuli, and trotted down to the ford. Kelene, Gabria, and Rafnir traded glances, but they would not ask any questions until Athlone was ready to talk. They fell in behind and thankfully recrossed the river.

As soon as they reached the opposite bank, Gaalney, Morad, and several chiefs came running to meet them. Athlone spoke a vehement curse and slid off Eurus. His anger smoldered in his movements and in his words. "The Shar-Yon is dead," he told the listening people.

"How did it happen?" Rafnir demanded.

The reply came hard and dagger-sharp. "The Turics think we did it."

"That's ridiculous!" Fiergan snarled. "They can't think

we're that stupid. That boy's the best thing they have."

Rafnir looked searchingly at his father-in-law. "Something made them think it was us. What was it?"

Athlone clenched his fists as if he were trying to crush his impotent wrath. "Oh, there was something all right. Something only seven of us here can use. Sorcery. The Shar-Yon was killed by the Trymmian force."

4

"Bad news comes in threes," the clanspeople often said, and the second piece of ill-tidings came at dawn on a frigid wind from the north. The temperatures, which had been falling steadily throughout the night, took a plunge, and the rain gradually slowed to a heavy drizzle and began to freeze. The sunrise came reluctantly, lightening the darkness to a gloomy morning heavily cloaked in cloud and mist that showed no signs of thawing the building ice.

The clansmen cursed and struggled against the freezing sleet to reinforce their tents, bring the horses into shelters hurriedly erected in the lee of the tents, and gather up any firewood that was not already encrusted in sheets of ice. Ice storms were rare on the northern plains, which made them that much more dangerous, and the clanspeople hated them almost more than the blinding blizzards that often swept the grasslands.

Across the river there seemed to be a furious swarm of activity in the Turic camp. Tents were coming down, wagons were being loaded, and horses were being saddled in spite of the weather. A constant, heavy guard patrolled the banks, and no one would answer Lord Athlone's frequent requests to meet with the Shar-Ja or any of his counselors.

The chiefs, meanwhile, tried to solve the mystery of the young Shar-Yon's death. He had been, Athlone reported, burned almost beyond recognition by a blast of the Trymmian Force, a power used only by magic-wielders.

"But that's impossible," Rafnir said for the third time. "We were all in our tents. Gaalney and Morad have witnesses to their whereabouts, Father was on watch, and the four of us were asleep."

The other chiefs, who had crowded into Athlone's spacious tent for a quick council, looked at one another in grim confusion. There were only seven known magic-wielders in their midst. Three of them had excellent alibis and the other four, while not necessarily witnessed by other clan members to be in their tents, were too well-known to be conceivable murderers.

"That leaves two possibilities," said Athlone. "There is either a clansman with the talent to wield magic whom we have not yet detected, or there is one we do know who is hiding close by."

Sayyed glanced up, his eyes unreadable in the dim light. "There is one other possibility, my lord." He paused and held up his own hands. "Another Turic half-breed with clan blood."

"Now how could any untrained Turic use the Trymmian force to kill?" Lord Terod wanted to know. Terod, chief of Clan Amnok, had no magic-wielders in his clan and little practical knowledge of magic.

Lord Sha Tajan of Clan Jehanan, on the other hand,

knew sorcery well. "The Trymmian force is easy to use, especially during a thunderstorm. It wouldn't take much skill to blast the unprotected Shar-Yon."

"There certainly wasn't much skill involved," Athlone growled. He remembered the seared corpse vividly. "Bashan was struck by an uncontrolled blow."

"Then, too, there is the question of why," said Bendinor the Dangari. Like most of his clan, he had a blue-dotted design tattooed along his forehead and down his left cheek. Unconsciously he rubbed at the dots as he deliberated aloud.

"We have no real motive to dispose of the most capable son the Shar-Ja has; that would be harmful to our own cause. But what if Sayyed is right? What if there is a Turic with enough talent to wield the Trymmian force and enough ambition to use it? Why kill the heir? Why make it look as if we did it? Perhaps someone wants to interrupt succession to the high throne, cause further trouble with the clans, or open the way for a new leader."

"The Fel Azureth have been threatening to do that for almost a year," Lord Athlone pointed out. "Maybe they found a way."

"So what do we do?" Rafnir grumbled. "We're in the middle of an ice storm, the Turics are preparing to leave without the treaty, the Shar-Ja won't speak with us, and the Turic nobles think we killed their heir."

"Short of attacking their camp and forcing our way in to the Shar-Ja's presence, the only thing we can do is keep trying to talk to someone in authority and make them see reason," suggested Bendinor reluctantly.

Cursing at the sleet, the ten chieftains, Sayyed, and Peoren mounted their horses, called the hearthguard warriors, and rode to the river ford. The Altai ran fast and turgid, swollen by the earlier rains. The ford was still serviceable, but the clansmen rode warily across, watchful of the current that now reached their legs.

On the southern bank, the tribal guards eyed the

riders suspiciously and stood in ranks across the road
with their hands on their sword hilts. A row of archers
stood in the line of trees by the bank and held their
crossbows ready to fire at a second's notice. The
Turics waited silently while the clansmen drew to a
halt at the water's edge.

This time the Lords Fiergan and Sha Tajan
approached the guard together. The big, red-headed
Reidhar and the tall, cool-eyed Jehanan presented an
attitude of determined commitment as they spoke to the
guards' commander.

This man was a different officer from the belligerent
one of the night before, and though he gave no orders
to move his ranks, he sent a man to deliver the chieftains' message.

With nowhere else to go, the clansmen sat on their
restive horses and waited impatiently in the steady,
freezing drizzle. They drew their hoods low over their
faces, but it did not seem to do much good. The wet
sleet soaked through their cloaks to their clothes, trickled down their boots, and spattered on their hands and
faces until all but the sorcerers were chilled and miserable. Athlone, Sayyed, and Rafnir were slightly drier and
warmer from the vibrant, glowing warmth exuded by
their big Hunnuli.

Finally a lone figure followed by a large and shaggy
brown dog wandered down the path to the guard post.
The person looked like a boy of twelve or thirteen, well
dressed and fine-featured, with thick black hair and an
irrepressible grin. He greeted the commander of the
guards with cheery enthusiasm. The officer saluted him
peremptorily and promptly ignored him.

Undaunted, the boy patted his dog and studied the
uncomfortable chieftains for a moment; then he called,
"Hello!" in a merry voice.

Sayyed lifted his head, surprised that the boy spoke
Clannish. He glanced at Athlone, who gave a nod, and

returned the greeting in Turic.

"Oh, please, speak in your tongue," the boy insisted. "I'm trying to learn it." He had a pleased, open expression that paid no heed to the weather or the tension around him.

Sayyed grinned. "What is your name?" he called back, raising his voice to be heard over the ranks of soldiers.

"Tassilio. Are you a chieftain?"

The sorcerer's grin grew wider. "No. They won't let me." Several guffaws came from the men around him, and Sayyed pushed himself a little higher on Afer's neck to see the boy better. "These men," he explained, pointing to the lords beside him, "are chieftains. They're waiting to see the Shar-Ja."

The light abruptly faded from the boy's face. He tilted his head as if listening to something beside him and shook it fiercely. "Tell them? Of course I can't tell them!" he shrilled.

The officer of the guard rolled his eyes.

"I can't take them to see him either, you know that!" Tassilio said forcefully to the empty air. "He's very sad. He won't talk to anyone. Why? I don't know why! No one ever tells me anything!" He suddenly turned on his heel and stamped back the way he had come, the dog close to his heels.

The clansmen watched him go in surprise, the boy's unhappiness obvious even from a distance. The Turics paid no attention.

When Sayyed asked the officer about the boy, the man shrugged and answered indifferently, "The Shar-Ja's son by a concubine. But he's a sandrat and a simple one at that."

Most of the northern chiefs looked blank when Sayyed translated that bit of news, so he explained. "A sandrat is another name for a bastard." He chuckled mirthlessly. "The concubine was probably not his own, but the Shar-Ja was honorable enough to accept the child."

"Too bad he's a simpleton," growled Fiergan.

To everyone's relief, a small contingent of counselors arrived at that moment led—to no one's surprise—by Zukhara. The elegant counselor tried to look apologetic for the first time since they'd met him. He marched his companions just to the first rank of guards and there stopped, once again keeping his distance and forcing everyone to shout.

"My lords," he called, "we have received your message. Unfortunately, the Shar-Ja is unable to accept visitors. His grief has taken a serious toll on his stamina and has forced him into seclusion."

"I'd like to bet on that one," muttered Fiergan.

"Then perhaps we can talk to you, Counselor," Sha Tajan shouted back. "The treaty we worked so hard to bring about is at risk. Grant us, we ask, time to work through this tragedy. We can prove to you that none of our magic-wielders is responsible for the murder of the Shar-Yon."

Zukhara replied, his words crisp and forceful. "I'm afraid that is impossible. The Shar-Ja is leaving tonight to return to Cangora for the burial of his son. His only words to me were that he would not sign the treaty until the murderer of his son was found and brought to justice."

The chiefs slumped in their saddles, discouraged and cold. They were at an impasse, and no one knew yet how to get around it.

"Counselor," Athlone tried again, "I give you my word that the magic-wielders in our camp had nothing to do with—"

"So you say, Lord Athlone," Zukhara interrupted through a thin veneer of civility. "But only clan blood carries the talent to wield magic, and magic killed Bashan. If you wish to make peace with us, *you* must find the killer! So the Shar-Ja has spoken." He sketched a bow to the clansmen, turned his back on them, and led his followers away.

Fiergan made a disgusted noise somewhere between a grunt and a snort. "So that's that."

A blood-red look of fury crept over young Peoren's face, and the Ferganan reached for his sword. Shaking with emotion, he kicked his horse past the chieftains and wheeled it around in front of the officer of the guard. The archers in the trees raised their bows, but Peoren, if he saw them, paid no attention. He flung his sword to the earth point-first, where it stuck upright in the mud, an emphatic confirmation of his outrage.

"The Ferganan called the Turics 'friend.' We have given your people our hospitality; we traded on good terms. We dealt with them honorably, and they slaughtered my family!" he shouted with all his despairing fervor. "Until the Shar-Ja fulfills his vow to pay the weir-geld, our clan will seek our revenge in Turic blood!"

The tribal guards surged forward to unhorse the boy, but their officer roared, "Stand off!" and thrust himself between Peoren and the angry men. "Be off, boy," he snarled to the Ferganan, "before your blood is spilled."

Not the least bit daunted, Peoren reined his horse around and galloped it back to the Ramtharin shore. The older men, subdued and grim, followed close behind.

* * * * *

The coals were hot, the herbs had steeped, and Gabria and Kelene settled down at last in the empty peace of their tent for the long-awaited cup of tea. The hot drink was a special mixture of Gabria's made with lemon balm, tea leaves from Pra Desh, a hint of wild mint, and a sweetening of honey. On this chilled, wet day the tea reminded the drinkers of summer and wild-flowers and simmering afternoons.

Kelene sipped carefully and sighed her pleasure. She made a mental note to ask her mother for some cuttings of lemon balm to grow in her garden at Moy Tura. A smile crept across her face at the thought of her garden. At Khulinin Treld, Gabria's herbs grew wild in the sun-warmed glades beside the Goldrine River. At Moy Tura, the plants, like the stone, the wood, and the earth, were shaped to men's will—an accomplishment clanspeople were still learning to perfect.

Kelene's thoughts were interrupted by Gabria's gentle laugh. "You and I have been together for days now, and this is the first quiet moment we've had alone. Tell me about Moy Tura."

So, over the tea, Kelene talked about their lives in the ruins. She told her mother about the temple, their house and garden, the guests who came and went so frequently, the numerous underground passages they had found under the city, Sayyed's excavations, and all the many problems they had had. She talked for a long time while the sleet pattered on the canvas over their heads and the brazier softly glowed.

Gabria listened and asked a few questions and watched her daughter's face. When Kelene's words finally dwindled to silence, the older sorceress squeezed her hand and said lightly, "What a tale to tell your children. You should have a bard there to record your adventures."

Kelene stilled. She had not said a word about her failure to have children or her hope that Gabria could advise her. She looked around at her mother almost apologetically and said, "What if we have no children?"

Gabria's fingers tightened over Kelene's. "I was wondering when you were going to talk to me about that. As much as you and Rafnir love each other, your city should be full of babies."

"I have tried everything I know," Kelene murmured sadly. "Prayers and gifts to Amara, herbal remedies. I

even went to Wylfling Treld last spring for the Birthright
to be blessed by a priestess of Amara."

"You found no help in the healers' records?"

A few tantalizing records, medicinal recipes, murals,
and healing stones had been found under the old
Healer's Hall at Moy Tura, but they had been sadly lack-
ing in pregnancy information.

Kelene wrinkled her nose at her remembered disappointment. "No. Nor have the healers who come to
study the old records." She broke off, feeling a sudden
prickle of tears behind her eyes. "Oh, Mother, to be a
healer and not know how to heal yourself! I don't know
what's wrong with me. Why can't I have children?
Rafnir and I wanted a big family to fill that shell of a
city with life! But I feel as empty as the ruin."

She fell quiet while her own words echoed in her
head. Empty. It sounded so final! So pitiful. She shook
herself and drove away the threatening tears. Self-pity
would get her nowhere; that lesson she had already
learned. But as she sipped the last of her tea and smiled
wearily into Gabria's loving face, she had to admit she
felt a little better for having poured out her worries to
her mother.

Gabria, meanwhile, listened patiently to the silence,
knowing for the moment there were no platitudes
Kelene would want to hear. Now that the pain was in
the open, they could ponder and study and maybe
work out a solution. Gabria fervently hoped so. Besides
the delight of having grandchildren, she cherished the
practical hope for an increase in the number of magic-
wielders to carry on the traditions of Valorian's blood.
Kelene and Rafnir were an excellent match, and should
they produce children, their offspring would be powerful indeed.

Their companionable silence lasted for a few precious minutes more before the two women heard the
sound of running feet. A head hooded in a gold cloak

abruptly thrust itself through the tent flap, and a male voice cried, "Come quickly! There's been an accident by the river." The speaker vanished just as hastily, and his footsteps pounded away before the sorceresses recognized him or could ask any questions.

"That was helpful," Kelene grumbled, gathering her healer's bag and her cloak. "He could've stayed long enough to say who or what."

"He did look very flustered," chuckled Gabria. She swept on her own gold cloak over her warm split-skirts, leather tunic, and boots. She gathered an extra blanket from the bed and hurried outside behind Kelene. The messenger was nowhere to be seen.

Nara and Demira stood side by side under the slanted roof of their shelter.

"Did you see which way that man went?" Kelene asked, squinting through the cold gloom.

Toward the grove of trees by the river, Nara responded. *He was in a hurry.*

Without complaint the two Hunnuli left their dry shelter and bore their riders along the faint trail left by the messenger's footprints down toward the Altai. There was no sign of the chiefs, but neither Gabria nor Kelene worried overly much. They half expected their husbands to be at the scene of the accident.

Both women peered ahead through the gathering twilight and saw little more than dark shapes and shadows. The temperature had dropped further during the afternoon, and now snow mixed with the sleet to form a slushy white coverlet over the freezing mud.

The Hunnuli bore left along the bank and trotted into a grove of cottonwood, wild olive, and shrub oak. The trees, barely budded, cluster thickly along an old bow of the river and formed a dense screen beside the bank.

Gabria glanced around. She could not see very much in the flying snow, and the clan camp was lost from view. "Are you sure he went this way?" she asked her mare.

"Over here!" a voice shouted. "Quickly!"

The two mares thrust their way through the thick undergrowth toward the sound of the voice until they reached the edge of the trees by the water. In the dull light they saw a body lying prostrate on the stony shore, and four or five men in clan cloaks bending over it.

The Hunnuli's ears suddenly swept forward in a single motion. Their nostrils flared red, and both mares dug in their hooves and slid to a stop. *Danger!* flared their minds.

Kelene caught a glimpse of two men whirling around and throwing what looked like dark balls at the horses. In the space of a heartbeat, she saw the balls burst into a dense yellowish powder directly in the faces of the mares. Nara trumpeted in rage, but the powder, whatever it was, filled her lungs. She staggered sideways and crashed against a tall tree trunk before Gabria could stop her. Two men immediately dropped from the trees and pulled the sorceress to the freezing mud. Another man roped Nara's head and neck.

Kelene had no time to react. Desperate to save her rider, Demira flung herself forward to free her wings from the crowded trees. Then the powder took effect, and she lurched and fell to her knees at the edge of the water, her eyes rolling. Kelene fell hard. Pain shot through her right arm and down her back. Fury and fear flamed her blood, but a hand clamped a damp cloth over her nose and mouth. Unable to speak, unable to use her magic, Kelene inhaled foul, metallic fumes from the cloth and felt her body go numb. The dim light faded to gray before it blinked out and was lost.

The men quickly flung their clan cloaks and the dead outrider into the river. Swiftly they blindfolded the dazed mares and roped them side by side. They flung the women's bodies over the Hunnuli's backs. Several more men and horses worked their way across the river. With the strength of the additional horses to steady

them, Nara and Demira were forced forward across the
rising Altai into the darkness on the opposite bank. In
less than a moment the river was empty, and Kelene
and Gabria were gone.

*   *   *   *   *

Across the clan camp, Eurus lifted his great head. He
stood in a huddle with Afer, Tibor, and the smaller
Harachan horses of the other chiefs, trying to keep
warm while the men conferred one last time in Sha
Tajan's tent before the darkness became complete. The
stallion stirred irritably and blew a gout of steam, like
smoke from a dragon's mouth.

Something was wrong. Eurus could feel it like an
ache in his belly. He slammed a hoof into the slush and
snow. The Harachan, though handsome, graceful animals, had little of the Hunnuli's intelligence, endurance,
or power. They rolled their eyes at the restless giant in
their midst and shifted nervously away from him.

Afer nickered to reassure them, and they settled warily back into their group. Only the Hunnuli could not
calm down again. Afer and Tibor both grew restive, and
after only a few minutes, the three Hunnuli sidled away
and trotted back to the Khulinin tents.

At first glance, everything looked normal to the Hunnuli. The tents were holding their own against the gathering ice, a few sheltered campfires were burning, the
guards were at their distant posts, and the camp was
quiet.

When the stallions came to the chieftain's tent,
though, their anxiety blew up into alarm. The two
mares and the women were gone, and their tracks,
already filling with snow, pointed down toward the
dark river.

Afer neighed a long, demanding clarion call that rattled the camp and brought men alert, but there was no

response from either Nara or Demira. Like black thunder the three stallions galloped along the mares' trail to the grove of trees. There they slowed to a walk and let their keen eyes and sharp sense of smell lead them through the dense undergrowth to the river's edge.

They caught the scent of Nara and Demira in the crushed grass and of Hunnuli blood mingled in the slush and mire of the shore. There, too, they detected traces of many men: churned footprints, a pool of human blood, and the scent of sweat and fear.

Another smell teased Eurus's nose, a scent that was pungent, powdery, and metallic. It made him dizzy, and he quickly snorted it out. He scented Gabria's faint scent in the brush by the trees and Kelene's on the rocks by the Altai. And that was all.

The riverbank was empty. The women and the mares had vanished.

Tibor and Afer wheeled and charged back the way they had come, while Eurus searched up and down the bank for some sign of his mate and her rider. At his side, the Altai tumbled and rolled in a muddy, heaving current that reached higher and higher up the shore, washing away the scent and sign of the attackers and their victims.

Troubled shouts and running feet crashed through the quiet of the grove, and hooded lamps bobbed their light in the deep twilight. The old stallion returned to meet Athlone, Sayyed, and Rafnir, who were out of breath and wild-eyed. Afer and Tibor came with them.

"Tell me," gasped Athlone. Other men, Gaalney and Morad among them, joined their chief on the bank, and Eurus told the five sorcerers what had been discovered.

Lord Athlone breathed long and deeply before he roared, "Sayyed, I want the entire camp checked tent by tent to be certain they are not there. Rafnir, take squads of men up and down the river to search the banks. The rest of you come with me!"

Without hesitation everyone leaped to obey. They searched for hours, as the darkness closed in and the sleet completed its change to driving snow, and yet they found nothing more of Gabria, Kelene, or the two Hunnuli mares.

In all the furor of the search, no one on the northern bank of the Altai saw the Shar-Ja's great wagon leave the camp, nor the long line of supply wagons and baggage vans that followed in its wake.

At last the men gathered in the center of the camp by a huge fire built as a signal on the slim possibility the two women were lost in the storm.

Rafnir's face was blanched when he reported to Athlone the dismal results of the searches. "Only one guard noticed them leave the tents, but they seemed fine to him and he thought nothing more about it. No one knows why they rode down to the river. We have found no more traces of them anywhere close by." He bit off his words fiercely as if to contain the worry and fear that ate at him. "Downstream, they found the body of one of our outriders washed up on a snag. His throat had been cut, and his cloak was gone."

Athlone, Sayyed, and Rafnir looked at one another, their minds coursing along the same track. Other chiefs and clansmen clustered around the roaring fire, but to the three men they seemed only a distant, murmuring part of the background. For the sorcerers there was only their common anger and burning anxiety for their wives and kinswomen.

Sayyed spoke first, his dark eyes glittering in the shifting light of the fire. "The Turics had some hand in this."

There was no firm evidence to back him up, and yet Athlone nodded in agreement. "None of the clans could profit by their capture."

"What about exiles or even strangers on our land?" Rafnir ventured.

Athlone pondered those possibilities, then shook his head. "It would have taken a fair number of men to capture and hide two Hunnuli, Gabria, and Kelene. They must have been taken by surprise. I don't think a large group could have slipped past all our outriders without leaving some trail. Whoever it was struck fast from close by and fled where we can't follow."

"What if they weren't captured? What if they're dead?" Rafnir said miserably.

The stallion Tibor laid his muzzle gently against the young man's chest. *I do not believe they are dead. I would surely know if Demira had left this world.*

And Eurus, who had run with Nara for twenty-six years, nickered his agreement. Hunnuli had the capacity to make powerful mental and emotional connections with their riders, so powerful that many Hunnuli sought death on their own if their rider died before them. This deep mental attachment was often extended to each other as well. Hunnuli such as Eurus and Nara, Tibor and Demira, whose riders were passionately in love, mated for life.

If Tibor said Demira was still alive, then Kelene must be, too, and Rafnir accepted his word wholeheartedly. He rested his brow on the stallion's wide forehead. "We will go after them," he declared.

"The council is over," Athlone said, sweeping his hand in a sharp gesture. "Pack your gear. We'll leave—"

Lord Fiergan bullied his way into their midst, and his commanding voice rang over the snap and crackle of the fire. "Don't be a fool, Athlone. You can't just ride into Turic territory and demand your women back. They'd either laugh at you or kill you. You don't even know who took them. Could have been the Shar-Ja, those crazy fanatics, or even that cold fish, Zukhara. Maybe the women were taken to lure you over the Altai and into a trap."

"Lord, he's right," Gaalney put in fervently. "And if

you crossed the river and tried to pass yourself off as a Turic, you wouldn't get far! You don't look enough like one. Please listen! You're too important to us to lose. You can't leave the clan for a venture this dangerous."

"Venture!" exploded Athlone. For once his temper got the best of him, and he turned on both men with fury raw on his face. But before he could vent his anger, another sound reached the ears of the clansmen, a sound that froze them where they stood and turned every eye to the east. Beyond the edge of the fire, in the swirling darkness, the dull drumming of hoofbeats pounded closer and closer.

"Lord Wendern!" wailed a frantic voice.

The Shadedron chief lunged forward several paces. "Here! I'm here. Is that you, Hazeth?"

"Lord Wendern!" the voice cried again, and out of the night, guided by the bright beacon of the fire, came a dark horse carrying an apparition of ice and snow and blood. The exhausted horse staggered into the firelight, its sides heaving and its nostrils red as flame. Steam poured from its drenched hide, and its legs shook from its effort.

The figure on its back, swathed in a snow-blanketed black cloak, slid sideways and fell into the arms of his chief. Blood from a head wound had frozen in rivulets down the young rider's face, and another wound on his shoulder had left a hard, icy crust on his cloak. Even so, in spite of his injuries and exhaustion, the boy struggled to remain on his feet.

"The treld has been attacked, my lord," he panted. "By Turic raiders!"

This time, the bad news had come in a set of four.

5

"Lord Athlone, please!" Wendern pleaded. "Please see reason. Hazeth says the raiders attacked yesterday before the weather turned foul. They could not have made it to the river yet. In this snow they'll be holed up somewhere, ready to bolt as soon as the sky clears. If we leave now, we can cut them off. We have a chance to put an end to this raiding for good!"

"Your logic is persuasive, Wendern, but you don't need me. I have to go seek my wife!" responded Athlone adamantly, and he squared his shoulders as if to fend off further argument. He turned his back on the Shadedron chief and continued to pack his gear with an urgency bordering on frenzy. The other chiefs had returned to their own parts of the camp to organize their men and prepare to leave at first light, but Wendern had followed Athlone to his own tent and stood shifting from foot to foot, the blood of his youngest warrior still staining his hands.

Wendern was one of the new chiefs, a robust, middle-aged man who had won his torque three years ago when the previous chief died in the plague. He was a strong, capable leader, but he had no experience in warfare and little idea how his clan had fared in the attack. He truly did need help, Athlone acknowledged, help that would have to come from someone else. Gabria and Kelene were more important.

Athlone slammed a waterskin onto his pile of gear and had just reached for the bag containing his flint and firestone when a sound at his tent flap interrupted him.

"What is it?" he growled, barely pausing in his activity.

A choked gasp from Wendern brought Athlone around, hand on dagger hilt, to see two Turics standing in the entrance. Their long-sleeved brown robes were starred with snow, and their burnooses gleamed white as the moon. They appeared to be unarmed. The first man stepped quietly into the tent, the second close on his heels. Because the ends of their burnooses were wrapped across the lower halves of their faces to protect them from the stinging wind, only the Turics' dark eyes could be seen. The first Turic's eyes seemed to crinkle in some sort of amusement.

He touched his fingers to his forehead and his chest in the Turic form of salute and greeted Athlone in the tribal language.

Athlone's hand dropped. If the garb wasn't familiar, the voice was. "Sayyed," he said, exasperated, "don't you think that's rather dangerous at the moment? Someone could take offense and put an arrow through you."

Sayyed chuckled as he pulled the cloth away from his face. "It proves my point though."

"Which is?"

"That I should seek Gabria and Kelene beyond the Altai, while you go after the marauders with Lord

Wendern."

"No. I am going to find Gabria."

"Athlone, listen!"

The chieftain hesitated, his attention caught by the intensity of his friend's voice.

Sayyed crossed his arms and said, "Gaalney had a point. You do not look like a Turic, nor act like a Turic, nor have any hope of ever speaking like a Turic. If you go over the river, you will be an invader, and no one will help you. Fiergan was right, too. We have no proof who took Gabria and Kelene. We need someone on this side of the border to eliminate other possibilities."

Athlone was still, his face unreadable, his big body held with such tight control that the knuckles of his hands were white. Wendern stayed wisely silent, leaving the arguments to a stronger voice than his. The second Turic, too, was quiet and watchful.

"I propose you go with Wendern and cut off the escape of the raiders. There are not enough warriors close enough to help. The Ferganan have their own troubles; the Wylflings and the Khulinin are too far away. There are only the chiefs and their men. They need a sorcerer to help."

"Gaalney and Morad can go," Athlone said forcefully.

"Gaalney and Morad are not leaders! They are not even wer-tains. They've never fought in battle. They are not Lord Athlone! If Lord Athlone, the renowned sorcerer lord of the Clans of Valorian, moves against the invaders of the Ramtharin Plains it will send a message to others who consider our people too weak to fight." He raised a finger and shook it at the chief. "And don't forget the Shar-Yon. Other Turics may want revenge against us for killing Bashan. If you are here defending the borders, the Turics may think twice about attacking us in force."

Athlone grunted. "You give me too much credit."

"That's dung and you know it. Wendern needs *you.*

Not Morad or Gaalney. Of course, if you capture those raiders, you might have a bargaining chip to ransom in exchange for Gabria and Kelene. Whoever took them took pains to remove even the Hunnuli. They wanted the women alive."

Athlone's expression lost a little of its ferociousness as Sayyed's words sank in. His friend's arguments made sense to Athlone's mind; it was just his heart that had to be convinced. "And what are you going to do if I go haring off after brigands and thieves?"

Sayyed bowed slightly. "My companion and I intend to infiltrate the Shar-Ja's caravan, learn of the women's whereabouts, and free them at our earliest opportunity."

"Your companion?" Athlone asked dryly.

The second Turic tugged his burnoose free and smiled wanly at his father-in-law. "Father thought it was time I learned more about the other side of the family," replied Rafnir.

Athlone's knees seemed to collapse, for he sat down abruptly on the cushions in the center of the tent. Gabria's teapot and the two cups were still on the low table where she had left them, and the coals in the brazier were still warm. The chief's gaze went from one man to another in a long, pondering stare, while his mind struggled to choose the best path.

"Eurus!" he suddenly bellowed. When the Hunnuli poked his head in the flap, Athlone jabbed a finger at Sayyed. "Did you hear what he said?"

The stallion's head bobbed yes.

"We must also consider Nara and Demira, so I ask you, what do you suggest?"

Eurus, one of the oldest Hunnuli in the clans and one of the few horses to have run wild with the King Hunnuli, had grown wise during his years with humans. He replied simply, *Sayyed has a better chance to find Gabria and Kelene. You would have a stronger hand against the Turics if the raiders are stopped.*

"And you're willing to let Afer and Tibor go without you?"

I would hardly tell you to go somewhere if I were not willing to follow.

"But," Wendern offered almost apologetically, "they can't take the Hunnuli into the Turic realm. The horses would be recognized immediately."

Rafnir gestured outside. "Come see. We've already taken care of it."

The men trooped out into the night. The wind had slowed a little, and the snowfall was lighter. With the help of the gods, Athlone thought, the storm would blow over by the next day. He patted Eurus and glanced around, expecting to see Afer and Tibor. All he saw were two large horses bridled, saddled with deep-seated Turic saddles, and tethered to the tent peg.

The horses seemed to be black, although in the darkness it was hard to tell. One had a small star on his forehead, and the other had two white socks on his forelegs. There was no sign of the Hunnuli's usual white lightning mark on their shoulders or any of the breed's power and grace. The two stood, noses down against the wind, looking anything but regal.

"Nice animals," Wendern commented. "Where did you find mounts so big?" Then to his amazement, one of the horses lifted its head and nickered at him. His jaw dropped.

"You can't be serious," Athlone chuckled. "How did you get Hunnuli to wear tack?"

It was Afer's idea, Tibor complained, shaking the saddle on his back. *Only for Gabria and Kelene would I do this.*

Sayyed laughed. "They even suggested the dye to hide their shoulder marks and the white paint to decorate their coats. If no one looks too carefully, and they keep their wits, they'll pass."

Athlone decided he could hardly fight such a united

front. He embraced his friend and his son-in-law in gratitude. "You have my permission to go," he said, too overcome with sudden emotion to say all that he felt he should tell them. But he did add one more admonition. "If I don't receive a message from you in the next fifteen days, I will gather the clans and march south after you!"

* * * * *

A pale glow softly tinted the eastern horizon by the time the clansmen discovered the Shar-Ja's entourage had already left. A heavy guard still patrolled the southern bank, but only a small camp remained where the day before the entire meadow was filled with the rounded Turic tents. Most of the wagons were gone, too, including the Shar-Ja's elaborate, covered vehicle.

Sayyed shrugged when he heard the news. "They can't have gone far in this weather. We'll find them."

The clan camp quickly disappeared as well, the traveling tents and supplies loaded in wagons or on pack animals. The snow still fell in fitful showers through air damp and cold, but it was the last gasp of a storm already dying. That morning the sky looked dove gray instead of the steely blue of the day before, and the wind had left to blow its mischief elsewhere.

As soon as it was light enough to distinguish detail and color, Sayyed brought his prayer rug out of his pack and laid it carefully on the bare patch of ground left by Gabria's tent. He knelt in the time-honored tradition of the Turic to pay homage to his god at sunrise. Twice a day he prayed, bowing to the south where his fathers believed the sacred city of Sargun Shahr was located. Although he had lived with the clans for twenty-six years and participated in some of their festivals, Sayyed still practiced the religious beliefs of the Turics and still carried the love of his god deep in his heart. He was grateful the clanspeople were not fanatical about their religion and had not tried to convert him. In respect to clan ways, he had allowed Rafnir to be raised in the traditions of Amara, Lord Sorh, Surgart, and Krath, telling his son only the meanings behind the different beliefs.

That morning, though, as he knelt in the cold light, he slanted a glance over his shoulder and saw Rafnir watching him. "Get a rug," he ordered. "You don't have to believe, but if you're going to be a Turic for a while, you need to pretend."

Rafnir gladly obliged. He spread out a horse blanket, knelt beside his father, and bowed his head. Wordless and attentive, he listened to the lines of his father's prayers. The words were ones he had heard as far back as he could remember. They were songs really, songs of praise and gratitude and hope for a new day, and they rolled off Sayyed's tongue with salutary humbleness and joy. There was comfort to be found in the phrases, and Rafnir found himself repeating them after his father. The deities addressed may have been different, but the heart-felt sentiments of each man's prayers were the same.

By the time they were finished, the chiefs had gathered their men to leave. Sayyed and Rafnir rolled their rugs, loaded their bags behind their saddles, and threw clan cloaks over their Turic garb. They joined the mounted warriors and rode with them toward the rising sun. On Council Rock, the huge tent sat empty and abandoned, its task unfulfilled. Across the Altai, the Turic rearguard watched the clans ride away.

The chiefs were forced to set a slow pace for the morning because of the drifted snow and the snow-encrusted ice beneath the horses' hooves. The warriors rode carefully, paralleling the Altai River toward the ruins of Ferganan Treld. If all went well, they would reach the sand hills south of Shadedron Treld in time to cut off the Turic raiders' retreat over the border river.

Sayyed and Rafnir rode with the clans for nearly an

hour until they reached the next passable ford on the swollen river. On a small knoll overlooking the Altai, they stopped with Lords Athlone, Wendern, and Bendinor.

Sayyed pulled off his cloak. He felt a genuine sadness when he passed it over to Athlone, a tug of regret he had not expected. True, he was secretly excited about returning to the Turic lands, but he had lived with the clans longer than the tribes, and he realized the Ramtharin Plains were now and forever his home. He grinned at Athlone, lively mischief suddenly glinting in his eyes, and he saluted his lord as a clansman. "Until we ride together again, Athlone." He waved, then urged Afer into a canter down the slope to the river. His voice, lifted in the wild, high-pitched ululation of the Turics, sounded eerily on the still morning air.

Rafnir tossed his cloak to Bendinor, sketched a salute to Athlone, and turned Tibor after Afer. The lords watched as the two black horses plowed across the river and emerged dripping on the other side. In a moment the two were gone, lost to sight beyond a belt of trees.

For a while Athlone sat rigid on his stallion, his gaze lost on the southern horizon. It took all of his strength to sit still and not send Eurus galloping after Afer and Tibor. Fear for Gabria clung to the Khulin Lord like a wet cloak, and he wanted to challenge it directly, not delegate such vital responsibility to someone else. But Athlone was shrewd enough to accept the truth: he would be more effective north of the border in his own territory.

Silently he breathed a prayer, to Amara rather than Surgart, that the gods keep watch over his wife, his daughter, and the two men who risked so much to find them. At last he nodded to his companions and turned Eurus east, his thoughts already ranging ahead to Shadedron Treld and the hunt for the killers of his people.

* * * * *

It was midafternoon by the time Sayyed and Rafnir caught up with the Shar-Ja's caravan. Sayyed had been right; it had not moved far in the snowy night, only going a few leagues deeper into tribal territory before stopping again. The huge cavalcade had been underway since early morning, traveling slowly along a beaten caravan road toward Cangora, apparently in no hurry to reach its destination.

A large covered wagon, draped in black and royal blue, carried the coffin of the dead Shar-Yon at the head of the caravan, and a procession of priests and royal guards surrounded it. Word of the death had already passed ahead, for the road was lined with mourners and spectators who came from nearby settlements to pay their respects to the royal dead.

The weather seemed to reflect the sad occasion with a low roof of clouds and a faint mist that teared everything in drops of glistening dew. As so often happened in spring storms, this one lost its ferocity on the northern plains. By the time it crossed the Altai and hit the arid, warm winds of the desert realm, its teeth were gone. The icy snow lasted barely five leagues into the Turic lands before it turned to mud and melted away. Only the clouds and the mist remained of the storm that had swept the Ramtharin Plains.

On the crest of a low hill, Sayyed and Rafnir sat side by side, watching the caravan pass by on the road below. They carefully studied the long ranks of warriors representing the fifteen tribes, the disciplined rows of royal guards, the mounted counselors and nobles who had stayed so reticent at the council meeting, the dozens of war chariots, the Shar-Ja's enormous personal retinue, and the innumerable wagons, carts, and baggage vans that followed in the rear.

"I don't see anything that even resembles a Hunnuli,"

Rafnir said glumly.

"Did you expect to?" Sayyed replied in a thoughtful murmur. His eyes were still on the caravan below, his brows drawn in concentration.

"Well, no," admitted the young man. "That would be too easy. If they're with this caravan at all, they'd have to be out of sight."

Sayyed scratched his beard. "Hmm. Maybe we're looking at this from the wrong direction. We've assumed Gabria and Kelene were taken to trap Lord Athlone or to incite the clans to war, but what if they were kidnapped for a more personal reason?"

Rafnir looked startled. "Why do you say that?"

"Just a guess, really. I was counting heads," Sayyed answered. "There are more men among the tribal ranks now than there were at Council Rock."

"Are you sure?"

The older man nodded. "Law requires each tribe to send a specific number of men to escort the Shar-Ja on official journeys. I counted forty men for the Raid tribe at Council Rock. The other tribes should have sent equal numbers, but some of the units have gained more men."

"That seems odd. I wonder who they are and why are they coming now?" said Rafnir.

"Two excellent questions."

"So you think someone in the caravan is expecting trouble and may have taken the women to protect himself?"

"It's possible. Two sorceresses are a powerful shield—or weapon." Sayyed grimaced as he pushed himself to his feet. The cold, damp weather had played havoc with his knees, and unbending them was a slow process. "We'll stay out of the way until dark, then join the caravan when it camps for the night."

His son sprang upright with the suppleness of youth. "What if they're not here?"

"We'll give it four days," advised Sayyed. "If we can't find any sign of them here, we'll ride north to find the Fel Azureth and start again."

Quickly the men returned to the Hunnuli at the base of the hill. They withdrew from the road into open country among the folded hills and scrub to follow the caravan at a safe distance. The afternoon wore away slowly. The mist ended before evening, and a brisk breeze sprang up to tear away the roof of clouds.

Shortly before sunset the royal caravan stopped in a broad, flat basin near the first of a series of big oases that lay like jewels along the golden string of the caravan route the Turics called the Spice Road.

The road was an old trail that passed on a long diagonal from the merchant city of Pra Desh in the Five Kingdoms southwest across the Ramtharin Plains and the Ruad el Brashir to Cangora, the seat of the Turic overlords tucked in the foothills of the Absarotan Mountains. The Absarotan, or Blue Sky Mountains, were a southern extension of the Darkhorns and rose like a giant's fortress above the Kumkara Desert.

The first stop along the Spice Road in Turic territory was the Tarzul Oasis. The staging settlement of mudbrick houses, inns, shops, and suppliers had grown up beside the wells of the oasis and served not only the locals but pilgrims, travelers, nomadic shepherds, and caravans as well. When the Shar-Ja's officers stopped the caravan for the night, a flock of people, excited children, and barking dogs rushed to the camp to help, watch, or just get in the way.

Sayyed and Rafnir watched the oasis from a vantage point on a nearby rise. The caravan's setup was quick and organized in spite of the confusion from the additional oasis people, but the two clansmen were pleased to see the Turics set few guards around the perimeter of the camp. Only the Shar-Ja's tent was under a very tight and heavily armed guard.

Just as the sun touched the tops of the distant range of mountains, the clouds opened a window in the west, and slanting rays of golden light swept across the basin and gilded the trees of the oasis. At that instant a horn sounded a long, sonorous call to prayer.

To Rafnir's astonishment, the entire bustling population of the Shar-Ja's camp, the oasis, and the village fell silent, turned to the south, and stood motionless, their heads bowed in prayer. Some kneeled, and a few lay prostrate on the ground. The young sorcerer stared, awed at the scene. He felt his father kneel beside him and heard him murmur the evening prayer. Slowly Rafnir sank down beside him and turned his thoughts to the gods in a wordless supplication for strength and wisdom.

The sun dipped lower; the golden light faded. A moment later the horn blew again, and the Turics bustled back into activity. Rafnir rose, feeling strangely comforted.

"Let's go," Sayyed said softly. They turned to the Hunnuli and removed their saddles and bridles. "I don't want to take the chance of leaving you two in the picket lines tonight. You'll be safer with the herds or on your own," he informed the stallions.

Thank you, Afer sent, grunting with relief as the tight cinch was unbuckled.

"But," Sayyed said, pulling two leather halters from his saddle pack, "you'd better wear these."

Why! snorted Tibor. *Those are humiliating.*

"Exactly. Even the Turic know Hunnuli will not wear tack. If you are seen, no one will suspect you are Hunnuli if you are wearing a halter."

Afer sighed gustily. *He is right, Tibor. Be grateful he did not suggest hobbles.*

Chuckling, Sayyed buckled the halters on their heads and sent them out to graze with the caravan herds; then he and Rafnir shouldered their saddles and gear. They decided to make their way down the back side of the hill and work their way around the base to the outskirts of the camp through a shallow gully lined with shrubs and high weeds.

They had covered barely half the distance through the gully when the first small sounds reached them through the quiet backdrop of evening noises. The two men halted and stood listening intently. One sound came again, a single metallic clink, like a blade hitting a rock, then a rustle of bushes, and the unmistakable mutter of subdued voices from somewhere in front of them.

Sayyed nodded to Rafnir and eased his load to the ground. They padded forward as quietly as possible through the undergrowth to the edge of an open space between several tall clumps of brush. Sayyed froze, his hand raised to warn Rafnir.

Dusk pooled in the shadows of the gully, but there was still enough daylight left in the clearing to see five men hunched together, speaking softly among themselves. They were dressed in the dark robes, high boots, and warm wool knee-length coats the tribesmen preferred for travel, and they were heavily armed with tulwars, knives, and hand axes. One man was busy sewing something to the front of his coat.

Sayyed jerked his hand back, and he and Rafnir retreated up the hillside where they could watch the clearing undetected.

"Now why were five tribesmen lurking in the bushes?" Rafnir whispered.

"Look!" Sayyed hissed in reply, and he pointed to the gully they had just left. One by one, the five men slipped out of their hiding place and split off in five different directions. In just a few minutes, all five had nonchalantly disappeared into the crowded camp.

"Who were they?" wondered Rafnir.

"Of that I'm not certain, but did you see the man sewing? He was tacking a tribal patch on his robe." Sayyed pointed to the embroidered lion of the Raid on his own chest. "Every tribesman wears his emblem on his clothes, so why was that man adding one at the last minute?"

Neither man had an answer to that puzzle, so they put it aside for the time being and proceeded back down the hill to the borders of the camp. Following the lead of the others, the two men casually walked out of the deepening twilight and into the Shar-Ja's camp. They left their gear beside a pile of other saddles near the picket lines where some of the horses were kept close by for quick use. The smell of roasting meat led them to a cook tent, where they got a meal of bread, cheese, meat, and dates.

When they were finished, they meandered around the enormous camp to see what they could find. They stopped to chat now and then with other tribesmen, shared a cup of wine beside a fire with some villagers from the settlement, and exchanged pleasantries with them. They stopped to admire the Shar-Ja's elaborate wagon, and they paid their respects to the dead Shar-Yon in his draped coffin. When they tried to get close to the Shar-Ja's tent, however, several guards blocked their path and suggested forcefully they go elsewhere. They caught a brief glimpse of the Shar-Ja's son, Tassilio, playing with his dog, and once they saw Zukhara striding purposefully through the camp.

They had heard the counselor had taken charge of the caravan in place of the Shar-Ja and that no one had seen the Turic overlord since the debacle at Council Rock. A few rumors circulating the camp whispered the Shar-Ja was dead, but nothing had happened to confirm that.

Sayyed observed how people fell back from Zukhara and how all but the royal guards warily saluted him. To Rafnir's shock, Sayyed called out a greeting and saluted, but the counselor barely acknowledged him and continued on his way, his tall form lance-straight, his face dark and resolute.

By dawn the clansmen were weary and disappointed. They had found nothing to indicate Kelene and Gabria were in the caravan, nor had they heard anything even remotely connected to sorcery or the kidnapped women. All the talk in the camp had been about the religious zealots in the north, the Shar-Ja's ill-health, and the growing unrest in various areas of the realm.

At sunrise, after the morning prayers to the Living God, the Turics broke camp to continue the journey to Cangora. Sayyed and Rafnir retrieved their saddles and whistled in the Hunnuli. Afer and Tibor reported they had been unable to scent or even sense the presence of the mares. Unhappily the sorcerers and the Hunnuli joined the groups of tribesmen riding in the caravan. No one commented on their presence or questioned their right to be there. A few eyebrows were raised at the size of the black stallions, but Sayyed explained they were crossbreeds from a certain breed of plowhorse. He suppressed a laugh when Afer whipped his head around to snap at a 'fly' on Sayyed's leg.

The caravan wound onward at the slow pace of the funeral cortege toward the next oasis on the trail. The Spice Road ran due south for a few leagues, then curved southwest toward the high foothills of the Absarotan Mountains.

Although Rafnir was not familiar with this territory, Sayyed had traveled this road several times in his youth with his father, the Raid-Ja, and he saw with deep misgivings that the tales he'd heard of the drought were painfully true. The area they rode through was still open range and usually rich enough to support sheep, cattle, goats, and the Turics' tough desert horses. In most years, spring rains refreshed this land, replenishing the stock ponds, bringing wildflowers to bloom, and enriching the tall, thin grass that would cure to a golden brown by summer.

But this year the green that should have carpeted the

broad hills had already faded to a dull, wilted tan. The grass was sparse, and the stock ponds, man-made ponds dug to catch the spring rains, were mere mud holes. The herds Sayyed spotted were thin and far between.

When he mentioned this to a man riding beside him, the man's expression turned mournful. "Aye, we've had to sell or eat almost everything. My family has only our breeding stock left. If we don't get rain soon, we will have famine by the Feast of the Prophets."

Sayyed glanced at the man's emblem and recognized him as a member of the Mira tribe that had its hereditary demesne to the northeast. He frowned in sympathy. The Feast of the Prophets was in nine months, in the cool season of winter. Not much time to save a population from starvation. "Haven't the priests stockpiled grain in settlements as they are supposed to do?" he asked curiously.

At that his companion turned red with ill-concealed irritation. "Perhaps the Raid have honest officials and no dealings with the Fel Azureth. But the priests of our lands have had to pay grain for taxes to the Shar-Ja's collectors, and what is left has been *claimed* by the Gryphon to feed his army of zealots."

Sayyed slouched in his saddle and tried not to look too interested. He had heard that name from Athlone as the title of the unknown leader of the Fel Azureth. Gryphon seemed an appropriate title for such a man, Sayyed mused. Real gryphons had once existed in the Absarotan Mountains and were known to be cunning, secretive, and fiercely loyal to their mates. "Have you seen the Gryphon?" he asked casually.

"Not face-to-face," the tribesman said glumly. "He sends his commanders to tithe the settlements and towns in the name of the Living God and the Prophet Sargun." The man suddenly realized his voice was growing louder with his anger, and he bit off his words with a harsh laugh. "Shahr keep the Gryphon in the palm of his hand, and," he tacked on in an undertone, "keep him away from my family." He clucked to his horse and rode forward, away from the curious strangers.

"That was interesting," Rafnir said. "Not all tribesmen are happy with the Fel Azureth either."

Sayyed stared thoughtfully ahead, far beyond the caravan, beyond the horizon, to things only his mind's eye could see. There was so much to consider, so many facts he did not yet have, so many nuances he could not put into place. He needed to talk to someone who knew the current news around the entire realm, someone who would not inquire in turn about his big horse or his lack of knowledge or his curiosity. But there was not one person he could think of, or anyone he could trust. He and Rafnir would have to continue their blind search without drawing the attention of those who might have Kelene and Gabria in their control. One slip could prove deadly for them all.

The sorcerer stifled a yawn. Time was precious, but he and Rafnir could not function much longer without sleep. They had spent three anxious days and two nights with virtually no rest, and the effects were wearing them down. Sayyed yawned again. His head felt heavy and ached behind his eyes.

He glanced at Rafnir and saw the same weariness dragging on his son's features. There was more there, too, a brittleness of worry and a tight-jawed self-control. Rafnir had said little of his fear for Kelene, but it was there to read in the banked fires of his dark brown eyes.

*   *   *   *   *

That night at the second oasis, called the Tears of Al Masra, the evening was much the same. The caravan halted in a level field and set up camp beside the string of shallow pools that formed the oasis. After prayers, food was prepared, the horses were herded out to graze under the watchful eye of mounted herders, and the travelers relaxed. Sayyed and Rafnir walked about, observing the activity and looking for something that would lead them to the missing women.

They saw little to help them. The Shar-Ja remained in seclusion. The counselors kept to themselves, and the tribesmen ate and rested. Tassilio seemed to be the only one in camp with a light heart. He ran with his dog, laughing and barking and chasing imaginary prey.

As night settled on the oasis, Sayyed saw seven more men slip out of the darkness and mingle in with the camp's inhabitants. They were like the first group, totally unremarkable except for their full complement of weapons. When Sayyed tried to approach one, a lean wolf of a man with a mole on his cheek, the tribesman glared at him and hurried away.

At last, exhausted, Sayyed and Rafnir sought shelter in a quiet place under the tall, slim trunk of an oasis willow. They slept undisturbed until morning, when they woke to horns calling the faithful to prayer.

That day followed much like the last. Three days were gone, and there was still no word or clue as to the whereabouts of Kelene and Gabria. That evening the caravan traveled late into dusk to reach the next oasis on the Spice Road, one unimaginatively called Oasis Three.

"There's one place we haven't tried yet," Sayyed told his son as they ate their meal. "The baggage train. We'll take a look in some of the bigger vans and wagons."

They waited until the night was late and the camp had settled into subdued nocturnal peace. The enormous dome of the sky arched over their heads, clear and afire with countless stars. In the pale starlight, the sorcerers crept to the supply wagons and began a slow, methodical search of the interiors of each one, large or small. Soft-stepping, they checked the first row then moved to the next.

Sayyed put his foot on the wheel of a large covered vehicle and was about to lift himself up to see inside when he heard the faint crunch of soft boots on sandy soil. He turned to warn Rafnir and glimpsed several shadows spring around the corner of the wagon. Balanced on one foot and with his hands on the wagon sides, he could not react fast enough to defend himself. He fell sideways, hoping to throw off the attackers long enough to form a defensive spell. Something flashed in the starlight, and a brilliant pain exploded in his head. He heard a muffled thud beside him, and as he collapsed he felt the body of his son fall silently on top of him.

6

Sayyed hung suspended in a black pitiless limbo somewhere between consciousness and oblivion. He could not see or move or speak; he could only dwell in the pain that racked his body. He thought at first the pain was only in his head, in a blinding crack behind his ear that threatened to split open his entire skull. But as he concentrated on that agonizing sensation, more of his senses became aware, and other parts of his body began to complain. His neck, shoulders, and arms ached for some reason he did not yet understand, and his shins and ankles felt battered. Confused at this unknown assault, Sayyed's mind scrambled farther out of the black fog to seek a way to end the pain.

He became aware of several things at once. First, although he knew his eyes were open, he could not see. Fabric had been wrapped around his head, effectively blinding and gagging him. Second, he realized his arms and shoulders hurt because someone had roped his arms up over his head and was dragging him, face-down, over ground rough with short shrubs, rocks, and small prickly cactus.

Groggily he struggled against the tight bonds on his arms, but his efforts brought only a vicious kick that landed on his ribs. He groaned and stayed still while he forced his mind to full alertness.

He briefly considered summoning magic to break his ropes; then he set that idea aside for the moment. He was still too groggy and could neither speak nor use his hands. Without those guides and the strength to control the powerful energy, he could cause more trouble for himself than he was in now. The magic could burst out of control and destroy all who were in the vicinity.

Instead, he let his body hang limply in his captors' hands and listened to the sounds around him, hoping to learn more about the men who held him and what had happened to Rafnir. As he concentrated, he discerned more footsteps, perhaps five or six pairs, and what could be the sound of another body being dragged close by.

The attackers moved swiftly and silently up an easy slope, then down a long, gentle incline to a hollow lined with gravel and short spindly plants that crackled under Sayyed's weight. There the unseen men stopped and dropped their captives on the ground.

"By the Path of Sargun, these brigands are heavy!" one voice complained. "Why did we have to drag them out here?"

A second, harsher voice answered, "He said no more killing in the camp. It'll start to be noticed."

Sayyed bit his lip to stifle a moan of pain. His arms were still up over his head and felt as if they had been racked from his shoulders. He felt the other body rolled over beside him, and to his relief, he heard a third voice say, "This one's still alive."

"Anyone know these two?" demanded the second voice, probably the leader.

Sayyed felt himself pushed onto his back, and the fabric was yanked away from his face, jarring his aching head. The groan he tried to stifle slipped out of his clenched teeth.

Six faces peered down at him, smirking and merciless. "He's Raid tribe, that's all I know," one dark face said. "He was probably looking for things to steal."

"Raid," another sneered. "Nothing but thieves and brigands. No wonder they do not follow the Path of Light and Truth."

"Kill them," ordered the leader.

Sayyed frantically tried to lick his lips, to swallow past a dry and bitter mouth. He had to take action now before the assassins slit his throat. Using all his will, he drew on the magic in the earth beneath him. He felt it surge into his body, a furious, energizing power that flowed through bone and muscle as easily as his own blood. He formed the magic into the only weapon he could use instinctively without forming a specific spell: the Trymmian force.

He saw the thugs draw their knives, the long, fat-bladed weapons the Turics often used, and he pulled his arms down to his chest. His muscles tensed; his heart beat hard against his ribs. One man stepped close to grab Sayyed's hair.

"Oh! Excuse me," a boyish voice called cheerfully.

Every man whirled and looked up to see a short figure standing halfway down the hill.

"Excuse me," the voice cried again. "I was just looking for my dog. He is big and brown and looks as ugly as you!" Swift as a hunter, the figure drew back his arm and fired a rock from a slingshot at the man closest to Sayyed. The missile struck the man's temple with such a crack, he fell sprawling, dead before he knew what hit him.

The leader yelled a curse and sprang up the slope after the boy.

"Tassilio!" a new voice bellowed and, to the astonishment of everyone, a black-clad warrior lunged down the hill, his tulwar drawn and ready. He charged past the boy into the midst of the surprised men and swung his curved sword with both hands into the belly of the leader. The assassins hesitated only a heartbeat; then the four still on their feet drew their own blades, circled around their lone attacker, and rushed in like wolves.

Sayyed struggled desperately to sit up and free his hands. A pale blue aura formed around his fists from the power of the Trymmian force, and he made use of a fraction of its searing energy to burn through the ropes on his arms.

In that instant he heard the boy cry out and a dog bark. Looking around, he saw the boy run furiously down the hill toward the warrior with the sword. The black-clad man had injured a second thug, but the others had pressed him so closely he tripped over an outcropping and lay sprawled on his back. The assassin's swords rose over his head.

Sayyed had lifted his hand to fire a blast of magic when suddenly horses' hooves pounded on the hillside, and the enraged scream of a stallion interrupted the thugs' intent. Two huge horses blacker than night, their eyes like moons of green fire, rushed into the three remaining attackers. The men screamed in fear and flung themselves away, but only one escaped the horses' trampling hooves. That man tried to break past Sayyed to escape to the relative safety of the distant camp.

A blast of the Trymmian force shot from the sorcerer's hand, flared a fiery blue path through the darkness, and scorched into the chest of the last assassin. The thug crashed on his back, his robe smoking.

A strange stillness sank over the hollow. The dead lay motionless in the settling dust. The warrior leaned on the hilt of his sword and gasped for breath. His small companion stood just above him on the hill, his mouth open and his eyes bulging. His dog pressed close to his knees. The two black horses sniffed the dead men lying at their feet, then swung their great heads to look at Sayyed, who bent over his son.

"By all that's holy," a wondering voice said softly. "Sayyed. It is you."

The sorcerer lifted his head. The voice, once familiar and remembered with pleasure, put a name to the unknown warrior. In the pale light of the icy stars, he saw a face he had not seen in twenty-six years: his brother Hajira, one year older than himself, the sixth son of the Raid-Ja and his wife, the clanswoman from Clan Ferganan.

They built a small fire in the hollow out of the way of the cool night wind. While Sayyed tended Rafnir, Hajira dragged the bodies out of sight into a thicket. Tassilio raced off to the distant camp and soon returned carrying a wedge of cheese, a box of sweet oatcakes, and a jug of *firza*, a drink made from fermented grain and dates. Rafnir was conscious by that time and nursing his pounding head by the fire. The two brothers sat on either side, unsure yet of what to say.

Grinning like a conspirator, Tassilio laid out his offerings with several plates and a pair of matching flagons.

Hajira rolled his eyes when he saw the things. "Tassilio may be son of the Shar-Ja, but he steals like a street urchin," he said as the boy sat close beside him.

The boy grinned and winked at Sayyed with such intelligent mischief that the sorcerer began to seriously doubt the general belief that Tassilio was "simple." Up close, the Shar-Ja's son was rangy, athletic, and the image of his father, with a straight nose, strong jaw, and two huge, wary eyes that stared unwaveringly at the two sorcerers.

"You're clansmen, aren't you?" the boy said to Sayyed

in Clannish. "Yet you speak Turic, ride with the caravan, and look like Hajira."

"You don't miss much, do you?" Rafnir said, offering him a weak smile.

To the clansmen's surprise, the boy slouched forward, letting his hair fall over his eyes. His mouth slackened into a loose-lipped grin, and the bright glint of awareness in his eyes dulled to a blank stare. He looked so much like the simpleton people thought him to be, Sayyed simply stared.

"It's amazing what you can hear when people pretend you don't exist," Tassilio laughed. He straightened and as quickly snapped back into his alert, cheerful self.

Hajira stirred for the first time. "Tassilio was the one who saw the thugs jump you at the baggage wagons. He came to get me."

Sayyed sipped his wine, letting the tart liquid soothe his dry and aching throat. He wondered where to go with this conversation. How far could he trust even a brother he had not seen in so long? Hajira knew him for what he was, and when they were boys Hajira would have died before betraying his brother. But what would this man do? Who was he now?

"How did you know I was here?" he asked Hajira after a short pause.

"I recognized you from that day on the riverbank," Tassilio answered for his companion. "So I told Hajira you were in the caravan, and he told me to keep an eye on you."

The Turic warrior lifted an eyebrow at this enthusiastic speech. He seemed to be as quiet and taciturn as the boy was voluble. "We've heard many tales about a half-breed sorcerer who rode with the Lady Gabria," he said finally. "But Father would never allow your name to be spoken after you left. I did not realize it was you until tonight. We always thought you were dead."

Sayyed shook his head at the memory of his father. A

stern, unrelenting man, the Raid-Ja believed that as leader of the Raid tribe he had to follow the exact letter of the law. When his youngest son revealed the unexpected and forbidden talent to wield magic, Dultar sadly but mercilessly disinherited him and exiled him from the tribe. The hurt of that rejection had dulled over the years, and after a time Sayyed accepted the results of that exile with gratitude. If he had not fled to the Clans, he would not have met Gabria and Athlone, nor his beloved Tam, nor would he have his handsome, if rather battered-looking son. In gratitude to the Living God who had watched over him so well, he leaned over and affectionately squeezed Rafnir's shoulder.

"Your son?" Hajira asked, eyeing his new nephew.

"Yes," Sayyed said. He leaned forward to study this brother he had known so long ago. Hajira did not look very different. He had matured, of course, but he still wore his mustache long to help elongate his broad face. His wide-set eyes were deep and large above a hawk-nose and a strong jaw, and when he stood, he still topped Sayyed by several inches.

What had changed, and what disturbed Sayyed, was the cut of Hajira's hair. His brother's long, thick hair and the intricate knot of a tribesman had been shaved off close to his skull—a cut that was usually reserved as a punishment for some crime of dishonor.

Sayyed took another sip of the wine and said, "And what of you? If you have heard tales of me then half of them are probably true and you know my life. How is yours? Tell me of the family."

Hajira laughed a short, sharp bark of amusement. "The family goes on as always. Alset is Raid-Ja now, and he is as unforgiving as Father ever was."

"Father is dead?"

"Four years ago. He died in his sleep."

"And Mother?"

"Well and happy and rejoicing in her grandchildren.

She will be overjoyed to know you live." He paused
and glanced at the two Hunnuli standing protectively
behind Sayyed and Rafnir before adding, "As for me, I
chose to join the Shar-Ja's guard, and there I have been
for twenty years."

Sayyed was impressed. The Shar-Ja's personal guards
were the elite warriors from every tribe. Initiates went
through several years of rigorous training and condition-
ing and had to swear undying loyalty to the overlord. All
would give their lives for the Shar-Ja. Almost unwillingly
his gaze lifted to Hajira's head, and his brow furrowed.

His brother recognized his unspoken question. He
cocked a half-smile. "Things have been changing in
Cangora the past two years. I made the mistake of voicing my opinion of Counselor Zukhara rather forcefully.
He could not dismiss me, but he had me reprimanded
and transferred to guard Tassilio—a huge step-down in
honor, he thought, sentenced to 'babysit the idiot.' " He
chuckled as he repeated the counselor's words in a
good imitation of Zukhara's sonorous voice.

A glow of humor lit like a lamp in Tassilio's face.
"Smartest thing Zukhara ever did, and he doesn't even
know it," Hajira went on. "This imp's mother sent him
to court a year ago. He took one look at the political situation and has been acting the fool ever since to save
his hide. He is the accepted, right-born second son of
the Shar-Ja, and his heir after Bashan. You saw what
happened to the Shar-Yon."

"The Fel Azureth have sworn to kill the Shar-Ja and
all his offspring," Tassilio said in a flat voice. "When
Father got sick, I pretended to go crazy. The law pro-
tects lepers and fools."

Sayyed blinked, both amazed at the boy's wit and
dismayed by the circumstances that drove him to such
desperate measures. "What does your father think of
your subterfuge?"

The boy looked away quickly, but not before Sayyed

saw the glitter of unshed tears in his eyes. "I doubt Father has even noticed. He saw only Bashan."

Sayyed sat straighter to draw the boy's attention back to himself. "Who do you think killed the Shar-Yon?" he asked Hajira and Tassilio with deliberate emphasis. His brother and the boy, young as he was, would make good allies in the caravan, and Sayyed wanted to put to rest any suspicions they might have.

"Perhaps we did. Do you think we are here to assassinate the Shar-Ja as well?" Rafnir put in. "As Zukhara said, only clan blood carries the talent to wield magic."

Tassilio squirmed and looked as if he would say something, but this time he waited and deferred to the warrior sitting beside him.

It was Hajira who spoke first. He put more fuel on the fire, poured more *firza*, and thought carefully before he made his answer. "I didn't know what to think when I heard a clan magic-wielder was in the caravan. The thought that this sorcerer was here to harm the Shar-Ja crossed my mind. But I know you. Twenty-six years would not be enough time to turn my brother into an assassin."

Tassilio's head shook vigorously. "Not the half-breed who turned sorcerer, fought gorthlings and plagues and stone lions, who tames the black Hunnuli and rides with the Lady of the Dead Clan," he blurted out. "Do you really have a diamond splinter in your wrist?"

Sayyed's lips twitched at the boy's outburst. He was amazed that Tassilio knew so much about his past and viewed it with such enthusiasm. Sorcery was supposed to be outlawed, but obviously the stories of the clans had traveled over the borders. Obligingly he pulled back the long sleeve of his robes and revealed a tooled leather wristband on his right arm. As soon as he loosened the lacings, the band slid off, revealing the pale glow of the splinter just beneath his skin. About two inches long, the slender diamond gleamed dusky red through the blood that flowed around it.

Tassilio's eyes grew wide. "So you are not here to kill Father. Why are you here?" he asked directly.

"To find Bashan's murderer?" Hajira suggested.

Sayyed pulled the armband back on. "If we can, and to find the Lady of the Dead Clan and the healer with the winged horse," he told them in a terse voice.

Both guard and boy sat up with a jerk and shared a bewildered look. "Lady Gabria and—"

"Kelene," Rafnir finished for them. "My wife. She and Lady Gabria disappeared the night your caravan left Council Rock. We are trying to find them."

Hajira did not ask why they had come to search the caravan. The fact that they had risked doing so gave enough credence to their news. "I can promise you they are not with the Shar-Ja or any of his immediate servants. Tassilio or I would know if they were there. Where else have you looked?"

Sayyed told him everything they had seen and examined so far. "We were checking wagons in the baggage train when we were jumped."

"Odd place for an ambush," Hajira said, scratching his neck thoughtfully. "I wonder if someone has something to hide and has set guards. They obviously didn't know you were sorcerers, or they would have killed you instantly."

"There are several big covered vans that could carry two Hunnuli," Tassilio pointed out. "We could check them tomorrow night." His sadness put aside, he turned his youthful enthusiasm to the thrill of the mystery.

His dark-clad guard turned on him. "What is this *we*? *You* will stay in your tent where you belong."

Tassilio drew a long, quivering sigh, but one eyelid drooped in a quick wink to Sayyed.

They doused the fire and thoroughly erased every sign of their presence in the hollow. With Tassilio and his dog leading the way, the two brothers walked side

by side back to the sprawling camp. Tibor carried
Rafnir, who still suffered the ill-effects of the vicious
blow to his head. Sick and weak, Rafnir decided to find
his blankets and sleep in a sheltered nook where Tibor
could watch over him. Sayyed helped him find a place
and settled him comfortably.

Tassilio dubiously eyed the big black horse standing
over Rafnir. "Is that your Hunnuli? Where is its lightning?"

Tibor obliged his curiosity by turning his right shoulder to Tassilio. The boy dug his fingers into the stallion's hair and crowed with delight when he found
white skin beneath the black dye. To the brothers'
amusement, Tassilio asked if he could join Rafnir, saying he'd rest better if a Hunnuli guarded his bed.

Hajira acquiesced, and Tibor gently sniffed the boy
all over and nickered his acceptance. Tassilio quickly
bedded down next to Rafnir, his dog cuddled beside
him, before Hajiral could change his mind.

Although his head pounded and his muscles felt sore
and weak, Sayyed did not want to sleep yet. Under
Afer's close watch, he and Hajira walked around the
outer perimeter of the camp, talking for hours about
everything that came to mind. Their companionship
pleased Sayyed, for the years seemed to fall away, and
he and his brother moved back into the easy, confident
relationship they had enjoyed before their father tore
them apart and sent Sayyed into exile.

For the first time since the plague, Sayyed found himself talking at length about Tam. While Hajira strode
silently at his side, he told him of their life together, how
Tam saved his life while still a girl, how he waited five
years for her to reach maturity, of her love for her animals,
her courage and strength, and at last, in a voice that still
trembled after three years, he told his brother of her death
in the plague tent and of the fatal grief of her Hunnuli.

When he was through, he drew a long breath and
slowly exhaled, feeling better somehow for opening his

thoughts to Hajira. He had kept his memories of Tam buried deep in his mind, out of sight where they would not hurt so badly, but now that he had brought them out fresh and shining for his brother, he realized he had been missing an important part of his healing. He needed to talk about Tam, to remember their love and joy together. To fail to do so diminished the life she had left behind.

When Sayyed's words trailed away and he lapsed into his own thoughts, Hajira laughed softly, his black, brilliant eyes filled a new measure of respect. "For years I have hated Father for sending you away. Now I see that, knowing or unknowing, he did you the greatest of favors."

They walked on peacefully for a while until they passed the cluster of luxurious tents set aside for the counselors and the tribal leaders who attended the Shar-Ja. As they approached the Shar-Ja's huge tent, several loyal guards on duty snapped to attention and saluted Hajira. The warrior did not return the salutes but nodded at the men's mark of respect.

The sorcerer noted the strange exchange and said, "You were more than a guardsman, weren't you?"

Hajira hesitated an instant, then drew himself up with a warrior's pride. "I was Commander of the Tenth Horse, the oldest and most honored cavalry unit in the Shar-Ja's guard. We were called the Panthers for our silence, our cunning, and our speed in the attack. Now I am a foot soldier in the lowliest ranks, whose only duty is obligatory guard on a simpleton of a sandrat." Bitterness shook the timbre of his deep voice, and his hands curled as if gripping an invisible weapon.

"But that's some sandrat," Sayyed remarked, hoping to ease Hajira's tension.

His words helped a little, for the warrior's hands relaxed, and he laughed ruefully. "That boy was a real surprise."

"What happened?" Sayyed asked. They had passed the Shar-Ja's tent and were walking by a large area of

tents and crude shelters. The escorts from all fifteen
tribes camped together, drinking, gaming, talking, and
bickering half the night. Girls from the oasis settlement
came to entertain them for coins, and enterprising
tradesmen brought trays of food and kegs of drink to
sell. Even at that late hour, a few fires still burned, and
occasional laughter and song could be heard mixed
with the mournful howls of wild dogs sniffing for food
about the edges of the great camp.

Sayyed remembered the six dead assassins and
wished the dogs a good meal. He glanced at his brother.
There was just enough distant firelight for him to recognize the stony set of Hajira's broad face, and he wondered if the warrior was going to ignore his question.

But Hajira had brought his anger under control and
fully regained his trust in the younger brother he had
once thought dead. "You know the Shar-Ja has been ill
almost a year," he began. "It was about that time that the
Gryphon and his extremists captured the holy shrine of
the Prophet Sargun and declared their intention to destroy
the Shar-Ja's corrupt court and return the leadership of the
tribes to a high priest. No one paid much attention to
them at first because the priests and the tribal councils
were too busy dealing with the effects of the drought and
the Shar-Ja's declining health. No one was able to find the
cause of his malady or a cure, so he turned over many of
his responsibilities to his son.

"For a while, Bashan did a good job. But then things
started to go wrong. Grain shipments to the cities disappeared; the tribal chiefs grew resentful; counselors were
murdered; violence on the roads increased dramatically.
Then news came that the Fel Azureth was spreading
across the realm and causing problems over the Altai.
The remaining counselors lost confidence in the Shar-Ja
and his son. Finally someone suggested Counselor
Zukhara replace the Shar-Yon and take control of the
royal council until the Shar-Ja returned to health."

Here Hajira paused, and a wry smile crossed his lips. "Royal guards, even Panthers, are not permitted to draw weapons in the council chambers, but when that weasel-eyed, honey-tongued Zukhara agreed and ordered the Shar-Yon to leave the council, I objected." He drew his long, curved tulwar and held it out at arm's length. "With this. If Bashan had not ordered me to stand down, I probably would have killed the counselor and paid for it with dishonor and disemboweling. Zukhara has hated me ever since." His arm fell, and the gleaming blade whispered back into its sheath. "Bashan saved my life that day, but I was not there to save his. For the honor I owe his father, I will protect his brother and I *will* find Bashan's killer."

Sayyed stopped. "Then we hunt the same trail, for the Turics will not give the clans peace until the Shar-Yon is avenged." He raised his right hand, palm upward, and extended it toward his brother.

Hajira's hand met his, clasped it tightly, and lifted both into a joined fist that wordlessly sealed their vow of mutual trust and commitment.

Together they turned and began to walk back toward the place where they had left Rafnir and Tassilio. Afer dutifully followed, looking for all the world like a simple horse on a lead line. Only Sayyed and Hajira, who had seen both the killing fury and the loving devotion in the glittering dark eyes, knew the stallion for what he was.

The two men found the younger ones wrapped in their blankets, contentedly asleep under the attentive watch of the Hunnuli and the dog. Exhausted at last, Sayyed threw himself down by his son and fell into a rightfully earned sleep. Hajira prowled around the perimeter of their sleeping area for several more minutes, the ingrained caution of years urging him to check the dark shadows one last time before he slept. At last, cocking an eye at the two black stallions, he stretched out near Tassilio and allowed himself to rest.

* * * * *

Just before sunrise and the morning horns, Hajira woke Sayyed. Without speaking, they left the Hunnuli and the other sleepers and strode purposefully in the direction of the baggage wagons. They climbed a short rise where they could see the wagons and vans parked row by row in the early light. Talking and gesturing to hide their true intent, they took turns studying the wheeled vehicles.

After several minutes of this, Hajira's expression turned thoughtful, and he said in a low tone, "Take a look at the large, covered van. Last row, near the end. There are several men lounging nearby."

Sayyed made a casual turn as if he wanted to look at something on the paling horizon. "I haven't noticed that one before. The brown one, wood roof, and some sort of red emblem on the side?" He felt a surge of hope. The van looked big enough to hold both the mares and the women.

"That's the one. It looks worn. It's probably a merchant wagon that was rented or borrowed. But those men down there do not look much like drivers."

"Hmm, no. They are dressed like the men who attacked us. More guards perhaps?" Sayyed suddenly stiffened, and he had to force himself to look naturally away from the men below. "I know one of those men. The lean one. He has gray in his hair and a mole on his cheek. I saw him slip into the caravan two days ago."

Hajira's face lost its friendliness, and his eyes turned hot and frustrated. "Have you seen others coming into the caravan?"

"Several groups," the sorcerer confirmed. "They were heavily armed and arrived at dusk."

The warrior frowned. "I was right!" he said fiercely. "Someone is fattening the tribal levies with mercenaries and fanatics. I have tried to warn the counselors, but no one will listen to me. I am dishonored!" he spat. "And other men are too afraid to talk. The Gryphon has sworn to call a holy war, and no one wants to get in his way."

Sayyed sucked in his breath. A holy war was a call to battle in the name of the Living God, a call that few Turics would ignore. Usually the holy war was used in times of invasion or war with other nations. Never had a holy war been called to incite rebellion within the Turic nation itself. "The God forbid," he murmured.

"Indeed. The Gryphon may be planning a coup before we reach Cangora in nine days." He turned on his heel and strode down the rise away from the wagons. Sayyed followed. "We'd better find your women and get them out. We certainly do not need two magic-wielders caught in the middle of a civil war."

Sayyed couldn't agree more.

They split up after that, Hajira taking his charge to the front of the caravan near the funeral wagon and Sayyed and Rafnir riding in the midst of the tribal escorts. For fear of attracting attention, they all kept their distance from the wagon train that brought up the rear.

The ride that day was long and hard, over a rolling, twisting road that reached to the rising Absarotan foothills. It was dark by the time the caravan stopped at the next oasis, the Impala Springs. The people were too tired to set up a full camp, so they put out crude shelters, ate cold food, and went thankfully to bed. Only the Shar-Ja and his counselors had their tents erected for the night.

Hajira waited only until the camp was settled before he sought out the clansmen. Ignoring Tassilio's protests, he left the boy with the Hunnuli and led Rafnir and Sayyed back to the parked wagons and vans. They did not have to search long before they made an alarming discovery.

The large wooden van with the red emblem on its side was gone.

7

Almost frantically the three men checked the baggage wagons again, from one end of the field of parked vehicles to the other. There was no brown van and no guards, only a few drivers tending to their wagons. Sayyed asked several about the van, but no one had paid much attention to one brown vehicle among so many, and no one had noticed it leave. The men then looked everywhere in the oasis village, around the stone-walled springs, in other areas of the camp, even in some outlying gullies, hollows, and dry valleys. All to no avail. The unremarkable brown wagon had vanished from the caravan.

Frustrated and upset, Sayyed and Rafnir returned with Hajira to the Hunnuli. The night was well advanced, but the men were too agitated to sleep. The allotted four days was gone, and their only possible lead had disappeared somewhere along the leagues of the Spice Road.

"We have several choices," declared Sayyed, his arms crossed and his face grim. "We can go back to the Altai and find the Fel Azureth, to learn if they have Gabria and Kelene. We can continue to search the caravan, or we can abandon both ideas and go in search of an unknown wagon that may or may not be holding the women."

"The road forks three ways," Hajira said softly. "Which way does the heart go?"

Tassilio put his hand on Sayyed's sleeve. "The Fel Azureth would not take them. They believe too firmly in their own righteousness. They would not stoop to coercing a power they believe to be heretical."

All three men gazed at Tassilio, astonished at the boy's astute observation. His earnest, eager face brightened under their stare, and he pushed a foot forward, crossed his arms, and lifted an imperious chin in such an excellent imitation of his father, Hajira nearly choked.

"He's right," the guardsman conceded. "The core of the Fel Azureth are extreme fanatics who despise any religion or power not their own. Of course, that doesn't mean someone else didn't kidnap the sorceresses to make trouble for the fanatics." He lapsed into silence and brooded over their lack of tangible results, his fingers drumming on the hilt of his sword.

Rafnir, too young and intense to bear his patience stoically, began to pace step after angry step between the men and the Hunnuli. "So where does that leave us, Father?" he demanded. "There's nowhere to go forward and too many places to go back!"

The older sorcerer rubbed his neck against the throbbing pain in his head. It had been a very long day and night, and he was still suffering from the aftereffects of the blow to his head. He closed his eyes and drew a long, filling breath. "I wish to sleep on this decision," he said. "I will decide in the morning which fork in the road we'll take."

The other men did not argue. There was little point wasting more time or effort on discussion when there was nothing they could do about it until daylight anyway. With Tassilio between them and the Hunnuli keeping guard, they rolled themselves in their blankets to wait for morning.

Deep in the night, Sayyed's dreams fled to the Ramtharin Plains. He rode frantically on a desert horse after a golden cloaked woman on a cantering Hunnuli. He chased her, shouting, until she slowed and waited for him. He expected to see Tam, but when he neared and the woman turned around, she pulled off her hood and revealed Gabria's face as she had been twenty-six years ago when he first saw her that spring day and fell instantly in love with her. Sayyed's heart ached at her loveliness. She smiled at him with all the warmth and love he remembered, and without a word she lifted her arm to point to a range of mountains. Abruptly she disappeared, and Sayyed found himself in a stifling darkness. He cried out, more at her loss than at the blackness that covered him, and he tried to lunge away from the constricting dark. He discovered he could not move his arms or legs. Something pinioned him from head to foot, something that groaned and creaked close to his head. Then he heard her voice, no more than a faint whisper in his head, "Sayyed."

"Gabria!" he shouted, and his own voice jolted him awake. He jumped to his feet and saw morning had already lit the skies with apricot and gold. Afer nudged him with his muzzle, and Sayyed leaned gratefully into the stallion's powerful shoulder.

Rafnir, with five days' growth of beard on his face, yawned and clambered out of his blankets. His eyes met his father's, and they locked in a long, considering stare.

"I think we should look for the wagon," Rafnir said quietly. "I don't believe they are here."

Sayyed said nothing, for he had looked over Rafnir's shoulder to the mountains northwest of the oasis. He had seen the peaks in the days before as the caravan slowly traveled closer. Last night, though, when they reached the springs, it had been too dark to see details of the great, gray-green chain of mountains that still lay perhaps ten or twenty leagues away. Now he saw them clearly, bathed in the morning light, and he recognized their rugged crowns as surely as he had known Gabria. She had pointed west to those same mountains in his dream. He pondered, too, the other elements: the meaning of the darkness, the creaking noise, and Gabria's voice.

Was a dream any more of a clue than a hunch or a guess or an idea? Was it a sign sent by Amara or just his tired mind furnishing a solution to his dilemma? Perhaps Gabria's talent was reaching out to him. Whatever its meaning or its source, he decided to follow its lead, for lack of any other evidence. "The wagon it is," he said.

Hajira, who had awakened with Tassilio, drew a small knife from a sheath hidden in his boot. Thin and slender as a reed, the blade fit easily into his palm. The handle was a tiny gryphon's head carved from a flat slice of opal so the beast's face shone with rainbow colors in the sun. Hajira handed the blade to Sayyed. "Keep this when you go. If you need me for anything, send the knife with your message and I will come." He put his arm around Tassilio's shoulders, a fatherly gesture the boy accepted gladly. "We will keep our ears alert. If anyone has the women close by, we will learn of it."

Sayyed ran a finger along the hilt. Although gryphons were extinct, they were still powerful symbols of loyalty and courage in the Turic faith. "A beautiful knife," he said.

"A gift from the Shar-Ja," Hajira replied, unable to

completely disguise the ironic bitterness in his voice.

The sorcerer tucked away the knife and took something from his saddlebag. It was a rope as thick as his little finger. "Many years ago magic wards were made of ivory or wood, carved into balls of great beauty," he explained to Hajira and Tassilio. As he talked he deftly cut a length of the rope and began tying an intricate knot in the middle of the section. "Unfortunately, I do not have time to carve. This will have to do for now." He laid the knot on the ground and before Tassilio's fascinated gaze, he touched the knot and spoke the words to a spell he had memorized from the *Book of Matrah*.

The magic glowed red on the rope knot for just a minute before it sank into the twisted fibers. Sayyed picked it up, tied it into a loop, and gave it to Tassilio. "This is not as strong as the old ones, but this magic ward will help protect you against all but the most powerful of spells."

Tassilio marveled at the gift. He accepted the knot without his usual blithe smile and hung it gratefully around his neck.

After morning prayers, the four ate a quick breakfast together, saddled the Hunnuli, and made their farewells.

"Watch your back," Sayyed told his brother. The two men embraced, both thankful for this unexpected meeting after so many years. The clansmen mounted and waved to the lone guardsman and his royal charge. Hajira lifted his arm in salute.

The Hunnuli unhurriedly trotted through the outskirts of the caravan camp toward the settlement. The camp bustled with preparations to leave, and everyone was too busy to pay attention to two tribesmen minding their own business.

Before long the camp and the oasis with its slow bubbling springs were left behind. As soon as they were out of sight of the camp, Rafnir and Sayyed split up, each taking a side of the beaten caravan road. The chances of finding the tracks of one wagon, particularly the right wagon, were very small. On the other hand, the men knew the conveyance had left the caravan somewhere between the Impala Springs and Oasis Three, and they planned to search every square inch of territory along the road until they found some trace of the missing van.

With the help of their stallions' keen sense of smell and their own knowledge of tracking, the men examined the Spice Road for leagues. It wasn't easy. The Shar-Ja's vast caravan had left a huge trail of hoofprints, wheel tracks, boot marks, trash, and dung piles, while subsequent traffic had added its own signs. Well-traveled side roads joined the trail here and there, and the route passed through two tribal settlements, each with its own collection of carts and wagons.

The clansmen asked for information at the tiny villages, and they questioned other travelers, but no one remembered seeing a wagon of that description. They fought a constant struggle between their desire to hurry in case the wagon was somewhere ahead of them on the road and the need for slow, careful scrutiny for tracks in case the wagon had been driven off the road to some remote destination. Through most of the day, the men forced their frustration aside and worked their way slowly northeastward.

The afternoon sun slanted toward evening when Sayyed and Rafnir returned to the road and walked their horses side by side. The caravan route passed through a hump of tall hills, forcing travelers to go through a narrow cut walled with steep slopes and shaded with fragrant cedar and pine. Father and son rode quietly, each occupied with his own thoughts, until they rode out of the hills and came to a long, rolling stretch of road.

There is another track to the left, Afer told Sayyed. The stallion was right. It was faint and overgrown, but a

two-wheeled track split off from the main road and
wended its way into the barren, brown range. The
horses followed the track a short distance and stopped
to allow Sayyed and Rafnir to dismount.

"Something heavy has traveled this way very
recently," Sayyed observed. He pointed to wheel marks
in the dirt and crushed clumps of grass.

Rafnir bent to look. "But is it our missing wagon?" He
looked back the way they had come toward the hump
of hills. "If you were planning to leave a caravan with
little notice, this would be a good place to do it."

Sayyed studied the hills and saw what Rafnir meant.
A wagon lagging behind could easily veer off the road
when the rest of the baggage train turned out of sight
into the tree-lined cut. "So, do we continue along the
road or try this track?"

"Try the track," Rafnir suggested. He shaded his eyes
with a hand and looked down the course of the trail as
far as he could see. If the track continued its apparent
direction, it would eventually reach the mountains.

The men mounted again, and the Hunnuli stretched
out into a slow, easy canter. There were few places a
wagon could leave that track, and the trail wound on,
clear and obvious even through the dry vegetation.
They had ridden for almost half an hour, one in front of
the other, when Tibor veered off the path so abruptly,
Rafnir was unseated. Reacting quickly, the sorcerer
grabbed the stallion's mane and hauled himself back
into the saddle.

Look! Tibor sent excitedly before Rafnir could voice
any of the words that came to his lips, and the stallion
nosed something on the ground.

Rafnir could not see the object over Tibor's big head,
so he slid off and pushed the stallion's nose aside. All
he saw was a thin strip of red dangling from the long,
sharp leaves of a dagger plant. His eyes suddenly
popped wide, and he whooped with delight. "It's

Kelene's hair ribbon," he yelled, waving the trophy in the air.

"Are you sure?" Sayyed's brow rose dubiously.

I am. Tibor neighed. *It has her smell.*

"They're just ahead of us!" Rafnir crowed. "She must have left this as a sign."

The two men grinned at each other. For the first time in five days they had a definite lead, and they did not want to waste it. Rafnir quickly tied the ribbon around his arm and leaped into the saddle. The Hunnuli sprang away.

The wagon had a day's lead on them, but no living creature could outrun or outlast a Hunnuli. The horses ran for the rest of the daylight hours, until the sun slid behind the mountains and night fell. They saw no more signs of the women, only the wagon track drawing nearer and nearer to the mountains.

As soon as the sun set, the Hunnuli were forced to stop. Although they could have run all night, a high veil of clouds covered the sky and hid the light of the moon and stars. The men were afraid to proceed for fear of missing another sign or losing the faint trail in the darkness. Reluctantly they made a cold camp and bedded down for some much-needed sleep.

Just before dawn the men roused, ate a quick meal, and made their prayers on bended knee. Rafnir felt comfortable now with this morning oblation, and he silently sent his plea to the mother goddess to watch over his wife and her mother. By the time the light was strong enough to see the trail, the men and the Hunnuli were on their way. The path went on before them, like two pale parallel ribbons that led ever westward into the foothills of the Absarotan Mountains.

Swiftly the land rose into bleak, rumpled uplands whose brown slopes lay bare to the arching sky. Dry creekbeds and gullies ran like cracks down the slopes, and rough outcroppings of weathered stone poked up like ancient ruins through the grass. Not far ahead the mountains reared their towering peaks above the parched plains and sat like brooding giants over their deep, unseen valleys.

A warm wind from the east blew steadily during the day and slowly piled clouds up against the mountains' lofty heads. By midafternoon, towering thunderheads began to form, and the elemental forces of a storm were spawned in the battle between air, stone, and fire.

On the ground the men and Hunnuli sensed the coming storm in the magical energies around them. In a phenomenon little understood by the magic-wielders themselves, thunderstorms strengthened the forces of magic and enhanced the sorcerers' ability to wield it. Even before the sky turned to steel and the first bolt of lightning streaked to earth, the two sorcerers could feel the tingle in their blood and the building exhilaration as the storm brewed along the mountain's face.

Worriedly they hurried on, but there was still no sign of the elusive wagon except for its tracks winding ever higher into the inhospitable flanks of the mountains. In the late afternoon they rode up a rocky ridge, crested the top, and stopped to look around. Although the van was nowhere in sight, they saw two shepherds hurrying a flock of goats down a valley below. Afer and Tibor quickly caught up with the shepherds, and the clansmen cordially greeted the two Turics.

The shepherds eyed them and the big horses suspiciously until they recognized the Raid crests on the riders' robes.

"The True God go with you, travelers," the younger shepherd said over the bleating goats. "We thought you might be taxers or collectors for the Fel Azureth."

Sayyed chuckled. "The Raid ride only for honor, which is why we're so poor."

The shepherds relaxed a little, but they shifted their feet, anxious to be away. Their goats, the long-legged, rangy mountain breed, crowded around them, noisy and impatient. Sayyed quickly asked about the wagon.

"Haven't seen it today," the older shepherd replied. "We've had the herd in the meadows up there." He pointed toward one mountain rather isolated from the rest, a savage, lonely peak with its crown buried in the clouds. "Had to bring 'em down early, though. The Storm King grows angry."

"The who?" Rafnir asked.

"You are strangers here." The shepherd grimaced. "Yonder lies the Storm King," he pointed to the same peak. "The old man can force ferocious storms when his anger is up."

"Well, do you know where that road goes?"

The shepherds looked at one another as if trying to jog each other's memories. "Doesn't it go to that old fortress?" the young one offered.

The other shrugged. "Could be. The main trail to the place is south of here, but I've heard there was a back road going up there. I just never followed this one. Won't go up there myself."

Something in his tone caused Rafnir to ask, "Why not?"

Both men were startled when the shepherds crossed their wrists to ward off evil. "There's something dark far back in those mountains. Some old evil that won't die away. Something I wouldn't risk for all the gold on Storm King," the old shepherd said.

"If you're going on that road," suggested the young one forcefully, "don't stray off it. Find your wagon and get out as fast as you can." Without waiting for an answer, the shepherds rounded up their herd and hurried away.

The Hunnuli returned to the track and resumed a canter. The men saw now that the trail headed toward the peak the shepherds had called the Storm King. True to its name, the mountain sat under a roiling gray-and-white mantle of cloud that obscured its upper slopes. Lightning crackled around its crown.

"We'd better find shelter soon," Sayyed called.

Faster now, the stallions galloped along the open path on the rising slopes of hills and ridges, but all too soon they reached the treeline and were forced to slow to a trot through the scattered groves of trees and heavy brush.

The hunters pushed on and on into the higher reaches, while the sky darkened and the wind began to roar through the trees. Dust and leaves whirled, and the warm, sultry air suddenly turned cold. Thunder rumbled in a continuous drumroll that echoed from peak to peak. The daylight died to a ghostly twilight.

Sayyed was scanning the trail ahead when a bolt of lightning snaked down from the clouds and exploded a tree close by. The thunderous shock wave nearly blew him from the saddle. Afer and Tibor neighed in pain from the horrendous sound. With that fanfare, the fury of the Storm King broke loose in a wind that came screaming down from the peak, snapping off branches and flattening grass.

Half-blinded by flying dust and grit, the men clung to the horses as the wind howled by them. The Hunnuli struggled on as best they could. In seconds, they had lost the trail in a whirlwind of dirt, debris, and leaves.

"Go on," Sayyed cried to Afer. "Find shelter!"

Obediently the old stallion plowed ahead, using his wits and his senses to locate any kind of shelter out of this terrible wind. Tibor struggled to stay close on his tail. Neither could see where they were going. All they could discern were darker shapes through the flying wind and the direction of the slopes under their feet. Lightning continued to explode, with shattering crescendos of thunder around them.

They had not yet found a safe place to stop when the hail came pelting down in curtains of stinging pellets. Mumbling an oath, Sayyed tied his burnoose tightly across his face and stopped Afer. He hunched down, his back to the wind, and waited for Tibor to come close.

"We don't have much choice. We'll stay here until the storm passes," he shouted to Rafnir. "Let's make a shield."

Rafnir nodded a reply. They started the spell to form a storm-proof dome against the wind and hail.

Afer lifted his head. *I smell something! I cannot tell what it is, but it smells man-made,* the Hunnuli told both men.

Sayyed grimaced. "Do we look for it?"

"Let's try. There's no knowing how long this storm will last, and shelter would be welcome."

Excitedly now, Afer plunged ahead into the wind and whipping ice. Using the magic they had already summoned, the men formed small shields of power and used the energy to ward off the worst of the weather. Tibor hurried after Afer along a saddleback ridge and down into a steep, narrow valley.

Dusk came and went too quickly, and an impenetrable night blanketed the mountains. The hail finally dwindled to a stop only to be replaced by a heavy torrent of rain. In moments Sayyed and Rafnir were soaked by the cold downpour in spite of their shields. Still Afer went on after the elusive scent, leading them farther up the valley along the banks of a small, tumbling stream. In the dense darkness and pouring rain, they were unaware that the valley walls were rising steeper and higher the deeper into the mountains they went.

Then, without warning, a towering shape loomed out of the darkness. Twice as tall as a man, thick and ungainly, it sat in the middle of the canyon floor like a misshapen row of large human heads set one on top of the other. The topmost head, its gruesome face nearly lost in the gloom, glowered down the valley at any who approached it.

It is stone, snorted Tibor.

"Yes, but what is it?" Rafnir exclaimed, not really expecting an answer. The huge statue was unlike anything he had ever seen.

"It is an ancestor pole, an ancient device used to warn evil spirits," Sayyed replied wearily.

Rafnir shivered in the icy blast of the wind. "I don't think it's working. Is this what you smelled?" he asked Afer.

Some of it. But now I sense other things, Afer answered.

So do I. Man smells on wood, stone, and smoke. Horses, too, added Tibor.

"Then let's go," Sayyed sighed. The need for shelter outweighed his caution and curiosity. They circled past the strange statue and pushed ahead up the canyon.

In the dark and the storm they did not see the top head turn slowly around to watch them ride up the valley.

Although they found a faint animal track that followed the course of the stream, the going proved very difficult. The path wound through heaps of boulders, rock outcroppings, marshy pools, and heavy brush. Sayyed and Rafnir had to dissolve their power shields because they could not concentrate on maintaining the magic and finding the path at the same time. Sayyed settled on a small globe of light instead. Once set alight, the magic sphere would glow without much attention, and its light was a welcome help in the storm-wracked night.

Barely an hour had gone by after they left the unknown statue when the canyon ended abruptly in a sheer wall of striated stone. At the foot of the wall, the stream bubbled up out of a deep, clear pool that steamed and frothed in the pouring rain. Instead of stopping, Afer turned left into a cleft in the walls that was so narrow the men would have missed it. The passage within was deep and dark and cut off nearly all the force of the wind and rain. The Hunnuli continued up the crevice without pause, ignoring the walls that closed in on both sides and towered nearly forty feet above their heads.

The men and horses walked in single file along the passage for several minutes, grateful for the respite from the weather. The Hunnuli's noses lifted high, and their ears strained forward to catch more sign of the humans they knew were close. They were so attuned to what lay ahead, they did not notice anything behind until they heard something akin to thunder followed by a rumbling, crashing noise from the mouth of the crevice.

Tibor neighed stridently, but in the flash of a moment, two ropes that glowed a pale silver in the darkness snaked down from above. The ropes looped around both men's necks and hauled them off their saddles. Jerking and twisting, they were pulled upward so swiftly the Hunnuli could only scream their rage and paw the empty air.

Hands grabbed at Sayyed just as he passed out, and for the second time he and Rafnir were taken prisoner by an enemy they could not see.

In the crevice below, the magic sphere died out, and the Hunnuli were left in darkness.

8

The gag bit deep into Kelene's mouth, drying her tongue and forcing her mouth open to such an impossible angle she could barely work her jaw. Her lips were dry and swollen, and her entire head ached with a pounding throb that brought tears to her eyes. Ignoring the pain in her right arm, she struggled again to reach the gag, but her hands had been tied tightly to her sides and the knots would not budge. Already her hands were swelling, and she could feel blood trickling down her wrists.

She had tried several times to break the ropes with magic, to no avail. Whoever had tied them knew magic-wielders well and had crafted bonds woven from the hairs of a Hunnuli's tail. Like the horse itself, the hair was impervious to magic. Briefly, Kelene wondered what horse the hairs had come from.

She subsided onto the pallet and thought of several vile curses she could heap on the head of the person who did this as soon as she worked her hands and mouth free. Close beside her she felt the heat and closeness of Gabria's body trussed in the same painful manner. She wasn't sure if her mother was asleep, unconscious, or simply biding her time. The older sorceress had awakened some time earlier, struggled against her bonds, and then slipped into a stillness without motion or sound.

Kelene sighed a short breath of frustration and looked through the dim light at her surroundings. She already knew by heart the few things she could see, yet she continued to hope she would notice something new that could help her. She and Gabria were in a wagon—that much she had realized the moment she regained consciousness hours ago. It was not a clan wagon, since the box was too big and enclosed with wooden sides and a slightly peaked wooden roof. One door at the rear allowed access into the wagon, and a tiny window opened under the roof for ventilation. The vehicle reminded Kelene of the merchant wagons she sometimes saw at the clans' summer gatherings, the kind that had room for sale goods and a small living space for the merchant.

She and Gabria were lying on a fold-down bed rather than on the floor, and from her place she could just make out a small table folded up against the wall and a short bench. The interior of the wagon was dark, except for a few pale glimmers of light that leaked in through a crack by the door frame and around the roof.

Just beyond their pallet, in the darker end of the van, stood Nara and Demira, side by side in a wooden stall Kelene guessed had been specially built for them. The wall separating them from the women was built from thick, heavy timbers that looked strong enough to contain even a Hunnuli. Neither mare had responded to

Kelene's noises, and she wondered if they had been sedated. If she lifted her head as high as her bonds allowed, she could barely make out the two horses standing with their heads facing the front of the wagon. Each mare wore a halter and Demira's wings appeared to be fastened to her sides by a wide strip of fabric. Someone had gone to a great deal of trouble.

Angrily Kelene struggled upright until she was sitting on the edge of the bed board. Knowing they were in a wagon was useful, but she still did not know who had taken them or why, or where they were going. She tried to think back to that night they were attacked by the river. Was it last night or two nights ago? She couldn't be certain. Everything that had happened since she and her mother rode to the riverbank was a blank. She remembered seeing several dark men coming at her, and she recalled the pain and fear when Demira fell. Her arm had been hurt when she struck the ground, and then everything had gone black. She did not know how she, Gabria, and the horses had been moved to the wagon, nor did she see who had done it. Her memory was blank until this morning, when she woke with a crushing headache and a desire to see the perpetrator drawn and quartered by teams of slow horses.

Outside the wagon she could hear the crack of whips, the thudding of many hooves, and the creak of other wagons. Dust from the road filtered between the old wall boards and swirled in the tiny, pale beams of light that shone through the cracks in the roof. Kelene guessed their wagon was part of a caravan, but without further clues she had no clear idea which way they were going.

The wagon gave a sudden lurch, and Kelene lost her precarious perch on the bed. Unable to catch herself, she crashed to the floor on her injured arm. The pain almost knocked her out again. She lay on her back and gritted her teeth on the gag while tears trickled along her temples. Her stomach felt nauseated.

On the pallet above her, Gabria rolled over to the edge and looked down. Her green eyes were shadowed and sunken in her thin face, but they gleamed with awareness and concern.

The creak of the door alerted both women, and they lifted their heads just as daylight flooded the interior. A dark silhouette stood balanced in the open doorway in a block of light so strong neither sorceress could see who it was.

"Good. You're awake," a flat voice said. The speaker ignored the fact that Kelene lay on the floor and went on in a cold, deadpan tone. "We will be arriving at an oasis soon. I will bring you food and water then. If you cause any trouble, try to raise attention, or cast any spell I will kill your Hunnuli." The figure stepped down and slammed the door shut without further speech.

The women's eyes met in a silent exchange of confusion, worry, and anger. Kelene lay back on the floor. It seemed better to stay where she was than to struggle painfully back to the raised bed. At least her arm had quit pounding with such intensity.

She closed her eyes and turned her mind inward to the spells she had used the winter before to repair her crippled ankle. She wished she had the healing stones from Moy Tura, for one was spelled to help set broken bones. Some medicinal herbs like comfrey or boneset would be nice, too, but those and the stones were in her healer's bag and the gods alone knew what had happened to that. Her bag, their cloaks, boots, and jewelry were gone, probably stolen or thrown away.

She concentrated instead on the magic, turning it inward to seek the damage to her upper right arm. At least that part of the arm had only one bone to work with, unlike an ankle and foot that were a puzzle of small bones and tendons. She knew the bone was not shattered, but it felt badly bruised and probably fractured.

Using only a small pulse of magic in her spell, she smoothed over the crack in the bone and gently increased her body's natural defense against pain.

The throbbing eased to a dull ache and, as the spell ended, Kelene became drowsy. In spite of the dust and the hard floor, she bowed to her own medicine and soon fell asleep.

* * * * *

Zukhara.

Kelene's eyes flew open in surprise at the name that appeared so clearly in her mind. She stared up through the darkness and wondered why she should think of the Turic counselor now. He was an unpleasant person who had little regard for the Shar-Ja or the peace council. He was well out of her life. Here, Kelene's thoughts faltered. Something had brought him to mind. Some memory or clue had jogged her overworked thoughts and brought him clearly and vividly to her attention.

She glanced around and saw night had come. The wagon had stopped swaying, and the world had fallen quiet beyond the wagon walls. The words of their visitor came back to her—he would be coming with food and water when the caravan halted at an oasis.

Kelene stiffened in her bonds. The words and the man's voice echoed in her head. The voice had meant nothing to her when she was distracted by her own pain and discomfort, but it struck a note of recognition now. Of course, she growled to herself. The silhouette now had a face: Zukhara's.

Soft footsteps crunched on gravel outside. The door opened, and the same lean figure climbed into the wagon and closed the door behind him. He was so tall he had to stoop under the wagon roof. He carried a small lamp, a waterskin, and several plates of food which he laid on the fold-down table.

Saying nothing, he bent over Kelene, picked her up, and set her effortlessly on the bench on the wall. Gabria, too, was shifted off the pallet and placed beside Kelene. Both women glared in unspeakable hatred at the man who had taken them prisoner.

Zukhara ignored their silent anger and set the food and water in front of them. He sat on the edge of the bed and let them stare for a long while at the refreshments set so tantalizingly close.

"Listen to me," he said finally. The tiny lamp flickered, sending harsh shadows shifting over the sharp angles of his face. "You are in the middle of the Turic realm. There is no escape. Your Hunnuli are safely sedated and will remain that way until we reach our destination. I know you will not leave them, but if you foolishly try to escape or cause any trouble while we travel with this caravan, I will not hesitate to kill them. Do you understand?"

Both women nodded, their eyes wide.

Zukhara continued, his words forceful and precise. "As long as you obey me, I will bring food and water twice a day. Defy me and one of you will die." He paused and pulled something out of the front of his robe. "I also have this." He showed them a small ball on a golden chain.

Kelene looked blank, but Gabria jerked in recognition. The ball was a beautiful piece of handcarved ivory, cut in a delicate tracery of interlocking knots. Within the ball were two more, one within the other, equally as intricate. Gabria had had a similar ball once, given to her by the high priest of the Cult of Krath. The balls, creations of an older age, were magic wards that protected their wearers from spells. There was no guessing how a Turic had found one or if he knew how to use it.

Zukhara acknowledged Gabria's recognition with a nod. "Now, if we understand each other, you may eat."

With surprising gentleness, he untied the horsehair ropes around their arms and carefully eased the gags from their mouths. He left their feet tied.

Kelene and Gabria could do nothing more for a while than work some feeling back into their hands and arms. Their jaws ached miserably from the release of the tight gags, and their mouths were so dry they could barely swallow.

Zukhara poured water in mugs for them and watched impassively as each woman painstakingly sipped the liquid.

The first question Kelene thought to ask as soon as she could voice a word was, "Why?"

The counselor stroked his long, elegant chin while he considered how much he wanted them to know. "Let's just say I have need of you and your abilities." He would not elucidate further, and the clanswomen were too desperately thirsty and hungry to force the question. They ate and drank as best they could. The food was stew, surprisingly soft and tasty, and the water had been drawn from the fresh, clean springs of the oasis. It tasted marvelous to their parched mouths.

As soon as they finished, Zukhara swept away the dishes and faced them both over the empty board. "I brought you here," he said without preamble, "because I need your help."

A look of surprise slipped over Kelene's face at the change in the counselor's attitude and tone. The belligerent aggression had been tempered by politeness; the cold harshness in his voice was gone, and the rigidity of his shoulders and limbs had relaxed into an almost neighborly slouch.

He leaned forward, his elbows on the table, and went on. "You must understand, it was not an easy decision to kidnap two sorceresses."

"Why?" Kelene said sarcastically and gestured at the wagon's walls. "You had plenty of room."

The counselor shrugged off the question as he might a fly. "I did not wish to disrupt the peace council, but after Bashan's death, I thought I had no choice. When the Shar-Ja left Council Rock last night, I brought you with us."

"We didn't kill Bashan," Gabria spoke for the first time.

"I know, Lady Gabria, but I'm afraid I do know who did and, because of that, I had to move fast." He smiled then, and Kelene drew a sharp breath at the amazing transformation. The predatory anger that lined his face was wiped away by a pleasant, disarming smile of friendliness and good humor. If Kelene had not felt his rage and seen the hate in his eyes at the council, if she had not spent the last twenty-four hours in misery and been threatened by this same man, she would have liked him for this smile alone. She knew then that Zukhara was even more dangerous than she imagined, for he was not only influential, powerful, merciless, and ambitious, he could wear charm like a beautifully crafted veneer.

"What do you want?" Gabria replied warily.

"You have in your clan a man who is half Turic and half clan. His parents had twelve children, yet only he inherited enough clan blood to be a magic-wielder." The man steepled his fingers and met Gabria eye to eye. "There have been other half-breed children along the border; this aberration could turn up again."

Gabria's expression tightened into a frown. "Of course that could happen again. But such a child has not yet been brought to my attention."

His mouth widened to what most people would have seen as an expression of delight. To Kelene and Gabria, his broad grin resembled more the victorious leer of a wolf about to eat its kill.

"Perhaps now, then," said Zukhara, and he opened out his palm, spread his fingers, and formed a small sphere of greenish light directly over his hand. The implications struck both women at the same time, and they shrank away from the harmless little light.

"How can you do that?" gasped Kelene.

"My mother was raped by a Wylfling while she was on a journey. She was so terrified of her husband's jealousy she told him the baby was his. It wasn't until he died a few years ago that she found the courage to tell me." He gave them another friendly smile. "It explained some questions that had been bothering me."

Gabria and Kelene said nothing to his revelation. The same suspicion was brewing in both their minds that the counselor knew more about magic than how to form a simple sorcerer's light, and they watched him quietly and waited for him to explain more.

Zukhara bounced the little light gently in his palm; then with a snap his fingers closed over the sphere and crushed it out. "I had thought to visit you these past few years to study sorcery with your clan students, but other matters kept me busy. Now there is little time left. I must control this power now, and for that I have brought you with me." The charm cracked from his voice, turning his words hard and bare. He turned suddenly and pointed a finger at Kelene. "I want you to teach me how to use my power, how to control it, and how to turn it to my will."

Kelene was so startled by his choice, she exclaimed without thinking, "Me? I'm no teacher. I'm a healer!"

"You know sorcery. It is enough to begin. Lady Gabria may watch and contribute if she wishes. We will start tomorrow." He stood then and pulled Kelene to her feet. With deliberate care he slipped the gag back into her mouth and tied her wrists tightly together. His eyes glittered in the lamplight as he stared down at her angry face. His hands lingered on her arms for a moment longer than she thought utterly necessary before he lifted her back onto the bed. Kelene did not even try to sense his emotions but shut her mind and turned her head away for fear of what she might find.

Gabria was gagged and tied again and returned to her place beside Kelene. This time Zukhara did not bother to fasten their arms to their sides. He picked up the lamp and dishes. "Until morning," he said pleasantly and climbed out, locking the door behind him.

His footsteps had barely passed away before Kelene pulled her bound wrists up and used her fingers to wrench the gag out of her mouth. "That—!" she spat furiously, too angry to think of a worthy epithet.

Gabria removed her gag, grateful for the small relief. "That man is crazier than a mad dog in the summer heat," she observed dryly.

"Half-clan!" Kelene hissed. "Gods' truth!" She lay beside her mother, trembling with rage. Although she could not bring herself to say anything to Gabria, she realized she was fuming not just because of Zukhara's audacious kidnapping or his demand that they teach him sorcery, but also because of the brilliant look in his eyes when he pulled her up and the slow touch of his hands on her skin. It was enough to make her flesh crawl.

Gabria tilted her head toward Kelene. "You know," she said slowly, "I would wager Nara that Zukhara was the one who killed the Shar-Yon."

"I won't take that wager," Kelene answered. "Mother, we *can't* teach that viper sorcery. He is already a menace to the Turics and the clans!"

"No, we must not if we can help it." She paused and thought of Athlone's description of Bashan's seared body. "But perhaps we should teach him the rudiments of control. Wild magic, in his hands, is more dangerous than a controlled spell."

"What if he pushes me to teach him more?"

Gabria's thin smile was lost in the darkness. "Then perhaps we should convince him that his abilities are not as strong as he hopes. If his spells were to go awry . . ."

Kelene gave a dry chuckle. "You're not suggesting disrupting his spells."

"Nothing blatant. Just a nudge here and there to sour the effect."

They fell silent, their thoughts heavy with their dangerous predicament. After a long, unhappy pause, Kelene whispered, "Should we try to escape him?"

"Would you leave Demira in his hands?" Gabria asked heavily, although they both knew the answer.

"No. So we deal with Zukhara until we can leave with the Hunnuli."

"Or someone reaches us."

Lying there in the darkness, tied hand and foot, far from home and desperately worried, Kelene felt very much the daughter in need of her mother's reassurance. "Do you really think they would dare search for us here?"

In the darkness Gabria felt for her daughter's bound hands and clasped them tightly in her own. "Athlone, Rafnir, or Sayyed will find a way. I know it."

The certainty in those words was enough to satisfy Kelene and reinforce her own belief in her kin. Calmer now, she set her mind on her immediate problems of teaching sorcery to Zukhara and dealing with captivity.

Suddenly she gave a rueful laugh at herself. "Just before Gaalney came to Moy Tura," she explained to her puzzled mother, "I was riding Demira above the city and feeling sorry for myself because things weren't going my way." She chuckled again and felt better for it. "Right now I would happily trade all of this to be back in that mere muddle. I promise, if we make it back to Moy Tura, I won't feel sorry for myself again . . . for at least another three or four years."

Gabria laughed softly with her, and their tension eased enough to let them rest. They slept fitfully through the night, until Zukhara returned at dawn. The Turic brought food to his prisoners, allowed them to attend to their needs, and waited while they ate their morning meal. Gabria and Kelene watched him like a pair of hawks, but the man remained mute and did nothing to give the women any hope of escape. His movements were brusque yet meticulous, and his eyes burned unabated with their fierce zeal.

As soon as the captives finished eating, their hands were retied, and they were returned to the pallet. Instead of leaving right away, Zukhara stepped to the barrier and glanced over at the Hunnuli. Kelene craned her head around to see what he was doing, and her heart jumped in hope when Demira tossed her head. A hoof crashed against the wooden gate, but the two mares were so crowded, Kelene could not tell which one had kicked.

Zukhara did not flinch at the impact. He drew a glass flask from a pocket in his dark blue robe and uncorked it. A pungent, medicinal odor filled the interior of the wagon, alerting Kelene's curiosity. She strained her neck to watch Zukhara pour some thick greenish liquid onto a cloth and rub it on Demira's haunch. Nara was treated with the same liquid, and shortly after, the mares' stall was silent again.

Kelene cursed under her breath. Whatever drug he was using to sedate the mares must be very potent to affect the big horses so quickly. The door slammed and locked behind the counselor, leaving the clanswomen in darkness again. Shortly thereafter they heard whips crack, voices shout, and animals call. There was a great deal of noise and some jerky starts as the baggage train sorted itself out; then the wagon bounced forward, once more under way.

The weather that day seemed sunnier, for the light shining through the chinks in the wagon's walls was bright and full. Kelene watched one whip-thin beam move slowly across the wall and down to the floor in a course that indicated they were moving south, deeper into Turic territory.

In spite of their thirst and discomfort, evening came all too soon for Kelene and Gabria. The light dimmed and disappeared into twilight; the caravan reached its next stop along the Spice Road. Unbeknownst to them, Rafnir and Sayyed were eating their meal and talking to Turics not more than several hundred paces away.

No one came near the wagon for a long while, and the sounds of the camp dwindled to sleepy tranquility. They heard several sets of footsteps pacing past their prison, but not one person stopped to look in their wagon or check on their condition.

Kelene squirmed against the Hunnuli-hair ropes that held her fast. Her hands were swollen, red, and painful; her body ached from lying on a jolting board all day. She dreaded seeing Zukhara again, yet she reviled him with every scrap of her fury for not coming and getting this ordeal over. Her tongue had dried to thick leather, and her throat burned with thirst. "Where is he?" she ground out between clenched teeth.

She felt her emotions kindle the power of the Trymmian force in her bones and blood. It burned like a spark on touchwood, ready to ignite at her will.

Without any warning, the door swung open, and a tall figure loomed in the entrance. In that split second Kelene's thoughts exploded with her pent-up fear and rage and, before she could control herself, a wild burst of the Trymmian force flamed from her hands. Kelene gasped in horror.

Gabria reared up and tried to evaporate the blast, but it flew too fast and struck Zukhara full on the chest, where it exploded in a cloud of blue sparks. The counselor staggered backward from the force of the blow. Only the ivory ward around his neck absorbed the searing power and saved his life.

Kelene's eyes grew enormous, and her heart beat painfully as Zukhara climbed to his feet. The tall Turic stepped back into the wagon, placed the tray he took from a servant on the table, and deliberately closed and locked the door behind him. Swift as a striking cobra, his hand shot out and clamped around Gabria's throat. His fingers found her jugular and her windpipe and began to crush her neck within his ferocious grip.

"No!" screamed Kelene. "It was me!" She tried to grab his wrists, to pull him away from her mother, but she might as well have tried to uproot a tree. Zukhara ignored her and sunk his thumbs deeper into Gabria's throat. The clanswoman's eyes bulged above her gasping mouth. She struggled and thrashed in vain to escape his iron hands.

"I warned you," Zukhara hissed in sharp, fierce anger. "You did not heed me."

"I didn't mean to! I was angry and scared," Kelene raged at him. "Get off her." She abruptly pulled up her tied feet and kicked at him with all her might.

Her feet landed on his ribs and slammed him sideways against the wagon wall, jarring his hands loose from around Gabria's throat. Kelene swiftly rolled over the older sorceress, knocking Zukhara's hands off completely, and she managed to use her body to shove her mother off the pallet to the floor.

Gabria was too weak to stand. Sobbing, she lay supine on the dusty boards and tried to draw deep, rasping breaths through her bruised throat.

The counselor angrily pushed himself upright until he was kneeling over Kelene. His long, lean shape loomed above her like a black, forbidding shadow.

"It was an accident!" Kelene insisted. "If you kill her, you lose your best lever against me, and I'll see you in Gormoth before I teach you even one spell."

Zukhara leaned so close his trim beard brushed her chin. His hands rose and fell over her neck but instead of choking her, his long fingers caressed her skin from her earlobes down the soft length of her throat. "Then I guess we are at an impasse, my lady," he said huskily in her ear. "If you do not obey, I will kill, and yet if I kill, you will not obey. A fine challenge."

Kelene quivered at his touch. His warm breath by her ear made the hairs rise on the back of her neck, and his weight on her shoulder and chest frightened her. She lay rigid and cold, her heart beating rapidly. "Then it would be best if we struck a bargain," she made herself say.

Zukhara settled more comfortably on top of her, his hands still resting on her bare neck, one thumb caressing the frantic pulse in the base of her throat.

"I will train you in sorcery—as much as you need to control your power—and when I am finished, you will let my mother, me, and our Hunnuli go home unharmed."

The man chuckled, warm and throaty. "A bargain struck in haste is oft regretted. I will think about it. Perhaps in time we will devise a better arrangement." He pushed away from her and untied her hands. "In the meantime, eat. Then show me what you have to offer."

Kelene gritted her teeth. There was nothing else to do but agree—for now. She helped her mother to the bench by the table where Zukhara had placed their meal and a small lamp. Kelene drew on her skills as a healer and tenderly eased the pain in Gabria's bruised throat. She wrapped a cool, damp cloth around her mother's neck and helped her sip a cup of wine.

From his stool, Zukhara observed them impassively.

After a while, Kelene coaxed Gabria to eat some soup and was pleased to see a little color return to the older woman's waxen cheeks. With the flush came a reawakening of Gabria's steel spirit. She covered her forehead with a limp hand, sagged back against the wooden wall, and surreptitiously winked at Kelene. The young woman smothered a smile and ate her own food gratefully.

The moment she was finished, Zukhara cleared off

the table and, in a lightning-swift change of mood, flashed his friendly, disarming smile. He pulled a small book out of his robes and laid it in front of Kelene. "Now, my lady. Where do we begin?"

Gabria and Kelene bent forward to look at the little volume in the light of the oil lamp. Although books were not common among the seminomadic clanspeople, both women had learned to read the old Clannish script from books preserved in the Citadel of Krath by the Cult of the Lash and from a few precious manuscripts unearthed at Moy Tura. To their astonishment, this book, no bigger than a man's hand, appeared to be a relic of clan history. It was made of white vellum stretched and scraped to thin, supple sheets and bound between a heavier cover of leather that, once dyed a rich red, had since faded to the color of old wine.

Kelene gingerly turned the front cover to the first page and heard her mother gasp. In a spidery, delicate script was written: Jeneve, Daughter of Lord Magar of Clan Corin.

Gabria's hands flew to the book, and she drew it closer to pore over the writing and illustrations on the following pages. "This is a spellbook," she breathed in surprise. "A personal collection compiled by Lady Jeneve! How did you get your hands on it?" she snapped at Zukhara.

He smiled again, a long, self-satisfied sneer. "The God of All delivered it to my hands to help fulfill the prophecy."

"What prophecy?" Kelene demanded.

Zukhara disregarded the question and tapped the book with his forefinger. "I can read this, so do not try to trick me. I simply want to know how to use the magic to control these spells."

Glancing over her mother's arm, Kelene read the names of some of the spells in the handbook. Most were simple day-to-day twists of sorcery that took only basic skills and caused little harm, such as firestarters, spheres of light, easy transformations, household aids, and simple medications. But there were others that a man like Zukhara could twist to his own purposes: a spell to paralyze an animal or human, spells of destructive power, a spell to summon wind from a gathering storm, and others she would be loath to show him.

Control first, she thought to herself. She had never taught anyone magic; that had always been Gabria's duty. But it seemed reasonable to start at the beginning where every magic-wielder had to start and take it as slowly as she dared. Perhaps, given the help of the gods, she and Gabria could find a way to escape before Zukhara pushed his training too far.

She traded looks with Gabria, then closed the book and pushed it aside. "We will start here," she said, tapping her own forehead, and she launched into her first lesson. "Will is at the center of sorcery. With every spell you create you are attempting to impose your will on the substance of our world. Magic is a natural force that is in every creature, stone, or plant. When you alter that force, even with the smallest spell, you must be strong enough to control the effect and consequences. The forces of magic can destroy you if you cannot control them."

She paused and stared at Zukhara's dark visage. Unconsciously she had been repeating Gabria's old lesson that she had listened to for years before the words took on real meaning. "The strength of will is the most important trait of a magic-wielder. Therefore you must know yourself, every measure and degree of your own being, so you can recognize your own limitations and know when sorcery has begun to bleed substance from your life-force."

Zukhara's hand suddenly grabbed Kelene's right arm and pulled her wrist out straight toward him. He touched her embedded splinter so hard she flinched in pain. "Enough of your childish lectures. I have the will of the Living God; there are no limitations other than my own lack of knowledge. I will have a splinter in my wrist in ten days' time or I will remove your arm at the elbow. Are we clear?"

Kelene gaped, aghast at his monstrous arrogance. He had no comprehension of his own weaknesses and therefore dismissed any possibility of them in impervious blindness. Perhaps she and Gabria wouldn't have to escape; perhaps all they had to do was wait for Zukhara to destroy himself in his own overwhelming self-confidence.

She hoped he would hurry and do so soon. She didn't want to have to tell him there were no more diamond splinters. Gabria had used the last one only a year ago and had not yet found a new source for the special, power-enhancing gems.

Kelene yanked her wrist out of his grasp and said firmly, "Fine. Then we will begin with control." She held out her fingers and demonstrated commands for Zukhara's first spell.

The Turic watched avidly, then followed her instructions until he had formed a perfect greenish-white sphere of light. Late into the night the sorceress and her pupil practiced and discussed, manipulated magic and worked on simple skills, until Kelene was exhausted and Gabria drooped beside her.

Indefatigable, Zukhara ordered them to lie down, retied their hands, and departed, his back still straight, his step as forceful as always.

"Oh, Mother," Kelene sighed when he was gone. "What are we going to do? He's at least as strong as Sayyed, and he's learning fast."

"I was afraid of that when I saw him work. He burns with ambition. But what is he planning? Why is he so determined to have a splinter within ten days?"

Kelene sighed and closed her eyes. She was so tired, and there was nothing left she could say.

Gabria's questions passed into silence unanswered.

9

Zukhara slammed his hand on the rough table. "What tripe are you showing me? Why will it not work?" he demanded. Stewing in frustration, he tried again to form a simple transformation spell to change a cluster of grapes into a handful of plums. He focused on the grapes and spoke the words of the spell for the third time.

On the bunk behind him, Gabria wordlessly moved her fingers and used her own will to throw his magic astray. The grapes on the table wavered a few times, then burst under the pressure of the vying sorcery.

The Turic spat a curse.

"Be patient," Kelene told him coolly. "Concentrate on what you want. You have to know exactly what you intend to create or the spell will go awry."

"I know what I want," he ground out.

"Then perhaps you are not trying hard enough to control the magic. If you cannot master these simple spells, you will never be able to control the more complex sorcery."

They eyed each other across the table, Kelene stiff and her head thrown back; Zukhara tense and angry, the lines pulled tight around his mouth and across his brow. In the flickering lamplight, he reminded Kelene of a black-and-gold adder, its large, dark eyes glittering, its lean head poised to strike.

"All right, try something a little simpler," she suggested, pushing the dripping grapes aside and picking up a flask of water. She poured a small amount of water into a dish and placed it before the Turic. "With a minor spell you can turn this water to ice," she said and showed him how to do it.

Zukhara tried the spell and managed to create a film of ice on the water before the pottery dish shattered and spilled water across the table. Kelene watched him impassively, like a teacher helping a pupil who cannot quite grasp an easy concept. He tried spell after spell, and no matter how hard he tried, everything went wrong.

An hour later he was struggling to create a flame on a candle when Kelene suddenly lifted her head. From somewhere nearby came the sounds of boots scuffling on the ground, several soft thuds, and the mutter of muted voices. Gabria didn't have to break the spell that time, for the disruption caused Zukhara to jerk his hand, and the candle sagged into a pool of melted wax. Muttering under his breath, Zukhara strode to the door, unlocked it, and stepped out.

Kelene followed him with her eyes and saw a dark-clothed man meet him just outside the door. "Counselor, we have found two more pilferers in the wagons," she heard the man say.

Zukhara looked at something out of Kelene's sight.

"Get rid of them," he ordered. "But not here. More deaths will draw attention. Take them out past the oasis."

The callousness in his voice chilled Kelene with a hollow foreboding. It could so easily be herself or Gabria he so casually disposed of. The counselor climbed back into the wagon, dusting his hands as if ridding his palms of some dirty annoyance. He settled on his stool across from Kelene and almost negligently flicked his hand and set the wick of the melted candle burning. He stared at the tiny flame for a long time, his volatile expression lost in thought. The silence built around him, thick as walls.

In one sudden movement and without warning, he sprang from his seat and delivered a stunning blow to Gabria's jaw. The fury of the assault snapped back her head, with an audible crack, against the wooden wall.

"Get back!" he roared at Kelene when she jumped to help her mother. With fierce deftness, he retied Gabria's hands and stuffed the gag back in her mouth. Mute with suspicion, he sat down and repeated the transformation spell Kelene had tried to teach him. The cluster of split grapes turned into a heap of delicate purple plums. He tried every spell they had practiced that had gone wrong, and each one worked perfectly. Kelene watched him, too terrified for Gabria to intervene.

"So," he hissed. "You thought to dissuade me from my goal by ruining my magic." He turned his baleful glare on Gabria. She lay half-stunned, her face white and her body limp. Blood ran down her chin from a cut on her mouth. She attempted to focus on him, her frustration and anger almost as potent as his. "You cannot stop me. Understand, fools, magic is part of my destiny. It is one of the weapons foretold in the prophecy."

There was that allusion to a prophecy again, Kelene realized. "What are you talking about? How can a clan power be any part of a Turic prophecy?" she snapped, her tone made sharp by her nervousness.

Zukhara seemed to swell before her eyes. Tall as he was, he straightened his spine, threw back his long shoulders, and jutted his chin forward arrogantly. "Five hundred years ago when your paltry horse clans were still settling the plains, the Prophet Sargun wrote *The Truth of Nine* from his prison in the dungeons of Sarcithia, while it was still part of the Tarnish Empire. When he escaped and returned over the mountains to his homeland, he founded the city of Sargun Shahr and gave his book to his younger brother. The city has since vanished. We still seek it today, but *The Truth of Nine* is in Cangora in the keeping of the Holy Order in the great temple of Sargun."

Kelene felt her mouth drop open, not at the lecture, for most clanspeople knew the generalities of Turic history, but at the conclusion she drew from his rhetoric. "Are you saying there is a prophecy about you in that book?"

He leaned forward, his hands on the table, and his daunting figure cast shadows over her still form. "The sixth," he said as cold as winter. " 'And the Gryphon shall rise to lay flame to the desert and feed on the blood of the unbelievers. Tyrants shall bow before him and nations shall fall at his feet.' " Zukhara's voice dropped to a low intonation, reciting the words of the prophecy as if breathing a prayer. " 'By these signs will you know him. In his hand shall be the lightning of the north, and the wind of the Living God shall uphold him. Drought, pestilence, and famine will open his way, and the copper gate will fall before his mighty strength. Before the eye of his chosen handmaiden, he will stand in the light of the golden sun, and a bastard will sit on the throne of Shahr.' " His words dropped away, and he stood poised, his thoughts running ahead to the future and the fulfillment of his dreams.

For once Kelene could think of nothing to say. His

audacity and conviction stunned her. The Gryphon. By the gods, she knew that name. "Fel Azureth," she whispered, unaware she had spoken loud enough to be heard.

Zukhara's head jerked up; his eyes glittered. "Yes, my lady. I am Fel Karak, the Gryphon, and the Fel Azureth is my sword. Already my plans are falling into place. There is but one weapon left to collect, and for that we shall leave the caravan tomorrow." He picked up the hair ropes, tied her hands behind her back, and steered her to the bed.

"Be glad, clanswoman, that you are here with me," he said softly. He touched her cheek, his fingers gently caressing. "Already the Gryphon sinks his claws into the north. When I gain the throne, I will claim the rich pastures north of the Altai for my own empire. With the lightning in my fingertips, your people will not withstand me. By year's end I will make *you* my queen and will lay the plains of Ramtharin at your feet as my wedding gift to you."

Kelene stared at him, her dark eyes enormous pools in her face. Although she could sense the stark power of his convictions through the touch of his skin on hers, she did not need her talent to grasp the reality of what she was hearing. "But I already have a husband," she said, too shaken to say anything more perceptive.

Zukhara's teeth flashed white against his black beard. "There is no law that says I cannot marry a widow."

With swift, sure movements he replaced Kelene's gag, cleaned the table, put out the light, and bid the women a good night.

Kelene listened to his footsteps pass away. Anger roared like a caged beast in her head, and she stared helplessly at the dark door, trying to bring her fear and rage under control. She wanted to shriek, to strike out at the man and his unshakable arrogance. She vowed to Amara, Sorh, Surgart, and Krath that she would find a way to stop him. There had to be something to thwart his plans. Not all prophecies come to pass as one would believe they should.

She turned her head to check her mother and saw tears leaking down Gabria's face. The sorceress had her eyes screwed shut and her pale face turned toward the ceiling.

Worry doused Kelene's anger as surely as icy water. As carefully as she could manage with her hands tied, Kelene used her long sleeve to mop away the blood on Gabria's swelling jaw and the tears that dampened her fair hair. Gabria forced a wan smile. Unable to talk, the two women pressed close and took solace in each other's company. Neither slept well that long, bitter night.

* * * * *

To young Peoren, the clatter of horses' hooves sounded unnaturally loud in the hushed twilight. He sat taller in his borrowed black cloak and tilted his head so he could hear the approaching troop. Beside him, his picked men—two Dangari, Dos his guard, and six Shadedron—stiffened like alert hounds, their attention pricked to the approaching sounds of horses, hushed voices, and the softer chink and rattle of arms.

To all appearances the ten clansmen appeared to take no notice of the troop approaching them up the long hillside. They had built their fires with care and set them so the vanguard of the Turic raiding party could see them and identify them at a distance that would still allow the clansmen time to run.

Peoren smiled a slow, assured smile as the first Turics topped the rise. The scouts had reported the disposition of the raiders perfectly. Five point riders rode ahead of the main body of men. As if on cue, they reined their mounts to a halt and stared at the ten men, their tiny fires, and the ten clan horses. Peoren and his companions jumped to their feet, as if in alarm. The Turics whooped with glee. One yanked up a horn and blew a signal to the riders coming up behind.

With an appropriate display of fear, the clansmen scrambled wildly to their horses, mounted, and set off along the side of the high hill to escape.

The troop of raiders was a big one, numbering over two hundred mounted fighters. Some brought up the rear with strings of stolen horses and laden pack animals, but the majority drew their weapons and followed the escapees at a rush. After all, ten men were easy prey, and ten clan horses were a prize worth pursuing.

Led by a Shadedron guide, the fleeing clansmen raced down the back slope to the mouth of a valley that plunged deep into a range of plateaus and towering hills. They paced their horses at a gallop just fast enough to stay ahead of the chasing band of marauders. Down they swept into the valley, swung right along the streambed, then cantered swiftly upstream toward the cover of the tree-clad hills. The Turics pushed their horses harder to catch the clansmen before they escaped into the night.

Twilight darkened to a dismal gloaming, obscuring detail and washing out color in a thickening blue-gray haze. Mist rose from the creek in curling tendrils that gathered in the hollows and spread out over the low-lying patches of bog. Snow still lay piled in drifts in the colder shadows of the hills.

The clansmen pushed on behind the Shadedron, a hunter who knew the hills as well as he did his own tent. Peoren brought up the rear and lagged slightly behind to taunt the Turic into continuing the chase over the poorly lit trail. The hillsides climbed higher above the stream, and the remaining snow grew deeper.

The clansmen were almost in range of the Turics' crossbows when the valley curved sharply to the left

and widened to form a fairly level open space devoid of
trees and lightly drifted with snow. In the dense twilight
the flat ground looked safe enough, and the Shadedron
led his companions across to the foot of a high embankment. The Turics, coming past the curve, saw their
prey's escape apparently blocked by a high bank and
yelled their battle cries while they spurred their horses
directly toward the milling clansmen.

In their excitement, the Turics did not notice a pale,
luminous glow on the ground beneath their horses' feet.
Camouflaged by the snow and the indigo twilight, the
glow covered the entire level up to the base of the high
bank where the clansmen waited with drawn swords.
Atop the embankment in a cluster of brush and rocks,
Lord Athlone watched the raiders and gauged his time.
Gaalney and Morad, across the valley, watched too, and
waited for the chieftain's signal.

The charging Turics raised their tulwars and prepared
to overwhelm the small band of clansmen. In the blink
of an eye, the earth sagged beneath their horses. The
pale fluorescence they had never noticed flicked out
with a wave of Lord Athlone's hand, and the hard crust
the Turics mistook for soil dissolved into a quaking bog.
The galloping charge turned into a thrashing, struggling,
screaming quagmire of men, mud, and horses.

A few riders at the rear of the troop had not yet ridden onto the bog, but when they tried to turn around, a
bright red wall of magic energy slammed into existence
across the valley, blocking their way out. They reined to
a stunned halt and watched over one hundred fully
armed and vengeful clansmen silently rise from their
hiding places and encircle the marauders.

The tribesmen still on firm ground guessed what
their fate might be in the hands of the furious clans and
chose to attack. They charged the nearest group of warriors and were brought down by arrows before they
reached the first man. Another bunch at the front of the

charge struggled toward Peoren and his men to cut
them down. The Shadedron, sick with rage, met them
hand-to-hand and killed several before Peoren stopped
them. He looked into a square-jawed face with a scimi-
tar nose and a killer's eyes, and he recognized the
leader of the band that had attacked Ferganan Treld.

This was a prize too good to lose. Peoren bellowed
to Lord Athlone and stood back from his opponent as
the sorcerer lord dropped down from his vantage point
and fired a burst of magic at the Turic commander. The
blue force laid the man unconscious. Twenty more
Turics were hauled from the mud and taken prisoner.
The rest either drowned in the black, clutching bog,
were crushed by the terrified horses, or were killed by
the clansmen.

By the time night was full, the ambush was over. The
clansmen rescued what horses they could, patched the
injured Turics, and left the dead to the scavengers. They
returned back up the valley, gathering the stolen horses
and plunder-laden pack animals as they went. They set
up camp by the stream and ate a robust dinner. They
were tired and saddened by the tragedies that had
forced their assault, but they had been victorious, and
one band of vicious marauders had been destroyed
without the loss of a single clansman.

After their meal, the men sat by their fires to sing and
tell tales and celebrate their success, while their chiefs
looked over the prisoners. Two guards brought the
Turic leader first, his hands and arms bound and his
dark eyes furious, to stand before the clan lords.

Peoren nodded once. "This is the man who killed my
father."

"He was at Shadedron Treld, too," said young Hazeth.

The Turic stiffened defiantly and glared at his captors.

"I have seen the horses they stole and the goods they
plundered," said Lord Wendern. "There is no doubt."

Lord Fiergan, the red-haired Reidhar, growled, "Who

are you? Why did you attack our trelds?"

There came no reply. The prisoner shifted on his feet, his expression sullen and determined.

Lord Athlone rose to his feet with the slow, deliberate intent of a stalking lion. No hint of emotion altered his cold features; nothing distracted his merciless stare from the prisoner.

The Turic's eyes snapped to the sorcerer; he recognized the chieftain and knew his power. His swarthy face turned noticeably paler.

Wordlessly the chieftains watched Athlone walk to stand in front of the Turic. The guards moved away, leaving the prisoner alone with the Khulinin lord.

"You know the punishments we can mete out to vermin like you," Athlone said in a voice as smooth and penetrating as steel. "You will wish for any one of those to end your agony if *I* am forced to deal with you."

The Turic, who was nearly as tall as Athlone, tried to meet his gaze and failed. He edged back from the chieftain and looked wildly around to see if anyone was going to intervene, but the clansmen stayed where they were, mercy long gone from their thoughts. The Turic began to sweat in the chilly night air.

Athlone raised his right hand, his fingers inches from the man's face. The Turic stared in growing fear. "Now," the sorcerer continued, "who are you? And what can you tell us about the Fel Azureth?"

The Turic visibly blanched. Athlone's fingers dropped until they lightly touched the prisoner's forehead. "Talk!" he commanded.

* * * * *

By dawn Kelene and Gabria were wan and sore. It had been a miserable night, and the coming day that softened the black shadows and sent delicate beams of light dancing through the chinks in the wagon wall did little to lighten the gloom in the women's hearts.

Still dozing, they were startled alert when the door slammed open and Zukhara strode in. His features looked thunderous but, without a word, he laid out their breakfast, freed their hands, and stood aside as they climbed stiffly to their feet. Kelene was ravenous and ate well. Gabria only picked at her food. Her jaw was swollen and discolored purple and blue; her skin was terribly pale. Only her green eyes blazed defiantly at Zukhara as she sipped the wine he had brought her.

No sooner had they finished than the counselor replaced their bonds, tying their hands loosely in front of them. Kelene had little time to wonder why before he pulled a strange vial from the pocket of his robe. Striking like an adder, he gripped Gabria's injured face and turned it upward. He forced the vial into her mouth and poured its contents down her throat before she could overcome her pain and spit it out. Terror crossed her face.

"What have you done?" Kelene cried.

Satisfied, Zukhara replaced the stopper in the vial. "I have had enough of your disobedience. You would not take me seriously, so I offer you a new bargain. I have given Lady Gabria a slow-acting poison. If you obey me in all things, in ten days' time I will give her the antidote. If you do not, she will die a long and painful death." He paused and smiled a slow, malevolent smile. "Do not think to escape me and seek the antidote on your own. The poison is of my own making, and only I hold its cure."

Indifferently he turned to the Hunnuli and slathered more of the thick sedative on their rumps. Giving the women a slight bow, he left them and locked the door behind him.

Even as the lock clicked into place, Kelene climbed to her feet. Her ankles were still tied, but the ropes had loosened enough to enable her to shuffle the short distance to Demira's side. She grasped the hem of her tunic and tore a long, narrow strip off the bottom where it would not be immediately noticed. Bunching it in her hand, she rubbed the place on Demira's hip where Zukhara had smeared his potion. To her relief, a thin film of greenish liquid came off on her cloth. She knew she had not removed all the sedative and that it would be a while before Demira revived, but this was a start. She carefully wrapped the fabric in a wad, the green stain hidden in the folds, and tucked it in her waistband.

She turned slowly and faced Gabria. "I do not trust Zukhara to keep his word. If Demira can escape, she can find Father, Sayyed, or Rafnir," she said almost apologetically. She knew she was taking a big chance with Gabria's life.

The sorceress nodded, her resolution clear. "This man must be stopped," she said simply.

There fell a silence neither woman wanted to break. Gabria lay down on the pallet, too weary to stay upright. Kelene braced herself on the little bench and kept watch through the hours of morning as the wagon lurched and rumbled its way south in the wake of the caravan. The dust grew thick in the little room, and the air turned warmer.

It was noon, judging by the grumblings in her belly, when Kelene realized the van had noticeably slowed. The sorceress waited, scarcely breathing the dusty air. A moment later the van made a sharp turn to the right and dropped onto a rougher road. Kelene had to grab the small table for support, and the mares lurched sideways in their stall. Kelene noticed a ripple run through Demira's hide from neck to tail, and the mare stirred her head before slipping back into her stupor.

The van stopped. In the quiet that followed, Kelene could hear the distant sounds of the caravan, and she was not surprised that the noises were dwindling away. Zukhara had said they would leave the caravan. Several voices murmured quietly outside, their tones too soft to identify.

Kelene glanced at her mother. Gabria appeared to be sleeping, so she decided not to waken her. But looking at her mother reminded her of Gabria's conviction that someone had come after them. Kelene's heart sank. If that were true, if Athlone or Sayyed or Rafnir had followed the caravan to find them, how would the men know where this wagon had gone? They could follow the Shar-Ja all the way to Cangora, hoping to find Gabria and her.

She would have to leave some sign and hope, slim as the possibility was, that someone would find it and recognize it. But what? If she left something of magic, Zukhara could see it and know her intent. It could not be anything large either, since she had no way to get a big object out of the van.

The wagon jerked and started forward along the rougher trail. Kelene's hands flew to her braid and her red ribbon. It hung limp in her hands, bedraggled and dirty, but it was all she had. On her hands and knees she searched the floor of the wagon for a crack wide enough to push the ribbon through. Unfortunately, someone had rebuilt the bed of the old wagon, perhaps to hold the weight of the Hunnuli. There was not so much as a seam. She finally resorted to a fingernail crack in the wall beside the door. It was painstaking work to feed the limp ribbon through the crevice, and she prayed no one was riding behind the wagon. At last the red strip fell away and vanished to fall somewhere on the trail. Kelene's prayers went with it.

They camped that night along the trail, and Zukhara brought their food and drink as usual. He spoke not a word to them, but roused Gabria, watched them eat, and swiftly returned outside.

As soon as she was finished, Gabria went back to sleep. Kelene lay beside her, worried at her mother's lethargy. Sometime during the night, Gabria tossed in her sleep in the throes of a powerful dream. Kelene woke to her mother's voice calling low and insistently, "Sayyed!"

The dream faded away, and Gabria lay still, her breathing so shallow Kelene had to strain to hear it. Was this another of her mother's visions? Was it Sayyed who had come after them? That made sense to Kelene. He had the best chance of making his way through Turic territory. She dozed again, thinking of Sayyed and, most of all, his handsome, dark-haired son.

Zukhara's entrance startled Kelene awake, and she lay blinking in the morning light that streamed through the open door while he laid out their food, dosed the mares, and departed, all without a word spoken. As soon as the door closed behind him, Kelene worked her way to Demira's stall, and again she wiped off the thick sedative onto her rag. She put her hand on Demira's warm hide. Her probing mind immediately touched the mare's consciousness straining against the drug that imprisoned her body.

Ever so gently Kelene formed a spell that loosened the fabric confining Demira's wings. The Hunnuli, sensing Kelene's closeness, shifted restlessly.

Be easy, Kelene soothed. *Wait and be patient. When you are alert enough, fly and escape.*

No! Demira's resistance rang in Kelene's head. The mare was fighting the sedative with every ounce of her will. *I will not leave you!*

Please, Demira, you must! Mother has been poisoned. She will die if we do not have help. I think Sayyed has come to look for us. Find him! Bring him to us! You are the only one who can.

I cannot leave you, Demira repeated, but her thoughts were weak and confused.

Kelene leaned her head on the mare's rump. "Please try," she whispered. She returned to their table, roused

Gabria, and tried to eat some food. Their breakfast that morning was simple—trail bread, dates, a wedge of cheese, and mugs of a sweet, red juice Kelene had never tried before. She eyed the juice suspiciously, wondering if Zukhara had slipped a poison or sedative into her drink. Thirst finally won over, and she drained the drink to the dregs. It was overly sweet but had a rich, fruity taste.

Gabria merely sipped hers and lay back on the pallet. Zukhara returned to gather the mugs and plates. He smiled his cream-eating leer when he saw Kelene's empty mug. "Did you enjoy the juice, my lady?" he asked pleasantly.

A warning buzzed in Kelene's mind; her eyes narrowed. "Why?"

"It contained a mixture I prepared especially for you." He moved close to her, trapping her against the wagon's wall. "If you are to be my chosen handmaiden, you must be receptive to my seed. I intend to father a dynasty of sorcerers with you." He brushed a strand of hair away from her face and softly kissed her forehead.

Kelene froze. The mingled smells of his clothes and the warmth of his body enveloped her; his tall weight pressed against her. She tried to struggle, but the ropes held her hands, and his strength trapped her helplessly against the wooden wall. "I can't have babies," she ground out between clenched teeth.

"You will," he chuckled close to her ear. "This is an old Turic midwives' remedy. It works well to light a fire in a barren womb."

"The better to burn your seed," she hissed.

Zukhara laughed outright. He stepped back and picked up the mugs. "Today we reach my fortress, where my last weapon awaits. There your work will begin . . . and our pleasure." Still chuckling, he left, and in moments the van jerked forward on its last leg of the journey.

Kelene could keep her anger down no longer. A raging scream tore from her throat, and she picked up the small bench and smashed it against the table. Both table and bench cracked and splintered into pieces. Outside, Zukhara's voice rose in derisive laughter.

The travel that day was long and difficult as the wagon lurched and bumped along a poor, unkempt road. Although Kelene had no idea where they were, the wagon seemed to be climbing ever higher. Hours passed. She felt the electrical energies of the coming storm long before she heard the muted rumble of the thunder.

The light in the wagon's interior dimmed to a grayish pallor. The wind began to pummel the vehicle's sides. Kelene could hear the crack of the driver's whip and the nervous neighs of the team. Voices shouted on both sides, and the thunder boomed closer.

In her stall Demira lifted her head. Her nostrils flared at the smell of the coming storm. "Patience," Kelene said to the mare.

The light was nearly gone by the time the wagon rumbled off the dirt road and clattered onto a stone-paved surface. The van made one final rush upward, then came to a stop. New voices called, orders were shouted, and Kelene heard the creak and thud of what sounded like a large door being opened. The wagon rolled forward a short distance.

Abruptly the door opened, and Zukhara climbed in. He untied their ropes and hurried both women outside. Gabria was hollow-eyed and groggy and had to lean on Kelene's arm. Kelene glanced quickly around. The storm was almost overhead, and the lightning cracked around them. She could barely make out a high stone wall with several dark squat towers, and to her left a long hall and a high keep.

"Bring the Hunnuli!" Zukhara shouted, turning to hustle his prisoners out of the storm. Rain splattered on the stone paving.

Suddenly a ringing neigh sounded above the wind's roar. There was a wild crash of hooves and a scream of terror. The Turic and the women whirled in time to see Demira rocket forward through a door in the front of the wagon. Hands reached to grab her halter, but she screamed and reared, flailing her hooves over the heads of her enemies. The fabric covering ripped and fell away; her wings spread like an eagle's, ready to launch.

"Catch her!" Zukhara shrieked. His words were lost in a crash of thunder.

The winged mare rolled her eyes at her rider. "Go!" shouted Kelene, and the mare obeyed. Like black thunder she charged the open gateway. Her legs were swollen from standing so long, her muscles were stiff and slow, and she was still slightly disoriented by the sedative. Yet carried by her desperation, Demira spread her wings and threw herself into the teeth of the storm. At once the clouds opened, and the rain poured down in blinding sheets. In the blink of an eye, the Hunnuli had vanished.

For one shattering moment Kelene thought she had pushed Zukhara too far. Quivering with furious passion, he turned on her and whipped out his dagger to press against her throat. His lean visage snarled at her like a wolf's.

"You didn't need her," Kelene forced herself to say calmly. "Like any horse, she will go home." She prayed he did not understand enough about Hunnuli to know they were not like any other horses.

Her cool words had some effect, for instead of ramming the blade into her neck, he spat a curse and dragged her inside the hall. She saw servants take Gabria away, but she had no chance to see where before Zukhara wrenched opened a door and flung her down a flight of stairs. Kelene scrambled to stay on her feet. The counselor's hand clamped more tightly about her wrist and dragged her down several more spiraling stairways that wound deeper and deeper into the subterranean depths of the fortress.

Silent and implacable, he hauled her on until her hand was numb and her legs were tired. At last he dragged her through a narrow archway and thrust her forward. She banged painfully against a low stone wall and had to grab at it to keep from falling.

A low, angry hiss filled the dark spaces around her. A strange smell lingered on the cold air. Zukhara snapped the words to a spell Kelene had taught him, and a bright white sphere of light burst into being. It hovered over their heads, casting its light over a huge stone ceiling that arched above.

"Down there is my weapon for the holy war I plan to launch. Unfortunately, it was injured during its capture. I brought you here to heal it and tame it to obedience. Do that, and your lady mother will get her antidote." Zukhara pointed down, over the stone wall.

Kelene turned. She saw they were standing on an overhang at the side of a large natural cavern. Slowly she let her eyes drop to the bottom, where a broad floor formed an amphitheater in the mountain's heart. Curled on the sandy floor, staring malevolently up at the light, was a creature unlike any she had ever seen.

"What . . ." she gasped.

Zukhara's anger receded before his pride. "That," he said, "is my gryphon."

10

"Father!" an urgent voice hissed in his ear. "Father, wake up!"

Sayyed stirred and groaned out of his stupor. He tried to move his arms until that same voice whispered, "No! Don't jerk like that. Stay still. Please, Father, try to wake up!"

The frantic urgency in that familiar voice penetrated Sayyed's groggy thoughts, and he closed his mouth and rested his aching limbs. Something seemed wrong though. Some strange thing had happened to his body that he couldn't understand. He could be wrong, yet he felt as if he were hanging upside down.

Sayyed opened his eyes. A brilliant morning sun illuminated everything around him with a clear, sharp light. The majestic mountains gleamed—upside down—in an endless sky of blue. Then he looked down, or was it up, and saw there was nothing beneath his feet but air.

The words he spoke were short and emphatic.

"Father!" hissed Rafnir's voice. "Please don't move!"

Sayyed's mind snapped fully alert, and he quickly recognized the precariousness of his position. He was tied back-to-back with Rafnir and hanging head-first over a very deep and very rocky ravine. Also, the rope that held them seemed dangerously frayed and was tied to a very fragile-looking wooden framework that over-hung the edge of the chasm. And, he noted in increasing annoyance, his weapons and most of his clothes were gone. Lastly, he realized there were voices other than Rafnir's speaking behind him.

"I'm telling you, Helmar, these are simply Turics. Uphold the law and get rid of them," demanded a male voice.

"Turics or not, why waste two healthy men?" a female voice cried. This speaker sounded older and more insistent. "You know we need new blood if our line is to survive! These two are strong and can father children. Let them leave their seed in our women before you kill them."

Sayyed was so startled by the gist of the conversation that he did not realize for nearly a minute that the speakers were talking in Clannish. Not the Clannish he was used to, but an old dialect combined with new word combinations and Turic phrases. He listened with both fascination and increasing anger.

"And what about you, Rapinor?" A third voice spoke. "You caught them. What do you say?" This third speaker was a woman whose voice was rich and self-assured.

Yet a fourth voice responded, "Lady, I don't know how to advise you. Yes, I found them in the Back Door, and they look and dress like Turics. But I swear they rode black horses bigger than any I've ever seen, and one man had a sphere of light."

"Are you sure it wasn't a torch he carried?" the first man said dryly.

"A torch on a night like last? No," the speaker said, the certainty clear in his deep, resounding voice. "The sphere was greenish-white like magic and went out when the man fell unconscious."

"There has to be a simple explanation for that," said the old woman irritably. "We all know magic is dead beyond the mountains."

Sayyed turned his head in an effort to see these people, and although he strained, he could not see around Rafnir. "What is going on here?" he said in Clannish.

His words caught the speakers' attention. "A Turic who speaks the tongue of the clans," said the first man. "All the more reason to kill them. They could get away and tell the clans."

Tell the clans, Sayyed wondered. Tell them what?

"Traveler," called the younger woman, "you were caught trespassing on land that is forbidden. Our laws automatically condemn you to death. However, we are having some doubts as to your identity. Who are you?"

Sayyed opened his mouth to answer, then closed it again. By the gods, how should he answer that? If he claimed to be Turic, these strangers would cut the rope and let him and Rafnir fall. If he said clan, they would probably do the same thing. His power itched to break the ropes that bound him and his son and set them on a more upright and equal footing with these people, but he decided to hold off exposing his talent until he absolutely had to. The speakers' opinion of magic was very unclear.

"We are looking for our family," Rafnir answered for him. "My wife and my wife's mother were kidnapped by someone we do not know. Yet the wagon that carried them came up into these mountains. We had almost found them when we were caught in the storm and lost the trail. If we trespassed, we did it unintentionally, and we humbly apologize."

The people remained quiet while they tried to understand Rafnir's unfamiliar dialect; then they burst into talk all at once in a babble of questions, demands, and angry opinions. Other voices joined in until Sayyed and Rafnir lost track of all the words.

"Who are these people?" Sayyed asked irritably. His head hurt from his inversion, and he was tired of all the arguing.

"I don't know. I can't see them either. They're just above us on a rock ledge," replied Rafnir.

Sayyed tried again to peer around his son and only succeeded in making their rope sway. He froze too late. He heard a creak and a snap, and in a sickening jerk, he and Rafnir began to fall.

"Lady!" the Rapinor voice shouted. "The rope broke!"

"Let them go!" yelled the first man.

Sayyed waited no more. He didn't care who those people were or what they were afraid of, it was time to show them that magic was very much alive and well. "I'll undo the ropes; you break our fall," he yelled to Rafnir.

The wind of their descent tore at his words, but his son heard them. Magic flared from Sayyed's hands, and the ropes dissolved into dust. With his arms free, Sayyed grabbed for Rafnir to keep him close. Rafnir's eyes closed as his lips formed the words to a spell he had used three years ago to catch Kelene in a terrible fall. The air thickened into a cushion beneath them. Their sickening speed slowed, and they tumbled gently onto a platform of wind and magic barely ten feet from the ravine's floor.

"Nice timing," Sayyed said, peering down at the boulders below.

"Gods," sighed Rafnir, "that was close. Let's get out of here."

"Not yet," Sayyed growled. He glared up at the ravine face where a group of people peered over the cliff's edge. "I want to know who *they* are."

He steadied himself on the platform of air while

Rafnir carefully steered it up to the level of the precipice
top. His arms crossed and his displeasure plain, Sayyed
stepped off onto the stone and faced the group of
people standing on the rocks. He looked them over and
felt his anger begin to recede. He had never seen such
a totally unanimous expression of astounded disbelief
and awed surprise in his entire long and adventurous
life. Not even the first and unexpected appearance of
his magical talent had produced such stunned surprise.
Every man and woman before him stared at him in
speechless shock. As one their eyes shifted to Rafnir as
he stepped beside his father and dissolved his spell;
then they looked at one another.

Sayyed counted twenty-one men and women of various ages gathered on the cliff top, including the four in
the forefront he assumed were the speakers they had not
been able to see. All the people were remarkably fair-
skinned, with light hair and blue, green, or gray eyes.
Whoever they were, Turic blood had not been in their
ancestry. In fact, if it were not for the location and their
strange clothes, he would think they were clanspeople.

He decided to try something to break the barrier of
tension and see what their reaction would be. His
burnoose, outer robes, boots, and belt were gone. He
had only his trousers and an undertunic left, so he
pulled the tunic off and transformed it quickly and skillfully into a golden clan cloak. He flipped the cloak over
his shoulders, stepped forward, and saluted the people
as a whole.

"I am Sayyed, sorcerer and Hearthguard to Lord
Athlone of Clan Khulinin. My son, Rafnir, and I have
come to these mountains only to seek our kin."

He was gratified when a woman stepped forward
and returned his salute. A tall woman, she stood before
her people, proud and fearless. The bright light of
morning flamed on a coiled mass of red hair and
gleamed on her wide forehead, arched imperious

brows, and wide, firm mouth. "I welcome you, Sorcerer. More than you know. I am Helmar, Lady Chieftain of the Clannad," she said in a clear, resolute voice.

She had a carriage of the head and a lancelike directness that reminded Sayyed of Gabria. And a woman chieftain? Gabria would appreciate that, too.

Sayyed bowed. "This was an interesting way to start the day, but I seem to remember we came with horses. May we return to them?" Despite his sarcastic choice of words, he kept his voice neutral, with none of the annoyance and mounting curiosity he was feeling.

As if a spell had been broken, the stunned silence evaporated into a flight of activity and astonished voices. Helmar gave a series of quick orders, and several people dashed away while others gathered around the two clansmen.

"This way," said a man Sayyed identified as one of the four. He was a giant of a warrior, muscular, burly, and softspoken. "I am Rapinor, swordsman and personal guard to the Lady Chieftain. Your horses are still in the back passage." He hesitated, his craggy face curious. "Are your mounts Hunnuli?"

"You have heard of those too?" Sayyed remarked. The more he learned of these people the more mysterious they became. How much did they know about clan magic?

"Softly, Rapinor," Helmar admonished. "There will be time for answers after we return the horses."

A thousand questions burned on the faces of all the people around them, but none gainsaid the chieftain as she led the strangers up a path to the crest of the ridge. There she paused and stretched her hand out to the west. "Welcome to Sanctuary."

Rafnir whistled softly, and Sayyed simply stared.

At their feet the ridge dropped away into a deep valley that lay like a green jewel in the cold heart of the mountains. Lush and verdant, it stretched for nearly five leagues east and west, nestled between three lofty peaks. Sunlight glittered on the waters of a small lake and a river on the valley's floor and picked out the white plumes of several waterfalls that cascaded down the western face.

"Look!" Rafnir said. His finger pointed toward the waterfalls, but it was not the water that gripped his attention. A huge ledge bisected the western face of the canyon wall midway up its height. On the ledge beneath a towering overhang was a cluster of buildings carved from the natural stone and sitting in eminence over the valley. Below, herds grazed in the meadows, and the tiny figures of more people could be seen moving about their tasks.

Helmar's eyes crinkled in her weathered face as she watched the reaction of the two clansmen. Her expression was calm but wary, and she studied the two men as thoroughly as they studied the valley.

Beside her, an older woman touched Sayyed's cloak. Small, bright-eyed, and quick as a bird, she was the only woman in the group wearing a long robe. The rest of the people, even the women, wore long, baggy pants, warm wool shirts, and leather vests or tunics. "Sorcerer, I am Minora, Priestess of the Clannad," she told Sayyed.

"Ah, yes," Sayyed said, flashing a smile. "The one who wanted to keep us for breeding stock."

Although Sayyed did not know it, he had a very charming smile that took any sting out of his words. Minora laughed, a ringing, delightful burst of humor. "And I still do. We are very isolated here. Good breeders are hard to come by."

He turned to look at the magnificent structure across the valley. "Did your people make that?"

The priestess lifted her chin to see his face. Short as Sayyed was, she barely reached his shoulder. "The ledge and the stone were there. We have simply worked it as we wished."

"We could certainly use these people at Moy Tura," Rafnir commented to his father.

A look too indescribable to understand passed over Minora's face, and the other people hesitated, their expressions still and hard.

"What is Moy Tura?" Helmar quickly asked.

But Sayyed sensed a nuance of familiarity in her tone that belied her ignorance. "An old ruin in our land. We are trying to rebuild it."

"Who—" she started to ask.

"My lady, you said no questions until the horses are released," Rapinor reminded her bluntly.

She chuckled, low and throaty, and led the group on a winding course along the top of the ridge and down a steep, tortuous trail to the tiny canyon where the stallions were trapped.

"When you entered the passage last night, we sealed the entrance," Rapinor explained. "We had no idea what we had caught."

Sayyed's fingers went to his throat. If his neck looked anything like Rafnir's, a blue and purplish bruise ringed his throat where the rope had hauled him off his Hunnuli. "Indeed," he said dryly.

Helmar cleared her throat in sympathy, and her lips twisted in a wry smile. "You must forgive our style of welcome. We do not usually allow strangers into our valley. If it had not been for Rapinor and his insistence that you were using a sorcerer's light, you would be dead already."

Sayyed shot a look at the burly swordsman. Stout as an oak, the lady's guard had not budged from her side since the two men landed on the ledge. Nor had his hand strayed far from the sword buckled at his waist. Another man, younger but more dour than Rapinor, stood on Helmar's other side. His heavy brows framed his eyes in a frown, and his thick lips were pursed with displeasure.

"How is it that you know so much about magic," Sayyed inquired, "what with your being so isolated in a realm that forbids its use?" And, his thoughts continued silently, *why is it so important to you?*

Lady Helmar cocked her head and gave him a wide, challenging stare from her green-gold eyes. "We hear things once in a while. We do not drop everyone over the ravine." She flashed a brilliantly disarming smile.

A short hike later, they reached the valley floor and trekked to the narrow entrance leading to the crevice where the stallions were trapped. Helmar and her two guards worked their way in, followed by Sayyed and Rafnir. They heard the horses long before they saw them, for ringing neighs echoed along the rock walls, punctuated by heavy crashes reverberating on something that sounded like wood.

The clansmen saw why a few minutes later. The high, narrow passage had been completely blocked by massive stone blocks fitted together to form a thick wall. The crashing sounds came from a wooden wicket gate set in the wall.

"The Back Door," Rapinor said. "Your horses obviously found it." He strode forward and, standing wisely aside, drew the heavy bolts. The door flew open, and Afer and Tibor charged through ready for battle. Their eyes glowed green with angry fire, their tails were raised like battle standards, and their hooves clashed on the stone.

Seeing their riders, both stallions stopped and snorted. *Where were you?* trumpeted Afer. *Who are these people?*

Before Sayyed could respond, Helmar stepped forward and boldly put her hand on Afer's arched neck. The stallion instantly stilled, his ears stiff and his nostrils quivering as he gently sniffed her arm and face. Tibor crowded over and smelled the chieftain from hair to belt, then nickered a greeting.

When she stepped back, the Hunnuli were satisfied and calmly went to join the sorcerers. A look of surprise passed between Rafnir and Sayyed.

Sayyed bent in the pretense of examining Afer's legs. "Are you all right?" he said softly.

I am and you are! And I am glad to get out of that crack. There was no grass in there, and I'm hungry!

As if she had understood what he sent, Lady Helmar bowed slightly to the two horses and the clansmen. "I would like to make amends for our poor hospitality. Would you care to stay the night with us and share our table?"

The dour young man beside her made as if to protest, until he saw Minora give him a hard look. He subsided, looking sullen.

Sayyed thought of the city in the cliff, of the hidden valley and the secretive people who inhabited it, of the veiled suspicion he saw in every person's eyes, and the gleam of excitement as if they could not quite believe what he and Rafnir had done. He thought of the Clannad's knowledge of Hunnuli, sorcerer's lights, and the "death" of magic beyond the mountains. These people with their pale skin and fair hair seemed different, and yet there was an undercurrent of familiarity he could not quite ignore. Surely one night here in this valley would make little difference in their search for Gabria and Kelene, and perhaps the Clannad could help by telling them where the wagon track went and how to find it again. He bowed to Helmar, and with Rafnir's consent, he agreed to stay.

The group rejoined the others waiting at the mouth of the passage, and everyone walked down a steep, narrow trail to the valley floor. Once there, they paused on a low rise at the western end of the valley and gazed at the land about them.

"Sinking River carved this basin," Helmar told her guests. "The waters come from the high peaks down those falls to the river, where it runs the length of our valley and spills into the lake." She pointed to the small lake that lay below the rise. Not much bigger than a large pond, the lake sat serene in a ring of slender trees and grassy banks. Clear water lapped its rocky shores and sank down into unseen depths. "The lake has no bottom that we have been able to find. The river is swallowed by the mountains."

The clansmen filled their eyes with the beauty of the valley. Having witnessed the bleak slopes of the rugged peaks and felt the fury of the Storm King, they could appreciate the lush serenity of this hidden realm where spring was in full bloom. Thick grass and vegetation carpeted the valley. Trees in full leaf grew in groves along the riverbanks and in scattered copses up the slopes to the towering valley walls.

A movement in the nearby meadow caught their gaze, and they turned in time to see a ghostly herd of horses sweep past a belt of trees and come galloping toward the rise. Both men drew their breath in wonder at the white animals that approached them. More than a hundred mares, stallions, and foals flowed like an avalanche up to the foot of the hill and neighed a welcome to the strangers.

Smaller than the Hunnuli, yet equally as graceful and beautifully proportioned, every horse was white, ranging in shade and intensity from dapple gray to the most brilliant snow.

A stallion and a mare cantered up the slope together. The mare, a starry white, went to Helmar with a greeting, but the stallion arched his neck, pranced to Sayyed and Rafnir, and sniffed them to familiarize himself with their scent. They rubbed his neck, which was the color of polished slate; then he went to Afer and Tibor. The two blacks touched him muzzle to muzzle, nickering their greetings. Sayyed removed the Hunnuli's saddles, and together the three stallions galloped down to the herd. The people and the mare watched them go until the horses spread out over a broad meadow and began to graze.

"Your horses are incredible," Sayyed said to Helmar.

"How did you manage to breed such a consistent color?"

"Fear, Clansman," she replied helpfully. With a graceful leap she mounted the mare's broad back, and an enigmatic smile touched her lips. "Bring them to the cliff, Rapinor. I shall go prepare a feast." The mare sprang away, as swift as a falling star. Minora chuckled to herself.

From the rise they walked down the valley to the waterfalls and the base of the great ledge. Rope ladders hung down the wall, connecting a series of small ledges, handholds, and narrow steps in several difficult trails up the cliff to the cave settlement. More people joined the group, their faces full of amazement and some disbelief at the arrival of the sorcerers. From somewhere above a horn sounded a summons. The sun was high by that time, and its warm light filled the valley from end to end, yet despite the business of the season, every person in the Clannad laid down their tasks and came at the call of the horn.

With a skill born from a lifetime's practice, the people clambered up the ladders to their home. Sayyed and Rafnir climbed up more slowly, and when they reached the top they were welcomed with the return of their clothes and weapons. The men were then led to a wide, circular gathering place near the edge of the cliff where a low stone wall had been built along the rim. A fire burned in the hearth at the center of the ring, and much to Sayyed and Rafnir's surprise, a real feast had been hastily prepared for their arrival.

Helmar's own handmaidens sat Sayyed and Rafnir beside the chief's seat and served them from platters of meat and fish, an interesting dish of cooked tubers, bowls of dried berries, and rounds of flat bread. Tall flagons of cooled wine and pitchers of ale were passed around.

As Sayyed gratefully ate the first hearty meal he had had in several long days, he let his eyes roam over his surroundings and the people around him. The settlement in the cliff was not as large as he had at first thought. While the buildings were large and numerous, the population was not. At a rough count he estimated there were about four hundred men, women, and children in the Clannad. Since he had not seen any other buildings, tents, or shelters within the confines of the valley, he assumed they all lived in this stone aerie.

The cliff buildings themselves were remarkable, some towering four or five stories above the floor level. From where he sat, Sayyed could see several artisans' houses, a gathering hall, what looked like a temple, and numerous multilevel dwellings, and while the buildings were not opulent, they looked comfortable and well maintained.

It was while he was looking at the narrow passages between the buildings that he made an interesting observation that only added fuel to his curiosity. Unlike a clan camp, this settlement had no dogs. Not a one, as far as Sayyed could tell. There were, though, cats of every color and age, lounging on windowsills, draped on walls, and padding along the walks.

One tabby boldly walked up to him and sprang into his lap. Pleased, Sayyed scratched her ears and the base of her tail, remembering Tam's cat waiting for him in Moy Tura. The cat settled on his knees and purred her song for him.

A soft laugh drew his attention, and he looked up into the green-gold eyes of Helmar. Now that he could see her close up, he saw that despite the similarities in character, there was little physical resemblance to Gabria. Helmar's face was square and strong-featured with a straight nose and an incongruous sprinkle of freckles. He guessed she had seen more than thirty summers, for years of sun, wind, and work had worn away the softness of youth. Her body was hard, too, from physical labor, and her hands were nicked and calloused from wielding a sword. She lounged on her fur-draped seat, as self-assured as any clan chieftain.

Unconsciously, he smiled back.

"You like our cats?" she asked.

"I have one at home. I miss her."

"Tell me about her."

And out of this simple, ingenious request came an afternoon of talk and tales and history. From the story of Tam's cat, Sayyed went on to tell his fascinated audience about Tam, the plague, and the clans. Rafnir took his turn, talking about Moy Tura, Kelene, and Demira. The people of the Clannad listened avidly.

When Sayyed described Gabria and her battle with Lord Medb, the people sat hushed and unmoving. Sayyed, looking at their faces, thought their interest went beyond mere politeness. In a whole afternoon, not one person left the gathering. Children napped in their parents' laps, elders dozed in their seats, but not one person walked away from the tales. When he was finished, a low buzz of conversation filled the circle. The sorcerer glanced around and was surprised to see the sun had gone behind the western peaks. Darkness filled the bowl of the valley.

The talking stopped as Lady Helmar rose slowly to her feet. She looked thoughtful and rather sad, but her voice was as firm as ever. "This Lady Gabria, this last Corin, is she the other woman you are trying to find?"

"She is Kelene's mother," Rafnir replied. "They were taken together."

"I should like to meet her. I think we will go with you to this fortress."

The younger guard beside her leaped to his feet and planted himself squarely in her way. "My lady, think again. It would be folly to leave the valley this time of year. Let them find the trail themselves."

Lady Helmar did not step back. Coolly she faced her guard and said, "Hydan, you forget yourself."

Jut-jawed and steely-eyed, Hydan pointed at the two

sorcerers like a man flinging an accusation. "What if they're lying? What if all we have heard has been a tale to save their necks?"

Sayyed felt Rafnir tense and stir, and he laid a restraining hand on his son's arm before Rafnir jumped into anything unnecessary. Helmar, he could see, was equal to the confrontation.

Eyes blazing, she ignored the rest of the gathering and pushed herself close to Hydan to make her point very clear. "And I suppose they faked the sorcery they used this morning," she said fiercely. "Truth or half-truth, they are here and they are magic-wielders." She threw a wild gesture at the stone city behind her. "Do you want to live like this forever? If we can find this Lady Gabria, she will confirm the truth."

"If there is a Lady Gabria," Hydan muttered.

"If you doubt, Hydan, then ride with me and learn for yourself."

As quickly as he had flared up, the young guard subsided, having rammed his feelings against the wall of his chief's will. Helmar, obviously used to his tantrums, turned back to Sayyed without a pause. "You said the wagon had a red emblem of some sort and took the trail up around the Storm King? I know that path. It goes to a fortress owned by an old noble family."

"The old stone castle?" Hydan put in, as coolly as if he had never shown his temper. "The latest resident is one of the royal counselors, I have heard."

"His name wouldn't happen to be Zukhara?" Rafnir guessed. Hydan didn't even have to answer that. Zukhara's name fit the trail of clues and events they had been following since Council Rock.

"You know this man?" Helmar asked.

Sayyed nodded once. "A dangerous adversary." He lifted his eyes to her face and met her forthright gaze. He thought briefly of offering to leave alone—surely he and Rafnir could find the fortress with a few directions—then he dismissed the idea and bowed to the determination he could read so clearly in those expressive eyes. Yet he couldn't help but wonder why she was so willing to help two strangers that only hours before she had planned to drop down a ravine. And why was it so dangerous for the Clannad to leave their valley? These questions and many more trooped through Sayyed's thoughts. It was a puzzle with too many pieces missing.

At that point, men brought torches to the gathering circle. The fire was stoked, and several people fetched their instruments to strike up some dance music. Like their language, the Clannad's musical instruments were an interesting blend of old clan, Turic, and individual designs, and the music they played was rollicking, toe-tapping fun. The people danced late into the night, breaking only to listen to a harper sing ballads of the white horses, the Sinking River, and the valley they called home.

Sayyed and Rafnir enjoyed the evening and the pleasant company of the cliff dwellers. It was a frustrating evening, though, for try as they might they could not lead anyone into answering more than basic questions about their daily lives. Minora was more than happy to discuss her duties in the temple to the goddess they worshiped, but she neatly skirted any inquiries about the origins of the white horses and her insistence on keeping the two men for breeding. Rapinor, too, was closemouthed about anything except his duties as swordsman to Lady Helmar. And the lady herself, when asked a question, more often than not answered it with another question. Sayyed found himself talking to her for nearly an hour about his childhood with the Turics and his decision to join Gabria. In all that time she said nothing about herself.

At last the chieftain clashed the hilt of her sword against a gong hanging near her chair and ended the gathering. The people quickly split up, going their separate ways back to their homes. Helmar took Sayyed and

Rafnir to quarters that had been prepared for them on the ground floor of a tall building and bid them goodnight.

When at last they were left alone, Sayyed drew a long breath and expelled it in a gusty sigh. "I still don't know who these people are," he said irritably.

They found pitchers of water set aside on a stand for washing and beds covered with woven blankets. The stuffed mattresses on the beds felt so delightful after days of sleeping on the ground, Rafnir threw himself on one and was asleep before Sayyed had removed his boots.

Bone-tired as he felt, Sayyed could not sleep yet. Too many things ran through his mind, whirling as fast as the melodies of the Clannad jigs. He thought of the clan cloak he had transformed earlier and remembered he had left it at the gathering circle. Barefooted, he walked silently through the darkened passages back to the open ring.

He took one step out from between the buildings and as silently drew back into the shadows. Someone was standing in the ring beside the cloak Sayyed had left flung over the place where he had sat.

He stared at the form, trying to see who it was. Night filled the huge cavern with velvet darkness, but beyond the stone walls a curtain of countless stars glittered their distant, silver light. The person turned sideways against the backdrop of stars, and Sayyed recognized the handsome, straight profile of Helmar. Ever so slowly she picked up the cloak and seemed to hug it tightly to her chest; then she turned and strode toward him. Sayyed pushed deeper into the sheltering shadow as she walked on past.

The sorcerer blinked in surprise. For just the wink of an eye, Helmar had been close enough for him to see her clearly, and in that brief moment, he had seen the shimmer of tears in her eyes.

Sayyed walked slowly back to his quarters deep in thought, and when he finally drifted to sleep that night, it was Helmar's face, strong yet sadly vulnerable, that colored his dreams.

11

Kelene crouched against the stone wall as far from the gryphon as she could manage and vehemently loosed a string of well-chosen words vilifying Zukhara's ancestry. Blood dripped from three long scratches on her arm, and a bruise spread over the right side of her face. She glared balefully at the gryphon, who hissed and glared back with equal ferocity.

"Stupid bird," she muttered to herself. Or whatever it was. Even after two days of being trapped in its vicinity, Kelene still wasn't sure if the winged creature was a bird or an animal. It was beautiful, she had to admit that. Its narrow head, wings, and the beaklike nose reminded her of an eagle, as did its piercing hunter's eyes and the bright gold fur that looked suspiciously like feathers covering its entire body. The legs, though, looked like those of a lion, powerfully muscled, sleek, and deadly. Its feet had large pads fitted with razor-sharp retractable claws. The beast had a long tail like a cat's, and Kelene had noticed that it used the tail to communicate its feelings much as Tam's cat did. It used its tail now, lashing it irritably back and forth as it lay on the floor and glowered at her. Its tufted ears lay flat on its head.

"Afraid of a few scratches?" Zukhara's voice reverberated through the cavern. The woman and the gryphon glared up with matching hatred at the overhang. That was one thing Kelene knew they had in common.

"The beast will not kill you," Zukhara called to her, the scorn clear in his loud voice. "It is chained and prefers the taste of horseflesh. You have had two days already, two days that your lady mother lies dying."

Kelene leaped to her feet, ignoring the gryphon's startled snarl. "How is she? Is she still alive?" she called anxiously.

"She is being cared for," the Turic said curtly. "And she is still alert enough to continue my training in sorcery. But you have only five days left until the poison completes its task." He lowered a basket to her and left, his words still echoing in her mind.

Five days, she thought miserably, and she was no closer to taming this gryphon than she'd been when Zukhara dumped her in the pit with it. On the other hand, she thought wryly, the company of a wild gryphon was certainly preferable to Zukhara and his plans for her.

She unpacked the food and a wineskin from the basket. He certainly was taking no chances that she go hungry. He had sent enough delicacies to last another day, and the skin was full to bursting with the same fruit juice he had given her earlier. She wrinkled her nose at the sweet smell. He had probably laced it with more of his midwives' remedy. For the briefest moment she hesitated and thought of her wish to have a baby. If this remedy worked, was it worth the chance? Could she rely solely on luck and her wits to keep her out of the counselor's bed? Then, almost fiercely, she changed the juice to water. She wanted a child desperately, but she wanted Rafnir's baby, not a child conceived in trickery and hate.

After she had eaten, Kelene repacked the basket and stood to stretch her back and shoulders under the wary gaze of the gryphon. As she moved, something fell out of her skirt to the cavern floor. She picked it up and recognized the wad of fabric she had used to wipe the sedative off Demira's rump. It had lain forgotten in her waistband for three days. Curious to see if the ointment was still damp, she unfolded the cloth, and the faint medicinal smell rose to her nostrils. The sedative, set in its oily base, had saturated the fabric through almost all the folded layers. Kelene grinned. If this hadn't fallen out when it had, she might have been drugged by the very potion she hoped to save.

She folded it again, wrapped it in another scrap from her already tattered tunic, and returned it to its hiding place. Unfortunately there wasn't enough to sedate the gryphon. It stood taller than a Hunnuli and probably weighed twice as much.

But she had other weapons for that beast. Kelene rolled up her sleeves. She had refrained from using more than a few minor spells in the presence of the gryphon for fear of injuring it further or scaring it beyond redemption. All she had received for her gentle concern were scratches, bruises, and snarling disdain. Well, time was too precious now to softfoot around this beast! She would have to take her chances with its sensibilities.

Kelene recalled the handbook of Lady Jeneve, and in her mind's eye she pictured the page she wanted and the words to the spell that paralyzed living creatures. She recreated the spell and released it, stopping the gryphon in midstride before it knew what hit it. It could still breathe, and its eyes glowed bright with fear and anger, but it did not move as Kelene came close.

Softly, gently, she spoke to the gryphon to ease its fear. She did not touch it yet; she merely walked around the creature to ascertain the full extent of its injuries. Fortunately most of the wounds were scrapes and scratches that were healing on their own. Only one long abrasion on the left hind leg looked swollen and festering.

Kelene fetched the water left in the wineskin and her healer's bag. The first night Zukhara imprisoned her with the gryphon, he had returned her bag, sent her new clothes, and provided a pallet for her comfort. Kelene had ignored the new clothes, preferring her own torn and dirty ones to the silk tunic and the form-fitting gown Zukhara had sent. She found a use for them now, taking delight in tearing them into strips to bandage the gryphon's leg. She laid out several jars of salves, a bowl of water, and the bandages. When she was ready, she took a deep breath. The gryphon, its huge eye rolling back to look at her, looked terrified by its inability to move. Laying a hand gently on the gryphon's warm side, Kelene closed her eyes and extended her empathic talent down her skin and into the creature's body.

Wild, hot, and fierce, the gryphon's emotions broke over her, making her gasp at the sheer force of its personality. At once she realized the gryphon was a female, young, barely of breeding age, and consumed with rage at her captivity. Kelene felt barbs of suspicion and bright red animalistic waves of fear. She probed deeper, soothing her way with calm thoughts and feelings of concern, toward the heart of the gryphon's emotions.

Ever so delicately Kelene let her thoughts touch the creature's mind. *Easy, girl,* she sent kindly. *You and I are in this together. Let us help one another.* She didn't know if the golden beast was intelligent enough to understand her thoughts and the concept of cooperation, but it was worth a try.

Much to her relief, the gryphon's vivid, tumultuous feelings began to settle down to calmer waves of wary curiosity.

I will not hurt you, Kelene continued. *I want only to treat your hurt.*

Her mental touch still lightly on the gryphon's mind, she began to clean the infected cut. Skillfully she salved it and bandaged the leg, all the while stroking the creature with her empathic touch.

When she was finished with the wound she added one more thought before she broke their bond. *I am a captive like you, and like you I have to serve the man. If you will help me, I will help you gain your freedom.* And with that she withdrew her mind and dissolved the paralyzing spell.

The gryphon shook herself and snarled irritably at Kelene, but although she still stood in range of the creature's powerful paws, the gryphon sat down, curled her tail around her feet, and contemplated the sorceress with eagle eyes.

"Think about it," Kelene said aloud, and she returned to her pallet to let the animal rest. Would the gryphon settle down and let her help? She didn't know, and she was too tired to think about it for long. Without intending to, Kelene fell soundly asleep.

The gryphon's growl woke her to darkness, and she bolted upright at the chilling sound. The sorcerer's light she usually maintained had gone out while she slept, leaving the cavern in impenetrable night. The gryphon growled again, low and full of menace. Her chains rattled in the darkness.

Kelene raised her hand to relight her sphere when a small handlamp flared to light in an entrance she had not seen before. A stone door, cunningly set in the rock of the cavern wall, creaked closed behind Counselor Zukhara. He set the lamp on a ledge and moved toward her pallet. Kelene sprang to her feet in alarm.

"I have been watching you and your progress with the gryphon. It is almost ready." Kelene said nothing and warily watched him approach. He paused an arm's length away and eyed her from head to toe. "You are not wearing the clothes I chose for you," he said levelly.

"I had other need for them," Kelene replied. Nervously she edged back, very much aware that Zukhara wore only a loose-fitting robe open to his chest and his ivory ward. Deliberately she turned to run and, under the cover of her more violent movement, she dipped her fingers in her waistband and palmed the wad of fabric.

Zukhara lunged after her. His hands closed on her shoulders and wrenched her off balance. Her tunic ripped across the back. Half-hauling, half-dragging her backward, he flung her to the pallet and pinned her down with the full length of his body. Kelene lay panting and wild-eyed. She struggled against his weight, and as she tried to heave him away, she clamped the rag with oily sedative against his upper arm.

To keep his attention on her, she screamed and fought with all her might and prayed the sedative would work. She could feel his passion exuding from him in a heavy cloying aura, and she desperately closed her mind to his touch, terrified of being overwhelmed by his need.

Zukhara forced his hand over her mouth and silenced her screams. In the sudden quiet, she heard the gryphon lunge against her chains. The beast's growl rose to a hair-raising cry that shivered to the vaulted ceiling of the cave.

Zukhara heard it and exalted. "Tonight, my chosen, we consummate our union in the presence of the sacred gryphon." Kelene lay still, her face marble-white, her fingers still fastened to his arms. "You are like the gryphon," he told her. "Untamed, fierce, and proud. I have waited a long time for this."

Kelene's eyes widened. Did his voice seem to slur a bit on those last words? No sooner had she thought that, than Zukhara's eyes rolled up in his head and he slumped over her, dead to the world.

The sorceress gratefully pushed him off. She wrapped the rag back in its cloth and grinned. The sedative was potent stuff indeed. She had no idea how long the drug would last, so she quickly went to work. First she tried the stone door, but as she had feared, it was locked with a powerful spell. Not that she was certain she wanted to escape yet anyway. She had no antidote for Gabria and no knowledge of where to find her mother, or Nara, or even a way out. Nor did she want to kill Zukhara yet, for those same reasons. There would be a better time to escape—a time perhaps when she could also free the gryphon. Instead she decided simply to play along with Zukhara's plans. Let the man think he had succeeded, she thought grimly; then maybe he would leave her alone for a while.

Setting one blanket aside, she mussed her pallet as if it had been vigorously used; then she draped the Turic's long body over the whole thing. Her fingers found the ivory ward, pulled it out, and she cracked it ever so slightly under her knee. The crack would weaken the ward's effectiveness, and if all went well, he would not notice the damage until too late. She pulled off his robe, averting her eyes in distaste, and dropped it in a pile with her own torn, dirty tunic and skirt. Then she transformed the spare blanket into a pair of riding pants and a thick, warm tunic similar to those she had worn before.

She looked around for a place to lie down away from Zukhara and was surprised to see the gryphon sitting at the end of her chain and regarding her with calm, friendly eyes. In fact, she was purring. She walked up to the creature, waiting for her perked ears to go flat, but the gryphon only lay down on her side as if inviting Kelene to join her. Kelene threw all caution to the winds. She curled up beside the gryphon's warm, furry-feathery side and waited for Zukhara to wake up.

She didn't have long to wait. The sedative was old and there hadn't been much to work with on the rag. In a matter of minutes, Zukhara stirred and sat up rather groggily. He looked around for her. Kelene huddled closer to the gryphon's side and tried her best to look like a wounded maiden. The Turic's eye roved from himself to the bed to their clothes to Kelene's miserable expression, and Kelene was rewarded by a flicker of confusion in the man's dark eyes. Finally he stood, donned his robe, and strode toward her. The gryphon's tufted ears snapped flat, and her warning growl stopped him in his tracks.

He lifted a sardonic eyebrow. "I see you have tamed the beast," he said to Kelene.

"She and I have something in common," Kelene retorted.

"She? I didn't realize." He smiled in pleasure. "How appropriate."

"I thought gryphons were extinct," she said, trying to keep the aggrieved tone in her voice while leading him to any subject other than what had *not* happened between them.

She needn't have worried. Zukhara's pride would never let him admit he didn't remember a thing. He thankfully accepted her lead to an area he could discuss with authority and assurance. "My hunters found one tiny pride so far back in the mountains it took days to reach them."

Kelene noticed the gryphon was paying close attention to their exchange, and she pondered just how much the animal understood. "Are the others still there?"

"As far as I know. I took only the one."

"But why? What use will she be to you?"

"You do not know the Turic religion," he said scornfully, "or you would understand. Gryphons are the sacred messengers of the Prophet Sargun. In our ancient tales, it was a gryphon who freed the prophet from his prison and carried him home. The gryphon is a powerful symbol to my people, and this one will be the vanguard of my conquest. When she flies, the people will know my armies are blessed by the Living God, and they will flock to my call."

Kelene merely nodded. She had given up being surprised by the scope of this man's plans. "And when you are finished with her, will you let her go?"

Zukhara's mouth lifted in a cold smile. He knew she was talking about more than the gryphon. "When I am finished, she may not want to go." He bowed slightly to them both. "Good day, my lady. Stay with the gryphon and be sure she will come at your call. Tomorrow we leave for Cangora."

Kelene jumped to her feet. "And my mother?"

"She comes with us." He laughed as he turned to leave. "And the antidote, too." He blew out his lamp, leaving Kelene and the gryphon in the darkness, and the door boomed shut behind him.

* * * * *

The Clannad mustered at daybreak in the meadow at the foot of the cliff settlement. Fifty warriors, men and women armed and dressed for battle, mounted their white horses and fell in behind their chieftain's standard. Sayyed and Rafnir, astride their Hunnuli, marveled anew at the beauty of the Clannad horses and their training. Except for simple saddlepads, the horses wore no tack of any kind, yet they obeyed their riders as well as any Hunnuli.

As soon as the ranks were mustered, Lady Helmar

raised a gloved fist. She rode her star-colored mare that morning and wore a shirt of silver mail that glistened like water in the pearly light. Her bright red hair hung below her helm in a heavy braid that dangled over her shoulder, and a bow and quiver were strapped to her back. She gave a single piercing call that was answered by fifty voices in a shout that rang across the valley. In the city above, those who remained behind waved and shouted good-bye.

The troop trotted down the valley, sorting themselves into a single file as they approached the passage of the Back Door. One by one they rode down the narrow crevice and worked their way down the rugged glen beside the tumbling stream. Even in the light of a sunny spring day, the going was slow. It was nearly midday before the first of the troop came to a halt by the tall, grotesque pole of faces that guarded the faint trail.

"Do you know anything about that statue?" Rafnir asked the rider closest to him.

The man looked up the length of the pole and grinned. "Those things have been in the mountains since long before us. But this one was found many leagues away. My grandfather helped move it here to guard the Back Door. The local shepherds are terrified of it and stay away from the valley."

The clansmen fully expected to travel the rest of the afternoon. The day was clear and mild, the trails were drying, and the traveling would be easy. But to their astonishment, as soon as the last Clannad warrior reached the ancestor pole, instead of mounting and moving on, Helmar led her riders into the shelter of a thick belt of trees and ordered them to dismount.

"Because," she insisted when Sayyed demanded to know why, "we always travel at night. The only reason we left early was to traverse the glen in the daylight. But now we're out of our territory. Now we rest the horses and travel at night." And that was that.

Sayyed and Rafnir could only swallow their impatience and wait. The stallions didn't seem to mind. Sayyed noticed Afer and Tibor had taken a strong liking to the white horses and apparently found something amusing about their company. When asked, though, neither stallion would give a definite answer.

Sayyed scratched his beard and tried to relax. It was not easy. The afternoon wore slowly on while the horses quietly grazed, the warriors dozed, and the insects droned in the undergrowth. Finally Sayyed brought out his tulwar and the special stone he kept solely to sharpen the weapon, and he began to run the stone smoothly along the curved blade. After several strokes, he felt the tingling on the back of his neck he always got when he was being watched, and he looked up into Helmar's intent gaze. Her eyes sparkled, green and intense, the color of sunlight in deep water. She met his regard with frank interest.

"Are you as good with that blade as you are with magic?" she asked, her voice lightly teasing.

He lifted an eyebrow and kept working. "You have only seen me use one spell, so you cannot know whether I am good or not."

Beside the chief, flat on his back, Hydan chuckled at the remark.

"If half of what you told us is true, then you must be one of the finest sorcerers in the clans," she said.

"He is." Rafnir spoke up from his resting spot by the trunk of a tree.

A hiss of humor escaped Sayyed. "All of what I told you is true," he said shortly. "Now tell me a truth. Where did your people come from?"

"Over the mountains." She shrugged. "We have been in Sanctuary for generations."

"Why did you decide to save us when you learned we were sorcerers?"

"You saved yourselves. We couldn't very well argue

with magic-wielders."

He grunted. "Where did you learn to speak Clannish?"

"We didn't know we were until you came along."

Exasperated, Sayyed put away his stone. He felt as if he were running into walls with every question he asked. Either they had a poor oral tradition, they simply didn't care about their ancestry or—and Sayyed was more inclined to believe this—they were deliberately concealing a secret they weren't ready to share.

He shoved his tulwar back in its sheath, crossed his arms, and leaned back against a tree, shutting his eyes to end the conversation. The Clannad would reveal their truths when they wanted, and until then he was not going to beat his head against their walls.

When night came, the troop ate a cold meal and continued across the mountain slopes toward the trail Sayyed and Rafnir had lost in the storm. The two sorcerers quickly acknowledged that the Clannad warriors were quite good at night travel and their horses were sharp-eyed and agile. But the darkness disguised details, drained color, and turned the world to shadow, and even the most seasoned traveler was slowed by night on treacherous paths in the mountain wilderness. Worse yet, the heavy rains of the storm two nights ago had washed out many sections of the trails they were trying to follow, and a huge, muddy landslide blocked one shortcut they tried, forcing them on a long detour out of one valley and up a traverse over a high, spiny ridge before they could find their way to the wagon trail. By dawn they were tired, muddy, and still leagues from the fortress.

When daylight painted the eastern horizon, the Clannad began to look for a place to shelter for the day. Sayyed, though, urged Afer close to Helmar's mare. "We can't stop now," he said bluntly. "Gabria and Kelene have probably been in that fortress almost three days. We have to get them out!"

"And we will," Helmar replied. "But the horses need a rest and we—"

"Do not travel in daylight. I know," he cut her off. "But we don't have that time to waste."

"I will not endanger my people for—"

"What is *that?*" Hydan exclaimed.

All eyes swept to the brightening sky in time to see something large and dark swerve toward them. A shadow swift as a storm cloud raced overhead and plunged out of the dawn light. The white horses neighed a warning.

Hydan's warrior instincts brought his hands to his bow and an arrow before he stopped to think. In a blur he nocked the arrow, raised the bow, and drew the string to his jaw.

"No!" bellowed Rafnir.

Tibor sprang forward and rammed into Hydan's horse, knocking the man's aim askew. The bow dropped, but his fingers released the string, and the arrow sang wildly into the group clustered around Helmar.

In the same second the downdraft from a huge pair of wings swept over the party and blew the shaft farther off course. *I found you!* trumpeted a Hunnuli voice.

"Demira!" Sayyed shouted in joy. Just as he spoke, the arrow pierced through his arm and into his side. Stunned, he looked down at the shaft that pinned his arm to his ribs, and a sickly smile twisted over his lips. "I knew I should have stayed in Moy Tura," he said and slowly sagged off Afer to the muddy earth.

Appalled, Helmar, Hydan, and Rafnir slid off their mounts and hurried to Sayyed's aid. While Tibor joyously welcomed Demira, the warriors carried the sorcerer into a copse of trees and laid him on the cloak Helmar had returned. There was no question now that they would have to stop.

Helmar snapped orders to her riders, and in moments every man and horse was out of sight in several scattered groves of trees. One man was a healer, and under his direction Helmar and Rafnir removed the shaft from Sayyed's arm. Fortunately that part proved easy enough, for the arrow had pierced straight through the muscle on the back of his upper arm. The difficulty came in removing the arrowhead from his ribs. Demira's wings had probably saved his life by slowing the arrow, but it still had struck with enough force to wedge between two bones. It took a long while to cut the skin, work the arrow free, and stitch the wounds. Although Helmar and the healer tried to be gentle, by the time they were through Sayyed was drenched with sweat and utterly exhausted. His hand reached out to grip Helmar's, and he thankfully passed out into healing sleep.

The lady stared down at his hand, still dirty from clenching the earth in his pain, and her fingers tightened around his.

Afer gently nosed her. *He will be all right.*

"I know," she murmured.

Rafnir looked up sharply. "What?"

She settled more comfortably beside the clansman, his hand still in hers, and sighed. "Just talking to myself."

Sleep, the healer's salves, and a warm meal soon bolstered Sayyed's constitution. As soon as he could stand without getting dizzy, he insisted on greeting Demira and making much over her return. The mare confirmed Gabria and Kelene were in Zukhara's fortress, and she told the men the sketchy facts she knew.

"Poisoned!" Sayyed said furiously. "Are you sure?"

That is what Kelene said, Demira replied. *She was certain someone had come after them, and she ordered me to leave.* Her mental tone still sounded aggrieved. *I have looked for you all over these mountains!*

Rafnir flung his arms around her neck, and that was all the thanks he needed.

The troop left the trees that night at Sayyed's insistence, but the loss of blood had left him weaker than he thought, and he could ride only a few hours that night. They stopped again the third day in a woods only a few leagues from the fortress. Sayyed was too tired to argue. Although his impatience pushed him on, his body would not obey. The puncture in his arm was healing well, but riding had pulled the stitches in his side. Blood oozed from his bandages, and the wound looked red and swollen. Sayyed knew he would be no good to Gabria and Kelene if he did not regain his strength, so he ate his food, swallowed a draught provided by the healer, and went to his bed without protest.

Just past midnight the next night, the troop climbed a rocky hillside and rode down into a steep ravine. There on a high plateau overlooking the ravine, they saw the stark outline of several squat towers and the high stone walls of a fortress. On one side of the castle the cliffs fell sheer to the ravine floor; on the other a pale road wound its way up the steep face to the entrance.

"Good gods," Rafnir breathed. "How do we get up into that?"

"By the front door," Sayyed growled.

He conferred with Helmar for several long minutes and, when they were agreed, the Clannad riders dismounted. Silently and nearly invisibly, the warriors began to work their way up the road toward the fortress. Demira pushed aside her fear of flying at night and flew a reconnaissance over the fortress.

It is lightly guarded, she reported when she returned. *And they are not paying close attention.*

Sayyed and Rafnir watched the descending moon and gave Helmar and her warriors another half hour; then Sayyed trotted Afer openly up the road toward the fortress gates. Rafnir mounted Demira, and she launched herself into the darkness.

Demira was right, the guards were very lax that night. Sayyed rode nearly to the top of the plateau close to the gate before a voice called out to challenge him.

Sayyed replied in Turic, "I have messages for the Supreme Counselor, Zukhara."

"Not tonight," grumbled a voice on the wall.

Sayyed shot a look over his shoulder to the dark, rock-tumbled edge of the road. A tiny flash, the reflection of moonlight on a dagger blade, signaled Helmar was ready.

"Sorry, but I really must see him now," Sayyed snapped, and he raised his good arm and fired a powerful blast of magic at the wooden gate. To his astonishment, the magic struck the wood and evaporated. The entrance was protected with magic wards!

This arcane defense was so unexpected, Sayyed stared in surprise. Shouts echoed on the walls, and feet pounded along the battlements. The sorcerer had wanted to surprise the garrison, and all he had succeeded in doing was rouse them all. He tried again with a more powerful bolt. That one shook the gate and boomed against the stone, but the wards were new and well made, and they held.

Sayyed took a deep breath. He was weaker than he imagined, and the thought crossed his mind that maybe he wasn't strong enough after all to break this gate. As if Afer had read his thoughts, the big stallion neighed, and someone slipped up beside the Hunnuli.

"Try again," Helmar cried to the clansman.

He pulled in all the magic he dared use, formed it into an explosive spell, and released it from the palm of his hand. Before he could even draw breath, a second bolt followed his across the night-dark space and exploded just behind his on the portals of the gate. The wards vanished in a clap of thunder, and the wooden gate cracked to ruins.

The Clannad warriors charged forward, their swords raised, their voices lifted in battle cry. Behind the walls, Demira came to land on the stone pavings, and Rafnir, in all the confusion, sprang into the hall to look for the women.

Sayyed looked down at Helmar, too startled to think of anything to say.

She smiled at him. "If you had been full-blooded, you might have learned that 'clannad' is an ancient clan word for 'family.' "

"Your ancestors were clanspeople?" he asked, feeling rather dense.

"A long time ago."

"But you have no splinter."

"There are no more," Helmar replied with a shrug. She touched his right wrist where his splinter glowed beneath his sleeve and ran to join her warriors in the fighting at the gate.

The garrison, undermanned and ill-prepared for a battle with sorcerers and sword-wielding warriors who came out of nowhere, quickly surrendered. As Sayyed and Helmar ended the assault and rounded up prisoners, Rafnir ran out of the hall, looking thunderous. "They're gone!" he shouted furiously.

Sayyed turned on the commander of the fortress. "Where is Zukhara? Where are the women he had with him?"

The Turic drew himself up in pride for his master. "The Gryphon flies, and Lord Zukhara rides to claim his throne."

"He did what?" asked Helmar puzzled. Sayyed had not gone into detail about the current unrest in the Turic realm. He assumed the Clannad knew.

"Lord Zukhara left this morning with the sorceresses," the soldier explained as if to a simpleton. "Soon he will call his armies and march on Cangora."

12

"A day!" Rafnir cried, totally frustrated. "We keep missing them by a day!" He paced back and forth in the hall of the mountain fortress, slamming his hand on a shield every time he passed it. The shield was a large one, hung on the wall for decoration, and it made a satisfying crash every time he hit it. "Why can't we leave now?" the young man demanded. "The Hunnuli could catch up with their horses."

He got no immediate answer. His father, Helmar, Rapinor, Hydan, and several other warriors sat around a long table in front of a roaring fire. A map of the Turic realm, unearthed in a storage chest by the garrison commander, lay unrolled on the table amid a scattered collection of flagons, pitchers, and plates. The rest of the troop rested, tended their horses, or raided the castle storerooms for food and drink. The fortress garrison kicked its collective heels in the dungeons.

Midnight had passed hours ago, and dawn would soon lighten the road, but Sayyed made no effort to move from his chair. There were too many forces in motion now to leap precipitously into action. He wanted time to think. He had already explained in detail to Helmar and her men what had happened at Council Rock and later in the caravan. They had been unpleasantly surprised. Still, in spite of their concern, Sayyed fully expected the mysterious Helmar to take her riders and return home now that their duty was done.

He was, therefore, startled when she spoke into an interval between Rafnir's rhythmic banging. "If you plan to go after Zukhara, you will need help."

A ripple of surprise passed through her men. Rafnir halted in midpace.

Instead of looking pleased, Sayyed's brows lowered in suspicion. "Why? It will mean leaving the mountains, traveling in daylight. Why do you offer that now?"

Helmar slowly rose. Her helmet had been laid aside, and her hair blazed red-gold in the firelight. She swept her hand over the map, then looked at her warriors one by one. When she spoke, her words were only to them. "For generations we have lived in Sanctuary thinking the world had abandoned us. Now the world has come pounding at our door, and we learn it has changed while we hid in our mountain fastness. Knowing what we know now, do we want to continue to hide and let the world go by without us? Or do we ride forth and embrace the possibilities of the future?"

Her question fell to every man, and there was silence while each one considered his answer.

Rapinor spoke first, the loyal, staunch warrior who would follow his chief to the grave. "I go with you."

"Have you considered the consequences, Lady Helmar?" asked another man.

"For the past three days, Dejion. I have also considered

the consequences if we stay home and turn our backs. As Minora keeps telling me, we have grown stagnant. Our bloodlines are dying from lack of new stock. If we go back, we could lose everything our ancestors tried to save."

"Then I will ride with you, and the gorthlings take the hindmost," the warrior laughed.

"I still haven't seen this Lady Gabria," Hydan grumbled. "But you make a good argument."

The others, too, agreed to ride with the clansmen, and Helmar nodded her satisfaction. "Then go. Talk to the warriors. Tell them why and say any who wish to go home may do so."

The men bowed and left, leaving Helmar with only her two guards and the clansmen. She pulled in a deep breath and sat down so quickly her sword clattered on the chair. "Does that answer your question?" she said to Sayyed.

He leaned back in his chair, his legs stretched out in front of him. His arm hurt and his side throbbed abominably, but he wouldn't go to his pallet yet. This night was too full of revelations. "What made you decide this?" he asked.

"The mare." Helmar nodded toward the open doorway where the Hunnuli rested in the courtyard. "When I saw her in all her beautiful living flesh, I knew you had been telling me the truth—all of it. I realized then that our stone walls would no longer be enough. It is time the Clannad shows its true colors."

Sayyed offered her a slow, conciliatory smile. "Will dawn be a good time to start?"

At that Rafnir's hands went up in annoyance. "Why wait until then? They like to ride at night; let's go now!"

"You may leave any time," his father told him, "because I want you to go back to the Ramtharin."

A bright flush swept over Rafnir's face, and he turned on his heel and stamped to the table.

Seeing the look on his son's face, Sayyed held up his hand. "I need someone I can trust to find Athlone. He said send a message, remember? Well, I'm sending you and Tibor. Get him to come south with the werods to help the Shar-Ja."

The audacity of such a suggestion took Rafnir's breath away. "You want him to bring the clans over the Altai? But the Turic will think they're being invaded."

"That's why I want you to go. With you at Athlone's side, you can tell the Turics you have been summoned by the Shar-Ja in accordance with the peace treaty."

"A treaty that was never signed!"

"A mere formality. Make a likeness of the Shar-Ja's banner. Dress like a Turic noble. Make it look official."

"What if the Shar-Ja doesn't want any help?" Rafnir demanded.

Sayyed rubbed his temples and said grimly, "I don't think he is in any position to argue."

Helmar had been listening to the exchange, her face thoughtful. "Can't you take your flying horse? It would be faster, would it not?"

Rafnir picked up a full flagon and put it down again, still too agitated to stand still. "No. She can carry me short distances, but I am too heavy for her to carry such a long way. Besides"—he cracked a crooked grimace—"I doubt you could get her any farther away from Kelene than she already is."

Helmar nodded as if she had already anticipated that answer. "Well, your journey back will be dangerous if you go alone across the open country." She traced a line north along the foothills of the Absarotans. "One of my rangers could lead you on mountain trails all the way to the border."

"Lady, that is generous, but I don't think your horses could keep up with a Hunnuli," Rafnir replied distractedly.

The lady chieftain laughed softly as if at a private

joke. "On the mountain slopes you have not been able to witness the full talents of our white horses, young Rafnir. Be assured, the whites will match your blacks."

Sayyed pursed his lips and looked thoughtful. "And I suppose your white horses are descended from clan stock, too."

She nodded, her eyes merry. "Of course."

When she didn't add more, Sayyed bent forward, cupped his hands over hers, and said earnestly, "One day will you trust me enough to tell me the full truth of your history?"

Helmar's eyes fell to their linked hands, and something flickered in the back of her heart, that same heart she thought she had hardened to the attentions of men. "One day," she said and pulled her hands free.

Rafnir went back to his pacing, but this time he did not slam the shield as he passed—a good sign, Sayyed thought. The older sorcerer continued with his plans, letting Rafnir stew over his duty. "There is another favor I must ask, Lady," he said, and hesitated before he went on. "It could be very dangerous, but it is important to me and maybe to the Turics as well."

"Ask."

"I need someone to get word to my brother, Hajira, in the Shar-Ja's caravan. He is the sole guardian of the Shar-Ja's only living son. That boy has to be protected at all costs."

Helmar steepled her fingers. "I know nothing of this boy or the Shar-Ja beyond what you have told us, but even that little shines brighter than what I have heard of this Zukhara. I will find someone willing to go."

"My lady, with your permission," Hydan said, rising to his feet. "I will go. I speak a little Turic, and I owe Sayyed a favor for shooting his arm and making us late."

The clansman looked around, surprised. He had not expected help from that quarter. "Can you find your way?"

"Hydan is one of the few who leave the valley on occasion to visit nearby settlements. He is a good man," Helmar added. "His only faults are a temper he can't control yet and an overreaching desire to protect what he values."

The swordsman's face turned red, but he did not waver when she asked, "You understand what you might have to face?" He nodded. "Then go with my blessing and ride safely."

After that was settled, Sayyed, Rafnir, and Helmar bent over the map again to finalize their plans. Although Sayyed had made most of the decisions to that point, he was very interested to learn Helmar had a quick grasp of the worsening situation and a sharp mind for tactics. She was the one who suggested sending other rangers out to gather news and who pointed out a rough trail over the Khidar Pass that would take them directly to the Spice Road and cut off leagues of extra travel.

One point confused her though. "What will we do when we catch up with this Zukhara? What if he's already joined his army of fanatics?"

Sayyed could only shake his head. The same thought had occurred to him with no brilliant inspiration to light its way. "I won't know until we get there," he admitted. "So if you have any ideas . . ." He yawned, too tired to finish.

The fire had burned low by that time, and everything that could be planned had been discussed. Sayyed's swarthy face had washed to a grayish pallor, and he moved with uncomfortable stiffness when he stood. Helmar took one arm and Rafnir the other, and they led him firmly to a bed. He was asleep before they had pulled a blanket up over his chest.

*   *   *   *   *

The castle bailey was bustling with activity when Sayyed woke the next morning. After a quick wash and a quiet moment for his morning prayers, he strode out into the sunshine in time to say good-bye to Rafnir and his guide.

Rafnir had not verbally agreed to leave the search for Kelene and Gabria, but Sayyed knew his son well enough to hope he would accept the reasons for this request. He stood out of the way, his arms crossed, while Rafnir buckled one of the Clannad's saddle pads on Tibor instead of the heavy Turic saddle.

"I'm trusting you to find Kelene," Rafnir said, his voice sharper than he intended. He modified his tone a little and went on. "I never fully understood how you could grieve for Mother for so long, but when I think what it would be like to lose Kelene, I begin to see." He clasped his father's arm and sprang to Tibor's back. "I will bring the Clans!" he vowed. He was about to go when he turned and tossed out one more observation. "Father! I think Mother would approve of Helmar." He waved, and in a clatter of hoofbeats, the black stallion and the white cantered out of the fortress and on their way.

"What was that?" Helmar asked, coming to stand by the sorcerer.

A quirk of a smile passed Sayyed's lips. "He said good-bye." He wasn't sure why Rafnir would feel inclined to say what he had, and yet he thought his son was probably right. Tam would have liked Helmar. A gust of wind flounced by, snapping his cloak and sending dust swirling around the bailey in tiny whirlwinds. The sky was achingly blue and cloudless, but the air this high in the mountains was thin and still chilly in the mornings. Sayyed shivered as a finger of breeze brushed past his neck. "Tam," he whispered. Then he glanced over at a straight nose, a dusting of freckles, and a pair of green eyes set in a frame of red-gold lashes—so different from Tam's delicate oval beauty—and he was glad Helmar was there.

Hydan left next, with Sayyed's message wrapped around Hajira's gryphon knife and tucked carefully in his shirt. He had scrounged some Turic clothes, including a shortcoat emblazoned with Zukhara's red emblem, and had saddled his reluctant horse with Rafnir's Turic saddle. He looked passable enough, if rather uncomfortable in the saddle, and he saluted his chief and trotted out in Rafnir's wake.

A short while later, Helmar led her troop out the fortress gates. To her delight and secret relief, every warrior chose to go with her on her quest to help Sayyed rescue the sorceresses. They took with them all the supplies and equipment they could pack on the backs of the garrison horses. Sayyed waited with Afer until the riders were out of sight; then he hurried down a winding stairs to the dungeon level. The prisoners crowded around the doors as he unlocked them.

"You have to the count of one hundred before this place is destroyed," he said calmly.

The Turics took one look at his face and fled the castle as fast as they could run. The clansman leisurely rode out the gates, counting as he went until Afer reached the bottom of the ravine. He turned and studied the cliff wall.

". . . ninety-eight . . . ninety-nine . . . one hundred."

Sayyed raised his good arm, pointed to the cliff at the base of the castle wall, and sent a long, steady beam of power into the rock. There were no explosions this time, just a rumbling sound that began beneath the beam and radiated rapidly outward. Suddenly an enormous chunk of the rock face slipped loose. Cracks appeared in the fortress walls; then the ground fell from beneath the structure. The hall, most of the outbuildings, several towers, and half the walls slipped down, tumbling and crashing in a cloud of stone, dust, and debris to the ravine floor. The remains of the fortress lay shattered, and the entrance to the narrow spiral staircase leading down to an empty cavern vanished in a pile of rubble.

Sayyed found the sight of the gaping ruins small satisfaction for all the trouble Zukhara had caused. Afer snorted in agreement. Swiftly they set off and soon caught up with the Clannad.

Now that the troop agreed to risk daylight travel, they made excellent time. They rode south at a brisk pace back the way they had come, and in less than two days they reached the back entrance to Sanctuary. Taking with her most of the packhorses and three of her warriors, Helmar left the others to rest and refresh themselves in the tumbled glen.

Sayyed did not know what she said to her people in the valley, but she came back the next dawn with twenty-five more riders and a glowing expression on her face.

"Minora sends her blessings," was all she would say.

She led her warriors up the slope of a high hill and stopped to watch them pass by. Sayyed paused beside her. The world before them lay bleak and unpeopled, the mighty peaks turbaned in cloud, the slopes mottled with forests and bare outcroppings of stone. Beyond the wild lands to the east where the mountains gave way to the arid plains, the horizon was swathed in mist, as if already obscured in the smokes of war. Behind the troop lay the narrow path to Sanctuary and all that name implied. Sayyed, who had seen for himself the beauty and security of the valley, marveled at the courage it took to step out of the protective walls and ride into a dangerous, troubled world. Some of the men, he knew, had never set foot outside their valley.

Overhead, Demira neighed to the people below and wheeled over the slower moving column, keeping a sharp vigilance from the sky.

That day and the next the Clannad rode in deadly earnest, first to the east to the less rugged and more open foothills, then south toward the Turic capital of Cangora, located on the fringes of the great southern desert. They rode hard, and for all their settled ways, they and their white horses endured as well as any nomadic band.

Their guide was an older man, a short, powerful warrior with the lively, quick glance of a curious child. While most men of the Clannad did not usually leave Sanctuary, a few trained as scouts or rangers and learned the mountains and the trails from tradition handed down from other rangers and from years spent exploring the great peaks. This man knew the trail Helmar had found on the Turic map and led his people unerringly on the shortest and safest route possible.

They saw smoke the second afternoon, a dark column of fumes that rose above the plains and slowly spread across the southern skyline. Demira flew to investigate, and when she returned, her message was dark and grim.

I saw a caravan, a big one, scattered along the side of the road for nearly a league. There were wagons burning and dead men everywhere.

Sayyed felt a cold fear grip his belly. "Can you describe any of part of it? Was the Shar-Ja's wagon there?"

I did not see that wagon, but I saw dead guardsmen with his colors, and I saw other wagons I recognized from Council Rock. Her tone faltered, and she dropped her long lashes. *Even the plague camp did not look or smell so awful.*

Sayyed and Helmar exchanged a long look, but neither could ask about Hydan or Hajira or Tassilio. Even if their bodies lay in the dust of the Spice Road, Demira could not have distinguished them from her place in the sky. They rode on toward the smoke and hoped that somehow the two men and the boy survived.

On the third evening, one of Helmar's scouts found

them as they rested the horses along the bank of a scraggly, half-dead stream. The rider trotted his sweat-soaked horse directly to Helmar and nearly fell off as he tried to dismount.

"The clansman was right," the scout said wearily. He was so tired he could barely stand. "I went down to the settlement at Khazar and talked to some of the merchants and shepherds. The news is spreading like locusts. They say the Fel Azureth have risen. The Gryphon has declared himself the true ruler of the Turic and has called a holy war to purge the land of unbelievers. Half the men in the settlement are leaving to join him, the other half are talking about fighting him. They say the Gryphon is marching on Cangora and that his forces massacred the Shar-Ja's caravan."

"Is anyone attempting to organize the resistance against him?" asked Sayyed.

"Not that I know of. I heard many of the tribal leaders who accompanied the Shar-Ja were killed in the massacre, along with most of the royal guards. The tribes are in confusion. The Shar-Ja's soldiers are leaderless, and no one knows what befell the Shar-Ja."

Sayyed leaned back against Afer's strong side. "By the Living God, this gets worse."

"Aye, it does," responded the exhausted scout. "They say the zealot's army meets no resistance because he carries the Lightning of the North."

"What is that?"

"I have never heard of such a thing. But I also heard a gryphon flies in the vanguard with a black-haired woman on its back. A woman reputed to be a sorceress."

Sayyed's eyes widened. "A gryphon? Do you mean a real one?" He whistled. "And Kelene on its back? No wonder the people won't fight him." His voice broke off, then went on. "Did you hear any news of the boy, Tassilio?"

The scout shook his head. "All I heard was that the

caravan was on the road when fighting broke out in the ranks of the tribal levies, and before anyone knew what was happening, the entire caravan was under attack. They never had a chance."

"Do you think Hydan had time to reach them?" Sayyed asked Helmar.

She knew who he meant, but she had no reassurance for him. "I don't know."

His hand fell to the hilt of his sword; his sharp gaze turned far away. "Are you sure you still want to go? This has become far more than a rescue of two women from an unknown assailant."

"We have gone too far to turn back now. I will ride with you, Sorcerer." She lifted her hand, and he clasped it with his own, making a joined fist to seal their vow.

"Besides," she added with a grin, "in the words of Hydan, "I still haven't seen this Lady Gabria.""

* * * * *

Kelene gripped the gryphon's sides with her knees and dug her fingers into the feathery-fur down to touch the creature's warm skin. After a lot of practice, she had learned that the best way to communicate with the creature was through the same sort of mental link she could establish with the Hunnuli. It was difficult and tiring, but the gryphon was much more likely to obey that than a mouthful of nonsense words shouted in her ear. *Down, young one. It is getting too dark to fly.*

A growl issued from the gryphon's throat, but she finally obeyed and began to spiral slowly to earth.

Kelene sighed. Riding a gryphon was exciting, because unlike Demira, the animal had been flying since birth. Exquisitely graceful, as skilled as any bird, she read the nuances of the forever changing currents and flew as if her body were a part of the wind. But she was also willful, resentful, and still very wild under the weak link of obedience Kelene had established. Unlike Demira, who adored her rider, Kelene knew the gryphon only tolerated her and waited for the day she would be set free. The sorceress understood how she felt and tried to be as kind as possible, but that did not make riding the gryphon over these long, hot days any easier.

Kelene would have given almost anything to fly the gryphon away—almost anything but Gabria's and Nara's lives. The gryphon, too, would have to pay a price too high, for Zukhara had fashioned a collar spelled to release a killing bolt if she flew beyond two leagues of his position. Kelene did not know how the collar worked, but she was not going to find out by testing it. There had to be some other way she could take her mother, Nara, and the gryphon and escape from Zukhara. She just had to be patient and keep looking.

Kelene glanced down toward the ground. Already Zukhara's army had stopped and made camp along the Spice Road. She sighed again and fought down the despair that seemed to hover over her with increasing potency.

When she first heard Zukhara's plans, a part of her mind had dismissed them as the ravings of a deluded man, but in the past four days, everything had happened as he had said it would. The moment he stood before his followers at Impala Springs and proclaimed himself the new, true leader of the Turic tribes, men had flocked to his call. Kelene had no notion how he spread the word so fast—unless he had preplanned it—but true to his word, on the tenth day after he threatened Kelene, he called his holy war, and men from all over the realm arrived to answer his summons.

Thank the gods, Kelene thought, he had not fulfilled his threat to remove her arm for the diamond splinter. After Gabria had explained that there were no more splinters, and he had satisfied himself that the women's could not be surgically removed, he dropped the issue for the time being and contented himself by awing his followers with demonstrations of his power, until everyone knew Zukhara did indeed carry the Lightning of the North in his hands.

In the meanwhile, Zukhara commanded Kelene to fly the gryphon at the head of his ever-growing army as it marched south toward Cangora. Even from the air the sorceress had seen the awe and the fear the gryphon's presence wrought. Some people bowed low to the golden creature, others stared in stunned surprise, and still others fled at her approach. No one tried to withstand Zukhara's army. The force of fanatics, rebels, and supporters marched unopposed along the caravan road. There seemed to be no one willing to make a stand for the Shar-Ja. Would it be the same in his own city?

The gryphon swept low over the parched grass. She was stiff and unwilling to land yet, so Kelene let her fly a few more minutes along the road. They had flown south only a short distance from the army when the gryphon's ears perked forward and her nostrils twitched at the warm breeze.

Suddenly a light gust swept by, and Kelene smelled it too, the heavy stench of rotting bodies. She almost reeled in her place. A sharp, piercing picture burst from her memory, an image of her return to the clan gathering during the worst of the plague. Her stomach lurched, and Kelene forced her memories back before they overwhelmed her self-control.

Ahead through the twilight, she saw several shadowy things on the verge of the road. She peered harder, and as the gryphon flew closer, the entire disaster became clear. Burned and broken wagons, vans, and chariots lay on both sides of the path for as far as Kelene could see in the dimming light. Their contents were scattered everywhere, already picked over by looters. Dead horses bloated among the wreckage, and wherever

Kelene looked, in the trampled grass, by the wagons, in small or large heaps, lay the bodies of dead men.

Kelene quickly turned the gryphon away and, ignoring her annoyed hiss, told her to return to the camp. They came to land in a clear space near Zukhara's tent. Her hands shaking, Kelene fastened the gryphon's chains as Zukhara had instructed, gave her a heaping meal of goat meat, and strode into Zukhara's tent. Whatever she had intended to say was immediately squelched by Zukhara's sharp gesture.

"Sit!" he ordered and pointed to a smaller chair near his. The man was seated in a large, ornate, high-backed chair near the center of his spacious tent. Bright lamps lit the interior, and beautiful woven rugs covered the floor. Zukhara had dressed in black pants and a black robe embroidered with a golden gryphon standing rampant. The clothes were simple yet rich and on his tall, limber frame, very elegant. He sat composed, waiting expectantly with his officers on either side.

Kelene reluctantly perched on the chair he indicated. By Amara, if she had to swallow any more resentment, Kelene swore she would burst. She hated being put on display like this! Being the Gryphon's "Chosen" had a few privileges, but they were all heavily outweighed by the disadvantages. She could only be thankful that he had been too busy to force his attentions on her again.

She heard the tread of boots outside, and eight men crowded into the tent. All but one saluted and bowed low before Zukhara. Kelene gasped. The one man who did not, or could not, bow was the Shar-Ja. If he had looked old and sick at Council Rock, he looked near death now. His once strong face sagged with loose folds of grayish skin. His red-rimmed eyes were nearly lost in the sunken shadows of his haggard face. He barely had the strength to stay upright, yet he fought off any hand that touched him and through some force of supreme will managed to stand unaided before Zukhara.

"Good," the Gryphon said, a short, sharp bark of approval. "You caught him alive. And the boy?"

One officer stepped forward. "Your Highness, we have not yet found his body, nor the guard who was with him."

A flicker of anger passed over Zukhara's features, but he merely commanded, "Keep looking. I want no loose ends."

"And what of me?" the Shar-Ja said scornfully. His voice had a surprising timbre to it that demanded Zukhara's attention. "Am I a loose end, too?"

The lamplight fell in the Gryphon's eyes and turned to black fire in a face as still and cold as ice. "No, Shar-Ja Rassidar. You are a very important part of my plans. Do you know the Ritual of Ascension?"

The old man gave a fierce bark of laughter and somehow stood straighter until he towered over the men around him. Kelene had not realized until then just how tall he really was, or how proud. "I am aware of the ritual. It was abolished several centuries ago."

Zukhara's smile came, quick and feral. "Yes, and in the name of Twice Blessed Sargun and to the glory of the Living God, I intend to resurrect the old ways, beginning with the Ritual." He gestured to his men. "Take him to his wagon and keep him there. No one is to see him or go near him." The men swiftly obeyed.

When they were gone, Zukhara turned his burning glance to Kelene. "You have done well, my lady. You and the gryphon have flown as successfully as I had hoped. I have a gift for you."

Kelene flung herself to her feet. "Mother has but one day left! The only gift I need is her antidote."

He stood and walked to his table where a small tray of multicolored glass bottles stood shining in the light. He picked up a small vial sealed with wax. "As you have undoubtedly noticed," he said, coming close to her, "I am very knowledgeable in the arts of medicines and poisons." He pulled the sorceress close and pressed her against his chest with one arm. With the other he held the vial up to a lamp. "Not only can I design a poison to suit my purposes, I also create antidotes and partial antidotes that delay the effects of the poison."

Kelene's jaw tightened. "Do you fulfill your promises?" she said between gritted teeth.

"Partially, my lady." He chuckled and kissed her fully on the lips before he handed her the vial. "This will keep the poison in check for another ten days or so. Continue your exemplary behavior, and I will give her more."

"What about the antidote?" Kelene exploded. Would he keep this game going indefinitely?

"I hold it close," he replied, and he pulled out the chain that held his ivory ward. There, hanging beside the ball, was a small, thin silver tube. "When I feel you have earned it, the reward shall be yours."

Kelene clamped her mouth closed and averted her face. At least, she thought, he had not noticed the crack in the ivory ward.

He kissed her again, long and languorously deep, until Kelene thought she would gag; then with a sneer he pushed her toward the entrance. "Not tonight, my lady. Though the thought is sweet. I have too many things to attend to. Sleep well."

Kelene did not bother to answer. She gripped the precious vial, whirled, and fled.

13

The Gryphon's army rose at dawn to another clear sky and hot sun. They knelt in the dust for their morning worship and bowed low to Zukhara, the figurehead of their reverent zeal. Their fervor ran high that morning as they broke camp and prepared to march, for by evening they would reach the outskirts of Cangora and perhaps meet their first resistance from forces still loyal to the Shar-Ja. At least they hoped so. Their blood burned for battle and the opportunity to give their lives in service to the Living God and his servant, Zukhara. After all, Zukhara, the Mouth of Shahr, had told them all that such a death guaranteed their entrance to paradise.

At the sound of the horns, the men took their positions. The Fel Azureth, the fist of Zukhara, took the honored place in the vanguard, their highly trained units riding like members of the Shar-Ja's own cavalry on fleet horses. Behind them rolled the Shar-Ja's wagon with its prisoner under tight guard. Then came the other combatants, some in orderly ranks on foot, some in mounted troops, still others—mostly rabble and hangers-on who had come for the loot, the thrill, or motives of their own—marched in crowds at the rear. Behind them were the supply wagons, camp followers, and a unit of the Fel Azureth who kept a vicious order on the trailing mobs.

The army set out under Zukhara's watchful scrutiny and soon reached the wreck of the Shar-Ja's grand caravan. Several days in the late spring sun had wrought havoc on bodies already torn by weapons and the teeth of scavengers. The stench along that stretch of road was thick and cloying and as heavy as the clouds of flies that swarmed through the ruins. The men wrapped the ends of their burnooses over their mouths and noses and pushed on, paying little heed to the dead.

Overhead, on the wings of the gryphon, Kelene tried not to look at the carnage below. She felt bad enough having to forward Zukhara's cause with her presence, without witnessing the bloody results of his ambition. She prayed fervently he would not order her to use her magic against the Turics. So far, his own power had been enough to awe and terrify his people, and she hoped that his pride would prevent him from seeking overt aid from a woman. But who was to say? If the city of Cangora bolted its gates against him and his army had to lay siege to it, he might be angry enough to force her hand. His arcane prowess was growing by the day, but the power of a fully trained sorceress could open an unwarded city in short order.

Kelene patted the gryphon's neck. Rafnir, she silently cried, I need you. Where are you?

She had no way of knowing that on that day Rafnir was far to the north, across the Altai with her father and the clan chiefs, preparing the werods for war.

* * * * *

That same morning, leagues behind Zukhara's army, the riders of the Clannad crested a high ridge and looked down on the dusty, beaten path of the Spice Road on the flatlands below.

"This is as far as I can lead you, Lady," the guide said gruffly. "I have never traveled beyond these hills."

Helmar studied the road from one horizon to the other, as far as she could see. At that moment it was empty. "You have done well, thank you. The trail is clear now for all to see."

Rapinor looked skeptical. "You want us to go down there?" All the warriors stared at the open road as if it were a poisonous snake.

"Too long a solitude makes a heart of fear," Helmar responded, and she urged her mare into a trot down the hillside. The warriors did not hesitate further but followed after her straight, unyielding back.

They have been hiding for so long, it has become habit, Afer commented.

"And how do you know that?" Sayyed inquired, still watching Helmar ride down the slope.

Helmar told me. I like her. Most of the Clannad are magic-wielders, you know. But she became chief because she proved herself to be the most talented.

"No," Sayyed said, almost to himself. "I didn't know. And did she also tell you how they came to be hidden away in the Turic mountains?"

Not yet, the stallion nickered. *But I could make a few guesses.*

"So could I," Sayyed replied thoughtfully. "So could I." He folded his golden cloak into a tight roll, tied it behind his saddle, and wrapped his burnoose around his head. If need be, he could pretend to be a Turic escorting new troops to Zukhara's war. He didn't know what they would find on the road ahead, and he did not want to give Zukhara any warning that more sorcerers were coming after him.

He glanced critically at Demira shifting impatiently by his side, and he realized there was no possibility of disguising her long wings. There was only one thing he could think of that might explain her presence.

A halter! she neighed. *That is humiliating!*

No more than this saddle! If I can wear tack, so can you. For Kelene! Afer told her severely.

So they left the mountains, a Turic on a big black horse, leading a winged Hunnuli mare. If anyone asked, Sayyed would tell them he had captured the mare and was taking her to the Gryphon.

Strangely enough, no one did ask that day, for though the road soon became busy, no one dared stop the strange troop of hard-eyed warriors jogging purposefully along the side of the road. Other groups of mounted or marching men traveled south toward Cangora, and a few refugees fled north. But not one person tried to join the troop or talk to any of its riders. They only stared as the white horses trotted by.

The sun was nearing its zenith when Afer, Demira, and the white horses flared their nostrils and began to toss their heads. An erratic breeze blew hot and dry from the desert, and on its skirts came the unmistakable smell of unburied dead.

In the open, nearly treeless land the riders saw the scavenger birds and the remains of the massacred caravan for a long way before they reached the first burned wagon and decaying bodies. A few birds squawked at the intruders and flew farther down the road to settle on another spot. Some of the dead had already been claimed and taken away for burial, but many more still waited on the sandy ground among the dead horses and scattered debris.

Helmar brought her troop to a stop. "We may not ever know if we do not look," she said to Sayyed, who was grateful for her concern.

They spread out in pairs along the long strip of road and carefully searched each wagon, body, and heap that belonged to the Shar-Ja's caravan. No one had a real hope that they would find Hydan, Hajira, or Tassilio among the wreckage, but if they found the bodies, at least they would know. Sayyed worked tirelessly in the search, since he and Afer were the only ones who could recognize Hajira and Tassilio, and while he saw a few faces he vaguely recognized, he found no one to match the description of the boy and his black-clad guard.

He reached the last cluster of wagons near what had been the front of the caravan and walked slowly among the ruined vehicles. Several of them had been stripped of anything usable by looters, but there was one on its side some distance from the others that looked familiar and still intact. He strode toward it, and suddenly two things happened at once. A horse neighed somewhere behind it, and a large dog leaped out of the interior and charged toward Sayyed. Its wild barking filled the quiet and drew everyone's attention. A warrior nearby drew his bow, but Sayyed yelled at him to put it away, and he held out his hands to welcome the dog. The big animal, whining and barking in delight, planted his paws on the man's chest and licked his face clean.

"Sayyed!" cried a familiar voice. A lean young figure burst out of the wagon's door and joyously flung himself in the embrace of the sorcerer. Between laughter and tears, Sayyed calmed down boy and dog enough to get a good look at them. They were both stretched tight with hunger and the shadows of fear, and Tassilio's face had lost what was left of its boyish innocence. But, the god of all be praised, he was unharmed.

He gazed up at the clansman with huge eyes, and every pent-up word came tumbling out. "Sayyed, you're here! I prayed you would come. And look at the horse with wings! Is that Demira? Did you find Kelene and

Gabria? Who are these people? Where is—"

Sayyed raised a hand to stem his rush of wild words. "Tassilio, where is Hajira?"

The boy led him to the wagon, talking rapidly as he went. "Hajira knew it would happen, you know. A strange man told him just before it started. Hajira stayed close to the Shar-Yon's wagon, and the minute he realized we were under attack, he threw the driver off and drove as far as he could before we were hemmed in by the fighting; then he loosed the horses, tipped the wagon over, and forced me inside. He thought no one would bother the funeral wagon."

He scrambled inside. Sayyed stooped to look in the covered vehicle. The Shar-Yon's sealed casket had been respectfully covered with the royal blue hangings and pushed to the side that had once been the roof, forming a narrow space between the wagon floor and coffin. There on a makeshift bed lay his brother, a crude bandage on his shoulder, another tied to his thigh.

"He was awake a while ago," Tassilio said, his voice quivering. "But now he won't wake up." Despite his strength and growing maturity, tears filled his eyes, tears brought on by exhaustion, grief, and overwhelming relief. He swiped them away with a dirty sleeve.

A grimace on his face, Sayyed stood to call Helmar and her healer. She was already there behind the wagon, standing with a crowd of her riders by a lone white horse and looking stricken. Something long and very still, wrapped in a shroud of royal blue, lay on the ground at the horse's feet. Sayyed felt a hand on his arm, and he looked down at Tassilio's unhappy face gazing at the mound.

The boy cleared his throat and said, "I don't know who he was. He came that morning, looking for Hajira. They were talking when the fighting started. He stayed with us and defended the wagon when some of the Fel Azureth came after us." Tassilio paused to wipe his eyes

again. Helmar and her warriors had turned to listen to
him, and he met the chief's regard directly as if he
spoke only to her. "He was very brave. He fought
beside Hajira, and he saved my life, you know. He took
a sword thrust that was meant for me. When the attackers went away, they thought everyone was dead. I
helped Hajira into the wagon, but I couldn't help the
stranger. I could only cover him and keep the vultures
away. I don't even know his name." The tears suddenly
came in earnest and slid unchecked down his cheeks.

The lady chieftain knelt on one knee in front of Tassilio and offered a cloth for his face. "His name was
Hydan," she said softly. "He was my swordsman, and
yes, he was very brave. Like you. I am glad to know he
died well, and I thank you for taking care of him."

Her simple, direct words were what Tassilio needed
to hear. He took the proffered cloth, giving her a tremu-
lous smile in exchange, and vigorously scrubbed his
face. When he emerged from behind the cloth, his tears
were gone, and he looked closer to his normal self.

Sadly the Clannad riders tied Hydan's wrapped body
onto the back of his horse. Helmar took the horse's
muzzle in her hands and leaned her forehead against
his to say good-bye. "Take him home," she murmured.
The horse neighed once, a grief-filled, lonely call; then
he trotted away with his heavy burden.

"Where is he going?" exclaimed Tassilio, astonished.

"He will take his rider home to be buried with honor,"
the chief answered, distracted by her own thoughts.

"How does he know where to go? Do you live close
by? Who are you, anyway?" Tassilio was definitely
returning to normal. He didn't even wait for an answer
but grabbed Helmar's arm and pulled her to the wagon
where Sayyed had returned to tend Hajira.

The Clannad healer quickly answered Helmar's summons, and willing hands moved Hajira out to a shelter
rigged by the wagon box that gave the healer more

room to tend the injured man.

After a thorough examination, the healer told Sayyed and Tassilio the good news. "His wounds are not dangerous. The worst of his malady is dehydration. He needs liquids and plenty of them. If he can get through the next few hours and stave off infection, he should be fine."

Tassilio whooped and danced around the tent with his dog.

True to the healer's word, Hajira revived under a steady treatment of water, honeyed tea, and finally broth. In the late afternoon, he surprised everyone by sitting up and insisting rather forcefully that Sayyed take him and the boy out of this stinking, fly-infested, pestilential wreck. The healer agreed, and the riders very thankfully obliged. They built a makeshift cart for the guardsman out of several broken wagons, hitched it to a horse, and left the massacred caravan behind.

Sayyed rode beside Hajira part of the way and told him what had been happening. The wounded man listened, his eyes half-closed, and when Sayyed completed the tale, his haggard face lit with amusement. "Only you, my brother, could go into those mountains to find two magic-wielders and come out with over seventy."

"Just not the right ones."

Hajira's mirth fled. "No. Not yet. This is worse than we feared." Ignoring the pain in his shoulder and leg, he pushed himself up against the back of the cart until he was propped upright. "Zukhara is using your women to help him fulfill an ancient prophecy from *The Truth of Nine* that he thinks applies to him."

"And you do not believe it?" Helmar asked.

Hajira snorted. He knew enough Clannish to understand her. "Prophecies are not exact. They can be bent to fit any number of events."

"What then is the Lightning of the North?" asked Sayyed.

"Where did you hear that?"

"From what little bit of news we have been able to gather. It is rumored Zukhara carries the Lightning of North in his hand."

Hajira shrugged that away with one good shoulder. "It must be Kelene and Gabria's sorcery."

Sayyed scratched his chin. That made sense, so he mentioned something else that had bothered him. "Did the Fel Azureth kill the Shar-Ja?"

"I doubt it. I saw them capture his wagon just before we bolted for the funeral van." He bowed his head to Helmar, who rode on his other side, Tassilio perched happily behind her. "Thank you for sending your man, Lady. He told me he had ridden day and night to reach us. I am sorry it was his doom to come at such an ill-timed moment."

She acknowledged his thanks and said, "There is one thing I would know. How have you two survived for two days?"

The Turic pointed a finger at the boy. "He is a most ingenious scrounger."

Tassilio blushed beneath his dark tan and blurted, "You would have done the same for me."

"True." Hajira's eyes crinkled with a smile then slid closed, and the man drifted to sleep.

Tassilio solemnly regarded his friend with something akin to adoration. "He wanted me to run away and leave him, but I couldn't do that! And he was right, too. No one came near the Shar-Yon's wagon after the battle. Many people came to loot or look for wounded or for the dead, but no one dared approach a royal coffin defended by a large dog and a horse as white as a ghost." The boy grinned at the memory and almost as quickly his smile slipped away. He sniffled, thankful that the worst part of his ordeal was over, and surreptitiously swiped a sleeve over his eyes.

Then his quick mind found another thought, and he reached back and patted the mare's white rump. "Hydan's

horse was something special, wasn't he? He seemed so
horribly sad at the death of his master, I could hardly
bear it. I told him I was sorry and I thanked him, and you
know the odd part, I think he understood."

"Most horses understand a kind heart," Helmar
replied.

"Don't try to get direct information from her, boy,"
Sayyed warned him dryly. "She is as secretive as a clam."

"All secrets are revealed in good time," Helmar
retorted. "And the reasons for them."

Weary and safe for the first time in a long while, Tassilio leaned against Helmar's strong back. "At least we'll
be in Cangora soon. I hope my father is there."

The adults made no answer. No one knew what they
would find in Cangora, and no one wanted to hazard a
guess.

The Clannad rode for the rest of the daylight hours,
following the beaten trail of Zukhara's army. Although
they saw other Turics along the way, most of the people
looked too suspicious or frightened to offer any further
news of the Gryphon. The riders came to the last oasis
on the Spice Road near sunset, hoping to find the army
camped there, but the oasis was empty, and the tiny
settlement close by was deserted. The reason for that
dangled in the few tall trees around the four walls. Ten
men of various ages, their hands bound and their robes
stripped away, had been hung not more than hours
before. An edict nailed to a tree forbade any man from
removing the bodies until they rotted off their nooses.

"So the Gryphon deals with those who do not accept
his will," Hajira said in a voice heavy with scorn and
disgust. "The families who lived at this oasis were Kirmaz tribe. Their leader did not travel with the Shar-Ja's
caravan. He is a stubborn man with a fierce sense of
tradition who did not get along well with Zukhara.
Once he knows about this"—Hajira jerked a hand at the
hanging men—"he will be hard to hold back. The

guard's words dropped off, and his face grew very thoughtful. "Cut them down," he said abruptly.

The lady chief started at his sharp voice. "What? Why? Would it not be better to let the families deal with the bodies? Do we risk the time?"

"It is probably already too late to catch the Gryphon before he reaches Cangora," Hajira replied, intent on his own thoughts. His piercing eyes swept the nearby foothills. The wells and springs of the Spice Road oases bubbled up from an intricate series of underground rivers and streams that flowed from the secret heart of the Absarotan Mountains. They were the lifeblood of the western half of the Turic realm and were granted for safekeeping—and often as favors—into the hands of the different western tribes. Even in times of drought, the oases usually had water. This particular set of wells was doubly important for its proximity to Cangora and its location along a prime road that led into high pastures in the mountains. It had been zealously tended by the Kirmaz tribe for several generations.

Hajira was familiar with their leader and knew his reputation as a firebrand. If he could get the man's attention, it could be worth the time spent. "The survivors are probably up there now watching us from that cover," he told Helmar. "They don't know who we are yet, but if we treat their dead with respect and leave a message for the Kirmaz-Ja, we just might earn a new ally."

Following Hajira's advice, the riders cut down the ten men, laid them carefully in a row in the shadow of a mud-brick building, closed their bulging eyes, and covered their bodies with blankets and then stones to discourage scavengers.

When the job was complete, Hajira hobbled to the mounds with Sayyed. "The families will return soon and can bury these men as they see fit, and they will know the Raid are not afraid of the Gryphon." The two men draped Sayyed's coat over the first mound where anyone coming to investigate would see the Raid emblem and understand.

After watering the horses, the Clannad continued their journey. They were not far from Cangora, and they wished to push on after Zukhara, in the hope that his army would camp before the gates and they would be able to find the women before the Gryphon entered the city. It all depended on whether or not Cangora would defend itself.

Yet the closer they drew to the capital, the more evidence they found of the Gryphon's brutal advance. An increasing number of small villages and farms were located along the road, and many had been raided to feed the voracious army. More bodies hung from trees or lay hacked in front of their abandoned houses. One building, a storehouse from the looks of its burned remains, had been blasted to splinters by what they all recognized was magic.

"Would Kelene do that?" Hajira asked, nonplussed by the amount of damage.

"If Zukhara held a knife to her mother's throat, she might," Sayyed said heavily.

"That is something I have wondered since you told me this tale," Helmar said. "Why don't Kelene and Gabria use their sorcery to escape? They've been held for days now, and we know they're alive."

"Zukhara has poisoned Gabria, but beyond that I do not know, and I have been thinking about it from the night we realized they were gone."

She is afraid of him, Demira sent. *I know that from her touch, but I do not know why. He kept me asleep for so long and then, when I woke, she made me escape.*

Sayyed shook his head. "So what hold does he have over her? Kelene has the courage of a lioness and the stubbornness of a badger. I hope she is just biding her time."

"And what will you do if Zukhara forces her to fight us?" asked Helmar in her quiet, husky voice.

"We will leave that to our gods," he replied, so softly she could barely hear him.

The road wound on along the treeless, rolling hem of the foothills. To the west the sun had dropped behind the massive ramparts of the Absarotan peaks. To the east a purplish haze settled peacefully over the flat, arid lands bordering the Kumkara Desert. Ahead of the troop where the road rolled south over a long, easy hill, the riders spotted the first gray clouds of smoke climbing on the still evening air. Soon they noticed a murmur as deep and threatening as thunder rumbling in the far distance.

The riders glanced uneasily at one another. Hajira sat up in his cart and strained to see ahead. The road was deserted now; the countryside was empty of life. A tension hovered in the air as palpable as the sounds that grew louder and more distinctive the closer the troop drew to the top of the hill. By now they could distinguish the din of thousands of voices raised in anger, the clash of weapons, and several large explosions.

The troop hurried forward to the top of the slope and there halted to stare down at the scene below. Cangora, the ancient capital of the Turic rulers, sat in a great bay in the sheltering arms of the mountains. Roughly equal in size to old Moy Tura, it climbed in gentle levels and terraces up the natural slope of the valley to a massive hump of rock that towered over the city and prevented attack from the rear. Cangora was also fortified with thick stone walls and high, domed towers that provided a solid line of defense across the bay. Its only large entrance was a massive gateway hung with the huge copper doors that gave the city its Turic name, "Copper Gate." After the vanished holy city of Sargun Shahr, it was the most important site in the Turic realm, a center of trade, religion, and art. Cangora had never been taken in battle.

The Gryphon's army had drawn up before the great city in shouting, seething ranks. They had no siege engines and not enough men to assault such a large fortification, but even from their position on the distant hill, the Clannad could see Zukhara's army would need nothing more than the one person who stood before the massive gates to open its way into the heart of the city. A distinctive blaze of fiery blue light seared from the person's hand toward the top of one of the towers. The dome exploded in a deadly blast of stone, melting lead, and burning timbers. Three other towers had already been destroyed.

"Is that Kelene?" asked Helmar in surprise and consternation.

Hajira leaned forward over the driver's shoulder, staring at the figure so far below. "No, by the Living God's hand," he answered. "That is Zukhara!"

A horrified hush fell over the watching warriors. The answers to so many questions fell into place.

"The Lightning of the North," snarled Sayyed. "It's not Kelene's sorcery, it's his!"

In spite of the darkness the watchers on the hill could see frantic activity on the walls. Weapons blinked in the torchlight, and people struggled to put out the fires before they grew out of control.

Just then a large, dark shape winged slowly over the city. Torchlight and the light from several fires by the front gate glowed on the golden wings of a living gryphon. On its back sat the figure of a woman, her dark hair unbound, her body unmoving.

Demira suddenly neighed in anger and would have sprung into the air if Sayyed had not seen the tension in her muscles and anticipated her intention. "No!" he bellowed and gave her halter such a tug, it yanked her off balance and into Afer's side. "No! Do not even think it. Not yet. Wait and see. We cannot rescue her in front of an entire army."

The mare neighed a strident peal of frustration. *Let me get her. I can outfly that thing!*

The black stallion snorted fiercely in reply. *No, you cannot. That is a creature born to the air. And if you will not think of yourself, think of Gabria and Nara!*

Demira pawed the ground. Her coat broke out in damp patches of sweat, and her tail swished a furious dance, but she accepted their logic and angrily clamped her wings to her sides—for now.

Another sound drew their attention back to the besieged city. The braying voice of a single horn echoed across the distance. The attackers fell quiet. The man in front of the gates blared out a thundering message. The troop could not hear his words, but they heard his exalting tone and knew what he demanded.

Nothing happened for a long while. The gryphon continued to cruise over the city; the army shuffled impatiently like a hunting dog waiting for the kill. Smoke swirled from the tops of the shattered towers.

At last another horn sounded, this time from the battlements of the city's wall, and the huge gates swung slowly open to allow a small contingent of men to exit the city. From their robes and the flat gold chains glinting on their chests, Hajira identified them as members of the Shar-Ja's council. They bowed low to Zukhara.

"That's it then," he growled. "If those men are negotiating, the city will surrender. I had hoped the governor would put up a fight, but they have probably killed him."

The words had no sooner left his mouth than the envoy turned to point to something, and two more men dragged a body out of the gateway and dumped it at Zukhara's feet.

A roar of triumph swelled from the ranks of the Gryphon's fanatics. They lifted their weapons high and crashed their shields together, making a cacophony of noise that filled the valley from end to end and shook the foundations of the city. The great gates opened wide. The Gryphon and the Fel Azureth entered Cangora in triumph.

14

A pall of mist shrouded Gabria's dreams. Dense and heavy, virtually impenetrable, it hung across her subconscious, obscuring the visions that formed in her mind. She struggled to get through the fog to a place where the air was clear and the light was as bright as the midday sun over the Ramtharin Plains, but there seemed to be no end to the clinging, gloomy mist. No beginning. No end. No life. Just dismal obscurity.

Then she heard a sound familiar to all clanspeople: the distant drumming of hoofbeats. A jolt of fear went through her. It had been twenty-seven years since the massacre of her clan and the inception of the vision of her twin's murder. She had suffered the same dream or variations of it several times since then, and it never ceased to cause her grief and pain. It always began in fog and always included the sound of hoofbeats. She half turned, expecting to hear her brother's voice, and found she was alone in the mist. No one spoke; no other sounds intruded into her dream. There was only the single beat of one approaching horse.

Gabria looked in the direction of the sound and saw a rider on a ghostly white horse materialize out of the mist. A Harbinger, her mind said. The immortal messenger sent from the god of the dead to collect her soul. Zukhara's poison had worked at last.

But her heart said no. Her heart still beat in her chest, faster now with growing excitement, and her thoughts, too, leaped at the vision coming toward her. Harbingers were male, as far as anyone knew, but the rider on this glorious white horse was a woman, and a magnificent woman at that, dressed for battle and bearing a sword. A helm hid her face, and the style of her clothing was unfamiliar, but behind her back, rippling like a chieftain's banner, flowed a cloak as red as Corin blood. The woman lifted her sword in salute . . . and vanished.

Gabria stirred restlessly on the bed. "They're coming," she whispered.

Ever alert even in sleep, Kelene roused and moved close to check her mother. "Who is?" she asked, but Gabria sighed and slipped back into deeper sleep.

The light from a candle by the bed flickered over Gabria's face and highlighted the sharp angles of her features with a yellow outline. Kelene bit her lip worriedly. Normally slender, Gabria had lost so much weight she looked gaunt. The poison in her system made her nauseated, and it had been all Kelene could do to persuade her to take liquids so she did not become too weak and dehydrated. Her long, pale hair, usually shining and meticulously brushed, lay in a limp and bedraggled braid. Her skin had taken on a grayish pallor, and her strength had ebbed, so she tired very easily. In fact, she showed so many of the same symptoms Kelene had noticed in the Shar-Ja, Kelene seriously suspected

Zukhara had poisoned him as well.

Wide awake now, Kelene slid off the bed and walked across the room to a window seat set in a deep embrasure. She didn't like sleeping on that high bed anyway; it was too far from the ground. A warm pallet on the floor made more sense and was certainly easier on the back than those overstuffed feather mattresses the Turics saw fit to put on their beds. Of course, this room was meant as a guest room for visiting nobility, not clanswomen accustomed to tents and stone ruins.

Kelene cast a censorious glance around the darkened room and curled her lip. The whole thing was too big, too elegant, too overdone. Large pieces of ornately carved furniture, murals, thick rugs, and pieces of decorative art had been arranged in the room by someone, Kelene was sure, with a very tense and cluttered mind. The effort had been made to impress, not to make comfortable, and she found the whole effect annoying.

Suppressing a sign, she drew back the drapes and unlatched the glass-paned window. Glass was a rarity among people who spent most of their lives moving tents around, but Kelene liked the feel of the smooth, cool surface and the way light could pass through. If she ever returned to Moy Tura, Kelene decided to find a glassmaker who could teach her how to create the panes and the beautiful colored glass bottles, vials, and jars she had seen the Turics use.

She leaned out over the sill and drew a deep breath of the night air. Far below her the city of Cangora dropped gradually down street after street to the great copper gates that now stood closed for the night. The city was dark, brooding in silence after its easy defeat by the Gryphon the night before.

After the surrender of the city, Zukhara had taken up residence in the Shar-Ja's palace at the foot of the magnificent buttress of stone that thrust out from the foot of the mountain and formed the foundation of Cangora's defenses. Kelene could not see the rock formation from her window, but she had noticed it from the gryphon's back and recognized its unopposable might. The Turics had recognized that strength long ago and built a large temple on the top of the lofty stone. That temple, Zukhara had told her, was the main reason he had come to Cangora. Unfortunately, he had not yet told her why.

Thankfully she had seen him only once since he locked her and Gabria in the room near his quarters, and then it had been for just a brief time while he displayed her to the remaining members of the Shar-Ja's council. In the meanwhile, he had been constantly busy, swiftly solidifying his position in the city and spreading his war throughout the realm. The city governor's body had been hung in a gibbet by the front gates and was quickly joined by three more city officials who protested Zukhara's right to impose martial law on the population.

He set a nightly curfew for all city inhabitants, and the Fel Azureth patrolled the streets in squads to ruthlessly enforce his brand of civil law. The rest of the army, those who were not billeted at the palace, moved into several inns and a number of large homes around Cangora, throwing out the inhabitants and plundering the stores. Zukhara did little to keep them in check, and anyone foolish enough to complain found himself talking to rats in the city's prison. Those who did not profess their belief in the Gryphon's holy calling also found their way to the dungeons.

It was hardly an auspicious way to begin one's magnificent reign, Kelene thought sourly. She lifted her gaze beyond the night-cloaked city to the heights beyond where the caravan road came down from a broad, open hill. Although she could not see the distant landscape, she remembered it well.

"They're coming," her mother had said.

Who was coming? Was someone out there riding to their rescue? Or was it something she could not yet understand, something Gabria had seen only in a dream? Kelene studied the place where the hill should be as if she could penetrate the blackness and see what was there. Last night she had heard something—or thought she had. There had been a brief sound that called for just a moment over the roar of the army and the crash of its weapons. It had risen so faintly she still wasn't certain it had been there, but it sounded so familiar, so dear. Maybe it was just wishful thinking that she had heard Demira's voice on the hilltop beyond the city.

Leaving the window open, she returned to the bed where Gabria slept peacefully and pulled a spare cover onto the floor. She folded the blanket into a pallet and stretched out close to the bed so she could be near if Gabria needed her. Her eyes closed and her body relaxed, but it was a long time before she slept.

*   *   *   *   *

Because of her restless night, Kelene slept late the next morning and roused only when servants brought trays of food into the bedroom and set breakfast on a table near the open window. She bounced to her feet, having slept better on the floor, and maneuvered the servants out the door when they insisted on serving the clanswomen their breakfast. Kelene closed the door in their faces. "Overfed, interfering females," she said irritably.

At least they had had one good idea—they had brought a pot of freshly brewed tea. Kelene prepared a cup, laced it with milk, sweetened it with honey, and took it to her mother.

Gabria was already awake, and she smiled as Kelene sat beside her. Carefully she drank the hot tea, letting it settle her queasy stomach between sips.

"Do you remember the dream you had last night?" Kelene asked after a while.

The older sorceress looked blank; then she tilted her

head in thought. "It is so vague. I feel as though I walked in a fog all night. But I do remember a white horse."

"A *white* horse?" Kelene repeated, alarmed. The color was unusual among clan horses because of its connection to sorcery and to the Harbingers' spectral steeds. "Was it a . . ."

"No," Gabria hurriedly reassured her. "I thought so too at first, but it was ridden by a woman."

"Who? And why would you say 'They're coming'?"

"Did I? I don't know. I don't remember anymore."

Kelene clicked her tongue. "Mother, some day, a long time from now, when you enter the presence of the gods, will you please ask Amara why your dreams are always so maddeningly unclear?"

The remark brought a smile to Gabria's face, and for a moment lit her dull eyes with humor. "I'll be sure to let you know the answer."

They were still laughing when their door banged open and Zukhara's majordomo walked into the room. A golden gryphon on his uniform identified him as one of the Fel Azureth, and the deep lines on his forehead and the chill black of his eyes marked him as a man of little humor.

Kelene glared at him and said coldly, "Were you born in a brothel that you do not ask to be admitted?"

He ignored her remark. His eyes slid over the room disdainfully and did not once look directly at her. "His Supreme Highness, Lord Zukhara, Ruler of the Faithful, expects your presence, clanswoman," he demanded in crude Clannish.

"I guess that means me," snapped Kelene.

"And he wants you in one of the gowns prepared for you."

Kelene spat her opinion of the dresses and stalked out of the room before the officer realized she was going. She still wore the clan pants and tunic she'd made in the cavern—that was good enough!

The officer hurried to catch up, his face a frozen mask. Without another word he led her to an airy room on a lower floor of the large and spacious palace, where Zukhara and several other older men and two priests in yellow robes stood together talking.

The Gryphon's distinctive eyebrows lowered when he saw Kelene. "I asked you—"

Kelene cut him off. "I am comfortable as I am."

The men looked shocked at her effrontery, but Zukhara snapped his fingers and spoke a brief spell. To Kelene's chagrin, she found herself clothed in a long blue gown with a bodice that clung to her form and a skirt that flowed like water to her feet. Silver embroidery decorated the neckline and the hem, and a silver belt tucked in her slender waist. Even her long hair was braided with silver ribbon and crowned with a simple coronet. She'd never felt so elegant, self-conscious, or humiliated in her life.

Zukhara suddenly broke into his charming smile. "You are lovely, my lady. And do not think to change it back, or you will stand before the city in nothing but your silky, pale skin."

Kelene swallowed hard. She had no chance to retort, for in the next minute a fanfare of horns blared close by. Zukhara took her hand. It was only then that she saw the magnificence of his clothes and realized he had arranged something important.

Heavy drapes were pushed aside by servants, and Zukhara, Kelene, and the other men walked out onto a large balcony overlooking the palace grounds. Crowds of Turics filled the huge, open space and overflowed down the promenade into the streets. Half of Zukhara's army was there, yelling loudly and prompting the sullen citizens into cheers. Fanatics began chanting Zukhara's name.

The usurper basked in the adulation before he held

up his hands and commanded silence. The crowds gradually quieted to hear his words.

"Rejoice, tribes of the Turic, your salvation is at hand!" Zukhara shouted. "Long have we been led down paths of greed, sloth, iniquity, and corruption at the hands of the Line of Festith. See how we pay for their evil! Our wells run dry; our animals die; our women and children starve. The grain we plant withers for lack of water. There is no help for us! The Living God has turned his countenance away from our pleas. As long as we allow the last Festith to rule as Shar-Ja, Shahr will not deem us worthy of redemption."

A few hisses and boos followed those words, but most of the crowd remained silent.

"See what happened when the Shar-Ja tried to forge a pact with the infidel horse clans? His evil and greed were repaid with treachery and his only son murdered. That was our sign, my people! Sent by our god to show us the way out of our darkness. We must overthrow the perverted power of the Shar-Ja Rassidar and as foreseen by the Prophet Sargun, place the Gryphon on the throne of the Turic realm."

The men of the Fel Azureth burst into cheers.

Kelene stared, wide-eyed, at the man beside her. She knew he was capable of concocting lies, of twisting the truth to fit his purposes, and of deliberately misleading his own people, but he executed his speech with such fervor and sincerity, in a voice that boomed to the edges of the throng with just enough pleading in it to show sympathy and concern for his audience. She might have believed it herself if she had not been a witness to the truth of his cruelty and manipulations.

Zukhara's voice cried out once more. "Behold the heretic who brings such affliction upon us." He pointed downward and out from the main doors came four men bearing a chair litter. Tied to the chair, in his ceremonial robes, sat the Shar-Ja, still alive and furiously silent.

The city dwellers looked shocked as the Shar-Ja was paraded up and down in front of the palace. Zealots pelted the ruler with rotten fruit and worse, but the citizens drew back as if from a leper.

"Four days from today, on the first day of the month of Janus, I and the priests of Sargun will perform the Ritual of Ascension to formally kill the Shar-Ja and prepare the throne for a new dynasty. As ordained in the sacred texts of the rite, that day I will take this woman as my wife and be ordained Celestial Monarch and Sacred Ruler of the Turic Tribes. As it was written, so let it be done!" He raised his arms to the roar of approval from his followers; then he thrust Kelene forward to the edge of the balcony just long enough for the crowd to see her. He turned on his heel and strode back indoors, dragging Kelene with him. As soon as he slowed down, the sorceress yanked her hand out of his grasp.

"I will not marry you!" she yelled. "I am already married and no widow." She knew it would do her no good to argue, but her temper had grabbed the bit and run away with her common sense.

He flicked a hand as if to swat away an unimportant fly. "Your marriage as prescribed by your people under your heathen gods is considered invalid in our land," he replied, his arrogance unruffled by her fury. "To us, you are not united to any man, except me."

She crossed her arms, feeling stymied. "It will do you no good. I have not been drinking the 'remedies' you send with my meals. I am still barren and can do nothing to increase the blood of Valorian in your descendants," she threw out for lack of anything better to say.

He laughed then in delight. "Of course you haven't. You have been eating it ever since the night in the cavern when I discovered you had turned the juice to water. That was clever. But not clever enough. By the time we consummate our wedding night, the remedy will have completed its purpose."

"There will be no wedding night," Kelene said very slowly and distinctly, as if each word were a dagger to plunge into his heart.

His hand flashed toward her, caught her braid, and wrapped it tightly around his fingers. He wrenched her head back until her throat was exposed. "You are so beautiful when you are angry. Do not change. It will be such a pleasure to break that spirit," he hissed in her ear. His fingers caressed her neck where the blood surged under her skin. "There will be a wedding night, and soon you will forget that worthless man who never gave you a son."

This time Kelene reined in her hot reply. Nothing she could say would change his mind or alter his plans one whit, and all she wanted to do now was escape from his sight and think. Four days, by the gods, that was so little time! Her hands itched to snatch the chain around his neck and run, but what good would that do? Even if she managed to kill him, she still had to fetch her mother, find Nara and the gryphon, who were housed somewhere on the palace grounds, and contend with an entire army. She needed help, at the very least a good distraction, but a rescue force of several magic-wielders would be most welcome.

Zukhara kissed her lightly on her throat, and a chill sped down her spine. If something didn't happen soon to precipitate her escape, Kelene knew she would have to choose between her own honor and her mother's life. Clan society frowned on adultery; some women had even been exiled for promiscuous behavior. But what if the cost of fidelity was death for Gabria? More importantly, what would Rafnir think? How would he feel if she submitted to another man? Would he under-stand? She groaned, her teeth clenched, and prayed he would never be tested like that.

Zukhara laughed at her. Still holding her braid, he dragged her along the corridors back to her room and wrenched open her door.

Gabria, already dressed and seated at the table, stared coldly at the Gryphon as he shoved her daughter into the room. "My lord counselor," she said before Zukhara could leave. "A boon I ask."

He hesitated, curious, and because he was feeling generous at the moment, he decided to listen. Although he would never admit it even to himself, he harbored a grudging respect for this clanswoman who had survived so much in her life. He considered it an honor and an achievement to be the one who would at last kill her. "What do you wish?"

"I would like Lady Jeneve's book."

Zukhara shrugged. He had memorized every word and every spell in the little book. There was nothing in it the sorceress could use to thwart him and no real reason why he couldn't give it to her for a short while. "Why do you want it?" he asked.

Gabria pushed herself to her feet and walked to Kelene's side. "It is a part of a clan long dead. I would simply like it as a memento."

The Gryphon bowed. He could be magnanimous. "Then you shall have it. I will send it to you today. Good day, ladies." He swept out, and the door banged shut behind him. They heard the unmistakable hum of a spell, and when Kelene tested the door, she found it barred with a powerful ward.

She leaned her back against the door and ripped the silver coronet off her head. "Four days, Mother. That's all we have left."

* * * * *

The moment the Gryphon vanished from the balcony, the citizens of Cangora hurried back to their shops and homes. Disgruntled and fearful, they paid little attention to the beggar boy with the idiot's smile who crouched with his bowl and his mongrel dog near a column in the promenade. He laughed and chattered to someone only he could see with his great black eyes, and merely grinned all the wider when his bowl remained empty.

At last the court and the promenade had emptied of everyone but the many guards who watched the palace. One of them strode over to the boy and told him to move on. The urchin nodded extravagantly, his mouth hanging open, and he shuffled away with the dog at his side. The guard frowned, thinking Zukhara should do something about the riffraff in the city.

The "riffraff," meanwhile, continued his way down the streets and eventually reached the Copper Gate. A large contingent of the Fel Azureth commanded the gates, led by a giant of a man whose very appearance gave most men no thoughts of arguing with his decisions. Under his harsh eye, the guards scrupulously examined every cart and wagon going through, interrogated everyone, and refused entrance to anyone they thought suspicious. Undaunted, the dirty urchin wandered over to the captain of the guards and held out his bowl.

"Go on, simpleton," the man growled, too busy to deal with the likes of street rats.

The boy grinned wider, whistled to his dog, and trotted out the gate. The guards didn't give him a second look. He continued on, apparently aimlessly, up the caravan road, past the fields and a few outlying buildings and businesses until he reached the high hill. At the top he paused to look back; then a triumphant smile replaced his idiot's grin, and he sprinted out of sight of the city. Laughing to himself, Tassilio raced his dog along the road and, as soon as the way was clear, he angled left into a wide dale partially obscured from the road by a belt of wild olive trees. The Clannad had set up camp there in a scattered grove of trees while they tried to decide what to do and Hajira and Sayyed mended.

Tassilio could hear Sayyed even before he reached the outskirts of the camp. He waved to the outpost guards and ran directly to the healer's tent where the brothers stayed under the watchful eye of the Clannad healer.

"Where is that boy?" Sayyed was yelling. "He has been gone since sunrise."

Tassilio understood the sorcerer's sharp, angry pitch the moment he sauntered into the tent. Sayyed was on his side, his back to the entrance, his fists clenched, while the healer tried to clean the infected pus and flesh from the hole in his ribs.

"You're a good man," the clansman said through clenched teeth. "But on the whole I'd rather have Kelene as a healer."

Before he could stop himself, Tassilio blurted out, "I saw her! With Zukhara."

His unexpected voice caused everyone in the tent to startle, including the healer who accidentally poked Sayyed a little too hard in the tender flesh.

The clansman uttered a vile curse even Hajira had never heard. Ignoring his aching leg, the guardsman neatly collared Tassilio and pulled him to a seat near Sayyed. "Do not ever sneak up on a sorcerer who is in pain," Hajira warned. "He might turn you into a toad."

Tassilio's eyes widened. "Could you do that?" he asked Sayyed breathlessly.

Sayyed glared at him. "Don't tempt me. Where in the name of Sargun have you been? And what do you mean you saw Kelene?"

Before Tassilio could answer, Hajira limped to the tent flap and called for Helmar. The lady chief came quickly, slapping dust from her pants and hands.

She cast a sympathetic glance at Sayyed and an irritated one at Tassilio. "Heir or not, young man, you do not leave this camp without telling one of us first," she admonished. "We looked everywhere we could for you, and I will not allow you to add further to our troubles by getting yourself lost or killed or captured. Do you understand?"

Momentarily chastened, Tassilio hung his head and kicked his bare feet at the ground. He knew he deserved the reprimand—he had snuck out without asking—but he felt his news was worth the risk. His irrepressible good spirits came bounding back. "Yes, ma'am," he said, his face alight with his tale. "But I did see Kelene. And Father, too. He is still alive!"

Helmar knew a lost cause when she heard it. "Then you'd better tell us," she said with a sigh and sat down by Hajira.

Tassilio told them in excited tones how he had entered the city that morning, learned of Zukhara's proclamation, and mingled in with the crowds at the palace. He repeated Zukhara's speech almost word for word and described exactly what his father looked like and what Kelene was wearing.

"She is so beautiful!" exclaimed the boy who was obviously verging on manhood. "And her chin goes up when she's mad, and her eyes are thunderous!"

Sayyed, bandaged and sitting upright, chuckled at Tassilio's description. "So she has not been drugged or broken yet. That is a good sign."

"But four days!" Tassilio exclaimed. "Zukhara said he will perform the Ritual of Ascension then. We've got to do something to help Father!"

"What is this ritual?" Helmar asked.

Hajira grimaced at the memory of the texts he had read about the rites. "It is an ancient ceremony that is intended to purge the throne of one monarch to make way for another. Ritualistic murder. Zukhara intends to behead the Shar-Ja and burn his body. He then takes a wife that same day and begins his own line on the throne of Cangora."

"Where does Gabria fit into all of this?"

"My guess is she is being used as a lever against Kelene," Sayyed answered.

"I hope she is still alive," Helmar said.

Sayyed sighed so softly only Helmar heard him. "So do I," he said.

Something in his tone unaccountably pricked Helmar's feelings. There was more than mere worry in his voice; there was what . . . yearning? She mentally kicked herself for thinking such a thing, let alone letting it bother her, but her self-inflicted reprimand did little good. Immediately an unbidden, jealous pang insinuated itself into her thoughts and reminded her that Sayyed himself had admitted to loving this woman once. How many men put themselves in such jeopardy for someone else's wife without good reason? Helmar flung herself to her feet before her thoughts got any more ridiculous. She strode out of the tent without another word.

In surprise, the men watched her go. Only the healer, an old and trusted friend of the chief, thought he understood. "She has never been married," he tried to explain. "She does not yet understand."

"Understand what?" wondered Sayyed.

The healer shrugged his bony shoulders. "How she feels about you."

Stunned, Sayyed looked at his brother, then at the healer, and he felt his face grow hot. Despite having deeply loved two women and having been married to one for eighteen years, he had not understood either. He liked Helmar and respected her more than he thought possible, but he had never imagined she would feel the same for him. After Tam's death he firmly believed there would be no other love for him. Now he examined his feelings and, for the first time, he realized his desire for love had not died but merely slept within his heart. Could Helmar be the one to revive it? He suddenly smiled. It was like discovering a beautiful box intact in the ruins and not knowing what he would find inside.

Intent on his own musings, he pulled on his loose tunic over his bandaged ribs and walked out of the tent in a direction opposite to the one Helmar had taken.

Tassilio grinned at Hajira and winked at Sayyed's departing back.

* * * * *

The sun shone hot when a lone horseman approached the Clannad camp later that day. At the first low-pitched warning signal, the riders grabbed their weapons and formed a line of defense at the perimeter of the camp.

The rider, a Turic on a chestnut horse, reined his mount to a halt and studied the warriors with approval. He held up his hand in peace. "I am Mohadan, the Kirmaz-Ja. I see by your dress and white horses you are the troop I seek," he said in Turic.

Hajira stepped out of the line of warriors and addressed the tribal leader as an equal. "I am Hajira al Raid-Ja, Commander of the Tenth. Why do you seek us?"

The stranger lifted an arched eyebrow and leaned his arm on the saddle horn. "These are hardly Turic soldiers, Commander, and as I heard it, most of the Tenth was slaughtered."

"Not all of us, Kirmaz-Ja. So we make do with what we have."

"And what are you planning to do?"

Hajira, who knew the tribal leader to be a man of honor, gave a short bow. "Perhaps you would like to join us. We could discuss possibilities."

The stranger dismounted and led his horse to the camp to meet with Hajira, Sayyed, Helmar, and Rapinor. The Clannad warriors stayed in position, relaxed yet alert while their chief led the Turic to the shade of several tall cedars. Cool wine and plates of cheese and dates were brought and served by Tassilio. The Kirmaz-

Ja sat wordlessly, watching the preparations with a fascinated eye. He seemed particularly intrigued with Helmar and her obvious authority.

"I do not know of you, Lady," he said in rough but credible Clannish, "or your people. You are like clan and yet not clan. And how is it that a woman leads a troop of warriors? Some of whom," he suddenly noticed, "are also women."

"Swords and bows are not our first weapons," Helmar replied. "Strength of arms is not as important as talent to us."

The Turic narrowed his eyes. He had smallish eyes deep set behind a thin nose, but they were not piggish eyes, for his face was too hard and narrow, and his gaze glittered with intelligence and wit. He had a grizzled beard trimmed close to his jaws, and his knotted hair was iron gray. He shifted his eagle's glance from Helmar to Sayyed. "And you, you are Turic no longer. I would guess you are the half-breed who turned to sorcery."

Sayyed merely lifted his cup in reply, impressed by the man's knowledge and intuition.

"Are you here because of the women Zukhara holds?" Mohadan wanted to know.

Briefly Sayyed and Hajira told the Kirmaz-Ja the events beginning at Council Rock and leading up to their arrival at the outskirts of Cangora. Sayyed only touched on his time in Sanctuary and the Clannad's offer to ride with him, but Mohadan's sharp attention missed nothing, and he studied the warriors around him with keen interest.

When the narrative was through, however, Mohadan drove straight to the point that had brought him to see them. "I was told yesterday what your men did for the dead at the Saran Oasis. The families were grateful that you defied the Gryphon's edict to let the men hang until they rotted. So tell me now, will you join your forces to mine and help me bring down the Gryphon?"

15

Hajira shared a glance with Helmar and Sayyed before he turned to Tassilio sitting close beside him. "Is it your will, Shar-Yon, that we unite with this man and the enemies of the Gryphon?"

For the first time, Mohadan's expression registered real surprise. He had paid little attention to the boy who had served the wine, and now he focused all his fierce regard on the son of the Shar-Ja. "You are the sandrat? Rumor said you were dead."

The boy looked startled at the name by which Hajira had called him, but he collected himself quickly. "No, Kirmaz-Ja," Tassilio replied with every ounce of his father's dignity. "I am the Shar-Yon, and I am very much alive."

Mohadan, the traditionalist, the man sworn to honor the throne of the Shar-Ja, had never once considered the possibility of winning the throne for himself. He greeted the unexpected appearance of an heir with sincerity and relief and bowed low before the boy. His gesture sealed Hajira's decision.

At a nod from Tassilio, Hajira drew a dagger from a sheath at his waist and jabbed it into the ground in front of Mohadan. By doing so, he followed an old Turic custom of offering his services to another tribal leader. If Mohadan pulled the dagger free and returned it, he would accept Hajira's services in an agreement as binding as a blood vow.

The Kirmaz-Ja looked at the blade quivering in the dry grass. "I welcome your assistance, Commander, but I must ask, does this also include the sorcerer and the lady and her warriors? I have a feeling that without them, we will stand little chance against Zukhara's power."

Sayyed answered first. "I have already sworn to my own lord that I will do everything I can to return the sorceresses to the clans. To that end, I will help you for as long as the women are held captive."

"Fair enough, Clansman." He turned to Helmar who was sitting beside her guard. "And you, Lady?"

Sayyed was taken aback by the bold look of interest in the man's eyes when he looked at the chief, but Helmar seemed to pay no heed. Unaffected, she tilted her chin and replied coolly, "I made my promise to Sayyed to help free Lady Gabria and Kelene. We will do what needs to be done."

The man's jaw tightened, and his eyes hardened under a thoughtful frown, as if he had just made an unwelcome observation. He glanced at Sayyed then nodded to himself in decision. Without further hesitation, he yanked the blade free and passed it hilt-first to the royal guard. Hajira accepted it back with a thin smile.

"Now," said Mohadan, jumping to his feet, "if you

will break camp and come with me, I have something
to show you."

They followed his suggestion, swiftly and efficiently,
and in less than an hour were riding in a column along
the caravan road toward Cangora. They bypassed the
city by a wide loop and trotted into the hills on the
southern end of the broad valley. Mohadan led them
into the first deep dale they reached and pointed them
toward a long meadow where a large, bustling camp sat
along the banks of a dry streambed. The yellow banner
of the Kirmaz floated above one of the tents.

"Most of those men are my own," said the Kirmaz-Ja,
indicating the camp with a wave of his hand. "Some are
survivors from the caravan. Others have been coming as
the word spreads. Not all goes Zukhara's way. There is
fighting along the coast and in the cities of Hazereth
and Shamani where the Fel Azureth have met resistance
from several tribes—including the Raid. Perhaps two
hundred men have gathered at my summons. More will
come." He indicated a place in the meadow where they
could erect their camp near his.

"If all goes as planned," Sayyed told him as they all
dismounted, "there will be more men soon. My son is
bringing Lord Athlone and the werods to aid the Shar-Ja
as promised in their treaty."

A second look of surprise spread over Mohadan's
face. Surprise, Sayyed thought, was not a common emotion to the hard-bitten leader, and today they had managed to shake him twice.

"They are coming to help?" Mohadan almost shouted.
"We thought they had crossed the Altai to take revenge
for the capture of the women and the raids on their
trelds by the Fel Azureth."

"I sent for them six days ago."

Mohadan gave a great, gusty snort. "They crossed the
Altai yesterday. A messenger bird brought the news
from a cousin of mine this morning."

"Yesterday." Sayyed looked thoughtful. "Then they are four or five days away—if they ride like the wind and no one stands in their way."

"I will see that no one does! I will send an escort and a safe-pass for the men of the clans."

"Kirmaz-Ja, that is an excellent idea, but may I suggest we send the safe-pass and an urgent message with the winged mare? Only she is swift enough to reach them quickly."

I heard that and the answer is no! Demira bugled before anyone else could respond. The mare pranced to Sayyed, her big eyes alight with anger. *I am not going away from Kelene again!*

Mohadan could not "hear" what she sent telepathically, but he understood what she meant well enough from her stiff-legged stance and her flattened ears. He gave a non-committal shrug. "Perhaps it would be better—"

Helmar cut him off by throwing an arm around Demira's neck. The mare rolled her eyes at the chief but did not pull away. "If you were not the best choice to reach Kelene's father, we would not ask you," she said in soothing tones. "If Hajira were healed and able to ride that far, he could go, though his horse could not travel fast enough. Some of my men would go, but they are not Turics and would be in constant danger. You have your glorious wings to fly swiftly above the trouble and reach Lord Athlone in time. Please understand. To have any chance at all of saving Kelene and Gabria, we need more men to attack the city."

The Hunnuli twisted her neck so she could regard Helmar with her star-bright eye. *Could I come back as soon as I find them?*

"As fast as you can," the chief promised.

Then I will take your message to Lord Athlone and Rafnir. She tossed her mane. *The sky is clear, and the road is open. I will try to fly all night.*

"She will take the message," Helmar said, relieved.

Satisfied, the Kirmaz-Ja hurried away to obtain what he wished to send to the clan lords, and the Clannad put up their shelters and ate their evening meal. Sayyed and Helmar made much over Demira, brushing her glossy coat, wiping the dust from her nostrils, and feeding her tidbits until the Turic leader returned.

Mohadan brought a rolled scroll and a yellow banner tightly wrapped in cloth. "Give these to Lord Athlone. They will clear his way along the Spice Road to Cangora. And tell him to hurry," he said to Demira and awkwardly patted her neck. He was not accustomed to talking to horses.

They fastened the banner and the scroll to Demira's back and watched as she lifted slowly into the deepening blue of the evening sky. When she was gone, a tense anticipation settled over the camp. There was nothing left to do but wait.

The next day came hot and dry, as had most of the days before it. The arid wind that blew from the desert sucked what little moisture there was from the ground and left the hills parched and brown. After morning prayers, the Turics spent their time readying for war. They repaired their tack and battle gear, checked their weapons, and practiced swordplay and archery in the scattered splotches of shade under the few trees. Most of the Clannad stayed to themselves out of nervousness and hesitancy, for they had never been in the company of so many strangers. A few wandered over to satisfy their curiosity and before long were drinking Turic ale, admiring strange weapons or ornaments or other objects that were new to them, and fumbling through clumsy conversations.

No one remained idle throughout the day. A regular rotation of guards kept watch on the perimeters of the valley and on the camps. Scouts rode to watch the trails and the caravan road. A steady stream of men traveled the roads around Cangora that day. Most rode on to the city to join the Gryphon's holy war, but word of Mohadan's resistance traveled as fast as Zukhara's proclamation, and a constant trickle of reinforcements flowed into the Turic camp all day.

After noon, Helmar, Rapinor, Sayyed, Hajira, and Tassilio joined the Turics in the shade of Mohadan's big striped tent, and they discussed with the leader and his officers everything that came to mind concerning Zukhara, his intentions, the layout of Cangora, and their plans.

"Is it true, Lady," Mohadan said to Helmar, "that all of your riders are magic-wielders? Why couldn't you blast your way into the city and bring it down around Zukhara's ears?"

The lady chief drank some water from a cup before she took a deep breath and answered. "We are, but not all of us have the same strengths. Some of my people rarely use magic. We have been isolated for so long, our ways have become stagnant and our bloodlines are weakening."

Rapinor started to protest, and Helmar laid a hand on his arm. "You know it's true. That's why you came. It isn't just our horses or our livestock that are threatened. It is us." She turned back to Mohadan. "Yes, we could open the gates with our magic and wreak havoc on your city, and we will do so if there is no other choice. But I would prefer to wait for the clans. It would be better if we had an army behind us to distract the Gryphon's forces while we try to save the clanswomen and confront Zukhara. Besides," she said, winking at Tassilio, "I do not want to be the only one to shoulder the blame for damages to the Shar-Yon's city."

The Kirmaz-Ja nodded at her wisdom and cracked a hard smile. "I understand. It would be better for us as well if we rode together. We have little hope of defeating the Gryphon alone."

"Exactly." She returned his smile with one of her

own, her eyes crinkling at the corners above the constellations of freckles. She lifted her cup. "To cooperation and allies. Something we have not had in generations."

More ale was brought, along with honeyed wine and ewers of precious water. The talk went on while several of Mohadan's men outlined a map of Cangora for the strangers, describing the streets, the palace and its barracks, and the pinnacle with its huge temple.

"Could we try infiltrating the palace in a small group?" Sayyed suggested.

Tassilio looked dubious. "The palace and the grounds are heavily guarded, and soldiers are everywhere. The guards at the gate check everything and everyone. I don't know how you could get past and still find Kelene and Lady Gabria. That palace is huge!"

"I still think a lightning attack is our best hope. We strike fast, ride to the palace, and stop Zukhara before the ritual," Mohadan stated emphatically.

"And what if he kills the women or the Shar-Ja before we get there?" Hajira asked.

The Kirmaz-Ja sighed heavily. "That is a chance we take no matter how we approach our attack."

The talking went on while each person had their say about tactics and ideas. Although Tassilio listened closely, Sayyed thought he looked rather thoughtful, and the clansman wondered what scheme the boy was hatching in his active mind.

At the same time, scouts brought reports from the city, and new arrivals brought news from other regions of the realm. Fighting had spread across the country as the few surviving tribal leaders, appalled by the massacre of their contemporaries, struggled to organize resistance against the Gryphon's rebels. Those tribes without leaders were riddled with strife and confusion. Mohadan had hoped other leaders would join him at Cangora, but as the time passed and more news filtered in, he had to accept that he would have to fight alone.

By the time the sun crawled to its rest beyond the western mountains, the Turic and the Clannad alike were weary and ready for the cool of night.

The second day followed much the same course of heat and talk and preparation. The loyalists struggled to strengthen their numbers, and the Gryphon worked tirelessly to tighten his hold on Cangora and his bid for control of the fifteen tribes. Tension's grip grew tighter over everyone while they waited for the first day of Janas.

Sayyed, especially, festered in his worry and impatience. Questions crowded into his thoughts almost unceasingly, like crows harrying a hawk. Would the clans arrive in time, or would the Clannad and Mohadan's small army have to go, alone, up against the big city, which was well defended by a host far larger than their own? How was Zukhara treating Kelene? Had Gabria died of the poison? Would he and the Clannad be able to reach the women before Zukhara killed them? That fear terrified him the most and kept him awake late into the night, debating ways to get to them in time.

The third night, after another hot, interminable day, Sayyed crawled from his pallet and left the tent he shared with Hajira, Tassilio, and the healer. The darkness embraced him in a cool breeze and laved his fevered thoughts in quiet serenity. He walked barefooted away from the camps, out into the meadows where the horses grazed. The white Clannad horses were easy to see in the starlight, but it took him a while to find the black shape of Afer, standing like a shadow close to Helmar's mare. Their tails idly swished at a few stubborn flies, and their heads hung in peaceful rest.

At Sayyed's approach, both horses lifted their muzzles and nickered a welcome. Gratefully the sorcerer pushed his anxieties aside and crowded in between the two horses, where their warmth and companionship were the balm he needed for his spirit. Unwilling to disturb the silence, he leaned against Afer and sought out the stallion's favorite itchy places. He rubbed and patted and scratched until the big stallion quivered with delight. A soft nose nudged his elbow, and without thinking, Sayyed turned around to caress the mare. He discovered quickly that she liked her back and withers scratched, and he dug in with all ten fingers to massage her itchy skin.

The mare stretched her neck, her eyes half-closed, her ears flopping. If she had been a cat, Sayyed mused, she would be purring.

Oh, that is wonderful, a light feminine voice sighed in his mind.

Sayyed grinned. He had suspected as much. "How about here?" He moved his fingers to the end of her mane, where the ridge of her withers rose under her silvery coat.

Yes, came the voice again. The mare leaned into him. *I like that.*

"So why didn't Helmar tell me you were Hunnuli?" Sayyed asked casually, still scratching her back.

The white mare stilled, then gave a snort of amused annoyance. *Well, it is too late now to play dumb. Do you know how hard it has been to keep quiet around you?*

"Why did you?"

Helmar told us all not to talk to you. Not until she was sure.

"Is she so afraid of me?"

Not of you. Of the clans.

"Why?"

I will save that, at least, for her to explain.

"All right." Sayyed chuckled. "But if you are Hunnuli, why are all of you white?"

The horses turned their heads and whickered a greeting to someone else. Helmar walked out of the darkness. She wore only a light, loose-fitting tunic that rippled around her thighs in the soft breeze. She leaned over the mare's back, her expression unreadable in the night.

"They're not true whites, Sayyed. Only their hair is white. Our ancestors took the color of the lightning and covered over the black. If you look under their hair, their skin is still dark as night." She patted the mare and stallion and softly chuckled her husky laugh. "Marron, my beauty, you stayed quiet longer than I thought you would."

He was scratching my back, the mare offered as an apology.

"Is the lightning still there?" Sayyed asked, fascinated.

"Yes, if you look closely enough." Helmar pushed in by Sayyed, parted the hairs on Marron's right shoulder, and said, "There, you can just see the outline."

The sorcerer eased close to her and peered at the place she indicated. Faintly in the darkness he saw the pale line of white skin beside black. In the days that followed, Sayyed never could decide if what happened next was deliberate or accidental—and Afer would never tell him. Just as he straightened, Afer and Marron shifted closer together, knocking into Sayyed and throwing him off balance. He took a step to catch himself and banged into Helmar. Her strong arms went around him to steady him. His wounded arm hit her shoulder, and by the time the pain ebbed and he realized what had happened, they were standing wrapped in a tight embrace.

Neither moved. They were so similar in height, their hearts beat against one another, and their eyes stared at each other's from only a breath away. They hesitated, both surprised by the sudden intimacy of their position. Helmar's hands trembled against Sayyed's back, and Sayyed felt his skin grow hot. In a flash of unspoken consent, their lips met, and they kissed so long and deep it left them gasping.

Marron playfully reached over and nipped Afer. The stallion stamped a hoof, his neck arched, and he nipped her back. In a flash of phantom white, the mare leaped away, her tail held high like a flag. Afer galloped after her, and the two people were left alone in the meadow. The velvet night closed softly about them.

They stood, neither wanting to say a word, neither needing to. Sayyed's hands untied the strip of leather that bound Helmar's thick braid and gently worked her hair loose until it floated in a waving mass down her shoulders and back. He inhaled her scent, a warm blend of leather, horses, sun, wind, and a special fragrance all her own. He buried his face in her hair while her arms pulled his hard body against hers.

They kissed again, and all their questions and worries were cast to the winds until there was nothing left to think about but the warm grass and the wonder of a love unlooked for that had found them both.

Beyond the darkened meadow at the edge of the Clannad camp, a slim figure and a shaggy shadow slipped out of the healer's tent and worked their way around the perimeter guards. Silent and unseen, they crept over the hill and disappeared toward the valley of Cangora. By dawn they were sitting at the city gates patiently begging and waiting for the day to begin.

* * * * *

Afer and Marron came back just before sunrise and woke the lovers in time to return to camp. The four of them walked back together, feeling very pleased with each other. Helmar and Sayyed stopped near the tents, not willing yet to end their time together. This was dawn of the first day of Janas. There was no more time to save the Shar-Ja or Kelene and Gabria. They had to attack Cangora today, with or without the clans, and the gods only knew how the day would end. Arms entwined, they looked to the east, where a pale gold band of light illuminated the flat horizon.

They were so engrossed by the beauty of the coming day, they did not see a dark shape come swooping out of the west. An eerie, shattering cry broke over the predawn's hush, and suddenly the valley was filled with the screams of terrified horses. The two camps awoke to stunned life. Guards came running; men tumbled out of their tents.

Sayyed and Helmar whirled in time to see a huge creature dive from the sky, its wings folded, its talons extended. Howling, it dove among the Turic horses, and with a sweep of its big paw broke the necks of two animals. The rest fled in a maddened stampede away from the horrendous beast. They charged in a panicked mass up the valley and, blinded by their own fear, plowed directly through the Kirmaz-Ja's camp. The thundering of hooves and the screams and shouts of men filled the valley.

The gryphon growled with satisfaction. Hooking a dead horse in her claws, she flew heavily away, back toward Cangora and the man who had summoned her.

The valley was left in chaos. Through the dust kicked up by the stampeding herd, Sayyed and Helmar could barely make out the shambles of the Turic camp. The hazy forms of men ran through the pale light. Others lay motionless on the ground.

Helmar took one long look and became a chief again. She quickly squeezed Sayyed's hand and ran into their camp, shouting for Rapinor and her warriors. Snapping orders, she quickly organized them into parties and led them across to the Turic camp.

Sayyed watched her go. She was so different from his quiet Tam, and yet the two women shared the same strength of character, the same ability to coolly handle a crisis. He thought for just a moment about their night

and the box in his heart he had opened. The contents
had turned out to be something he would treasure for
as long as he had left to live. He put his hand on Afer's
shoulder. "Go," he commanded. "Gather the Hunnuli
and round up those horses. Zukhara started the hostili-
ties this morning, but we are going to finish them."

Afer and Marron neighed their agreement and galloped away to do his bidding. Hajira found him then,
and the two brothers hurried to the Turic camp to do
what they could to help. In the middle of the wreckage
stood the Kirmaz-Ja, unharmed and punctuating his
shouted orders with fierce gestures. Mohadan was in a
towering rage that turned his dark eyes to black fire and
his face to a mask of insulted fury.

"He thinks to stop us," the Turic snarled to Sayyed
and Hajira, "by driving off our horses and occupying us
with disaster. But I will attack Cangora today if I have to
crawl there on my hands and knees!"

The dust slowly settled, and the Turics and the Clannad worked to bring some order to the chaos. They
were relieved to find there were not as many dead and
wounded as they had feared. The first cry of the
gryphon had alerted most of the tribesmen, who had
managed to get out of the way of the stampede in time.
In all only six bodies were placed together under a tree
for burial, and fourteen men had to be treated by the
healers for abrasions, lacerations, and broken bones. A
broad swath of the camp lay in trampled ruins, and it
took several hours to sift through the debris for enough
clothes, weapons, and battle gear to equip the men able
to ride. The sorcerers helped as best they could to
repair or transform the needed equipment, but it still
used more time than they had to spare.

The Hunnuli soon calmed down the Turic horses and
herded them back to the mouth of the valley. Eager
warriors brought their mounts in to the picket lines and
began to saddle them.

As order slowly returned, Mohadan calmed down. A cold, deliberating anger replaced his earlier temper, and he gathered his officers, Helmar, Hajira, and Sayyed for a meeting.

"There has been no word from the clans," he said bluntly. "We must assume they cannot arrive today. Yet this is our last day to save the Shar-Ja. By sunset he will be dead, and Zukhara will sit on the throne. We are all that stands between that madman and the power of the crown. Do we attack today or wait until the other tribal leaders join us and the clans arrive?"

"Today," Hajira said forcefully.

"Even with the reinforcements and the Clannad, we number barely eight hundred. The Gryphon has amassed closer to seven thousand, and he holds the fortifications."

"We know that, Kirmaz-Ja," said one of the officers. "But I would rather die attempting to save our rightful ruler than sit by and let that usurper murder him."

Mohadan glanced at the lady chief. "Are you still willing to ride with us?"

Dirty, disheveled, and still dressed only in her light tunic, Helmar's authority and self-confidence shone as clearly as any accoutrements of war. "Of course. Our objectives may be slightly different, but our destination is the same."

"So be it," the Kirmaz-Ja stated. "We ride within the hour."

A sudden clamor made them all jump. "It's coming back!" a guard bellowed just before several horns blared a warning. Everyone froze, their eyes searching the sky.

"There!" shouted Hajira.

Faster than an eagle, the gryphon had circled around to attack the camp from a different direction. She dove on the picket lines, screaming her ear-piercing cry. The horses erupted into a rearing, pitching panic.

"The horses!" shouted Mohadan, and his men shook themselves from their motionless fear and awe and raced to defend their animals. Archers armed their crossbows with the short, barbed quarrels that could pierce armor. They fired a deadly flight, but the gryphon swerved at the last minute and roared her derision at the puny missiles. She swooped again over the meadows and harried the horses into terrified flight. Only the Hunnuli ignored her attempts to panic them and steadfastly tried to hold the frightened herds together.

The gryphon saw the white horses and understood what they were doing. She stooped low, her wings humming in the speed of her dive, and sank her claws into the back of one white Hunnuli. Before she could get it off the ground, three others and Afer charged her. The black, larger than the others, bared his teeth and drove his hooves into the gryphon's shoulder.

Hurt and furious, the gryphon let go of her prey. She crouched, ready to pounce on the black that had hurt her when another force hit her in the side and knocked her off her feet. Her baleful eyes sought the source of this new hurt, and she saw a man fire a blue blast of magic at her. Catlike, she twisted to her feet and sprang into the air. She was all too familiar with the effects of that powerful force. More bolts chased her into the bright sky.

Helmar and other Clannad magic-wielders joined Sayyed, and together they kept up a barrage of magic that forced the gryphon to circle higher and higher above the camp.

One rider, tears running down his face, ran to help his wounded Hunnuli.

Meanwhile, the Turics and the Hunnuli calmed the other horses enough to get them saddled and ready. The gryphon still circled the valley, but as long as the magic-wielders continued firing at her, she did not dare approach any closer.

"God of all," Sayyed gasped when he paused to wipe the sweat from his forehead. "That creature is strong. The Trymmian force hardly rattles it."

Helmar agreed. "It will be tough to shake it if it chases us all the way to Cangora."

"The Turics will be ready soon," Sayyed pointed out, eyeing her inadequate clothing. "You'd better prepare the Clannad."

She graciously accepted the hint, kissed him on the cheek, and took half the warriors with her. They came back shortly, dressed in mail and fully armed, and sent the rest back to do the same. By the time the Turics were mounted and ready to ride, the Clannad had whistled in their Hunnuli and waited to join them.

Sayyed looked around for Hajira to say good-bye. Hajira had chosen to keep Tassilio in the camp, despite the boy's pleas, and Mohadan had wholeheartedly agreed. A city consumed in desperate fighting was not a good place for the Shar-Ja's last son. But Hajira came running out of their tent, hurriedly buckling on his sword and looking so mad he could have spit lightning bolts.

"He's gone! And that mangy dog with him!" the guardsman yelled. He grabbed a saddle and threw it on the nearest spare mount with such force the frightened horse jumped out from under it, and Hajira had to calm it down before he could try again.

"What do you mean? Wasn't he here earlier?" Sayyed demanded.

"I thought he was, but things were so crazy, I don't know now. His bed is empty, those rags of his are gone, and he and that dog of his are nowhere in camp. I'll wager my next ten years of life he has gone to Cangora." Hajira's voice was laden with both anger and frantic concern. He managed to settle the skittish horse and mount without too much difficulty. "If the Fel Azureth don't kill him, I just might," he growled and kicked his horse to join the others.

Flanked by the magic-wielders, the Kirmaz-Ja led his small army out of the valley. The gryphon, seeing them leave, dropped close to harry the column, but the sorcerers drove her back with oaths and spheres of blue energy.

Hajira, Sayyed, and Helmar joined Mohadan at the front. "The Copper Gates will probably be enspelled with wards and be the most heavily guarded," Sayyed said. "But the straightest, quickest road to the palace and the citadel runs from there."

The Kirmaz-Ja nodded, his grizzled beard jutting from beneath his helmet. "We'll attack there." He glared at the sun, now nearly overhead. "Damned gryphon. It delayed us too long. We had no time to get anyone inside, and now it's almost noon. The Ritual of Ascension was always begun when the sun reached its zenith. We have very little time to fight our way through. At least it is a long ritual."

"And we probably do have someone inside," said Hajira irritably. "For what little good it will do us."

The column left the valley behind and trotted down the hills to the broad vale where the level fields rolled up to the foot of the city's wall. The gryphon wheeled and screeched overhead. The sun beat on the men's armor. The column spread out into a long line, eight horses deep, and moved forward at a canter. The yellow banner of the Kirmaz-Ja floated over the head of his standard bearer.

Sayyed hesitated a moment; then he unrolled something he had brought with him. A gold clan cloak spread over his knees. He fastened it on, glad at last to be able to wear it openly and proudly before the Turics. A flash of color caught his eye, and he turned his head to see Helmar pinning a cloak to her own shoulders. The cloak did not surprise him, since the Clannad had been clan at one time, but its color did. Bright and bold

and fiery red, Helmar wore the color of Clan Corin. He
gaped at her, wondering why she had chosen that
color; then she drew her sword in a signal to her riders
and yelled a piercing war cry that was immediately
echoed by a bellowed Turic command.

The horses, Turic and Hunnuli alike, stretched out
their necks, pinned back their ears, and sprang forward
into a gallop straight toward the gates of Cangora.
Horns blared on the city walls. The tribesmen and Clannad answered back with horns of their own that sang a
challenge that reverberated throughout the city. The
Turics lifted their voices in a wild, high-pitched ordula-
tion that sent chills down Helmar's back. The polished
gates, already closed and barred, gleamed like a beacon
in the sun.

The Clannad warriors, those most talented, drew
together behind Sayyed and Helmar. Others spread
themselves along the charging line. As the horses thundered closer to the city wall, the magic-wielders drew
on the omnipresent magic and shaped it to their will. At
Helmar's command, they fired as one at the massive
Copper Gates and at selected places along the wall.

The wards Sayyed had predicted were in the gateway, and they were even more powerful than the sorcerer had feared, yet they had never been meant to
withstand the sustained power of so much magic. The
wards groaned and sparked and held for several precious minutes until at last, in a thunderous explosion,
they gave way, and the attackers' magic blew out huge
sections of the towers on either side of the gate. The
copper doors themselves sagged and slowly toppled to
the ground in a resounding boom. Other sorcerers
breached the wall in two more places, opening new
entrances into the city.

The Kirmaz men roared with triumph and charged to
the breaches. The Clannad followed more slowly. They
had expended much strength fighting the gryphon and

destroying the wards, and they were starting to tire.

Stunned by the blasts, Zukhara's forces hesitated a few vital minutes, allowing the attackers to gain a foothold just inside the wall. The Fel Azureth, already accustomed to Zukhara's sorcery, recovered first and rallied their forces into action. Men from every quarter of the city rushed to beat back the invaders at the wall. All too soon the Kirmaz-Ja's charge bogged down under the overwhelming numbers of rebel troops that surrounded them. The warriors were forced to dismount and fight hand to hand in a vicious, bloody struggle to maintain their positions. Archers fired down on them from sections of the wall and buildings nearby. Swordsmen charged their defenses. A small mangonel was brought down the main avenue and used to batter the Kirmaz-Ja's force with chunks of rock and deadly spiked balls.

Only the sorcerers of the Clannad kept the tribesmen from being decimated. They were spread out among the three attacking groups along the wall, and they desperately worked to deflect missiles, provide cover fire, and protect the loyalists as best they could with defensive shields of energy. But the magic-wielders were tiring from the unending struggle. A few had already had to stop and rely on their swords for protection; several had already been killed.

In the Kirmaz-Ja's troop, Sayyed felt his energy flagging. He had not imagined the Gryphon's forces would be so relentless. They pushed forward, regardless of the cost, and slowly but steadily wore down the loyal Turics. Try as they might, the Kirmaz could not move forward or backward. They were trapped in a steadily shrinking circle that could end only in death.

16

The war song of the horns soared up the mountain's bay, carrying farther and longer and louder than any other sound from the battle at the city wall. The citizens heard it in the streets and in their houses. Some answered the call and marched down to join in the fighting on one side or the other; some listened to it and barred their shops and homes.

One boy, dressed as a beggar, lifted his head for the blink of an eye, the mindless grin on his face slipping to reveal a shining flash of excitement. Clutching his bowl, he ambled up the road, closer to the palace.

The music soared on ever higher and lapped against the high walls of the palace where the Gryphon's guards heard it and readied themselves—just in case.

Zukhara paused once in his preparations and recognized the horn music for what it was. The puny loyalist force had somehow evaded his gryphon and come knocking at his door. Let them knock, he sneered. His army and his gryphon would soon annihilate them. He had more important things to do this day of days.

In her room high in one of the palace wings, Kelene flung open her window and leaned out on the sill. "Listen, Mother!"

Gabria joined her on the window seat. Her smile lit even her dark-ringed eyes. "They're coming," she murmured.

Kelene stared down toward the gates, hoping to catch a glimpse of something or someone, but all she saw were the sandstone buildings marching down the slope to the distant wall, where smoke drifted above a few rooftops. A winged shape floating over the lower city caused her to catch her breath, and her fingers gripped the sill. "The gryphon. He's set the gryphon on them," she cried, torn between her fear for the attackers and for the gryphon. She hadn't seen the wild creature since Zukhara locked her and Gabria in their room, and Amara only knew what he had done to the beast since then.

"She will be unharmed," Zukhara's voice said from the doorway. "I would not endanger a thing so precious without some protection."

Kelene spun around, ready to heap four days' worth of frustration and anger on his head, when she saw him and nearly choked on her words. The counselor stood in the doorway in front of a retinue of priests, officers, and supporters. He wore ceremonial robes of royal blue velvet tipped with white fur and decorated with hand-sewn pearls and silver threads. A silver mantle draped his broad shoulders, and a simple crown ringed his jet-black hair. Tall, slim, and elegant, he looked to all who beheld him the quintessential monarch. Only the icy glitter of his impersonal eyes gave any hint of the cruelty beneath.

"Are you ready, ladies?" he said without preamble. He held out his hand to Kelene.

Kelene forced back her temper and did not demur. She was dressed now in a red gown trimmed in gold, ready for whatever would come. The sorceresses looked at one another in silent understanding, and Kelene gave her mother an almost infinitesimal nod. She ignored Zukhara's hand and took Gabria's arm instead to help her mother out the door. They walked down several flights of stairs and to the south end of the palace, where the throne room sat in sunlit splendor.

The room was part of the oldest wing of the palace, built nearly three hundred years before Zukhara's time. Its architect had used white stone to build the walls and designed the floor into a mosaic of tiny tiles of lapis lazuli, agate, and marble. Delicately carved buttresses held up a vaulted roof tinted black and ornamented with paintings in blue, white, and silver to represent the firmament—from whence came the name, the Celestial Throne. Between the buttresses were long, narrow windows that had been thrown open to the morning sunlight and wind. Light poured in brilliant bars into the room, reflecting off the gleaming floors and shining on the great sun throne of the Shar-Ja.

Hunkered over a broad dais, the heavy wooden seat was covered entirely in beaten gold that reverent hands had polished to a brilliant sheen. In the wall behind it was a huge, round stained-glass window that depicted a golden sun. Blue hangings were draped above the throne, and two men, dressed in the blue of the Shar-Ja's personal guard, stood beside it. It wasn't until Kelene had passed through the shafts of sunlight and stood at the foot of the throne that she realized the two guards were dead and merely propped there before they accompanied their slain ruler to his grave.

She closed her eyes. She didn't know if the clan gods would be present among a people who did not believe in them, but she prayed fervently that Amara could hear her plea. "Help me find the right moment," she silently begged the mother goddess.

Zukhara's voice startled her out of her reverie. "Welcome, Shar-Ja. Come, sit on your throne."

Three men entered from the big double doors. Two were garbed in the black and gold of the Fel Azureth, the other was the Shar-Ja, struggling to stay on his feet. They hustled the old man up the steps of the dais, set him on the throne, and tied his arms to the armrests.

The priests with Zukhara set quickly to work, lighting pots of incense and sprinkling the throne with water and sand to bless the proceedings in the name of Shahr, the Living God, and his prophet Sargun. Their chanting filled the room with their low pitched voices.

A small crowd of servants, Fel Azureth, and spectators from the city began to gather in the throne room near the entrance to witness the ancient rites. No one paid any attention to the boy in the stolen shirt and baggy pants who slipped into the rear of the crowd to see what was happening.

The priests ended their prayers and blessings for the throne and paused before beginning the next rite to purify the Shar-Ja for death. In that brief moment of aching silence, Kelene strained to hear something, anything, outside that could help her choose her moment to act. Her heart skipped a beat. She tried not to react, but her fingers tightened around Gabria's arm. The chanting began again and drowned out anything she could have heard on the wind. But it had been there, she would swear to it. Faint and far away she had heard the unmistakable clarion call of the Clan horns.

* * * * *

The horns sounded again, although Kelene did not hear it that time, on the heights of the caravan road above the valley. Pure and sweet and powerful as the north wind, their music rolled down the dale and washed over the city wall. Those on the battlements and in the towers heard the horns and hesitated. Those on the ground locked in the wild melee could not hear the song over the clash of weapons, the frenzied shouts of fighting men, and the screams of the dying.

But Afer heard it. His great head went up and his ears swept forward. He neighed a trumpeting call over the noise of the fighting. *They come!* he cried to all who could understand.

Sayyed and the warriors of the Clannad took heart and passed the word to the Turics. "The clans are coming!"

High on the fortifying wall men shouted, and several horns blew a warning. Surprised, the Gryphon's army hesitated and drew back a step to see what was causing the uproar. Nearly everyone who could snatched that pause to look out through the gaping holes in the wall.

A dark line of horsemen stretched across the valley, coming at a breakneck gallop. The sun glittered on their spears. Their numbers were obscured by the dust that billowed up from the horses' pounding hooves, but Zukhara's forces did not need to count. The colorful banners of the clan chieftains in the forefront and the four black Hunnuli horses in the lead were enough to make them blanch.

"Back!" bellowed Mohadan to his men. "Get out of the way!"

Frantically the Kirmaz and the Clannad grabbed their horses and their wounded and scrambled to get out of the way of the charging clan werods. The Fel Azureth pulled back too, and rallied their men to barricade the streets.

Abruptly the air reverberated with the heart-stopping war cries of all eleven clans. The ground trembled under the hooves of the horses. With lightning preci-sion, the line lowered its spears and split into three groups, one for each breach, and pounded through the gaps in the city wall. Lord Athlone and Rafnir led the horsemen through the ruined gateway and smashed head-on into the defenders' lines. The Fel Azureth could not hold. Although the clansmen were fewer in numbers and weary from days of relentless travel, their ferocity and momentum carried them irresistibly over the enemy. The spears gave way to swords and battle-axes, and the battle was joined.

Mohadan gave a shout to his men, and the Kirmaz plunged back into the fight. The Clannad, weary from the magic they had wielded, followed close behind.

Many of the Gryphon's volunteers broke and ran under the combined assault of tribesmen and clansmen, but the trained fanatics of the Fel Azureth had their master's orders: hold the city at all costs. They begrudgingly fell back before the werods and the Turic loyalists. They regrouped, fought, and regrouped again, struggling against every step they took backward. Yet even they could not withstand the power of the clan sorcerers for long. Backed by the riders of the Clannad, Lord Athlone, Rafnir, Gaalney, Morad, and Sayyed pounded their way slowly but steadily up the streets of Cangora toward the Shar-Ja's palace.

Helmar rode with the clan sorcerers for a short while as the fighting swept into the streets; then gradually she began to fall back. A strange sense of fear and urgency settled in the pit of her stomach. She shot a look up the broad avenue that she knew led toward the palace. Lady Gabria was up there—a woman she had never met, but the only woman left in the entire population of clanspeople who was of direct lineage to the Corin Clan. She was also a link in the tragedy of the Purge that had massacred so many magic-wielders. To Helmar, that link was vitally important.

She glanced up the road again. The clansmen were moving steadily closer to the palace, but not fast enough.

Someone should get there faster in case Zukhara panicked and disposed of his prisoners. A shadow swept over the ground, and she saw the gryphon winging toward the upper levels of the city where the palace lolled at the feet of the massive stone bastion.

Demira, Helmar remembered. Where is Demira?

"Marron, can you call the winged mare? Is she close?"

There. She is above the walls, responded the white mare. *She follows the gryphon.*

Helmar followed Marron's directions and saw Demira not too far away. "Call her! Tell her I need her! Please, my beauty. She can carry me above the fighting to Kelene and Gabria."

Marron understood and obeyed. She neighed a pealing call that reached over the battle and caught Demira's ear.

Helmar cast an apologetic glance at Sayyed, who was fighting by Lord Athlone's side, and swiftly ducked Marron down a side alley that was momentarily clear.

No one saw her go but Rapinor. Startled by her abrupt departure, he turned his horse to follow. From out of an open window, a man leaned out with a cocked crossbow and fired it wildly into the struggling men below. The swordsman, intent on following his chief, did not see the quarrel until it embedded in his chest. He looked down at it, feeling rather silly, and slowly toppled from his stricken Hunnuli.

Helmar went on, unaware of Rapinor's fate. She and Marron found an open square wide enough for Demira to land. As soon as the mare touched down, Helmar explained what she wanted. Demira's reply was immediate. The chief climbed onto her back, grabbed a handful of mane, and held on while Demira cantered forward into her take-off.

Marron watched the direction they went. Helmar had not told her to stay or go, so she scudded after them like a cloud blown on a stormy wind.

* * * * *

In the celestial throne room of the Shar-Ja, the spectators were growing restive. The breeze that wafted in the open windows blew a faint clamor of war from the city below that disturbed the sacred dignity of the rites. Only the Shar-Ja and Zukhara seemed unaware of the increasing din.

The ceremony had reached the moment that signaled the death of the current monarch. The sword for the beheading had been blessed, and the priests stood by with a basket for the head and wrappings for the body. A soldier stepped behind the Shar-Ja's throne and pulled Rassidar's head up and back to expose his neck.

Zukhara grasped the hilt of the sword with both hands. It was a two-handed broadsword of great weight and antiquity, yet he handled it as skillfully as a master. His eyes on the Shar-Ja, he walked to the throne and raised the sword over his shoulder.

A boy, of no more than thirteen years, darted around the crowd. He drew back his arm and, with the accuracy earned from months of practice, fired a rock from a slingshot at Zukhara's head. The missile missed the Gryphon's temple by a mere inch and hit instead just above his right eyebrow. The man staggered from the surprise and pain of the blow; the sword fell from his hand and clanged on the floor.

Swift as a striking hawk, Kelene snatched the moment. She took two steps away from Gabria, gathered the magic around her, and aimed a sphere of energy at the ivory ward beneath Zukhara's robes. The power hit him hard and knocked him into the dead guard by the throne, but it wasn't quite enough to break the ward. Furiously he lashed back, sending a fistful of stunning blasts at Kelene and the boy. The people in the crowd screamed and ran for safety.

The first blow took Kelene in the chest before she

could defend herself and sent her spinning against the wall. She sagged to the floor, unconscious. Gabria choked on a cry and ran to her side. A second ball of energy caught Tassilio and threw him skidding across the floor.

The priests and the guards looked at each other uneasily. Zukhara spat a curse. Blood dripped down his face from a cut on his forehead. He yanked out his dagger to stab the Shar-Ja, and another rock cracked into his arm.

Tassilio knelt on the floor, looking very much alive and very aware of what he was doing. He pulled a knotted piece of rope out of his shirt and jiggled it tauntingly at the Gryphon.

Zukhara recognized it for what it was. His face grew livid. "Sandrat!" hissed Zukhara.

"That's right!" Tassilio yelled fiercely, sliding another rock into his slingshot. "A bastard, just like you! But now I am Shar-Yon and that is my father, the rightfully ordained ruler of the Turic. You are nothing but a traitor, Zukhara, and I will see you dead!"

The Gryphon raised his hand to strike down the loathsome boy. With surprising strength, the Shar-Ja twisted his body and lashed out with his foot. He caught Zukhara on the back of the knee and knocked the leg out from under the usurper. The Gryphon fell heavily down the stairs. He pushed himself upright, shaken but uninjured, and glared malevolently at the old ruler.

"They're coming," a hollow voice intoned close by.

Zukhara spun around and saw Gabria standing upright and staring blankly at the large double doors. From somewhere in the corridors came the sounds of screams and the hard clatter of approaching hooves. He wasted no more time. He dashed to Kelene and lifted her over his shoulder. Gabria was too weakened by the poison to fight him off, and a backhanded blow knocked her to the floor. In a daze she watched him go behind the throne and disappear; then hoofbeats pounded outside the room and the doors crashed open.

A red-haired woman in full battle dress and wearing a red cloak rode in on a black winged Hunnuli. Gabria smiled through her tears. The horse wasn't white, but Demira was quite good enough.

The remaining priests and Fel Azureth must have thought so, too, for they took one look at the furious sorceress and fled, leaving only Tassilio and the Shar-Ja with the two women. Tassilio ran to his father and used the dagger to cut him free. Demira skidded to a stop on the patterned floor and Helmar slid off.

Her heart in her throat, the chief ran to Gabria's prostrate form. The older sorceress stared at the stranger as if she were still a vision. Her hand grasped the red cloak. Helmar was shocked by Gabria's thin body and shadowed face. Blood oozed from a cut on her cheek, and her hands trembled. But anger smoldered deep in Gabria's jewel-green eyes, and she managed to push herself to a sitting position.

"You," Gabria gasped. "By Amara's grace, where did you come from?"

Helmar steadied her and helped her rise to her feet. "Out of the past, Lady Gabria."

Kelene! Where is Kelene? Demira neighed. She clattered around the room to look for her rider.

Tassilio guessed what she wanted. "He took her out that way," he cried and pointed to the hanging blue drapes behind the throne. He hurried around to show her the door and found it closed and locked.

The Shar-Ja leaned his frail weight heavily on the throne and told them, "It leads to the courtyard outside and the path to the temple. He probably had horses waiting to take them up to the pinnacle."

Tassilio tried to work the lock; Demira tried to kick in the door. But it was wasted effort. The door was solidly barred. Frustrated, the mare took another circuit around the room and saw there were no more doors and the windows were too narrow for her bulky wings. Before anyone could gainsay her, she suddenly turned and cantered out the double doors to find another way to reach Kelene.

"He's taking her to the citadel," Gabria said fiercely. "She needs more help than Demira can give her."

The sounds of fighting had grown nearer since Helmar's arrival, yet it had not lessened in intensity. The Fel Azureth fought like wolves and still had the slight advantage of numbers and familiarity with the city streets. It could still be a while before Lord Athlone or Sayyed or Rafnir could subdue them enough to come and help, and that might be too late.

"Take me up there," Gabria pleaded.

Helmar exhaled sharply. "But, Lady, you are too weak. If you tried to use magic—"

"I am too weak to destroy him. Not to distract him."

More hooves pounded in the hallway, and Tassilio's dog bounded into the room just ahead of Marron. Barking and wiggling, the dog leaped delightedly on the grinning boy.

"Cal, I told you to stay outside," the boy laughed.

Well, you did not tell me to stay, Marron huffed to the chief. She was breathing heavily and hot with sweat.

"And glad I am I didn't," exclaimed Helmar. "We must still try to free Kelene."

"A *white* Hunnuli," Gabria breathed. She held her hands out to the mare and let Marron sniff her hands and face.

Helmar snapped her fingers. "Nara! We need her. Is she still alive?"

"Zukhara may be many things," replied the Shar-Ja dryly, "but he is not wasteful of things that are valuable to him. I heard he has the black Hunnuli under guard in the palace stables."

Marron stamped a hoof. *I will get her. I saw the stables on my way up here.*

"Pity the guards who stand in the way of that horse," the Shar-Ja said in wonder as he watched her go.

Tassilio ran out then and came back with a pitcher of water. "It was all I could find," he said, offering some to the women and his father.

The Shar-Ja took a sip of the proffered drink and smiled at his son. "By the Living God, where have you been? Zukhara told me you were dead, too."

Tassilio blushed at the warmth in his father's voice, and for once the voluble boy was tongue-tied. He grinned and shifted from foot to foot. "I was helping my friends," was all he could say.

The Hunnuli mares came back, sooner than the women expected. *The guards were gone,* Marron explained. *The palace is almost empty. Everyone has either left to fight or to hide.*

Nara said nothing but pushed close to Gabria, sniffing her all over and whickering her joy and relief. Whatever sedative Zukhara had given her had worn off, and she looked thin but fit. Gabria threw her arms around her mare's neck, burying her face in the black mane. With Helmar's help, she climbed onto Nara's broad back.

"When Sayyed and the others reach here, tell them where we went," Helmar told Tassilio.

The boy nodded fiercely. "Take the first left hallway, go to the end, and turn right. There are doors there that lead outside."

A quick salute and the sorceresses were gone, their Hunnuli's hooves echoing away down the corridors. Tassilio softly closed and locked the doors behind them and returned to wait with his father.

Helmar led the way along the opulent hallways. She noticed Marron was right—the palace seemed deserted. No one tried to stop them as they trotted the horses through the corridors.

Tassilio's directions proved accurate, and the women found themselves out in the bright sunlight on a broad, grassy esplanade. In front of them the towering bastion of stone soared high into the blue sky. On its top, like a red and green crown, sat the temple of the prophet Sargun.

Built originally as a citadel, the redstone buildings had been consecrated as a monastery and a temple a few generations after the death of the holy prophet. It housed a magnificent library, gardens, the royal crypt for the Turic shar-jas and a population of perhaps one hundred contemplative monks and active priests. It was used by the Turics only in times of the most sacred rites. A narrow road rimmed by a stone fence zigzagged its way up the steep face to the top. There was no sign of Zukhara or Kelene anywhere, and nothing moved in the sky but a few wisps of clouds.

Marron and Nara hurried off the esplanade and found the beginning of the temple road at the end of a long courtyard. Together they trotted up the steep way.

17

Kelene was too groggy to understand what was happening. All her whirling mind could recognize was the pain in her chest and stomach and the difficulty of breathing. She concentrated on her lungs and the effort of pulling in the air. Her chest seemed so sluggish, even heavy, as if something were pressing it down. Her stomach hurt from something that pushed into it, making her nauseated. She seemed to be moving by some outer volition, certainly not on her own feet, and her head felt strangely heavy and swollen.

She opened her eyes and looked at something fuzzy and dark brown. Her vision rocked sickeningly, so she closed her eyes, took a slow breath, and tried again. This time her eyes focused a little better, and the brown, fuzzy blur became clearly a horse's belly. With that understanding came full realization. Zukhara had thrown her over a saddled horse and was leading it somewhere uphill.

Struggling did little good because he had tied her to the saddle. Those same Hunnuli hair ropes, Kelene thought sourly. She lay still and tried to sooth the pounding in her head while she waited to see what he would do. It wasn't easy. Zukhara seemed to be in a desperate hurry. He rode a second horse and cantered the mounts as often as he dared up the steep grade. By the time they reached the top of the incline, both horses were blowing and lathered in sweat. He urged them through a strong-looking gate and brought them to a rough stop in the cloistered courtyard at the main entrance to the citadel buildings.

Leaving the horses where they stood, he ran back to close the gates. Kelene could not see what he was doing, because he had his back to her, yet he seemed to take an inordinate amount of time just to lock a gate. Finally he came back, tugged Kelene off her mount, and carried her over his shoulder into the forecourt of the front entrance. Several priests ran to meet him.

"Where is the Tobba?" he roared at them. "Bring him to the Chamber of Unity."

Kelene's mind whirled. What did he intend to do? Didn't he realize his cause was lost? The Shar-Ja was still alive. Cangora was falling into the hands of the loyalists, and his fanatics were being defeated. "What are you doing?" she said aloud.

The Gryphon heaved her over onto her feet and held her bound arms in an iron grip. "I failed to kill the Shar-Ja today, but without the antidote, he will die shortly anyway. The throne will still be mine. I am Fel Karak, the Gryphon, the anointed servant of the Living God!" he ranted. "And you are still my chosen wife." He wrenched her forward and dragged her with him through the corridors of the outlying buildings toward the inner sanctum of the temple grounds.

The sorceress struggled to bring her thoughts under control. It was time to act, to fight back, but her head and chest hurt so much from the earlier arcane blow that her wits felt addled and her vision was still blurry. She could hardly form a single coherent thought, let alone a strategy to defeat a sorcerer with a functioning ward. She staggered after Zukhara, paying little attention to where they were going.

After what seemed a very long time to Kelene, Zukhara pushed open a door adorned with vines and wooden roses and tugged her into the Chamber of Unity, the chapel used by members of the royal family for marriages and betrothals. Zukhara did not bother to explain anything to his captive, he simply placed her in front of a tiny, wizened old man and wrapped his fingers around her wrist.

The old man, the Tobba, was the spiritual leader of the community of priests and monks at the temple. He was very familiar with the Gryphon and his methods, and he did not even murmur a complaint at the hasty and unorthodox arrival of the man and his intended bride. He stretched out his skinny arms and lifted his voice in supplication to Shahr a   texts of Turic matrimony.

Kelene did not need a translator to tell her what the priest was doing, nor a witness to interpret the self-satisfied smirk on Zukhara's face. She had to get away from him now, before she became married to him in the eyes of Turic law. She glanced around the room, hoping for some bit of inspiration. She knew she was not strong enough to fight Zukhara physically. He was a powerful, athletic man who could overpower her all too easily. Nor could she use spells against his body as long as he wore the ivory ward. Perhaps, she thought, she could manipulate something around him that would give her a chance to slip away. She knew him well enough by now to know he would come after her, and she hoped he would. She still wanted the antidote hanging around his neck. She needed time only to untie her hands, clear her mind, and perhaps get some help.

The Chamber of Unity, she noticed, was more like a garden than a room. The walls were hung with pink silk handpainted with delicate white roses. Living roses grew in pots in every corner, along a small ornate altar, and in hanging baskets around the ceiling. To the right, wide doors sat open to the sunny warmth of a magnificent rose garden where rosebushes of every color filled the air with a sweet, heady fragrance. In the quiet of the afternoon, Kelene heard the gentle hum of bees.

A slow smile tickled the corners of Kelene's mouth. A spell came to mind, a simple, ordinary, everyday spell from Lady Jeneve's book: a spell to attract bees to a new hive. She breathed the words to herself and worked the magic into a gentle spell; then she shifted just enough to let her fingers touch the edge of Zukhara's ceremonial robes.

The magic worked faster than she thought it would. The Tobba had just finished his first set of prayers and ___ ___ ___ strip of linen over their joined wrists when ___ ___ ___ ___ ___ .he room and settled on the ___ ___ ___ ___ cheek. He brushed it away only to have ten more suddenly buzz about his head. All at once the room was filled with honey bees whirling in a cloud around Zukhara.

The Tobba fell back in a panic. The usurper yelled, waving frantically with his free hand at the determined insects. His flailing arm angered them, and they flew at him aggressively. He pulled his hand off Kelene to slap at several bees crawling down his neck, and she hoisted her long skirts and bolted into the garden.

Zukhara's furious shout rang out behind her, but he was too occupied with the bees to give immediate chase. She raced down the grassy paths between the raised beds of roses until she was completely out of

level of the temple and flew up on racing feet. She caught a glimpse of men running toward her through the gardens and ran along the outside walkway to the stairs going up to the second story. The steps were broad and solid and easy to navigate, but they were staggered along the side of the temple rather than climbing in a straight line up to the top.

A sudden blast of the Trymmian force exploded on the steps beside her. Kelene stumbled up to the next level, turned, and stared down the stairs.

Zukhara stood on the level below, glaring up at her. His hand was raised to fire again. "Come down, my lady. There is no escape."

Kelene did the only thing she knew he could not tolerate. She laughed at him.

His eyes ablaze, he fired a sphere of the Trymmian force directly at her. This time a red shield of defensive energy crackled into existence in front of her. The blue sphere ricocheted off into a wall. The sorceress turned and ran to the next set of stairs, her shield still intact and hovering close behind. Zukhara hurried after her. Temple guards came up behind him, but he waved them back. The sorceress was *his* prey.

The hunt continued up the side of the temple, like a crackling, booming thunderstorm. Kelene led Zukhara on, taunting him into using his power. Zukhara was strong, Kelene knew, virtually invincible as long as he wore the ward. On the other hand, he was arrogant and inexperienced. His ward would be little protection against his own magic if he lost control of his spells.

On the fifth level she slowed down and shot a few bolts of power at him, which he easily dodged. Sneering, he instantly returned a barrage intended to shatter her shield. Kelene gritted her teeth and intensified her defenses, then rushed on ahead of him. She climbed up and up, ever higher along the sides of the temple, past the hanging garden boxes full of ferns, flowers, and tiny trees. She was panting by the time she climbed to the ninth story. Her legs hurt after so many days of inactivity, and the pain had returned to her head. She hoped Zukhara was as tired as she felt, but when she looked back, he was striding up the stairs at the same relentless pace. Kelene stopped to catch her breath, and she waited at the foot of the last staircase for the Gryphon to reach her level.

He bared his teeth in a wolfish smile when he saw her. "There is nowhere left to go, Clanswoman. Submit to me before I am forced to break you."

"I'd rather break this," she retorted and pointed her hand toward him. Instead of firing at him, though, she ⟨...⟩ased a blast at a huge plant box hanging over his ⟨...⟩. The wood exploded in a hail of shattered frag⟨...⟩ and bits of plant. Zukhara was knocked ba⟨...⟩ the shock of the blast.

Ins⟨...⟩ Kelene lowered her aim and sent a sustained, specific beam of energy toward his chest, where his ward lay concealed. She felt a pressure there, fighting against her power, and she concentrated, forcing her magic deep into the intricate curves of the ward to find the crack and break it open. Blinded by the shower of dirt, Zukhara struggled to regain his balance and fight off her assault with a shield of his own.

Something shifted beneath the pressure of Kelene's spell. The ivory ward, although designed to resist intense amounts of magical energy, had been weakened by the crack in its surface, and now it wavered in the force of Kelene's power. The crack widened.

Zukhara hunched over, his arms wrapped around himself to protect his ward as he tried to form the shield. Kelene pushed harder. She imagined her hand closing around the pale white ball, the feel of its delicate weight on her palm, and the satisfying crunch as she crushed it in her fist.

There was an audible pop. In disbelief, the Turic

pulled the silver chain out of his robes and gaped at the shattered bits that fell out onto his hand.

Kelene stared avidly at the small silver tube that still hung on his chain. She did not want him to take revenge on the loss of his ward by destroying the antidote, so she moved quickly to distract him. "Sorcerer!" she sneered. "Ha! Now we're even. No false protection. Only our own skills. Try to break me now." And she dashed up the stairs to the very top, the roof of the temple.

Her ruse worked. Zukhara dropped the broken ward and sprinted after her. They came off the stairs onto the large flat, tiled roof. There were no potted plants growing up here. It was bare and unadorned and open to the vast sky. A small altar faced the east, and several stone benches sat along the low wall that framed the roof placed there for the priests who came to study the stars. The view of the mountains was breathtaking.

Kelene ran to the far end to look for another set of stairs in case she needed an escape. Instead of stairs, she discovered that the end of the temple edged the rim of the rocky pinnacle. From the temple's lowest floor, the ground fell away in a precipice that dropped nearly a thousand feet to the valley floor. Kelene sucked in a lungful of air and whirled to face Zukhara. He had finally completed his shield and stood across from her, enclosed in a dome of glowing energy.

Kelene pursed her lips. He was showing his inexperience. A full dome of shielding required a great expenditure of strength and concentration to maintain and was hard to move about. Kelene had learned that a simple shield, even one as small as the battle shields carried by warriors, was easier to use and needed less attention to keep intact.

Her thoughts stopped short with a jerk. What was that? Something, a presence, nudged her awareness. Not Demira. Then a high-pitched screeching cry sounded overhead, and a large golden shape wheeled over her.

The gryphon. The creature screeched again in a jarring, nerve-racking tone that sounded both angry and annoyed. She curved her wings and gracefully back-winged onto the roof between Zukhara and Kelene. Crouched there, she hissed at them both. Her ears lay flat, and the hairs rose on the back of her neck.

Kelene stared at her, outraged. "What have you done to her?" she cried to Zukhara.

That the gryphon had been abused was obvious. Her ribs poked out of her golden sides; her coat was matted and dirty. Raw wounds encircled her legs where she had fought against her chains, and red, oozing welts covered her face and shoulders. Worst of all were the singed circles on her sides where someone had used the Trymmian force against her. Kelene remembered seeing the gryphon earlier, flying over the city wall when the fighting started, but if any sorcerers had been with the attackers, she doubted they had caused the damage to the gryphon. The burn wounds looked several days old and were already crusted over.

Something else looked different, too. The gryphon wore a new collar, intricately woven in knots. A ward, Kelene decided; Zukhara had sent the gryphon out with a ward.

As if to confirm her suspicions, Zukhara snapped a command in Turic to the gryphon. She snarled, a low menacing sound of fury. He shouted again and raised his fist. The gryphon winced away. She looked at Kelene, and if there was any recognition in her slitted eyes, it died when Zukhara evaporated his dome and fired a blast of magic at the creature.

The gryphon screamed, more from fear than pain since the collar protected her from most of the blast, and she pounced at Kelene, her talons extended and her teeth bared. The sorceress dove out from under her.

"No, girl," Kelene cried. The sorceress held out her hands to signal peace, but the gryphon jumped toward her again. Kelene swerved sideways too late. The animal's paw caught her back, and she fell sprawling near a corner of the low wall.

Zukhara laughed, a low sound as full of menace as the gryphon's growl. He formed spheres of the Trymmian force and fired at Kelene to drive her into the corner. She scrambled back until her legs banged into the stone wall. She flicked up a shielding dome against Zukhara's bombardment and the gryphon's teeth, and tried desperately to think of some way out of the trap. She could not stand there forever holding up an arcane shield, yet she could not fend off the gryphon and fight Zukhara at the same time. She did not want to hurt the gryphon either, unless she was forced to.

The creature snapped at the red power, then ripped her claws over the length of the small dome. Her breath hissed. Her lips curled back from her long incisors. She paced around, staying well away from Zukhara.

All at once another dark shadow scudded across the roof. Kelene shot a look at the sky and saw Demira silently stretch out her long forelegs and dive directly at the gryphon. The winged beast half turned, startled by the mare's appearance, and caught a kick on her face from the horse's back hooves. The kick did not injure her since Demira had no real force behind such a maneuver in midair, but it hurt, and it infuriated the already angry gryphon. She sprang off the roof and streaked after Demira.

"Oh, gods," Kelene panted. She knew the Hunnuli had only a slim chance to evade the flying predator. For one desperate and blind instant she turned her gaze to follow Demira's escape and forgot about Zukhara.

He lashed out instantly with a spell that did not touch her or even her shield. It landed on the square of tiles beneath her feet and transformed the slate to a sheet of glaring ice. Caught unprepared, Kelene found her feet slipping on the sheer surface. She fell, smashing her head against the low wall.

Two blows in one afternoon were too much, her mind thought through a haze of pain and whirling bits of light. Her shield faltered and went out. She knew she should renew it, but at that moment she could not remember how. Zukhara's face swam in front of her. It smiled at her with such a gloating smirk that it would have made her queasy if she weren't already feeling very ill. She felt his hand on her face and sensed her death in the hatred and fury that steamed from his touch.

"Zukhara!"

Kelene blinked in surprise. She hadn't said anything.

The Turic flinched as if something had struck him. With an oath, he jumped to his feet and faced Gabria. The sorceress stood at the top of the stairs, looking like one of the plague dead. Her hair hung loose, as wild as any hag's. Her face was ghastly white and streaked with dark rivulets of blood. More blood smeared her torn and tattered skirts.

Zukhara, in his arrogance, rejoiced. Gabria could not fight him; she was too weak, yet she could watch her daughter be crushed beneath his power. He would not kill Kelene's body; he still wanted that for breeding. He would destroy her personality, the spirit that made her so unique. He leaned over Kelene again and lowered his hand to her face.

The little silver tube hanging loose on its chain dangled forgotten from his neck. It twisted and danced in a gleam of sunlight and shone like a tiny sun in Kelene's blurry vision. It beckoned to her hand to reach for it. Just as Zukhara's fingers touched her cheek, Kelene grasped the tube and yanked hard. The chain dug into the man's neck and broke with a snap.

He yelled in fury but, before he could snatch the tube back, Gabria formed a spell—a simple, devilish one that required little strength from her failing body—

and flung it at him. A small green ball of power flew through the space between them and smacked into his shoulder. It clung there like a bur. Immediately tiny tendrils of green energy burst out of the ball and skittered over his torso like streams of angry fire ants.

Zukhara arched backward, stunned by the itching pain of the magic. He scratched frantically at his arms and chest and back; he pulled at the little green bur, and all his efforts only made the burning stings worse. He staggered back from Kelene to the wall and screamed for the gryphon.

Free of his weight, Kelene grabbed the stones by her head and hauled herself to her knees. She was just high enough to peer over the low wall and see the ground below, where the gryphon crouched close to the temple wall, flanked by two furious Hunnuli mares. Demira had been clever enough to realize she could not outfly the winged predator. As soon as she saw her mother, Nara, approaching the temple, she had landed and sought the older mare's help. Now the gryphon had two large and powerful horses to contend with, and she was discovering they were not such easy prey. At Zukhara's bellow, she bounced into the air and beat her way up to the top of the temple.

Kelene saw her coming. Summoning all her strength, she willed her hurting body to walk toward Gabria. Her mother stumbled toward her. They met in the middle, and their arms went around one another.

Zukhara finally pried the green bur off his shoulder. He threw it to the ground and stamped on it. "Kill them now!" he shrieked at the gryphon. The creature wheeled, reluctant to obey the man's demands. She hissed at him and slowly came to land near the women. "Kill them I said!" he screamed again.

Kelene snatched at the one chance she had left. Letting go of Gabria, she threw herself at the gryphon and caught one of its long legs. Surprised, the animal jerked back, but Kelene held tight to the warm, furry limb. Her fingers clasped tight against the skin. Using her empathic talent, she reached into the gryphon's turbulent mind to touch the bond of familiarity she had forged during their time together. The gryphon growled a rumbling note.

It's all right, beautiful one, she sent softly, reassuringly. *It is me. I will not hurt you. I promised to help free you, remember?*

The creature's growl slowed and faded. Her nose sniffed Kelene's scent.

"No!" Zukhara yelled at her. "You are mine! You will do as *I* say. Now kill them both." Overcome with embittered rage, he lashed out at the gryphon with a whiplash of fiery magic.

Without the ward the spell would have killed her. As it was, the lash caught the gryphon on the haunches like a flick of lightning. She reared up, breaking away from Kelene, and screamed a shivering cry. Her wings beat the air; her eyes burned with white-hot fire. In one powerful leap she sprang at the man she hated above all other men.

Zukhara's arrogance proved his undoing, for even as he saw her come he could not believe the gryphon sent to him by his god would turn on him. By the time his brain thought to react, her powerful talons had ripped into his stomach. He screamed once before she crushed his head.

Kelene turned her eyes away. She walked back to Gabria, and for a time they simply stood together in utter exhaustion. Relief, release, and happiness formed a potent brew of feelings that began to revive Kelene's battered form, and she became aware of several details. The first thing she pointed out was the blood on Gabria's face and clothes.

"Most of it is not mine," Gabria said unhappily. "It is Helmar's and Marron's." She held up her hand to forestall Kelene's questions. "The tale is too long to explain now, but as soon as you're able, please go to them. Zukhara booby-trapped the citadel gate, and it blew up in their faces."

Kelene nodded. "There is only this; then we will go." She held up the silver tube she had torn from Zukhara's neck. "The antidote."

Years of aging dropped away from Gabria's face at the touch of a brilliant smile. With shaking hands she took the tube, unscrewed the top, and swallowed half the contents. "I will save the rest for the Shar-Ja," she said. "I could tell just by looking at him that he had been poisoned the same way."

"I hope it is enough. Amara only knows if there is any more."

A grumbling sound drew their attention back to the gryphon. Demira and Nara came clattering up the stairs, and the gryphon crouched, snarling at their presence.

Kelene skirted the remains of Zukhara's body and calmly patted the wild gryphon. Even hungry as she was, the creature had not tried to eat the man's corpse. Gently Kelene unfastened the collar on the gryphon's neck. Stroking her back, Kelene extended her magic into the gryphon to ease the pain of the animal's burns and injuries. *Thank you*, she told her. *That is twice you have saved me. I keep my promise. Go home and find your family.*

The gryphon's tufted ears snapped up and, without a backward glance, she leaped off the roof into the afternoon. Wild with joy, she called once and flew faster than the wind toward the western peaks. They watched her for a moment, until her golden shape disappeared in the distance.

Silently the sorceresses mounted their Hunnuli and left the temple roof, where Zukhara's trampled body lay alone and unmourned.

18

While they rode back to the front gate, Gabria told Kelene the little bit she knew about Helmar.

"A red cloak?" Kelene said in amazement. "Where did she come from? Do you think she is a Corin?"

"I don't know. All I can tell you is that she and her Hunnuli risked their lives for us, and I don't want to lose her now." Gabria's reply was iron-firm, a sure sign that her strength was starting to return.

Kelene said nothing else. She worked instead on her own condition to clear her battered mind, still the pain, and bolster her energies. By the time they reached the cloistered courtyard, her headache had eased from blinding agony to a dull ache that was tolerable, and her limbs felt strong enough to deal with what she had to do.

A small group of yellow-robed priests clustered under the shade of the arched cloister near the remains of the gate. Gabria went to them and gestured to Kelene.

The young sorceress slid carefully to the ground. She patted the mare, delighted beyond words to have her back. "Demira, I must ask one more favor. Please go back to the palace and find my healer's bag in our room. Third floor, west wing. And see if you can find Rafnir, too."

I will look for Sayyed, as well. I think he loves Helmar.

Kelene barely had time to register that surprising remark before Demira sprang aloft and dropped over the rim of the citadel's wall. Kelene hurried to help Gabria.

Priests from the temple had brought the unconscious woman to a resting place on a low cot out of the sun. They had been afraid to carry her any farther. A healer skilled in the arts of surgery and medicine had already begun the difficult task of stopping the bleeding from lacerations on her head, neck, and chest. Kelene looked at the bloodied face and marveled that the woman was still alive.

The healer said something in Turic, and Gabria made an understandable reply. The healer nodded to Kelene. She knelt down by Helmar's head and set to work. Although she did not speak very much Turic and the healer knew no Clannish, they were able to meld their efforts into a swift, efficient treatment. Kelene removed the wooden splinters and debris and cleaned the wounds while the healer priest deftly stitched the worst lacerations closed before the chief lost too much blood. It was a long, difficult process.

Helmar roused once and tried to twist away from the healer's sharp needle, but Kelene laid her fingers on the woman's forehead and eased her gently back to sleep. The Turic healer nodded with approval. They were nearly finished when Demira returned from the palace with Kelene's bag in her teeth and Tassilio on her back.

"Hajira and Mohadan are with Father, so I came to help," he announced, hopping off the mare's back. "Demira told us what happened. Lord Athlone, Rafnir, and Sayyed are on their way up."

Kelene smiled her thanks. "A gift for your help, Shar-Yon." She handed him the silver tube of antidote.

Recognition ignited Tassilio's face into an incandescent grin, and he quickly handed the precious vial to one of the priests. "Give this to my Father at once!" he commanded. "Tell him I will come as soon as my work here is done."

Kelene gratefully took her bag back to Helmar's bedside. Most of the immediate work to save Helmar had been done, but the woman faced a long siege before she could fully recover. Shock, blood loss, dehydration, and infection were side effects she would have to battle in the next few days. Fortunately she had suffered no broken bones, and as far as Kelene could tell, no internal injuries. Even so, neither Kelene nor the Turic healer who had helped her knew if Helmar would survive the devastating blast. Only time and her own strength could help her now.

To improve her patient's strength, Kelene brought out a carefully wrapped packet. Using some warm water brought by a monk, she made an infusion from a special combination of herbs that she always kept prepared and readily available in her bag. The recipe was an old one she had found in the ruins of Moy Tura, and its invigorating potency had helped restore many people to health. With Tassilio's help, she explained to the healer what it was, and he watched with interest while she mixed the tea with honey and dribbled it between Helmar's lips.

Kelene glanced around the courtyard for her mother and saw Gabria kneeling by something on the other side of the gate. Oh, gods, she had forgotten about the Hunnuli. She passed the cup to Tassilio and went to check on the horse.

Gabria had treated many wounds in her life, but she was the first to admit she was not a healer. It was apparent to Kelene as she joined her mother that the older woman felt overwhelmed by the extent of Marron's injuries. With one hand Gabria pressed a strip of cloth torn from her skirt over a gaping wound in the mare's chest and with the other tried to stem the flow of blood from a gash on the mare's neck.

Dismayed, Kelene dropped her bag and knelt beside the bloodied horse. The priests, assuming the mare was dead, had left her where she had fallen after the gate blew up, and she lay on her side, bleeding slowly into the dust from dozens of punctures, slashes, and abrasions.

"I don't think we can save her," Gabria said in a voice thick with tears. "She reared up and took the full force of the blow to save Helmar."

Kelene touched the mare's gray muzzle where the black skin showed through the short white hairs. The skin was warm and her eyelids flickered, but Marron was dangerously close to death. And if she died, Kelene knew Helmar would probably die, too.

"We need water, lots of it. Cloth, blankets, and a big bucket of hot water." She pointed to her bag. "If that tea helps humans, maybe it will help a Hunnuli, too."

Gabria fought down her worry and went to gather the things they would need. Demira and Nara stood close by Marron, their noses almost touching her. Kelene leaned forward to rest her cheek on the mare's face and said, "Marron?"

A flicker of consciousness flared in Kelene's mind—not the vibrant, alert thought of a healthy Hunnuli, but at least it meant Marron was still alive and, on a subconscious level, still aware. Kelene probed deeper into the horse's mind to reach her understanding. She extended her power over Marron's body, lessening her pain and soothing her fear.

Marron. I am Kelene, Demira's rider. Helmar is alive. Do you understand? The Hunnuli's thoughts burst brighter in recognition. *She is alive. But you must stay alive, too. Do you hear me? If you die, she will lose her will to fight. Please stay with us! We will take care of both of you.*

The mare's thoughts sparkled a weary acknowledgment, then slowly faded into the dim, pulsing glow of deep sleep.

Kelene heard horses approach, and she lifted her head to see one of the most welcome sights she would ever remember in her life: her father, her husband, and her father-in-law on their Hunnuli cantering almost neck and neck toward the citadel gates. Their three stallions slid to a stop, and the men dropped off in one unbroken movement.

Kelene stood up, took one step forward, and found herself engulfed in her husband's arms. She buried her face in his shoulder and held him as if she would never let him go. His clothes were filthy, spattered with blood and coated in dust, reeking of sweat and smoke. A dark beard framed his jaws, and his face was too thin, but Kelene thought she had never seen him look so wonderful.

Sayyed paused long enough to see she was safe; then he looked closely at Marron, and his face turned a sickly paste color. He ran into the courtyard to find Helmar. Afer joined Nara and Demira in their vigil over the white mare.

Lord Athlone came out of the gates, helping Gabria carry the water, buckets, and bandages. His clothes were as bad as Rafnir's, and his hair and beard were unkempt. His face was lined from days of worry, and his expression was sober after seeing Helmar. But underneath it all, like a light burning in a worn and weathered tent, glowed a joy too bright to mask. It was matched in its luminosity only by the happiness in Gabria's eyes. He set down his burdens and silently hugged his daughter. Words would come later when the wounded were cared for and the most immediate tasks were done.

With Gabria and Rafnir close by to help, Kelene settled down to the task of repairing Marron's torn chest and shoulders. She felt sometimes as if she were piecing together a shredded blanket of black skin, white hair, and too much red blood. It was a wonder the horse's jugular had not been punctured. The gods, Kelene decided, had kept their hands over Helmar and Marron.

When at last she was finished, Kelene felt worn to a single thread. Her hands shook as she slathered Marron's wounds with an ointment made to fight infection and keep the skin soft so the stitched wounds would heal without crippling scar tissue. If Marron survived, she would always carry scars, but Kelene wanted her to heal as unimpaired as possible.

Since they could not leave the mare lying in the road, the sorceress gradually roused Marron out of unconsciousness. Ever so gently, Afer and Nara nudged her onto her stomach, then helped her ease to her feet. Standing on either side of the swaying mare, they propped up her weight as she tottered into the citadel to the shady cloister near Helmar.

At Tassilio's insistence, the priests agreed to allow the chief and her Hunnuli to stay in the cloister where they could be close together. Straw was brought for Marron, and she lay down again, her eyes closed and her muzzle near Helmar's shoulder.

Kelene steeped a bucket of the restorative for the mare, leaving it where she could reach it without difficulty. She also fixed cups for herself, Gabria, and the three men. They all drank it gratefully.

Sayyed sat, like a man in a daze, beside Helmar. He wiped her face with a cool cloth and slowly fed her sips of her tonic, but a haunted shadow grayed his face, and his limbs were tensed with a terrible anxiety.

Gabria watched him worriedly. He had had that same look in the plague tent when he watched Tam die. She had no idea he had fallen so deeply in love with this woman—perhaps he hadn't either until now. But gods above, Gabria sighed, how would he survive if he lost another love? She leaned into the embrace of her own dearest husband and thanked Amara with all her heart for their reunion.

As soon as Helmar and Marron were as comfortable as they could be, Kelene found the nearest place to sit down and began to shake. Tears filled her eyes. Her strength was gone; her will was depleted. Her head pounded like an overworked drum. She had nothing left in mind or body but a strong desire to lie down and cry. Rafnir scooped her up in his arms. The last thing she remembered for a long time after that was the softness of a bed and the warmth of Rafnir's body as he held her close and comforted her to sleep.

She roused late in the afternoon of the following day in a chamber she soon learned was in the citadel. Rafnir had left, but Kelene was delighted to see a new clan tunic and skirt draped over the foot of the bed and a tray of stuffed meat rolls, cheese, grapes, and wine on the table. Kelene discovered she was ravenous. As soon as she had dressed and eaten, she hurried through the corridors to the front entrance. No one was there but Sayyed and his patients under the cloister. Twenty-four hours had brought little change to Helmar or her horse, and if Sayyed had left her side once, Kelene saw no sign of it. He still wore his filthy, rumpled clothes, and dark shadows circled his eyes from the lack of sleep.

Kelene kissed his forehead. "Thank you for coming after us," she said.

He cracked a semblance of a smile. "You led us on a merry chase."

"Tell me," she asked as she bent over the chief. So while Kelene examined Helmar and Marron and made more of the tea, Sayyed told her about the long journey from Council Rock. Once he got started, he seemed compelled to keep talking, and he told her everything about Sanctuary, the Clannad, Hajira, the ride to Cangora, and most of all, like a man astonished by what he was saying, he talked about Helmar.

Kelene listened quietly. Her father-in-law was not usually so verbose; in fact she had not heard him talk so much in years. She knew it was a measure of his fear for Helmar that made him confide so much of his feelings, and a measure of his love for his daughter-in-law that he chose to share his thoughts with her. Kelene was more grateful than words could tell.

After his tale had wound to an end, Kelene stayed with him. She brought him food and tea and made sure he ate it. She gave him clean clothes. She tended Afer and Demira, who stayed close by, and she conferred with the Turic healer to find the best ointments and pain relievers for her patients.

Lord Athlone and Gabria had returned to the palace, where Gabria and the Shar-Ja were slowly recovering from the effects of the poison. Rafnir had gone down to help Athlone, but he came back in the evening full of news.

"The last of the Fel Azureth surrendered this afternoon," he announced with deep satisfaction. "Mohadan's men routed them out of an old storehouse. The Gryphon's army in Cangora has been completely destroyed."

Kelene looked involuntarily in the direction of the temple. "And what of Zukhara?"

"The Shar-Ja ordered his body brought down from the temple and hung on a gibbet at the front gate. He is spreading the word that the Gryphon died a traitor's death."

The sorceress thought of the golden gryphon and the faith and loyalty she symbolized to the Turics. "He did," she replied shortly.

Rafnir glanced at his father. "Hajira has been restored to his command with full honors. He is reorganizing the survivors of the Shar-Ja's guard. Tassilio told his father everything, and the old man is so grateful to have his son restored to him, he would give Hajira the world if he asked for it."

Sayyed only nodded a reply.

A hush settled over the courtyard. The evening sounds became subdued and distant in the tranquil peace before sunset. The cloister basked in the last of the day's glow.

Helmar's gasp came as a surprise to all three of them. Her mouth opened and closed; then her eyes widened in surprise. She held up her bandaged arms and felt the stitches on her face. "Sayyed?" her voice croaked.

He took her hands in both of his and tenderly pressed them to her chest.

"Don't try to talk," Kelene advised. "Your face is still bruised and swollen, and there are stitches on your jaw and along your forehead. Just rest, and we'll tell you everything later." She fixed more restorative tea for Sayyed to give Helmar, this time laced with a dose of poppy juice to help her sleep.

When Helmar slept again, Sayyed looked more hopeful. "This is the first time she has tried to talk."

"That's a good sign," Kelene told him in all sincerity. "She is strong and healthy. She knows you are here, too. That will help."

Kelene was right. At sunrise the next morning she went out to the courtyard and found Marron lying on her belly, her legs tucked neatly under her, nibbling hay from a pile under her nose. Helmar lay awake, her eyes fastened on Sayyed's sleeping face.

Her alert gaze followed Kelene around while she checked Marron's stitches, changed her bandages, and fed her a small bucket of bran mash.

"Will she be all right?" Helmar whispered anxiously in a voice dry and raspy from disuse.

"As right as you," Kelene replied softly. She examined Helmar's wounds, too, and gave the chief a reassuring smile. "It was not your day to die. The Harbingers must have been too busy to catch you. Both of you were badly injured, and you will carry the scars. But your wounds are clean and healing well. I think you'll be able to go home soon."

"Home," Helmar echoed. Her eyes followed Kelene back into the building before they returned to Sayyed's face. "Home," she repeated, but the happiness she should have felt at such a thought was missing. There was only uneasiness and the fear of impending loss.

Two days later the Clannad carried Helmar on a litter down the road to the palace. Accompanied by the clan magic-wielders, she was escorted to a chamber beside a quiet garden where Marron was settled comfortably on a soft green lawn of grass. It was then the chief heard of Rapinor's death and learned the casualties of her troop. Fifteen riders had died in the battle at the gates; twenty more had been wounded. Helmar turned her face to the wall to hide her tears.

From that day on she had a constant stream of visitors, from the Shar-Ja and Tassilio to Lord Athlone and the clan chieftains who had come with him. From all her visitors she began to piece together the full tale of the past days.

"Now let me see if I have all of this," she said to Sayyed one evening. "Lord Athlone captured a raiding party of the Fel Azureth and learned about the Gryphon and his plans."

"Right. Zukhara had sent his fanatics to cause trouble on the border, hoping we would do just what we did— call for a council. We walked neatly into his trap, bringing Kelene and Gabria with us. Once Athlone learned what was going on, he convinced the other chiefs to support a move over the Altai to help the Shar-Ja. He had already gathered the werods of five clans before Rafnir found him. With those and the men from Council Rock, they rode here in less than four days."

"Four days," she breathed, awed by such a feat. "And is Mohadan doing well?"

"He is in his element." Sayyed laughed. "The clan lords have been staying out of the way and leaving restoration of the government to Mohadan and the Shar-Ja. Mohadan is making himself indispensable. He's already brought news that the extremists' rebellion is failing. Without Zukhara there are no other leaders to take firm command, and word that the Shar-Ja is recovering and has announced a new heir has strengthened his position. There is still a deep loyalty and respect for the Shar-Ja."

"Will he fully recover?" she asked.

"It looks as though he will. He and Gabria both grow stronger every day."

Helmar leaned back against her pillows and sighed. Through the open doors of her room she could see Marron grazing, and she winced at the red lines that crisscrossed the mare's white neck, chest, and shoulders. Helmar hadn't seen a mirror lately, but she imagined she looked equally as rough. Her eyes turned back to Sayyed.

He had hardly left her side the past few days, except to clean off the grime of war and deal with his own needs. The rest of the time he had stayed with her, changing her bandages, feeding her broth and tea, telling her stories and news, or just keeping her company in the quiet hours when she rested.

Anyone else spending so much time with her, she probably would have thrown out, but Helmar found she craved Sayyed's company. She missed him horribly when he left, and she cherished every moment he spent with her. Kelene had told her about Tam and Sayyed's vigil at her dying, and Helmar realized he was terrified of losing her, too. The knowledge strengthened her will to recover and forged her feelings for him into an abiding passion.

As the days rolled into the hot Turic summer, Helmar rapidly improved under the care of Sayyed, Kelene, and the Turic healers. One morning she felt strong enough to walk around the garden with Marron. The walk was glorious, but it made her realize how weak she had become. She began to walk every day, exercise with her sword, and retrain her muscles to regain her former strength and agility. The day the stitches came out she celebrated by going for a ride. Afer offered to carry her, since Marron was not yet ready to carry a rider, and Helmar delightedly rode the big stallion around Cangora to see the sights.

Much of the damage caused by the fighting had been repaired by city builders and the Clannad riders whose magic helped speed things along. Rafnir helped, too, learning at the same time much about construction and architecture. He and the other sorcerers had rehung the copper gates and rebuilt the walls.

Zukhara's body had been taken down by that time to be burned and his ashes thrown to the winds. A few of his officers languished in the dungeons awaiting trial.

A month passed in peace and growing optimism. At last the time arrived when Lord Bendinor and the other clan lords prepared to leave for the Ramtharin Plains and the summer gathering. Lord Athlone decided to postpone his return until Gabria and Helmar were strong enough to travel. Savaron, he knew, was quite capable of taking the Khulinin to the gathering.

Two days before the clansmen were due to leave, the Shar-Ja called for a council to be held in his audience chambers the next day. When Helmar heard of it, she asked to speak to Lady Gabria alone. Gabria came, bringing Lady Jeneve's book and the red cloak. They talked for several hours, and what they had to say to each other they kept to themselves. As soon as Gabria left, Helmar called her riders. She brought them all into her room and talked with them for several hours more. When they had said all there was to say, she bid them go to the Shar-Ja's council.

The council began at midmorning in the large, airy chambers off the celestial throne room. It was quite crowded, for the Clannad riders, the clan chiefs, the Kirmaz-Ja, a unit of royal guards, the Shar-Ja's newly appointed counselors, and Kelene and Gabria were there.

The Shar-Ja entered with his son and sat on a chair at

the head of the room. The antidote and days of activity and optimism had worked a miracle on the Turic overlord. His pride and vigor had returned, bringing health to his poison-wracked body and energy to his work. His skin had lost its pallor, and his eyes gleamed with intelligence and wit. Part of his healing had included finding his oldest son's body and bringing it home to Cangora for a royal funeral. The grief for his dead son still lingered, but the pride he felt for his intrepid younger son went leagues to heal his aching heart.

He rose and bowed to the assemblage. Standing tall, his white hair uncovered and his head unbowed, he expressed his gratitude to all who had helped preserve his throne. "Especially I owe my deepest gratitude to the people of the Dark Horse Clans and the Clannad, who rode to help a neighbor when no obligation was owed and no oath of fealty had been given. To you, the lords of the clans, I offer you this—better late than never at all."

A scribe stepped forward with four rolled scrolls and handed them to Lord Athlone. He passed the extras to Lord Jamas, Lord Wendern, and Peoren, then opened one and read it aloud to those around him. Written in both Clannish and Turic, the scrolls bore word for word the treaty they had completed at Council Rock. At the bottom of each scroll was the official seal and signature of the Shar-Ja. Quills were passed around and each chief signed his name to the scrolls. Lord Athlone returned two copies to the scribe. He bowed low to the Turic overlord.

"You rode a long way to get those," Rassidar said with a touch of humor. "I did not want you to go empty-handed. And you, Peoren," he said to the young Ferganan. "I was not so befuddled by Zukhara's poisons that I forgot my promise to you. I will pay your compensation in horses, stock animals, cotton, and spices to be delivered at a date of your choosing. Will that be sufficient?"

Peoren bowed to the Shar-Ja, his face red with pleasure. "That will do well indeed, your majesty, and I will call off the blood feud. May this be the end of any hostility between clan and tribe."

Lord Athlone said, "Shar-Ja, our offer still stands to help if we can during this drought."

"Unless you know a spell to bring rain, you have done more than I could ever have asked for. But we're not in the dire straits Zukhara led us all to believe. He and the Fel Azureth had been stealing and hoarding grain for the past two years. We have found enough to keep the people fed for a little while longer than we'd hoped. Perhaps you could ask your gods to send us some rain." He turned to regard the crowded room and saw the Clannad standing in a quiet group near the back of the chamber.

"Lady Helmar," he called and waited until she came forward. "You came out of our mountains like a legend. No one has ever reported your colony or any people like you in our midst. I hope you will not disappear again into the misty peaks. I have heard a great deal about you these past days from those who have gotten to know you, and because of what I have heard and what you have done for us, I would like to grant the Clannad perpetual ownership of the valley you call Sanctuary, to keep and hold as you see fit with no obligation or debt owed to the throne of the Shar-Ja."

The Clannad riders stayed strangely silent behind their chief, creating a quiet unified support for Helmar as she turned at an angle to look at both the Shar-Ja and the clan lords. Her voice rang out through the chambers so every person could hear. "Some of you have probably guessed how the Clannad came to be in the Turic mountains, but for those of you who do not know us well, I will tell you. Generations ago, during a summer clan gathering, my ancestress Lady Jeneve received a secret message that the magic-wielders had been slaughtered at Moy Tura." She paused when a gasp of surprise and understanding spread from the crowd around her. Only Lady Gabria watched her quietly and bent her lips in a knowing half-smile.

Helmar continued, "Lady Jeneve guessed what would happen if the murderers reached the gathering, so she took her family, her pet cats, a few friends, and their Hunnuli and fled south into the Turic mountains. They found Sanctuary by the grace of the gods, and for two hundred years we have slowly multiplied and lived in terror that someone would find us and give away our settlement to the clans. We did not know until Sayyed and Rafnir stumbled into our back door that sorcery had been resurrected by Lady Gabria. Shar-Ja, if we may wait to accept your generous gift, I would like to talk to my people and to the chiefs about returning the Clannad to the Ramtharin Plains. My lords," she said directly to the clansmen, "we would like to go home."

The clan chieftains stared at her. Some looked shocked; some appeared pleased. "But where will you go?" Lord Fiergan asked sharply. "Do you wish to join a clan or start a treld of your own?"

"Well, we can talk about that later I suppose—" Helmar started to say.

Sayyed began to grin as the possibilities lit a fire in his mind. "My lords," he said, cutting into Helmar's reply. "The Clannad could come to Moy Tura. They are used to living in buildings, and we are in desperate need of help." He winked at Helmar, and she beamed back. She had hoped he would make such an offer.

"I must talk to the rest of my people," she said firmly, "but I think that is a suitable solution."

"Then I will accept your answer whenever you decide," the Shar-Ja told her. "And I will count you as a friend wherever you go."

Kelene whooped with delight.

The clan chiefs left the next day with the Shar-Ja's treaty and Helmar's petition to rejoin the clans. They promised to take the news to the gathering and encourage the clanspeople to accept. Sayyed went with them.

Although he wanted to stay with Helmar, he felt he would be a good advocate for the Clannad at the gathering, and Lord Athlone agreed.

Before he left, though, he presented Helmar with a betrothal gift of a bracelet woven from hairs taken from Afer's and Marron's tails. "It is just a simple thing," he explained, "to remind you of me until you say yes."

She kissed him, grateful that he did not demand an answer yet. How could she decide until she knew where her people would go? She watched him ride away over the foothills back to the plains of the clans, and her heart ached to go with him. Oh, Amara, she wondered, what will I do if the Clannad says no?

Ten days later Lord Athlone, his men, Lady Gabria, Kelene, Rafnir, Helmar, and the Clannad riders bid farewell to the Shar-Ja and Tassilio and Hajira. Their farewells were long and pleasantly sad and full of promises to visit. They trotted out of the city, onto the Spice Road, and turned north toward the mountains and the valley of Sanctuary.

Kelene turned back just once to looked beyond the pinnacle and its green and red temple to the peaks beyond, hoping, foolishly she knew, for one last glimpse of the gryphon. Then she sighed and cast a sidelong glance at her husband.

"Do you know how many people are in the Clannad?" she asked, her tone deliberately innocent.

"Yes, about three hundred and eighty-two. Or so Helmar said," Rafnir answered.

"Good, then if they come, we will have three hundred and eighty-three new inhabitants in Moy Tura."

He was slow to catch on. "Three hundred and—" His voice caught, and he stared at her. The delight blossomed on his face. "Are you sure?"

She grinned then, shining like a star. "Yes! Zukhara's midwives' remedy actually worked! And that," she said, her spirit exalting, "is my best revenge!"

Epilogue

The following year proved another turning point in the history of the Dark Horse Clans. Bards marked its events in the Tale of Years; clanspeople talked about it for seasons afterward. It became known as the time of the Return of the Dead Clan.

That summer, a season marked by plentiful rains both north and south of the Altai, Sayyed and Rafnir decided to go to the clan gathering and take their people with them. They were one of the last groups to arrive, but they had planned that deliberately to honor their chieftain, Lady Helmar, and the three hundred and eighty-two members of the Clannad that would attend a clan gathering for the first time in over two hundred years.

The other clans crowded along the rivers and on the hillsides to watch them come. The Khulinin waited near the big council tent. Lady Gabria sat on Nara and felt the tears stream down her face, but she didn't bother to wipe them off. She thought of her father and her brothers and the other Corins who had died twenty-eight years ago. She wished fervently they could have been there to watch the return of the Clannad.

The first riders came over the distant hill from the north, and Gabria recognized Kelene, who rode with her baby daughter bundled in a carrier on her chest, and Rafnir. Behind them rode Sayyed close beside his wife, Helmar, on her star-white mare. Just to their right, bouncing along like a puppy on stilts, was Marron's month-old colt, a handsome baby Hunnuli with a black coat, the white lightning mark and, like an omen from the gods, a white mane and tail.

Then came the others, in a trailing column of carts, horses, and excited people—each and every one of them wearing the red cloak of Clan Corin.

The main body of the clan rode to the old Corin campsite along the Isin River, but Helmar, Sayyed, Rafnir, and Kelene trotted their Hunnuli to the council grove and greeted the other eleven clan chiefs.

Lord Bendinor stepped forward and spoke so all could hear. "Do you, Lady Gabria, as last surviving heir to Lord Dathlar and the line of Corin, acknowledge these people to be descendants of Lady Jeneve, daughter of Lord Magar of Clan Corin?"

Gabria looked up into Helmar's shining face. "I acknowledge them with all my heart."

Bendinor nodded to several people by the tent and, as Gabria watched through her tears, the scarlet banner of the Corin clan was raised for the first time since the massacre and took its rightful place among the twelve clans of Valorian.

A Brief Glossary of the Dark Horse Clans

The Clans	Chief	Cloak Color
Corin	none	Red
Khulinin	Athlone	Gold
Geldring	Hendric	Green
Wylfling	Jamas	Brown
Dangari	Bendinor	Indigo
Shadedron	Wendern	Black
Reidhar	Fiergan	Yellow
Amnok	Terod	Gray
Murjik	Geric	Purple
Bahedin	Ryne	Orange
Jehanan	Sha Tajan	Maroon
Ferganan	Tirek (Peoren)	Light Blue

Hearthguard: A chieftain's personal bodyguards. These men are the elite warriors of the clan and are honored with this position for their bravery, skill, and loyalty.

Hunnuli: Magical black horses that can communicate mentally with their magic-wielding riders.

Meara: The king stallion of the clan's herds, one that is chosen for its ability to defend the mares and foals.

Treld: A clan's permanent winter camp.

Valorian: Ancient hero of the Dark Horse Clans.

Weir-geld: Recompense paid in the form of gold or live-stock to the family of a person who was murdered or killed in a personal duel.

Werod: The fighting body of a clan. Although all men are required to learn the rudiments of fighting, only those who pass certain tests make up the werod.

Wer-tain: The commander of the werod. These men are second in authority only to the chieftains.

If you have enjoyed Mary H. Herbert's story about Kelene and Gabria and their magical Hunnuli, be sure to read these other volumes about the Dark Horse Clans.

In **DARK HORSE** the entire Corin clan is massacred. A young Gabria assumes her brother's identity and becomes a warrior to exact revenge upon the chieftain who ordered her family slain. But the chieftain, Lord Medb, has resurrected the forbidden art of sorcery and plans to destroy all who oppose him.

With the help of an intelligent, magical horse, the young warrior-woman goes against tradition and law to learn sorcery, an act punishable by death, all in the hope of thwarting Medb's evil plans of conquest.

(ISBN 0-88038-916-8)

Gabria's magical duel with Lord Medb seems to have done little to change opinions of sorcery among the clans who inhabit the Dark Horse Plains. But when the problems of the faraway city of Pra Desh threaten to spill over into the plains, Gabria is asked to intercede.

LIGHTNING'S DAUGHTER finds Gabria and her companions setting out on a difficult journey to seek a priceless tome of magic. If, with the help of the magical Hunnuli horses, Gabria can overcome the threat to Pra Desh and the clans, she may be able to win a place for magic in her world—if not, the Dark Horse Plains will be destroyed.

(ISBN 1-56076-078-8)

The tale of **VALORIAN** goes back nearly five hundred years, to a time when the last remnants of the once great clans struggle to survive under the cruel heel of the Tarnish empire. Only one man, Valorian, has the vision to dream of freedom and a new life for the clans. Few are willing to listen.

It is not until Valorian receives a gift from the goddess Amara that he is able to begin his quest. If Valorian is able to unite his people and escape from the ruthless General Tyrranis, he may find a new destiny for the clans. But if he fails, the clanspeople will face certain death.

(ISBN 1-56076-566-6)

It is a time of peace at last in the Dark Horse Plains. Under the leadership of Lady Gabria and Lord Athlone, the onetime outcast magic-wielders have gained a tenuous acceptance among their clans. But when a devastating plague sweeps over their people, old suspicions of sorcery flare.

The clans' only hope of survival rests with Gabria's daughter Kelene and a handful of young magic-wielders who journey to the ruins of Moy Tura, the ancient and feared **CITY OF THE SORCERERS**, in a desperate search for a cure.

(ISBN 1-56076-876-2)